Smoke Bitten

Patricia Briggs

ORBIT

First published in Great Britain in 2020 by Orbit

1 3 5 7 9 10 8 6 4 2

Copyright © 2020 by Hurog, Inc.

Map by Michael Enzweiler

The moral right of the author has been asserted.

A CIP catalogue record for this book
is available from the British Library.

HB ISBN 978-0-356-51359-1
C format 978-0-356-51360-7

Printed and bound in Great Britain by Clays Ltd, Elcograf S.p.A.

Papers used by Orbit are from well-managed forests
and other responsible sources.

MIX
Paper from
responsible sources
FSC
www.fsc.org
FSC® C104740

Orbit
An imprint of
Little, Brown Book Group
Carmelite House
50 Victoria Embankment
London EC4Y 0DZ

An Hachette UK Company
www.hachette.co.uk

www.orbitbooks.net

For Clyde, who played games with passion
but never took them too seriously.

For Jean, who has a beautiful heart and kind
spirit—and a gift for fun.

For Ginny, who can herd cats and make them like it.

My wonderful siblings, who taught me
to love stories. Thank you.

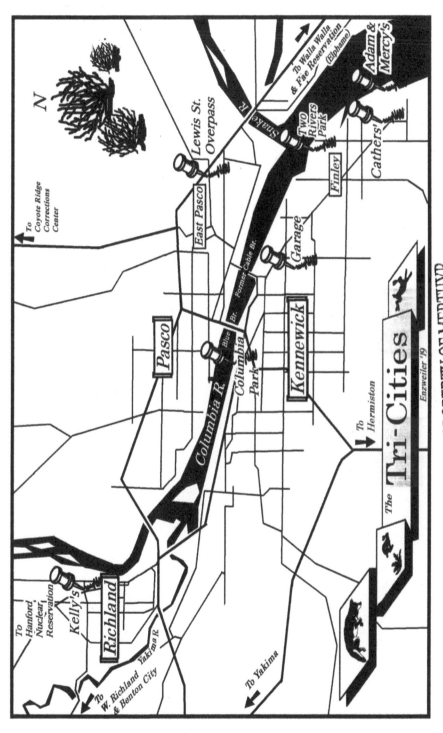

N

To
Coyote Ridge
Corrections
Center

Lewis St.
Overpass

To Walla Walla
& Fae Reservation
(Elphame)

Adam &
Mercy's

Snake R.

Two
Rivers
Park

East Pasco

Finley

Cathers'

Garage

Former Cable Br.

Pasco

Blue Br.

Kennewick

Columbia
Park

Columbia R.

To
Hermiston

The Tri-Cities

Richland

Kelly's

To
Hanford
Nuclear
Reservation

Yakima R.

To
W. Richland
& Benton City

To Yakima

Enzweiler '19

1

"ARE YOU OKAY, MERCY?" TAD ASKED ME AS HE DIS-
connected the wiring harness from the headlight of the 2000
Jetta we were working on.

We were replacing a radiator. To do that, we had to take the
whole front clip off. It was a rush case on a couple of fronts. The
owner had been driving from Portland to Missoula, Montana,
when her car blew the radiator. We needed to get her back on the
road so she could make her job interview tomorrow at eight a.m.

The task was made more urgent by the fact that the owner and
her three children under five were occupying the office. She had,
she told me, family in Missoula who could watch her children,
but nobody but her alcoholic ex-husband to watch them in Portland, so she'd brought them with her. I wished she had family
here to watch them. I liked kids, but tired kids cooped up in my
office space were another matter.

To speed up the repair, Tad was taking the left side and I was working on the right.

Like me, he wore grease-stained overalls. Summer still held sway—if only just—so those overalls were stained with sweat, too.

Even his hair showed the effects of working in the heat, sticking out at odd angles. It was also tipped here and there with the same grease that marked the overalls. A smudge of black swooped across his right cheekbone and onto his ear like badly applied war paint. I was pretty sure that if anything, I looked worse than he did.

I'd worked on cars with Tad for more than a decade, nearly half his life. He'd left for an Ivy League education but returned without his degree, and without the cheery optimism that had once been his default. What he had retained was that scary competence that he'd had when I first walked into his father's garage looking for a part to fix my Rabbit and found the elementary-aged Tad ably running the shop.

He was one of the people I most trusted in the world. And I still lied to him.

"Everything's fine," I said.

"Liar," growled Zee's voice from under a '68 Beetle.

The little car bounced a bit, like a dog responding to its master. Cars do that sometimes around the old iron-kissed fae. Zee said something soft-voiced and calming in German, though I couldn't catch exactly what the words were.

When he started talking to *me* again, he said, "You should not lie to the fae, Mercy. Say instead, 'You are not my friends, I do not trust you with my secrets, so I will not tell you what is wrong.'"

Tad grinned at his father's grumble.

"You are not my friends, I do not trust you with my secrets, so I will not tell you what is wrong," I said, deadpan.

"And that, father of mine," said Tad, grandly setting aside the headlight and starting on one of the bolts that held in the front clip, "is another lie."

"I love you both," I told them.

"You love me better," said Tad.

"*Most* of the time I love you both," I told him before getting serious. "Something is wrong, but it concerns another person's private issues. If that changes, you'll be the first on my list to talk to."

I would not talk about problems with my mate to someone else—it would be a betrayal.

Tad leaned over, put an arm around me, and kissed the top of my head, which would have been sweet if it weren't a hundred and six degrees outside. Though the new bays in the garage were cooler than the old ones had been, we were all drenched in sweat and the various fluids that were a part of the life of a VW mechanic.

"Yuck," I squawked, batting him away from me. "You are wet and smelly. No kisses. No touches. Ick. Ick."

He laughed and went back to work—and so did I. The laugh felt good. I hadn't been doing a lot of laughing lately.

"There it is again," said Tad, pointing at me with his ratchet. "That sad face. If you change your mind about talking to someone, I'm here. And if necessary, I can kill someone and put the body where no one will find it."

"Drama, drama," grumbled the old fae under the bug. "Always with you children there is drama."

3

"Hey," I said. "Keep that up, and next time I have a horde of zombies to destroy, I won't pick you."

He grunted—either at me or at the bug. It was hard to tell with Zee.

"No one else could have done what I did," he said after a moment. It sounded arrogant, but the fae can't lie, so Zee thought it was true. I did, too. "It is good that you have me for a friend to call upon when your drama overwhelms your life, *Liebling*. And if you have a body, I can dispose of it in such a way that there would be nothing left to find."

Zee was my very good friend, and useful in all sorts of ways besides hiding dead bodies—which he had done. Unlike Tad, Zee wasn't an official employee of the garage he'd sold to me after teaching me how to work on cars and run the business. That didn't mean he was unpaid, just that he came and went on his own terms. Or when I needed him. Zee was dependable like that.

"Hey," said Tad. "Quit chatting, Mercy, and start working. I'm two bolts up on you—and one of those kids just knocked over the garbage can in the office."

I'd heard it, too, despite the closed door between the office and us. Additionally, just before the garbage can had fallen, I'd heard the tired and overworked mom try to keep her oldest from reorganizing all of the parts stored (for sale) on the shelving units that lined the walls. Tad might be half fae, but I was a coyote in my other form—my hearing was better than his.

Despite the possible destruction going on in the office, it felt good to fix the old car. I didn't know how to fix my marriage. I didn't even know what had gone wrong.

"Ready?" asked Tad.

I caught the cross member as he pulled the last bolt. A leaking radiator was something I knew how to make right.

BEFORE I'D LEFT WORK, I HAD SHOWERED AND CHANGED to clean clothes and shoes. Even so, when I got home, I'd gone across the back deck to go in the kitchen door because I didn't want to risk getting anything from the shop on the new carpet.

I'd disemboweled a zombie werewolf on the old carpet, and one of the results of that was that I'd finally discovered a mess that Adam's expert cleaning guru couldn't get out of the white carpet. All of it had been torn up and replaced.

Adam had picked it out because I didn't care beyond "anything but white." His choice, a sandy color, was practical and warm. I liked it.

We'd had to replace the tile in the kitchen a few months earlier. Slowly but surely the house had been changing from the house that Adam's ex-wife, Christy, had decorated into Adam's and my home. If I'd known how much better I'd feel with new carpet, I'd have hunted down a zombie werewolf to disembowel a long time ago.

I toed off my shoes by the door, glanced farther into the kitchen, and paused. It was like walking into the middle of the last scene in a play. I had no idea what was causing all the tension, but I knew I'd interrupted something big.

Darryl drew my eye first—the more dominant wolves tend to do that. He leaned against the counter, his big arms crossed over his chest. He kept his eyes on the ground, his mouth a flat line. Our pack's second carried the blood of warriors of two continents. He had to work to look friendly, and he wasn't expending any effort on that right now. Even though he knew I'd come into the house, he didn't look at me. His body held a coiled energy that told me he was ready for a fight.

Auriele, his mate, wore an aura of grim triumph—though she was seated at the table on the opposite side of the kitchen from Darryl. Not that she was afraid of him. If Darryl was descended from Chinese and African warlords (and he was—his sister, he'd told me once, had done the family history), Auriele could have been a Mayan warrior goddess. I had once seen the two of them fight as a no-holds-barred team against a volcano god, and it had been breathtaking. I liked and respected Auriele.

Auriele's location, which was as far as she could get from Darryl and remain in the kitchen, probably indicated that they were having a disagreement. Interestingly, like Darryl, she didn't look at me, either—though I could feel her attention straining in my direction.

The last person in the kitchen was Joel, who was the only pack member besides me who wasn't a werewolf. In his presa Canario form, he sprawled out, as was his habit, and took up most of the free floor space. The strong sunlight streaming through the window brought out the brindle pattern that was usually hidden in the stygian darkness of his coat. His big muzzle rested on his outstretched paws. He glanced at me and then away, without otherwise moving.

No. Not away. I followed his gaze and saw that the door to Adam's soundproofed (even to werewolf ears) office was shut. As I turned my attention back to the occupants of the kitchen, my gaze fell on my stepdaughter's purse, which had been abandoned on the counter.

"What's up?" I asked, looking at Auriele.

Maybe my voice was a little unfriendly, but Jesse's purse, the shut door of Adam's office, Darryl's unhappiness, and Auriele's expression combined to tell me that something had happened. Probably, given the people involved and my insight into a few things going on in Jesse's life, that something had to do with my nemesis, Adam's ex-wife and Jesse's mother, Christy.

The bane of my existence had finally returned to Eugene, Oregon, where I'd optimistically thought she might be less of a problem. But Christy had a claim on my husband's protection and a stronger claim on my stepdaughter's affection. She was going to be in my life as long as they were in my life.

Christy's strikes on *me* seldom rated a level above annoyance. She was good at subtle attacks, but I'd grown up with Leah, the Marrok's mate, who had been, if not as intelligent, infinitely more dangerous.

I would pay a much higher price than dealing with Christy to keep Adam and Jesse. That didn't mean I was going to be happy about her anytime soon. *I* might be able to take her on just fine, but she hurt Adam and Jesse on a regular basis.

Auriele's chin rose, but it was Darryl who spoke. "My wife opened a letter meant for someone else," he said heavily.

"This is your fault," she snapped—and not at Darryl. "*Your* fault. You have Adam, *her* place in the pack, the home that *she* built, and you still won't let Christy have anything."

I might like Auriele, but the reverse was not true because Christy had a way of making everyone around her hyperprotective of her. Auriele was a dominant wolf, which meant she started out protective anyway. Christy just put all of Auriele's instincts into overdrive.

Still, I couldn't see her opening anyone else's mail because I was Adam's wife instead of Christy. I decided I didn't have enough information to process her accusations.

So I asked for clarification. "You opened a letter from Christy? Or for Christy?"

"No," said Darryl, staring at his mate. "She opened a letter for Jesse."

Auriele glanced at the table, and I noticed, for the first time, that on the table in front of Auriele was a stack of mail. On the top of the stack was a white envelope with Washington State University's distinctive cougar logo—and all the pieces clicked.

I pinched my nose. It was a gesture that Bran, the Marrok who ruled all the packs in North America except ours, did so often that it had spread to anyone who associated with him for very long. Since I'd been raised in his pack, it was bound to get to me sooner or later. It didn't help with the frustration, though I felt like it helped me focus. Maybe that was why Bran used it.

"Oh, for the love of Pete," I said. "Jesse told me she was going to call her mom a week ago. Let me guess—she put it off until yesterday or this morning. And Christy called you. You came over, found the letter from WSU on the table—"

"In the mailbox," said Darryl.

I raised my eyebrows, and Auriele's chin elevated a bit more and her shoulders stiffened. Yep, even in her current state of Christy-born madness, she was a little embarrassed about that one.

"We got here just as the mail carrier left," she said stiffly. "I thought we could take the mail in."

"You found the letter in the mailbox," I corrected myself. "And, given the urgency and trauma that Christy expressed to you about her daughter's change of plans, you had to open it to find proof that dire shenanigans were afoot."

Jesse had been accepted to the University of Oregon in Eugene, where her mom lived. She had also been accepted to the University of Washington in Seattle, where Jesse's boyfriend, Gabriel, was attending school.

Both were good schools, and she'd let her mother think that she'd been debating about which way to go. Adam and I had both been sure she intended to follow Gabriel—boyfriends outranked parents. I understood why Jesse hadn't wanted to tell her mother— witness the current scene with Auriele. Though putting it off had just been postponing the explosion.

But all of Jesse's schooling plans had changed thanks to recent events. Our pack had acquired some new and very dangerous enemies.

A week ago Jesse told me she'd decided to stay here and go to Washington State University's Tri-Cities campus. I'd agreed with her reasons. Jesse was a practical person who made generally good choices when her mother wasn't involved. The only advice I'd given Jesse was that she needed to tell Adam and Christy sooner rather than later.

"Hah," Auriele said with bitter triumph, pointing at me. "I told you it was Mercy's idea."

I opened my mouth to retort, but the door to Adam's office jerked open and Jesse stalked out, her cheeks flushed and her fists clenched. She glanced past me at Auriele and gave her a betrayed look that lasted for a long moment until she rounded the corner and took the stairs at a pace that was not quite a run.

I started to go after her and had made it to the foot of the stairs when Adam barreled out the door of his office. The pause between Jesse's escape and Adam's pursuit told me that he'd tried to let her go, but the wolf drove him to pursue her.

I turned so I was blocking the way up the stairs.

"Move," said Adam, his eyes bright yellow. "I will talk to you about this later."

I could feel the push of his dominance, let it wash on by me without effect. I am a coyote shifter, not a werewolf. Adam's Alpha dominance didn't make me want to drop to my belly in instant obedience—it made me want to stick out my tongue or smack him on the nose. A month ago, I might have done that.

Today, I restrained myself to a simple "No."

Adam took in a deep breath and made an effort to control his wolf; the resulting tension seemed to gain him another inch or so in height and breadth. Under other circumstances, I might have enjoyed a little battle with Adam. I don't mind a fight as long as no one gets hurt.

But Jesse had already been unnecessarily hurt. That made me mad, so I didn't trust myself to poke at Adam. It wasn't, I told myself firmly, that I didn't trust Adam.

"What result do you want?" I asked him in a calm voice. "You might be able to bully her into saying she will do what you want her to do—whatever that is. Is that really the shape you want your relationship with your daughter, who is an adult now, to take?"

"You might consider that I am madder at you than at Jesse," he bit out.

That surprised me for a moment—and then I realized that he thought Auriele was right, that I'd done something to influence Jesse's decision without talking to him. Hurt flooded me—he should know me better than that. But I stuffed that hurt down to look at later. Jesse was the important one at the moment.

"You calm down enough that your eyes aren't gold, and I will step out of the way," I told him.

"Fuck me," he growled, then turned and stalked back to his office. He shut the door with a softness that fooled no one about his state of mind.

Adam never swore around me. Not unless all hell was breaking loose. I stared at the door—thoughtfully, I told myself. I wasn't angry, because we already had too many angry people here. I wasn't hurt, because *that* I took care of in private and not in front of enemies. And Auriele apparently saw me as an enemy— I wasn't hurt about that, not at all. Not here where she could see me, anyway.

"You might want to consider," Darryl told his wife in a soft voice, "that Adam told us all that anyone who said a word against his wife, his mate, he would kill."

My stomach dropped to my toes—all the hurt that I was pretending not to feel was suddenly secondary. Yes, he had, hadn't he? Oddly, because that declaration sometimes chafed me like wet wool underwear, I hadn't brought that to bear on the current situation. And he wouldn't go back on his word simply because he was mad at me.

Killing Auriele wouldn't just be stupid; it would break him. *And that, children, is why ultimatums are a bad idea*, said a memory speaking in the Marrok's voice. I think he'd been talking to one of his sons, but it had stuck in my head.

Urgently, I asked Auriele, "Did you say something against me? Or did you just repeat what Christy said?"

She didn't answer, but Darryl did. "I think," he told me, "that he will let us leave rather than fight me. And I won't let him kill my mate without a fight."

Auriele frowned at him. "What? Why? *Someone* had to tell him what was going on beneath his own nose." From the tone of her voice, it was apparent she didn't think it would be a problem. Darryl glanced at me and then away. He was worried.

"Jesse," I said, then stopped because my own voice was a little shaky. Control was one of the things that werewolves respected. When I spoke again, my voice was quieter, a trick I'd learned from Adam because it made people listen.

"Jesse told *me*," I said, "that she'd decided, on her own, to apply to Washington State here in the Tri-Cities. The events of the past few months demonstrated to her that if she goes elsewhere, she will be a weakness for her father's enemies to exploit."

I let that hang in the air a minute. Saw them think about it.

"Eugene doesn't have a werewolf pack," I said, telling them what they already knew. "Vampires aplenty—but no werewolf pack we could call upon to watch over her. Worse, the vampires are a loosey-goosey bunch of misfits." The vampire Frost had hit the Oregon vampires a few years ago and left not much organization behind. Bran had briefly moved the Portland werewolf pack to Eugene, away from Frost's direct assault. After Frost had been disposed of, Bran had allowed the pack to return to Portland, leaving Eugene in the hands of the vampires Frost had left standing. "Those vampires have no central power, not that I've heard of, who could be negotiated with for Jesse's protection."

"That means that Christy is in danger," said Auriele, her eyes widening. "Why did you make her leave here if you knew Christy would be in danger?"

"Christy is an unlikely target," said Darryl before I could.

Which was good, because Auriele was more likely to believe him than she would me. "We've discussed this, 'Riele. Adam's ex-wife will not be seen by most powers as a good hostage. Their relationship never included a mating bond."

Auriele sucked in a breath at this—but she didn't say anything. I knew that the lack of a mating bond had been something that Christy had been bitter about throughout her marriage with Adam.

Darryl gave her a moment, then said, "Most Alphas would not protect a woman with whom they shared a temporary legal arrangement. If Christy had been his mate"—Darryl glanced at me—"it would be a different matter. But if she had been his mate, he would never have let her go in the first place. She is in a very safe position. Attacking her or taking her hostage would net no gains. They don't need to know that hurting Christy or scaring her would mean that Adam and the pack would go there to teach stray vampires a lesson they would never forget."

Her expression made it clear Auriele didn't want to agree that Christy was safe. But they had already, apparently, discussed the subject. Auriele knew as well as everyone else in the room did that Christy was probably safer away from the pack than she would be living here—unless she physically lived with the pack. But with her in Eugene, Adam's enemies would look closer to home for Adam's weaknesses.

When Adam's door opened and my mate stepped out, I ignored him even though his movement didn't sound angry anymore. One mostly unsolvable problem at a time.

"*Christy* is safe in Eugene," said Darryl heavily, repeating himself for Adam's sake, though he didn't look away from his wife. "*Jesse*, who is Adam's only child, and publicly known as such, would be another matter entirely."

"She worked out her college plans last spring and applied then," I said. "But that was last year, when our pack was allied with the Marrok, and we—Adam, Jesse, and I—determined that it wouldn't have been too dangerous."

The Marrok, Bran Cornick, was a Power in the world. It would take creatures stronger and more rash than the vampires in Eugene to try to defy him—even given that he mostly stayed in the backwoods of Montana. He had people he could send to mete out justice or vengeance. It wasn't just the werewolves who were afraid of his son Charles—or the Moor—or a number of other dangerous old werewolves in Bran's pack.

Last summer, Adam and I had discussed sending a pack member or two as a bodyguard for Jesse, rotating them out. But our pack had to be more defensive now that I'd painted a target on us by making it clear that we looked upon the Tri-Cities as our territory—and all of those living here, human and not, as our charges. It had seemed, had *been*, the right thing to do. But it had changed things for us. Jesse's ability to go to school wherever she wanted to—within reason—had been one of those things.

Sending a couple of pack members out to protect Jesse might mean that the pack would be two warriors short if we needed them—and without the umbrella of the Marrok's protection, it would take more than two werewolves to ensure her safety. There was no sense discussing it now because Jesse wasn't going to Seattle or Eugene.

"We don't have the Marrok at our back anymore," I said. "But it might not matter if we had. The Hardesty witches have shown themselves to be willing to take on the Marrok in his own territory—and we can argue how much good it did them. The point is that we, our pack, are a target for those witches. Given time, we might be able to teach them to respect us and our people. But after this last encounter, how safe do you think Jesse would be from them?"

Auriele paled and bit her lip. "I hadn't thought about the witches." For the first time she sounded uncertain.

Christy had this uncanny ability to blind people to common sense and make everything about her. Not that I was bitter or anything.

"Jesse thought about them," I said. "And she didn't want to hurt her father by making him tell her she couldn't follow her dreams, or that she'd have to find different dreams. So she took matters into her own hands. She met with a counselor at WSU and, though freshman admissions were officially closed, he managed to get her admitted. She told me she was worried that he pulled strings for her because of who her father is."

The Tri-Cities had been treating Adam like he was their own personal superhero. He accepted accolades with dignity in public and with frustration, laughter, and (on a few memorable occasions) rage in private.

"I told her she should accept what help having us behind her could give," I told them. "We certainly have cost her enough."

She'd broken up with Gabriel, her boyfriend. She'd told me that it had been one thing to ask him to wait a year for her, and an entirely different thing to try to limp the relationship along long-distance. He had, she told me tearfully, found a new girlfriend not a week later. He thought that Jesse would like her.

Sometimes even smart men could be stupid.

But that was Jesse's story to tell—and I wasn't sure that Auriele, who had babysat Jesse in diapers and served as surrogate aunt, still had the privilege of knowing Jesse's private pain. Not after she opened that letter and took sides with Christy against Jesse. If I were feeling more charitable, I would admit that Auriele likely didn't look at it that way. She would have put Jesse on Christy's side with me as the evil stepmother.

"She chose," said Adam slowly. "Jesse chose. Because of—" He glanced at Darryl, at Auriele, and lastly at Joel, who returned his gaze with eyes that held a little more fire than they had when I first came into the kitchen. "Because of the pack."

That hadn't been his first thought, though.

Did he blame himself? Or me?

He hadn't looked at me. I'd pushed the pack into a different role that had attracted the attention of some higher-level bad guys. So it was, in that sense, my fault that Jesse had to change her plans.

His tone had been deliberately bland and our mating bond had been shut down tight for weeks. I couldn't tell what he was thinking. I wasn't sure, just now, if I *cared* what he was thinking.

My first impulse was to say something biting in reply, something that would betray how hurt I was at how easily he'd fallen into Christy's story line. But I didn't *want* to trust him with my feelings just then. I curbed my tongue and, as I turned my head to look at him, tried to think of something more neutral to say. I came up blank.

In the middle of that tense silence, full of unspoken words, Aiden opened the back door.

Aiden was . . . a member of the family, though if pressed, I wasn't really sure I could have pinpointed the moment that had happened.

He'd arrived in my life dirty, defensive, and owed a favor for helping to rescue Zee and Tad.

Zee, when he wasn't twisting wrenches at the garage, was an old and powerful fae that even the Gray Lords treated with wariness, if not actual fear. Tad, his half-human son, was a power in his own right. And *Aiden*, who would have blended into a third-grade classroom so long as he kept his mouth shut, had rescued *them*.

He had looked, then, like the boy he'd been when some fae lord had stolen him to bring to Underhill, the magical land where the fae ruled—or thought they did. I don't know if humans just don't age in Underhill, if that long-gone fae lord did something, or if Underhill herself preserved the human visitors for company when she exiled the fae, but, like Peter Pan, Aiden had never grown up. In all the centuries—he had no idea how many—he'd lived in Underhill, mostly on his own, in a land full of the monsters the fae had imprisoned and Underhill had freed, he had never grown an inch. Last week we'd had to go out and buy him new clothes. He could still blend in with a class of third-graders, but it looked like now he was going to grow up someday. A fact he was pretty cheerful about.

He was incredibly dangerous. Possibly to keep him alive—more probably for reasons of her own—Underhill had gifted him with fire. But we were dangerous, too, so we'd taken him into our family and largely treated him like the child he appeared to be. He seemed to take comfort in that, maybe even enjoy it.

Entering the house, he could have been any abnormally dirty human child. He appeared to have gotten wet, at some point, then rolled in the dust that was our dirt in late summer. One of his grubby hands was firmly gripping the equally ragged and dirty girl who was about an inch shorter than he was.

He paused, having yanked the girl halfway into the kitchen

with irritation bordering on anger. He appeared to set all that aside as he observed the room and read the emotions with a brain that was not remotely childlike.

"I'm sorry," he said. "This is a bad time."

But the child he'd dragged in suddenly became cooperative and took another step into the room.

"No," she told him. "It's a wonderful time. I love battles. Blood and death followed by tears and mourning." She scratched at her matted hair, gave me a sly look, then smiled delightedly at everyone else.

"Underhill," Adam said dangerously, "what are you doing here in my home?"

Underhill was an ancient magical land. She was powerful enough to chew the fae up and spit them out again—even the fae who had the power to raise the seas or split the earth were cautious when dealing with her. She was capricious to the point of maliciousness, and when she chose, she manifested as a girl Aiden's age. While Aiden had been a child, trying to survive in Underhill's realm, she had joined his small group of friends as a fellow survivor. Eventually he'd figured out who and what she was, but she continued to treat him as a friend. I still didn't know exactly how Aiden felt about her—it was possible that he didn't know what he thought about her, either.

She was, understandably, not worried about facing down an irate Alpha werewolf.

"I heard you were inviting *everyone* in," she said disingenuously. "The Dark Smith and his misbred but powerful son. The coyote and the tibicena-possessed man." She smiled, displaying dimples. "The vampire—you know, the crazy one?"

She meant Wulfe.

The night the witches had died, Wulfe had been injured. Not physically, but mentally or spiritually or something—and it had been my fault. We brought Wulfe back with us, unconscious and babbling by turns, and Ogden, the pack member who was carrying him, had brought Wulfe into the house.

I found out later that he'd had no idea he was carrying a vampire. He didn't know Wulfe personally, and something—probably my whammy—had affected his scent. But Ogden shouldn't have been able to just bring Wulfe into the house. A vampire must be verbally invited into a home by someone who lives in that space. I suspect, given the function of our home for the wolves, that any member of our pack could invite a vampire in—but Ogden swore he hadn't said a word to anyone.

So Wulfe could come and go in our home anytime he wished. Maybe he'd always been able to.

"That's your fault, too," said Auriele, looking at me.

I don't know how she figured that, other than that I was the one who had knocked Wulfe silly so he could be carried into the house. True enough, I supposed, if you were looking for reasons to blame me for the sun rising in the east.

I looked at Auriele, then Darryl. I looked at Aiden and Underhill, a primordial being who was relatively powerless here in our world. "Relatively" being the correct word, as I had no doubt she could destroy our home and everyone in it with very little effort on her part. I looked at Adam, who was not looking at me—my *mate*, who had said nothing to contradict Auriele.

And I was done.

Without a word, I slipped around Underhill and Aiden and

out the open back door, grabbing my shoes on the way out. No one tried to stop me, which was good. I'm not sure that I would have responded like a mature adult.

Our backyard was set up for pack gatherings, with scattered picnic areas and benches landscaped into the yard. There was a new huge wooden playset with a pirate ship's lookout on top, complete with Jolly Roger.

We'd had all the pack and their families incarcerated here for a few days and decided that something for kids to play on would be a good idea. I hadn't expected the whole pack to play on it, but they loved it.

The logs bore scars from werewolf claws, and the Jolly Roger had a tear on one corner from when a couple of the wolves had fought over it.

I paused to look at the other new thing in the yard.

Part of a wall, six feet or so high, had been constructed in the corner of the property. The stones were river rock, mostly gray and all uncut. They were set without mortar, the shape of the stones matched to hold the wall together like pieces of a jigsaw puzzle. The wall ran for about twenty feet on either side of the corner of the lawn.

About three feet from the corner, on the side that ran the border between what had once been only my property and Adam's, was a battered oak door—even though with very little effort anyone could have walked around the wall.

The wall and its door hadn't been there when I came home from work, not an hour ago.

And I knew why Aiden had been so hot when he'd come into the kitchen. Underhill had made the wall, so she could have a door.

When Aiden had left Underhill, she'd missed him. After a misadventure in Underhill's realm, we had made a bargain. A couple of times a month we escorted Aiden to the Walla Walla fae reservation, where there were many doors to the magical land.

Now there was a door to Underhill in *our* backyard.

At another time, I would have run back into the house. But the thought of all those hostile faces . . . of Adam's hostile face was too much for me. My stomach churned and my heart hurt. Let Adam, Darryl, and Auriele deal with Underhill.

I hopped over the old barbed-wire fence, which continued where the stone wall left off, and strode through the field of sagebrush and dead cheatgrass toward my old house—or at least the house that stood where my old place had been.

A jackrabbit jumped out from somewhere, and my inner coyote took notice. There must have been something off about the rabbit for the coyote to be so excited by it when I wasn't hungry at all.

I glanced at it again as it ran away. There was a ragged edge to the rhythm of its movement—not quite lame, just oddly awkward. But jacks are pretty fast, even sick ones, so it was out of sight before I could pin down what was wrong.

I stopped by the old VW Rabbit I'd originally placed just so to get back at Adam when he overstepped his bounds, back when we were nothing more to each other than neighbors. Adam was one of those people who walk around straightening paintings in museums. The old parts car with its various missing pieces had been nicely calculated to drive him crazy.

I thought about doing something else to it—but the Rabbit was part of the play-fighting that Adam and I did now. I wasn't mad at Adam, wasn't fighting with him—I would be mad tomorrow, maybe, when my heart didn't ache. Today, I was just bewildered and sad. The old car couldn't help me there, so I walked on.

I was pretty sure that Adam's withdrawal from me had something to do with the witches, I reminded myself.

He'd seemed all right for the first few weeks after we killed all the witches. He'd had nightmares, but so had I.

I didn't know when he'd decided to keep our mating bond closed because, to my shame, I didn't notice at first.

I was bound to my mate, to my pack, and to a vampire. And if I thought about any of them too hard, I understood why animals caught in the jaws of iron traps sometimes gnawed their own limbs off to get free. Of the three bonds, the one with Adam bothered me the least. And when, a short time ago, it had been obstructed—I found out that I had become . . . completed by that bond.

Still, I had made very little effort to learn how it worked, leaving that to Adam. It was usually open only a little, just enough to let me know that Adam was okay and tell him the same about me. Sometimes he left it open wide—usually when we were making love, which was both amazing and overwhelming.

We weren't living in each other's heads, but I generally knew when he was having a good day—or a bad one, though only strong emotions made it through. I could tell where he was and if he was in pain or not. And he could tell the same about me. But his keeping it tightened down left us both some privacy. That way, he told me, I wouldn't try to chew off my foot to get free.

Sometime after the witches, he had closed it tight and I hadn't noticed until a few days ago. Once I noticed, then I could look back and realize it had been weeks since I'd felt much from our bond. The way it was now, I could not tell anything except that he was alive.

He had been working long hours—and so had I, my business freshly reopened and requiring more time than usual because of it. How little time we were spending together hadn't seemed abnormal until I stopped to think about it. He had been spending a lot of hours at work, but he'd still had time to take care of pack business, and the problems of various pack members. But our time, the space he and I carved from our days and weeks, had disappeared.

I didn't know when, exactly, it had happened or why, but I *had* been sure it was some kind of aftermath from the witches, from Elizaveta's death. But tonight, his reaction, his willingness to believe I'd urge Jesse to change her plans without telling him, left me thinking that maybe the problem was *me*.

Was he finally tired of the trouble I caused? Or at least seemed to be surrounded by?

We hadn't made love in weeks. My husband was a twice-a-night man unless one or the other of us was too beaten up. I found that with him, I was a twice-a-night woman, so it worked out well.

I leaned down to pat the old VW and then continued my walk. I didn't want to think anymore, and movement seemed the right thing to do. I had no particular destination in mind other than away.

I stopped by the pole barn I had used as a secondary base of operations the whole time my garage was being rebuilt and glanced inside. It looked oddly empty, most of the tools moved back to the garage in town. The main occupant of the building was my old Vanagon.

I'd put a white tarp down and driven the van on top to see if I could find the leak in the coolant lines that ran from the radiator in the front of the van to the engine fourteen feet away. It was a last-ditch effort to find the leak before pulling all the lines and replacing them with new ones. I wasn't hopeful, but I really wasn't looking forward to taking the whole van apart.

I closed the door without checking the tarp and walked to the little manufactured home that had replaced my old trailer. The yard was in better condition than it had been when I'd lived there, Adam having installed an automatic watering system and added my house to his yard man's routine.

The oak tree, a gift of an oakman, had escaped the fire that destroyed my old home. It had grown since I last paid attention to it, a lot more than it should have, I thought—though I was no gardener or botanist. Its trunk was wider around than both of my hands could span.

Impulsively, I put my tear-damp cheek against the cool bark and closed my eyes. I couldn't sense it, but my head had to be quieter for me to listen to the subtle magic the tree held.

"Hey," I told it. "I'm sorry I haven't visited for a while."

It didn't respond, so after a moment I turned to the little manufactured house that I had never lived in. My old trailer had burned down and I'd moved in with Adam. Gabriel, Jesse's ex-boyfriend who had been working for me when they met, had lived in it until he'd gone off to college. He'd planned to stay all summer, but a few weeks ago he'd moved his stuff out. At the time he'd told me that it didn't make sense for him to take up space here when he was living in Seattle.

I'd known that there was something more, something that put sadness in his eyes, and I'd been pretty sure it had to do with Jesse by the way she didn't come over to help him move. But I'd figured it was something that they would tell me when the time was right. So I hadn't been surprised when Jesse had told me that she and Gabriel had broken up because she would not be joining him at school in Seattle.

I had Gabriel's keys hanging on our key holder in the kitchen, and I wasn't going back for them. The fake rock was still sitting next to the stairs—one side was blackened and melted a little and I could still smell the faint scent of the fire.

Adam had nearly killed himself trying to rescue me. I had not been in the house, but he'd thought I was. Even a werewolf can burn to death. Crouching beside the wooden steps, I remembered the burns that had covered him.

But I also remembered the look in his eyes today when he'd told me, if not in so many words, that he believed I would go behind his back on something that I knew was important to him. That I would talk his daughter into an important life-changing decision without discussing it with him first.

I closed my hand on the plastic rock and found a shiny new key. Gabriel had put his spare key the same place I had. Adam, who ran a security company, would have chided us both had he known.

I opened the door.

Gabriel had cleaned the house before he left—and then his mother and sisters came and cleaned it again. She explained to me, "Gabriel is a good boy. But no man ever cleaned a house as well as a woman."

And with that sexist statement, she proceeded to prove her point. The house smelled clean, not musty as do most places that are left empty for very long. The carpet looked new; the vinyl in the kitchen and bathrooms were pristine.

There was a white envelope on the counter of the kitchen marked *Jesse* in Gabriel's handwriting. I left it alone. Someone had already opened Jesse's mail today—I wasn't going to do that again.

The manufactured house was larger than my old trailer had been, and better insulated, too. Even though the day had been hot and the electricity was off, the house was a bearable temperature.

Walking through the empty, clean house wasn't making me feel any better. I was starting to think that I'd abandoned the fight in the middle—which wasn't like me at all. I stared out the window of the master bedroom over at my home. My real home.

Time to go back and fight for it, I decided.

I strode out of the bedroom—and there was a woman standing in the living room with her back to me. Her hair was long and blond and straight. She wore a navy A-line skirt and a white blouse.

"Excuse me?" I said, even as I was wondering how she'd gotten into the house without me noticing her at all. I could smell her now, a light fragrance that was familiar.

She turned to look at me. Her face was oddly familiar, too. Her features were strong—handsome rather than lovely. A face made for a character actor. I'd have said "memorable," but I couldn't remember where I'd seen her before. Her eyes were blue-gray.

"I don't understand," she said. "He loves me. Why would he do such a thing?"

And upon her words, blood began to flow from wounds that opened on her body—shoulder, breast, belly, one arm, and then the other—and the smell of fresh blood permeated the house.

2

IT WAS HER VOICE THAT I RECOGNIZED. MY OLD NEIGH-
bor, Anna Cather. I'd seen her just the day before yesterday at the
gas station. The reason I hadn't known her immediately was that
the Anna I knew was in her seventies. The woman who stared
at me while her blood pooled on the gray carpet, turning it black at
her feet, was in her twenties.

Ghosts were like that.

I felt a rush of grief and though I knew better—of all people,
I knew better—I hurried to her side and reached out to her. Her
shoulder under my hand was as solid as any living person's would
have been, solid and cold as ice. Much colder than an actual
corpse's would have been.

She was dead, my happy neighbor who liked to eat my cookies
and bring me bouquets of flowers from her garden.

Seeing ghosts was the *other* thing I did besides turn into a
coyote. I knew that merely by paying attention to her, I made the

ghost more real, gave her power. Gave *it* power—though I hesitated a lot more when I said "it" around ghosts than I used to. I was no longer convinced that all ghosts were nothing more than the shed remnants of the people they had been—things without feelings or thoughts. What exactly they were, I wasn't sure, but I was doubtful that anyone else knew, either.

That I had noticed her was bad, but touching her was worse. If I didn't want her shade haunting this house for years to come, I needed to walk away. But Anna was—had been—my friend.

So instead of turning my back on her, I left my hand where it was. "Anna, what happened?"

Tears slid down her face as blood started to trickle out of the corner of her mouth. She raised her hands to cover her mouth, then hugged herself with those bloody hands, hunching slightly as if her stomach hurt. She looked at me with horror-filled eyes.

"Why?" she asked me, sounding bewildered. "Why did he do it? He is the gentlest soul—you know how he is. He even takes *spiders* outside instead of killing them."

"And live traps the mice," I said in disbelief. "Anna, are you saying that *Dennis* killed you?"

Dennis, Anna's husband, loved her with all of his gentle soul. They didn't have a perfect marriage. I knew she took once-a-year vacations on her own, and that after his retirement left him following her around like a devoted dog just waiting for the next thing requested of him, she'd started volunteering at hospitals, animal shelters, and anywhere else that would get her out of the house. But she loved him, and he loved her—so they worked it out.

She hunched over and looked at me. "Why?" she said again. "Why did he do it? He is the gentlest soul—you know how he is. He even takes *spiders* outside instead of killing them."

She wasn't talking to me; she was on repeat.

Ghosts sometimes interacted with me as if they were still the person whose shade they were. But only sometimes. Sometimes they were locked into a particular moment, or sequence of moments. That Anna had repeated herself so exactly indicated that she was one of those. She had no answers to give me.

"Anna," I said, knowing nothing I said could possibly make any difference. "I am so sorry."

The wounds on her body might have been analogous to actual wounds—in which case someone (Dennis didn't feel possible, despite what she had indicated) had attacked and stabbed her. But ghosts were not tied to physical reality. The wounds could represent what she felt when she died, or how she felt about death.

A 9mm gun spoke, breaking the normal early-evening sounds of light traffic, birdsong, and dogs barking. Anna and I both turned to look toward her house, though repeaters don't usually notice things outside their narrow reality.

The sound of the gun left me with a heavy certainty in my chest, though gunfire in this rural neighborhood wasn't uncommon. I felt sick. Anna's face lit with a relieved smile.

"Oh," she said. "Dennis?"

The blood disappeared from the carpet and from her body. The dark stains faded from existence between one breath and the next as if they never had been—because in some ways they had not. Only the tears on her cheeks and the lingering scent of fresh blood remained.

"Dennis?" she asked a second time, but this time her voice sounded like someone who hears a door open and is fairly sure of who has come in.

Her body softened with happiness. I stepped away, letting my hands fall from her. She took a step forward, not toward me, but toward something I couldn't see. She lifted both of her hands, her whole body leaning to rest upon . . . Dennis, I supposed.

"My love," she said, looking up—Dennis had been a great deal taller than she.

And I was alone again in the living room.

WASTING NO TIME, I RAN TO THE CATHERS' HOUSE. IN the short time I'd been inside, dusk had turned to night. The darkness didn't bother me—I can see as well in the dark as any coyote. It did provide me cover so no one would notice that when I ran full speed, I was faster than I should have been. The Cathers had been my closest neighbors, other than Adam, but they were still nearly a quarter of a mile away.

No one else seemed to have been disturbed by the sound of the gun going off. But no one else had had Anna's ghost in their living room, either.

When I reached Anna and Dennis's yard, caution made me stop to get a good look around. Someone had shot a gun over here, and though I had my suspicions of what had happened, I couldn't be absolutely certain. There might still be an active shooter.

Dennis's gray Toyota truck was parked next to Anna's silver Jaguar in the carport. Everything was neat and tidy except . . . I stopped by one of the big raised garden beds that Dennis had built for Anna. On one of the timbers that edged the beds was a box with a new sprinkler head. I could see that someone had been digging a hole—presumably to fix a sprinkler—but hadn't gotten far.

Dread in my heart, I climbed up the steps to the front door. The Cathers' house, like many in Finley, was a manufactured house—a much larger and grander version than the one I'd just left. Painted tastefully in gray and white, the house suited the Cathers, being neat and tidy. The only extravagance was the graceful wraparound porch.

I was wondering if I should wait for the police—and that meant I had to call them first—rather than open the door. If I just went in, I might ruin evidence. But if I waited for the police, they would go in first and mess up the scent markers that might allow me to figure out what had happened.

The front door, I noticed, was slightly ajar.

Trying to be as unobtrusive as possible, I pushed the door open with my foot, but it only opened about ten inches—stopped by a jean-covered leg on the tile floor. The smell of death washed over me—Dennis, and then a few seconds later I could smell Anna.

I'd been almost certain that Dennis was dead when I'd heard the gunshot. Closer to certain at Anna's last words. I hadn't realized how much I'd hoped I was wrong until I opened their door and found the body.

Faced with the reality that both Dennis and Anna were dead, I found that I was not very concerned with fingerprints and pristine crime scenes anymore. I slid through the narrow opening between the door and the frame, stepping over Dennis's leg and into the Cathers' living room.

Dennis's body lay crumpled midaction, as if he'd been walking toward the door when he'd shot himself. He *had* shot himself. The trigger finger of his right hand was still caught in the trigger guard. He'd done it right—put the gun in his mouth and blown out the back of his head.

My ears and nose told me that there was no one alive in this house—and no one dead except for Dennis and Anna. She wasn't in the living room, but she wasn't too far. The danger, whatever the danger had been, had passed.

I knelt beside Dennis, staying clear of the blood spatter and resisting the urge to close his death-clouded eyes. I could justify, if only to myself, my need to figure out what had happened. But altering the scene, even by a little, would be wrong.

Without touching him, then, I examined his body with all of my senses.

As far as I knew, this had been the first time Dennis had ever had a gun in his hand. It was an STI Trojan, a 1911 model chambered in 9mm. Anna's gun. She and I had gone target shooting a few times over the years—the Trojan was her favorite. Dennis had refused to go with us, his dislike of guns unyielding. Anna had told me that her father had been a Marine and had taught all of his daughters how to shoot. She was a better shot than I was, and I wasn't terrible.

What had happened to Dennis that he'd decided to change a lifetime of habit and conviction this afternoon? Drugs or alcohol would be my first choice. As weird as it was to contemplate that Dennis had gotten drunk (he did not drink to my knowledge) or tried drugs, that wasn't as weird as Anna having an affair or doing something that had made Dennis feel that a gun was his only recourse.

I couldn't smell any alcohol near his face or on his clothing, but if he'd ingested it more than an hour ago or if he'd been drinking somewhere else, I wouldn't be able to scent it from a distance. If he'd been drinking enough to go on a shooting spree, I should be able to smell it on his skin, but it might be subtle and I'd need to get close.

The wound was a host to strong smells—blood, gunpowder. If I was going to smell for drugs as well as alcohol, for something, anything wrong, I needed to find skin as far from the gore as I could. He'd been wearing a short-sleeved shirt and his left arm was outstretched from his body.

As I put my face near his arm, I noticed that he'd been bitten by something recently. I hesitated. There were two distinct marks, recently made, with small bloody smears on the surrounding skin. They looked as though he'd been bitten by a tiny vampire. Maybe that was why the hair on the back of my neck was crawling.

It could be from a snake, I thought, remembering the abandoned repairs in the yard. Rattlesnakes were scarce around here, in my experience. Bull snakes would bite, but they had no venom. Not that it mattered; no snake venom I knew about would turn a person into a murderer. I was no expert—maybe there existed a snake whose bite was hallucinogenic, but not any snake anyone would encounter around here.

It didn't look that much like a snakebite, anyway. What it *really* looked like was a rabbit bite. I have had my fair share of rabbit bites—when I am a coyote, rabbits are fair game. But Dennis wasn't a coyote shapeshifter, and they didn't have rabbits.

For some reason I thought of the jackrabbit I'd seen, the one my coyote had taken notice of because there was something wrong about it. Had it been headed in this direction? Maybe.

Could it have been infected with rabies? Rabies was a disease that rabbits could carry, I knew. Other than being traumatized by *Old Yeller* when I was a child, I didn't have any experience with it. Dogs, I thought, at least in Old Yeller's case, foamed at the mouth and bit people. It seemed like a long way from that to causing someone to kill his wife and then shoot himself.

Deciding it was unlikely that venom or rabies was the culprit, I resumed my examination for some chemical cause. I closed my eyes and inhaled, looking for the scent of alcohol, drugs of some sort—or illness. Despite my care, my nose touched Dennis's skin as I inhaled.

Magic filled my nose, burned into my sinuses, and brought tears to my eyes as I jerked back from the burn. I opened my eyes as I lost my balance, narrowly avoiding falling onto Dennis's body—which glowed with the magic that still bit at my nose like menthol oil.

Adam was of the opinion that it wasn't really my nose that allowed me to detect magic—otherwise he and the other werewolves would be able to smell it, too. He thought that my perception of magic felt like a scent to me because I had no other way of processing it, a sort of synesthesia. He may have been right, but that didn't change that it was mostly my nose that told me when there was magic around.

Usually, though, with magic that affected me this much, I'd have been able to smell it from the front door—maybe from the road. My fingers buzzed with it, my nose burned—and to my eyes, Dennis's whole body glowed. I didn't understand why I hadn't noticed it until I smelled Dennis's skin. No. Until I *touched* his skin. A lot of magic reacted to skin on skin.

Given that there was a brand-new door to Underhill in my backyard, not a quarter of a mile away, my initial suspicion would have been that it was fae magic at work. But it didn't smell like fae magic.

I can sort witchcraft from fae magic, werewolf from vampire magic. This wasn't anything I was familiar with. I had once gone to an exhibit of South American artifacts, and the whole room they were displayed in smelled like magic I'd never sensed before—dark and complex. The magic in Dennis's dead body was closer to that than to fae magic. Though not an exact match. It also reminded me of the magic that I'd scented around a sorcerer who had made a bargain with a demon—and a little, very little, like Underhill herself. No, not like Underhill—but there was some of the same lingering feel to it that I'd felt the whole time I'd spent in Underhill—something primordial.

I didn't know what it was. I did know what it wasn't. It wasn't witchcraft. It wasn't fae—though that was a little less definite. Some of the fae shared far less similarity to each other than I did to a milk carton. It didn't smell like the magic I had sensed from any fae I had encountered, anyway. With a nod to the faint resemblance to something about Underhill—and I wasn't sure that Underhill counted as fae—it was not an exact match to any kind of magic I'd ever run into before. It certainly hadn't belonged to Dennis because he hadn't had a molecule of magic to call.

"No, Anna," I murmured, though she wasn't here that I could tell. "It wasn't Dennis who killed you." It had been, I was sure, given how well I knew Dennis, whatever had left so much magic in him.

I got to my feet and moved away from the body until my hands quit tingling, and then I went in search of Anna. I found her in the kitchen, collapsed on the white tile floor. She had fallen face-first, her blood pooling around her. At the edge of the dark pool was a white-handled French chef's knife.

When I touched her body, it was still warm, and there was no bloom of the magic that saturated Dennis. Feeling confident that I'd found everything I was going to discover on my own, I pulled out my phone and called 911.

I SAT ON THE LAWN BY THE HOLE DENNIS HAD DUG AND watched the police carry out their business. Adam showed up about the time the coroner's office carried Anna's body out of the house.

He stood beside me, watching the proceedings without speaking for a while. It seemed to me that he was trying to figure out what to say, rather than playing any kind of power game.

I thought of him, of all of the ways that he had risked his life since I'd met him. The image that had come to me earlier when I'd thought of my old home burning, the memory of Adam's burned body in the hospital, lingered still. He had thought I was inside the inferno and nothing could stop him from diving in to find me. He'd nearly died to save me—and werewolves are hard to kill.

That man, that man I had to believe in. I had to believe that there was something going on that I did not understand—yet. Something that would explain why my mate was keeping me shut out of his life right now. Something other than the possibility that he didn't want me anymore.

I hadn't done more than glance up at Adam when he'd come over. I hadn't even explained what had happened. It said a lot about our current relationship that he hadn't asked me. How had we come to this? How had I let this happen? Because a relationship is a two-way street. It took both of us to let it get this bad.

I might not have been looking at him, but I felt him there, tense with uncertainty—even if our bond was shut down tight, I could still feel that much. It was not any lack of love, I decided, with the memory of his burned body fresh and real in my head, that had mangled our relationship.

Adam did not desert the people he loved. And he loved me. I would have faith that there was nothing wrong we could not fix.

I reached out and wrapped my hand around his ankle.

"Did you find them?" Adam asked, as if my touch had forced words out of his mouth. His voice was gruff.

I glanced toward my other side, where Anna's ghost worked in her garden, pulling weeds only she could see.

"Sort of," I told him. "Anna found me."

"Murder?" he asked. He knew about me and ghosts.

"Oh yes," I said.

The muscles in his leg tightened. "And you didn't call me?"

Hurt, I thought—and an edge of anger. *Too bad for you*, I thought without sympathy. I might love the man, but that didn't mean there weren't consequences for the way he'd been acting.

"The danger was gone," I told him—and then wondered if I was right about that. Since I try not to lie to Adam, even by omission, without good reason, I added, "As far as I could tell."

And when that last increased the tension in his calf muscle, I wasn't the least bit sorry. Petty of me, maybe—but I'd learned in a hard school that I couldn't let a werewolf, especially a dominant werewolf, get away with pushing me around.

I told him what I knew, starting with Anna's appearance in the living room of my manufactured house and ending with my calling the police. By the last bit, he'd calmed down about my not calling him. He didn't know the Cathers very well. He didn't go out making friends with the neighbors; he had enough to do running his company and the werewolf pack. I didn't know the neighbor up the road from the pack house, either, for much the same reason, though I did make sure to send them something— flowers, candy, fruit baskets—every time there was a disturbance at our house. My relationship with the Cathers predated my relationship with Adam.

"Detective Willis was not best pleased with my entering the residence before they got here," I told him, finishing my story.

"But I don't think he was serious about charging me with obstruction of justice."

He gave another grunt, this one sounding a little amused. He hadn't commented on the magic that had permeated Dennis's body, or my possible imminent arrest, but the amusement was promising. I thought it was safe to change the subject.

"So are you going to kill Auriele?" I asked. "Or did you figure out a way around it?"

"Darryl should have his own pack," Adam said, which wasn't a yes. But it also wasn't a no.

It was my turn to grunt. That made him laugh a little, though it was somber amusement, nothing that would draw attention when people were carrying bodies out of a house.

"Auriele was only a weapon Christy aimed at you," Adam told me, his tongue apparently loosened by my imitation of his usual grunt. "Extenuating circumstance enough that I decided it wasn't going back on my word to let her live. I explained to Auriele that it was time to practice some better judgment about what Christy has to say. The next time . . ." He sighed. "Hard to punish her for something I fell for as well. Of *course* you wouldn't tell Jesse what to do. Of *course* she would use you as a sounding board before she confronted Christy or me. And it was Jesse's place to inform both me and Christy."

"Damn straight," I growled, borrowing a phrase from my cowboy friend Warren. "So why did you fall for it?"

He didn't answer my question. Instead he said, "Auriele apologized to Jesse. I'm not sure that took. Punishment enough maybe, for Auriele. At least as far as opening Jesse's mail is concerned. She isn't often in the wrong."

True.

"I apologized to Jesse, too," he said. "I think that went over better."

"You didn't open her mail," I told him. "And Jesse knows how her mother works."

"And that's why she accepted my apology," Adam agreed. "And why she talked to you about school before she brought it to me or her mother."

"Jesse could have avoided all of this if she'd discussed matters with you before she talked to her mother," I told him. "But Christy was easier. She'd only be hurt because Jesse wasn't moving to Eugene. You were going to be hurt because you, and your position as Alpha of our pack, are the reason she doesn't have more choices about where to go to school."

Adam grunted again.

The coroner's van pulled out of the driveway with the two bodies inside. As Anna continued to work in her flower bed, some of the real weeds got pulled. Only strong ghosts affect the physical world like that. Maybe she would haunt her own house instead of mine. I could hope.

"I can't afford to lose Darryl now," Adam said. "I talked to him alone about that. I apologized because, especially after this incident, he should be cut loose to get his own pack. Do you know what he told me?"

"He likes his job here," I said, because I'd talked to Darryl about this a few weeks ago. "As far as the one with the salary is concerned, he could probably work remotely if he couldn't find a job wherever his new pack would be located. It's not like think tanks are available in every town. But he doesn't want to work remotely, because he likes to meet face-to-face with his team and with the people who use his team's work." Like me, a werewolf gets a lot of information from scent and subtle body language cues.

"And—" I glanced up at Adam. This part Darryl hadn't said, but I knew him. "He really loves the action our pack has been facing. He's an adrenaline junkie. A new pack might be interesting until he got settled in, but I don't think there is a pack in the US, other than maybe the Marrok's, that is in for as exciting a time as ours."

"That's more than he said, but I think you have it right." He smiled. It wasn't exactly a happy smile, but it wasn't one of those smiles I'd been getting lately that weren't really smiles. He reached down and held out his hand.

"You are making me really uncomfortable sitting at my feet," he told me.

"And you're starting to get funny looks from the cops," I said, taking his hand.

He laughed as he pulled me up. It was a quiet laugh—and this time I think he consciously pulled it down to suit the circumstances.

"Thank you," he said when I was standing.

"I can just see the headlines," I told him. *Alpha Wolf Makes Wife Kneel at His Feet.*"

His mouth quirked up. "Don't forget the 'Human Wife' part of that. There are still a lot of people who think you are my sex slave."

"You wish," I told him to the last part. "And it would be 'Human? Wife.'" I lifted my voice on the end of "human," so he could hear the question mark.

The newspapers had indeed begun to question just how human I was. That was a problem because one of the reasons the pack had been accepted so easily by the mundane population of the Tri-Cities was that people viewed me as one of them. It was only a matter of time before someone figured out that I wasn't—strictly speaking—human. But I hoped that by then, they'd be happy with us because we were the good monsters who protected them from the bad ones.

"Back to our previous conversation," I said, "we get to keep Darryl and Auriele."

I was sorry when the slight smile slid away from his face and his expression regained its grim neutrality.

He said, "Or at least we put that off for another day. Auriele understands what she nearly caused to happen, though I don't think she is apologetic about anything except for hurting Jesse. And *that* she still believes is your fault."

I blew out a breath. "Figures."

"You haven't asked me about Aiden and Underhill," he said.

"Do I want to know?" I asked.

Before he could answer me, Detective Willis approached. Willis was moderately tall, and graying, and carried himself like someone who'd been in a few fights. He was closer to retirement age than to his rookie years, but not by much. He was one of those men who used his size and his anger to intimidate people he thought needed intimidation, but he was capable of toning his presence down to gentleness when caring for trauma victims. He was smart, dedicated—and we got along all right for the most part.

"Generally speaking," he said, "when either of you show up at a scene, it's because something is afoot." He stopped in front of us, his hands on his hips—but he knew better than to stare into Adam's eyes. Instead he stared at me.

"My people tell me this looks like a classic murder-suicide," he said.

"No," I said. "Magic."

He grimaced. "God *damn* it. I knew it had been too quiet around here."

"I might believe it if Anna had stabbed her husband and then shot herself," I told him. "But Dennis was possibly the least violent person I know."

"And that's why you think there was magic involved?" asked Willis, sounding hopeful.

"It is all over Dennis's body," I told him. "I've never seen anything like it. He is lit up with magic—I wouldn't be surprised if someone could see him glowing from space." A thought occurred to me. "You might want to be careful with his body."

"Are you thinking witches and zombies?" asked Adam.

I shook my head. "Not witches, I don't think. But there is a lot of magic in Dennis's body—he wouldn't want to hurt anyone else."

"I'll speak to the coroner's office," said Willis. "Do you have any idea what got him?"

I shook my head.

"Of course you don't," he said. "And you wouldn't tell me if you did."

"I don't," I told him. "But you might be right about the last. Your guys aren't exactly the stand-back-and-let-the-werewolves-take-care-of-it kind of guys. Some things a gun works just fine on—and some things you need grenade launchers for."

"And werewolves are the grenade launchers?" He sounded a little amused. He didn't argue about my assessment of his people.

"That's about right," said Adam mildly.

Willis glanced back at the house. "Murder-suicide would be a lot easier than unknown magical cause."

"It wasn't a murder-suicide," I told Willis. "Don't let their kids think that it was."

He nodded, his mouth softening. "We'll call it an 'under investigation' situation. When you figure out just what happened, we'll let the family know." He started to leave, but paused. "It looked to me like he was heading out that door when he killed himself."

"That's what I thought, too," I said.

"You think he stopped himself from killing anyone else?" Willis didn't sound like an experienced detective. He sounded like someone who needed to believe in good guys.

"I don't know," I told him. "But he picked up the gun after he killed Anna—and if whatever had him had just intended for him to kill himself, that knife could have done the job. Dennis was the kind of person who would have killed himself to prevent anyone else getting hurt."

Willis nodded, as if I'd answered a question for him, then continued back to his car.

Adam and I left the Cathers' house. I started off at an angle, heading home, but Adam veered toward my manufactured house. I gave him a puzzled look, but he didn't seem to notice.

"I see that Underhill decided to redecorate the backyard," I told him.

He growled low in his throat. "That gate has to stay for a year and a day," he said. "Then she can remove it, if we still wish her to."

I laughed, I couldn't help myself—I think I was mostly just

punchy. But there was something funny about the disgruntled way he repeated Underhill's words.

"Holy doorways, Batman," I said. "We have an entrance to Underhill in our backyard."

He looked at me then, though he didn't quit walking. "Are you sure that it wasn't fae magic that caused Dennis to kill his wife?"

I quit laughing and looked at the border wall between Adam's house . . . Adam's and my house and my old place. The stone wall, even incomplete, looked better than the old barbed-wire fence had.

"I've never felt magic exactly like this," I told Adam. "It didn't feel fae."

"Coincidences happen," Adam said. But he didn't say it like he believed it.

"It smelled a little like Underhill—but not like Underhill," I told him. "I suppose it could be something that came through her door. But it also smelled a little like that vampire who was also a sorcerer. More that than Underhill. It didn't smell fae to me."

"He was bitten," said Anna, walking beside us.

"Bitten by what?" I asked her. "Was it the rabbit?" I was going to end up with my house haunted. Maybe I could make that a feature and rent it out as an Airbnb.

Adam didn't ask me who I was talking to—he'd gotten used to it. Instead he said, "You're going to end up with Anna haunting you if you aren't more careful."

"Most of them haunt places, not people," I said uneasily. Because I knew of at least one case in which a person was haunted. That one had had some fae magic thrown in to help the weirdness along, but there was magic afoot here, too.

Anna hadn't answered me. She was scuffing her shoes in the dirt and squinting up at the sky. "Looks like rain," she said.

The skies were clear. Maybe they looked different if you were dead.

"*Smoke.*" Dennis's voice in my ear made me jump.

I turned around, but he wasn't visible. And Anna was gone, too.

"What?" asked Adam.

I shrugged, but unease left over from that whispering voice in my ears made me look around.

"I think I'm going out hunting a jackrabbit tonight," I told him. Finding the rabbit would make me feel better. I was still pretty sure it was just an ordinary rabbit—but I wanted to make certain. I thought I would have noticed something that could pour that kind of magic into Dennis, notice it with more than the mild interest my coyote self had evinced. But then I hadn't sensed the magic in Dennis's body until I'd touched it.

"Did you get a reply?" asked Adam. "About what bit Dennis? I assume it was Dennis who was bitten."

I nodded. "I don't know that he was answering me. He just said, 'Smoke.' They are both gone now—not that ghosts are good at communication."

"How can you be bitten by smoke?" asked Adam. "And why would that mean that you need to go hunting jackrabbits?"

I explained about the rabbit I'd seen and how the marks on Dennis's wrist looked like a rabbit bite. We had reached the porch of my little house by the time I finished. Adam opened the door I'd left unlocked without saying anything about it.

"Anna told me, 'He was bitten.' I am assuming she was talking about Dennis—especially since I saw the bite myself. But that might not have anything at all to do with her death, just a leftover thought. It was Dennis who said, 'Smoke.' Then they both left. I don't know if one had to do with the other."

Adam closed the door behind us but didn't step farther into the house. He bowed his head for a moment before meeting my eyes.

"I am sorry," he said. "I know I hurt you today. I have been angry and short-tempered and I took it out on you. On you and Jesse."

"Okay," I said. "Let's talk about this. What is up with you? Why the shutdown of our bond? Why no time together? Why no—" I was trying to keep my voice clinical, but if I'd said "no making love," I would have had trouble doing it. So I said, "—sex?" And my voice wobbled a little anyway.

He nodded, as if he'd been waiting for those questions.

"The short answer is that I don't know," he said. "But something is wrong." He thumped his chest.

I frowned at him. "With your wolf?"

He shook his head, but then said, "Maybe? It doesn't feel like that—though the wolf is part of it."

I raised an eyebrow at him.

"See?" he said. "It doesn't make sense out loud."

"Is it me?"

He huffed out a humorless laugh. "I promise that this is not an 'it's not you, it's me' speech." His eyes brightened to gold. "I won't let you go."

"Not your choice," I told him. "But as it happens, you'd have a hard time shaking me off. You are mine, and I'm pretty stubborn about things like that."

His whole body relaxed with an odd shudder. He closed his eyes. My stomach settled for the first time in a few days. We could work this out.

And then he said, in a voice that was not his own, "*You'd leave if you knew what was inside me.*"

The wolf, I thought, after a weird moment. It was just Adam's wolf. We'd spoken a time or two. But it hadn't sounded quite right for the wolf.

"Nope," I told him—wolf and man. "Not happening."

"*You should leave.*" This time I was sure it was the wolf who spoke. "*It would be safer for you.*" And then Adam's yellow eyes opened, but he gave a half laugh. "Yes, I know, that just guaranteed you are going to stick around until bodies start dropping."

"Are bodies going to start dropping?" I asked.

"Mercy," he said. "I don't trust myself. I've been a werewolf for longer than you've been alive, and it's been decades since I've had trouble with it. But now I wake up and I'm in my wolf's shape—without remembering how I got there."

Two weeks ago, I thought. He'd been a wolf when I woke up. I'd just assumed that he'd had a restless night; we both were prone to those after the witches. Sometimes on bad nights we'd go out for a run—on two legs or four. I'd thought he'd decided to let me sleep. It *had* been after that night that the odd distance he'd forced between us had happened; it might have been right after that night.

He saw me remember and nodded. "Yes. That time. But it doesn't feel like the wolf is trying to take over. I know how to control that."

"*We cannot keep the people around us safe from ourselves,*" growled his wolf.

I couldn't find it in myself to be frightened of Adam—though I remembered clearly the look in his eyes when I confronted him on the stairs. He hadn't hurt me then—and he would never hurt me. But I wasn't the one who needed convincing.

"Is it something to do with the witches?" I asked tentatively.

"I don't think so," said Adam. "It doesn't feel like magic."

"*Yes,*" contradicted the wolf—startling Adam.

It was pretty weird having a three-way conversation when there were only two of us in the room. Adam and his wolf were usually more integrated than this.

"Okay, then," I said. "Do we believe your wolf? It was something the witches did?" They had made him obey them—it was a gift one of the Hardesty witches had. One of the nightmares Adam had after that night was that under the witch's orders, he killed me or Jesse.

Adam shook his head. "I don't think he knows anything I don't."

"Okay," I said, though I wasn't sure I agreed. "Now that we have all that out in the open, how about you open up our mating bond?"

"No," Adam said with emphasis. "I don't want this spilling out on you."

"*No,*" agreed the wolf.

"All of what spilling out on me?" I asked.

Adam flattened his lips.

"Adam?" I asked.

"No," he said.

He backed up against the door when I tried to put a hand on his shoulder. I raised both my eyebrows and stalked forward until he was flat against the wall and I pressed myself against him.

He could have pushed me away. Instead I could feel him try to pull himself back, as if he wished his body could dissolve through the door so we would no longer touch.

He turned his head from me, his eyes . . . ashamed.

"To hell with that," I muttered. He was only about four inches taller than I was, which meant that if he was trying to keep his lips away from me, there was still a lot of him I could reach. I kissed the skin under his jaw, soft but for the bristly hint of beard growing in. Then I rested my face against his neck and just breathed.

Gradually, his breathing matched mine and his body relaxed, melting into mine. Finally, his arms wrapped around me.

"I'm sorry," he told me, his lips on my temple. "I'm so sorry."

"Don't be sorry," I told him. "Fix it."

His chest huffed with a silent laugh, though the expression in his eyes hurt me. "I don't know how."

"Figure it out," I told him. "The first step might be letting me in." And I tugged lightly on the mating bond between us so he would be in no doubt about what I meant.

"No," he said adamantly. "There are things . . ."

"What kind of things?" I asked.

He shook his head. "Just things." His arms tightened around me and we stood, wrapped around each other like two children in the dark.

But he would not let me in.

3

I WENT UPSTAIRS WITH THE INTENTION OF WASHING up, but as I walked past Jesse's room, I hesitated. Light edged the bottom of her door. I knocked.

"Who is it?" she asked.

"Me," I said, then, in case she thought Adam was with me, "just me."

"Come in," she said.

I don't know what I expected, but it wasn't a completely cleaned room (though the carpet still needed vacuuming and some spot stain remover). It was dark outside, but I wouldn't have thought we'd been away from the house long enough for Jesse to have accomplished tidy in her room—but here it was. She took on her room once a month, and she was about a week out from her usual weekend cleaning frenzy.

Not only that, she'd had time to dye her hair—and freshen her makeup.

With her newly teal hair still wet, lip gloss and eyeliner intact, Jesse was sitting cross-legged on her neatly made bed, where she had been reading something on her phone. She set her phone aside when I came in and motioned for me to shut the door. It didn't guarantee privacy, but it did mean that any werewolf in the house wouldn't overhear us whether they wanted to or not.

Her eyes were puffy, but her lips quirked up. "I thought I'd try rage-cleaning. You are right, it does help. You were also right when you warned me I should tell them up front about changing schools."

"To be fair," I said, "I didn't expect this level of fireworks— and I'm not sure it would have been any better if you had told them both the day you made the decision."

"It might have kept Mom from bringing Auriele into it," Jesse said.

I snorted. "You underestimate your mother's ability to get people to perform in the Stupid Olympics for her."

"Hah," she said. "Maybe."

"I didn't come up to talk about that," I said, waving my hand. "From what Adam said, all of the offending parties have apologized for being stupid without proving they won't be stupid again. Which is all you can expect from people who are basically truthful."

She smiled. "To be fair, Mom can get me to compete in the Stupid Olympics, too. I can't afford to be too judgmental. But if someone is keeping achievement award points, for the record, I think Auriele won, hands down." Her mouth tightened, but she continued, "So what did you come up here for?"

"Gabriel left you a note when he moved out of my place." I held out the key to the house and then tossed it on the bed. "Your father didn't see it, I don't think. I left it where it was and didn't open it."

Her face paled and her nose reddened. She wiped her eyes carefully so as not to smudge her eyeliner. I could have told her that was a lost cause. "This day just couldn't get any better," she muttered.

"I never challenge the fates that way," I told her.

She smiled absently and focused on my face. "Did you and Dad have a fight?"

I glanced at the mirror on the top of her bureau. Jesse wasn't the only one who looked like she'd spent some time crying.

Damn it.

"Not as such," I said.

I caught myself before I told her that Adam was working out some issues—though he'd been frustratingly unclear about exactly what those issues were. I wasn't going to invite her into our marriage any more than I'd discuss things with Zee and Tad.

"I hope you set him straight," Jesse told me. "He's been unreasonable and grouchy for long enough."

"Can't argue with that," I muttered, wondering if I was breaking my rule about involving Jesse in my relationship with her dad if she was the one doing the commenting.

"So why have you been crying?" Jesse asked. "Did he say something?"

No. At least not the way she meant it. Her father was shutting me out, but I wasn't going to tell her that. That had been only one of the reasons I'd broken down and cried all over Adam tonight.

I said, "Dennis and Anna Cather are dead." And I teared up again, damn it, this time for my friends.

We hadn't done a lot together after Adam and I got married. Part of that had been the change in proximity. Though Adam's house was no farther from theirs than my old one had been, it was on a different street—no more driving past their house every day on the way to work and waving at them as they ate breakfast on their front porch. Like me, they had been early risers.

Mostly, though, I'd limited our interactions out of concern for them. For years I'd flown under the radar of the bigger nasties around. Once I'd married Adam, flying low had no longer been an option. I was exposed to the supernatural community—and even among normal people I drew attention. I didn't want to give the bad guys any more targets than necessary, so I'd restricted the amount of time I spent among people who couldn't defend themselves from the kinds of enemies I now attracted—like the Hardesty witches as only the most recent example.

I don't know why I hadn't considered that angle on their deaths earlier. I'd been thinking it had something to do with Underhill's door. Had the Cathers been targeted because they were connected to me?

Jesse jumped off the bed to hug me. "Mercy. Oh jeez. Anna and Dennis? What happened? Car wreck?"

She hadn't known them well, but she knew who they were.

I hugged her back and stepped away. "Stop that or I'll turn into a wet noodle and I need to keep it together."

She gave me a sympathetic nod. "Boy, do I know how that feels. Joel sent his wife up. Lucia's a hugger, which is awesome, but that's why my eyes look like this. I managed to deflect her with helping me clean or else I'd still be bawling." Which explained the mystery of how fast Jesse's room had been cleaned. "What happened to Anna and Dennis?"

"Magic," I told her, and then I gave her the full story as I knew it. If there was something running around that could cause Dennis to kill Anna, I wanted everyone I cared about to know about it.

"Witches?" she asked.

I shook my head. "Wrong kind of magic, I think. At least it doesn't feel like any witchcraft I've ever been around. And there aren't any witches around here anymore." Not that we knew about, anyway. We'd killed them all. "It didn't smell like fae magic, either."

"Well, that shoots down my other thought," she said. "With a door to Underhill in our own freaking backyard, I thought maybe something other than Aiden's dangerous best friend had come strolling out."

"I wouldn't rule anything out about Underhill," I said darkly. "But it's a lot harder to get out of Underhill than into her." I looked at the key that Jesse had clenched in her fist—and thought about her going past Underhill's door to get to my mobile home.

"I hate to say this," I told Jesse, "but I think that maybe you might want to wait until daylight before you go over to the house to retrieve the letter."

She shook her head. "Nah. I needed to get out of this house tonight, so I called some friends and we're all going out to a movie. One of them has a thing for Tad. It's doomed, but it's not my place to tell her that. But that's why I invited him, too. I'm working on the theory that exposure will cure her of her crush from afar. Anyway, Tad offered to take us all in his new old van."

Tad had just finished a build on a VW bus; well, mostly finished. Mechanically it was sound and the interior was completely redone, but he hadn't decided on a paint job yet so it was still primer gray.

"He's picking me up first," Jesse told me. "He'll be by in about fifteen minutes. I'll have him stop at your house to pick up the letter."

"Okay," I said. If Tad couldn't keep her safe, no one could. He was a good shoulder to cry on, too. "Have fun. Your dad and I are going out to chase rabbits."

Finding the jackrabbit I'd seen was mostly an excuse to search. Something had hit Dennis with a lot of magic, and Dennis mostly just hung around his house, so whatever had happened had probably occurred nearby.

Jesse snorted; she knew that we weren't hunting dinner. But she only said, "You two have fun killing cute fuzzy animals."

I gave her a thumbs-up and headed out.

"Hey, Mercy?"

I stopped in the doorway and turned back.

"Be careful."

"Always," I told her—which might not have been entirely true. Her laughter was a little sharp.

"I always try not to die," I told her more truthfully.

"Okay," she said. "And, hey, Mercy? Thanks for not reading Gabriel's note." There was an edge of bitterness I didn't care for in her voice.

"Don't give me too much credit," I told her. "Your mother doesn't willingly talk to me. If she did . . ." I shrugged. "She might have had me checking out his underwear drawer before I knew it."

"Hah," Jesse said, pointing at me. "I think you are the only person in this house who is totally immune to her."

"That's because I love you and I love Adam," I told her in all seriousness. "That makes it impossible for me to love Christy." That was probably more truth than I should have given her, but it had been a long day.

Her mouth turned sad. "Yeah," she said. "I get that."

———————

I WASHED UP IN MY BATHROOM, RESTING A COLD washcloth on my eyes until they weren't so puffy. I looked in the mirror and decided I was good enough, and headed downstairs.

I could hear Adam talking on the phone; I was pretty sure it was someone from work. Nothing important or he would have shut his office door. But if he was on his phone, then he wasn't changing to his wolf. That gave me time to go talk to Aiden about the door to Underhill.

Aiden's room was in the basement, so I just continued down the next set of stairs. He lived in what had previously been the pack's safe room because Adam and his happy contractor (who said that fixing the damage routinely experienced by our house from a pack of werewolves had already paid for his kids' college and was working on his grandchildren's) had decided that it would be the easiest room in the house to fireproof. Aiden tended to have nightmares, and when he did, sometimes he started fires. There was a fire extinguisher in every room of the house and two in the main basement— one of them near the stairs, and the other on the wall next to Aiden's bedroom.

Construction had begun on another safe room in the far end of the basement. Werewolf safe rooms kept everyone else safe from the occupant (presumably an out-of-control werewolf) instead of the other way around like safe rooms in human houses were intended to do.

A safe room started out as a cage constructed from silver-coated steel bars. Then it would be covered with drywall and turned into a fairly normal-looking room because cages don't help anyone calm down. Our new safe room was still in the cage stage.

Aiden's door showed its origins in that it was solid metal, but it no longer locked from the outside. I knocked on it twice.

Aiden opened the door. His hair stuck out in medium-brown swirls as it tended to when he got upset, because he ran his fingers through it and occasionally would grab and twist. Sometime since I'd left the house, he'd changed his clothes and cleaned up.

As soon as he had the door open, Aiden started apologizing.

"I am so sorry, Mercy. I had no idea Tilly was planning on this."

"Not your fault," I told him. "When an ancient powerful force of magic decides to do something, people like you and me don't get much of a say in it."

He didn't look as though I'd relieved him of guilt. "If you hadn't let me stay—"

"We like you," I told him. "We'll take you how you come."

I'd told him that before. He was, I thought, starting to believe it.

He took a breath, then frowned at me doubtfully. "Ancient powerful forces of magic and all?"

"Yup. You're in good company in this family." I gave him a rueful smile. "Joel is possessed by a volcano spirit. I have Coyote, who likes to show up and make trouble whenever he chooses. Even Adam comes with Christy baggage that just keeps on giving."

"Okay," he said. "You are all cursed, and I fit right in."

I laughed. Aiden learned fast. Anyone listening in would never think that he'd been trapped for who knows how long in that magical land and had only popped out just a few months ago. Jesse credited it to her tutoring with the aid of Netflix.

"I did come down to ask about Underhill's door," I said.

He nodded. "I already talked to Adam a little about it. She told me she put it there . . ."

He frowned trying, I knew, to recall Underhill's exact words.

Exact words were important to the fae—and Underhill, as far as I'd been able to tell, followed the rules that governed the fae. "She said, 'I need a door to Mercy's backyard. I miss you. The fae aren't playing nice and I don't want to owe any of them anything.'"

"Why would she owe the fae anything?" I asked.

Aiden shrugged. "I don't know. But it wasn't specific, so maybe it was something she said to distract me from the fact that she put a doorway in our backyard."

"Can anyone else use the doorway?" I asked.

He nodded. "Me and Underhill. I made her spell it that way as soon as I saw it. She guards her doorways pretty zealously anyway, but there are monsters in Underhill and sometimes we get out."

"Yep, well, there are monsters on this side of Underhill's doors, too," I told him briskly. "Don't get feeling too special."

He started to smile at me—and then his gaze grew suddenly intent. "Mercy, what happened?"

"My eyes aren't swollen anymore," I said, a little indignant. "I spent time with a cold washcloth."

He reached up and put a hand briefly on my face—his hand was warm. "Your eyes are sad, Mercy. Washcloths can't help that."

I told him about my neighbors. I included the jackrabbit and the ghost. I left out my interlude with Adam.

"Their deaths hurt you," Aiden said when I finished. "I am sorry for your loss." Frowning, he leaned against the door. "There are a few things that can use a bite—use that blood contact to make people do their will. Vampires, for instance."

"Marsilia would never permit it."

Aiden shook his head. "Not Marsilia's seethe. The ones in Underhill wouldn't owe her any fealty."

Like the rest of us, his thoughts had immediately gone to the door in our backyard when looking for a culprit.

"There are *vampires* in Underhill?"

Aiden said, "Everything you've told me about your neighbors' deaths could have been done by the fae. Other than a few of the less powerful fae—and creatures like the goblins, whose control of glamour is different—they could all take on the form of a jackrabbit. And while the fae don't use blood as often as, say, the witches do, there is a lot of magic in blood. But you told me that it didn't smell like fae magic to you. That still leaves other options. When the fae were driven out, there were still servants, curiosities like me, and prisoners left behind in Underhill. Tilly opened the prisons when she exiled the fae who were their caretakers. Most of the prisoners were—or had been—fae, but not all of them were. There are some weird things roaming around. Weirder even than I am." He shivered.

I was still stuck on vampires. "Vampires? Really? In Underhill? That's like finding coyotes in ancient Egypt."

"There weren't coyotes in Egypt, right?" he asked.

"Not unless Coyote—" I held up a hand. "Sorry. Let's get back to the idea that something escaped from Underhill through the door in our backyard and killed my friends." I had a thought powered by his tales of creatures set free by Underhill. "How many escapees could there have been?"

"If something escaped, it would have had to be before I found the door," he said. "I could believe that one creature escaped— but she doesn't like to lose her captives."

"It wasn't there when I got home," I said.

"Good," he said. "That makes multiple escapees even less likely."

"Would she know if something escaped?" I asked. "And more

importantly, would she know which something escaped?" And hopefully give us more information on what it was and how to kill it.

He nodded. "I think so. But she will know that I'll be mad at her over it—so getting her to tell us if something escaped will be hard. I'll call her and see what she will tell me. It might take a while for her to answer."

He didn't mean that he'd use the phone.

"Okay," I said. "Thank you." I started to go, then paused. "I should let you know that Adam and I are going out hunting jack-rabbits."

He frowned. "I think I should come along," he said. "Just in case. Let me get my tennis shoes on."

BY THE TIME WE WENT BACK UPSTAIRS, ADAM WAS waiting for us in his wolf form.

"I talked to Aiden. He agrees it might be something escaped from Underhill," I told Adam. "He has decided to come help."

Adam looked at Aiden, who gave him a cool look and said, "You are lethal, no doubt. Mercy is quick. But I lived in Underhill for a long time, and I made some friends there as well as enemies. Some of them . . . I know what they did in Underhill, but I have no idea what they could do out here. Magic works differently out here. Maybe we'll run into someone I know and we can chat. And if not—well, most things burn when I want them to."

Adam huffed a reluctant agreement. We didn't like using Aiden as a weapon. He was under our protection, not the other way around.

But he was right—he knew things we didn't.

"Okay," I said. "But if I say run, you run."

He gave me a look. It was probably not a look of agreement. Who was it that said leadership is a matter of never giving orders that you know will not be obeyed? I figured that his silence was the best I was going to do.

I stepped into Adam's office to change. Modesty was a thing that I'd left behind a long time ago, but Aiden looked like a kid. Unless there were dying people involved, I would strip naked out of his sight.

Once I was changed into my coyote self, Aiden let Adam and me out of the kitchen and closed the door behind us. They followed me through the backyard. Night had fallen and the stone fence looked strange in the light of the waxing moon, out of place and mysterious. We all climbed through the old barbed-wire fence instead of climbing over the stone.

I HAD THOUGHT THAT I REMEMBERED EXACTLY WHERE the jackrabbit had been. But though I could smell a mouse somewhere nearby—and Adam scared up a pair of rabbits of the regular variety following the only rabbit trail we could find—there were no jackrabbits.

We went to the Cathers' house and sniffed around the garden. I found a rabbit trail, but it was crossed and recrossed by a dozen people walking over it. I finally found a bit of it that led off the property, and the three of us set off through fields and backyards to find out if it was a jackrabbit.

Rabbits of all kinds smelled like rabbits. I could tell one *individual* rabbit from another—but to my nose there was no difference between a Flemish giant and a cottontail.

As soon as the trail took us through private property belonging to other people, Adam called pack magic to make us harder to notice. I didn't argue; people shoot at coyotes and I had the buckshot scars on my backside to prove it. The danger was reduced because it was night—but there were three of us, and a 250-pound werewolf and a boy weren't as good at stealth as a coyote was.

Rabbits don't travel in straight lines, and this one had rambled all over. Our bit of hometown was a patchwork quilt of large fields and once-large fields broken up into odd-shaped properties with homes ranging from 1960s trailers to modern mansions and everything in between, as well as a few industrial plants on the river.

We passed by or through hayfields, marijuana farms, organic farms, berry farms, and a few small vineyards, though the best vineyard country is on the other side of the Tri-Cities, and we ran through a lot of backyards, too. There were horses, cows, goats, chickens—all of whom ignored us, wrapped as we were in pack magic. The cats saw through the magic, as did the foxes. But they only watched our passing without sounding any alerts.

At one point we jumped into a backyard that was full of old cars. Most of them were rotted husks, with kochia, tackweed, and Virginia creeper growing up through the old floorboards—but there was a row of cars next to the house that were covered in tarps, and one of them . . .

I ducked my head low and tried to see under the tarp without being too obvious about it. Adam nipped me lightly on the hip and Aiden laughed. A light went on in the house and we all scrambled to get out of the yard before the back porch light turned on.

Fortunately, there was a break in the fence big enough for

Aiden to get through, and even more fortunately, that was the hole the rabbit had used to get out, too.

Trailing prey by scent for long takes a lot of concentration, even when there aren't mysterious tarps hiding what I was pretty sure was an old Karmann Ghia. Adam and I started trading off who was following the trail every ten minutes or so.

Rabbits are usually more territorial than this one was. I'd trailed rabbits in circles before, but never such a long trail over new territory. We didn't run into any old trails where the rabbit crossed its own path, as it would if this were its usual haunts. It made me think we might be on the right track.

The trail eventually took us across a road and into Two Rivers Park, a swath of green space along the river where the Snake joined the Columbia. Two Rivers wasn't all that far from our home, but we hadn't taken anything like a direct route here. Some of the park is groomed for picnics and recreation, but a fair bit is left wild with trails shared by equestrians and hikers. That was the part that the rabbit led us to.

Aidan stopped by a big sagebrush. "Hey. Over here," he said. "I think I've found your rabbit. Parts of him, anyway."

We trotted over to him but we didn't get quite there before we discovered something else. I froze, but Adam growled, the silvery ruff around his neck rising up, as did the hair along his spine.

I changed into human. I was taking a chance because we weren't out of sight of the road, but it was dark. Humans would need more light than that to see that I was naked. Nonhumans probably wouldn't care.

Aiden could see just fine in the dark. But we needed to communicate and it was a lot faster for me to change than for Adam to do it. He could, if the occasion warranted, pull on the pack for power to make the change more quickly, but then he'd be stuck walking home naked. A lovely sight, sure, but also illegal.

"Werewolves," I told Aiden. "Strangers." I glanced at Adam when I said this. I didn't know the three wolves I'd scented, but he was older than I and had traveled more among the werewolves. He knew a lot more of them than I did.

Adam just looked at me.

"Strangers to me, but Adam knows them." And he wasn't happy about it.

"Invaders," said Aiden.

"Yes," I agreed.

"Is this your rabbit?" Aiden asked me, gesturing at the bits of dead cottontail he'd found. It wasn't the jackrabbit, for sure. But we hadn't been certain we were following the jackrabbit's trail.

My nose isn't as good in human shape. I glanced at Adam, who stuck his nose closer to the rabbit—and shook his head.

"No," I told Aiden. "This isn't our rabbit. They left this one as a challenge and a test. We're too close to pack headquarters; they wouldn't have killed something unless they were investigating how well we patrol our territory." I looked at Adam for confirmation.

He growled, the sound rumbling deep in his chest. He bumped me with his shoulder, pushing me toward home.

"But what about the jackrabbit?" I asked him.

He gave me an impatient huff.

"Something made Dennis kill his wife," I said. And, damn it all, I teared up again. "That rabbit is a clue."

"How do you know that the rabbit we've been chasing is the

jackrabbit you saw?" asked Aiden reasonably. "It could be any old rabbit. Do you smell magic? I don't feel any."

I shook my head. He was right.

"Even if it was that rabbit, Mercy . . . there is not, right now, any proof that the jackrabbit had anything to do with the killing of your friends. Though parts of Underhill are infested with jackrabbits—and the creatures that feed upon them—I don't know of any killer bunnies."

I gave him a narrow look. "Is that a reference to Monty Python?"

He grinned. "I *like* Monty Python. I understand the jokes. So if there is danger out here that isn't related to whatever it is that attacked your friends, maybe we should listen to Adam and go home to regroup."

"Three wolves," I muttered, though I knew better. "I'm not worried."

Adam gave me a look and I threw up my hands. "Yes, all right. Okay. I know. Where there are three, there could be more. We could be looking at a pack. And yes, I don't want to meet a hostile pack when it is just you, me, and the firebrand." I glanced out toward the river in the direction that the rabbit we'd been trailing had run. "But the rabbit we've been following isn't acting like a normal rabbit and I want to know why."

Adam sneezed.

"Home," I told Aiden, resigned.

Back in coyote form, I led the way home with Aiden in the middle and Adam following from behind. We took a more straightforward way home, but since we also went by road instead of through fields and backyards, I wasn't sure it was any faster.

"Do you feel that?" asked Aiden almost soundlessly. "Someone is watching us."

By the pricking of my thumbs, I thought, though in this form I didn't really have thumbs. But Aiden was right, I could feel the hair on the back of my neck spark with the feeling that we were being observed. I glanced upward but didn't see anything in the night sky except for stars.

Adam huffed agreement and pushed us into a jog. We weren't running away, but the faster pace might force the person or people—or rabbits—following us to break cover. It was harder to stay hidden at speed.

We turned down the road that led to our house, and whatever or whoever was following us was still behind us. Adam waited until a small grove of big old trees hugged the road, and he disappeared into the shadows there without a sound. He must have pulled a little more pack magic out, because the ground around the trees was covered with crackling-dry leaves and even Adam wasn't good enough to get through those without making some noise.

Aiden and I kept to our jogging pace as if nothing were wrong—and a jackrabbit leaped out of the bushes and bit me on the neck, really sinking its teeth in.

I snapped back at it and missed but gave chase as it bolted through the underbrush and into an alfalfa field. We both tunneled through the bushy stuff using the furrows where the alfalfa grew thinner. A werewolf—I could hear Adam crashing behind me—wouldn't be able to run through this at the same rate.

Jackrabbits are built for speed. They can run as fast as an ordinary coyote. I was not an ordinary coyote—and I was determined this rabbit wasn't going to get away from me. I felt, faintly, as though there were a pressure on my head—like an incipient headache—but the sensation was lost in the greater drive of the hunt.

I pounced and snapped my teeth on flesh and fur. I had it between my teeth, though it didn't feel or taste quite right, not like a rabbit. And then it was gone. Not run away—gone. It turned from flesh into smoke in my mouth, an acrid-vinegary smoke that burned my lungs and tasted like the magic that had filled Dennis's body.

I dropped to the ground gasping and choking. My eyes burned and my throat felt like I'd tried to swallow a hot coal, and I curled up into a ball with the force of my coughing. I couldn't breathe, couldn't . . .

Cold arms picked me up and began running with me slung over a shoulder. I heard a wolf growl—and the vampire carrying me growled, too, and said words I was not able to pay attention to. I didn't have a clue where the vampire had come from and I was too busy trying to breathe to care.

The next thing I knew I was flung through the air and cold water closed over my head. It should have made everything worse—water not being conducive to breathing, either—but as soon as it surrounded me, the burning went away.

Survival instincts kicked in and I started trying to swim—and a wolf shoved his head under me and tossed me out of the water. We must not have been too deep because although he didn't get me all the way out of the river, I landed on solid ground with only a few inches of water rushing around my legs. And I could breathe.

I stood there for I don't know how long—probably not as long as it felt—just letting the sweet cool air rush in and out of my lungs as water swirled around my paws and dripped off my fur. Adam stalked out of the river to stand beside me, his teeth bared in a snarl aimed at the vampire standing on dry ground.

"Don't be dramatic," said the vampire. "I was just saving her life. You should be thanking me." He gave a sad sigh. "I am afraid that Marsilia is correct when she says that good manners are a casualty of this modern age."

"Why the river?" asked Aiden in a mild tone. He was standing on the shore, but he was wet, so he must have jumped in after me, too. I hadn't noticed.

"Everyone who ever read Washington Irving knows that running water can wash away magic," said the vampire. "Or is that story the one that says evil can't cross running water? I forget."

"Huh," said Aiden, keeping a wary eye on Wulfe. "How fortunate that you were here."

Wulfe was the scariest vampire I had ever met—and I'd met Bonarata, he who ruled Europe. But Bonarata was predictable to a certain extent—which Wulfe was not. I'd known that Wulfe could work magic, too, that he was a wizard—able to manipulate nonliving things with magic. I had known he could do a little of other sorts of magic, but I'd always assumed that it was something to do with being a vampire, a very old vampire. And all that might be so, but I'd recently learned that he was also a witch.

I was afraid of witches. I was afraid of vampires. I was very, very afraid of Wulfe.

The night all the witches had died, I'd used my affinity with the dead to lay an army of zombies to rest. I'd gathered them up in my magic and told them, "Be at peace." They'd all been released from the hold the witches had bound them with. As one, they had dropped to the ground and left their corpses behind. Wulfe had been touching me at the time—and he'd dropped to the ground, too.

I'd been worried that I'd killed him . . . destroyed him. I needed to figure out a word that encompassed what happened when a vampire ceased to exist. "Dead-dead," maybe? An end to living death? But Wulfe had recovered, leaving me caught between relief (he had been there because he was helping me) and worry—Wulfe alive was a lot more of a problem than the guilt I'd have felt for inadvertently ending his vampiric existence.

Whatever it was I had done had interested him very much. Ever since the night of the witches, I'd been catching his scent around our yard when there was no reason for him to be there. I'd even caught a glimpse of him now and then, when he wanted me to know he was nearby.

I'd treated him as I preferred to treat ghosts. If I didn't pay attention to him, maybe he'd go away.

"Not fortunate," demurred Wulfe, answering Aiden with a coyness that would have been more appropriate from a Southern belle in an old movie. In old movies, overacting was standard fare. "*Not* mere luck. I am stalking Mercy. Of course I was around, because that's what stalkers do, or so I've read. It's my new hobby."

I stared at him, and then I coughed up some river water, which felt a lot better than that smoke had but was still not fun. Then I stared at him some more—and started shivering. It might have been the water and the night air.

With his words, Wulfe had destroyed my ability to ignore his lurking. Stalking. My friend Stefan, who was also a vampire, had warned me that Wulfe thought I was interesting. And that had been *before* I'd done whatever I'd done to him.

Wulfe smiled at me. To someone who didn't know him, hadn't seen him with enslaved victims he was slowly killing, that smile might have been sweet. But I knew better. His expression sent cold chills into my chest. There was intent in his eyes. He was hunting and I was his prey.

When I get scared, it sometimes manifests as anger. I wanted very badly to shift back to human so I could tell him what I thought about his hobby. I didn't, though. I didn't want to be naked in front of him. It wasn't modesty. Naked is vulnerable in front of predators like Wulfe.

Adam moved between me and Wulfe and met the vampire's gaze. It wasn't something I'd have advised; vampire powers work just fine on werewolves. But I could feel Adam draw on the pack ties, so he must have done it as a deliberate show of power. I hoped he was right, that the pack had enough juice to neutralize the vampire's magic.

Wulfe raised an eyebrow and his smile grew sharper. He stared at my mate. It felt to me as though it might have been hours, but I think it was less than ten seconds before Wulfe looked down. He was still smiling.

"Oh goodness," he said. "A challenge. What fun." He looked at me. "Are you going to live? You'll have to tell me how you ran into a field chasing a rabbit and ended up enspelled and dying." His smile widened. "And then I saved you. You owe me for your life."

"You will leave her alone," said Aiden, and his voice was no longer mild.

I looked over. Aiden might be dripping with water, but he didn't look cold, though the night air had an edge of chill that preceded true autumn. In fact, as I watched, steam was starting to rise off him. He was standing much, much too close to the vampire.

Wulfe's eyelids lowered and he smiled. "Make me, Fire Touched. Make me."

Aiden was too close to the vampire, too far away from Adam and me for either of us to prevent what happened next. Aiden reached out and touched the vampire's arm, and Wulfe was engulfed in fire.

The vampire screamed, a high-pitched, terrified sound, his body so bright with fire that it hurt to look at. He flailed his arms as if trying to put the flames out—or trying to fly. He stumbled backward, away from Aiden. Sparks started drifting from his burning body, landing among the dry leaves and weeds, which started to burn.

Still screaming, Wulfe rolled on the ground, but it did no good; the flames continued undaunted. His flesh bubbled up and blackened—the air began to smell like someone was holding a barbecue. The warmth from the fire brushed my skin.

Unlike a gunshot, screams were not common around here, but no lights went on and no dogs barked. I realized that Adam must still be holding on to the pack magic that kept people from noticing us.

And still Wulfe burned.

Adam climbed onto the bank and bumped his shoulder lightly into Aiden's side and the boy reached over (not down, because Adam is a werewolf and Aiden is not very tall) and put his hand on Adam's back, closing his fingers on Adam's fur. Other than that, the boy looked unmoved by the gruesome sight of Wulfe burning.

I came up on Aiden's other side more slowly.

Wulfe rose to his knees and reached out as if to touch Aiden— but lacked the strength to close the distance between him and us. "Please," he said. "Please. I don't want to die . . ."

And he lied. I had become much better at telling truth from falsehood. It used to be that vampires were difficult. It used to be that I needed scent to smell the lie. But now, sometimes, I could hear it.

I took a step forward, ignoring Adam's growl.

Wulfe dropped to the dirt, facedown. He stopped moving, but his body still burned, flesh blackened and smelling like burned fat.

Then he turned his head and looked up at me. In an entirely normal voice he said, "Too much, right?"

The flames around him died, leaving us all in the dark as Wulfe bounced up to his feet.

I had never seen something that Aiden could not burn. I'd seen him melt metal and crack stone with his fire. A vampire was not metal or stone. Vampires are *vulnerable* to fire.

There were not a lot of ways to kill a vampire. Fire was the best one I knew of. I had trouble pulling air into my lungs again, but this time it wasn't magic that caused my difficulties—it was fear. I would not have thought that anything could make Wulfe more terrifying to me before this moment. I had been wrong.

The skin and burned muscle tissue reknit itself as Wulfe dusted off the remnants of his clothing, which seemed to have fared a lot better than they should have, given all the burning that had been going on. His pants were nearly intact, if blackened and smelly. He looked at Aiden and the smile died away from his face. Aiden stepped closer to Adam.

"Child," he said. "I gave you your chance. I won't give you another."

He looked at me, hugged himself, and rocked back and forth to the rhythm of my heartbeat because creepy was what Wulfe did. In a fade-away voice he said, "Well, boys and girl, I think my stalking is done for tonight. This was much more exciting than I thought it would be. Ta."

He waved a hand, then turned on his heel and walked back down the road. We all watched him go. I didn't think it was an accident that, at the same bunch of trees that Adam had used to disappear, before the rabbit had bitten me, Wulfe blended into the shadows and was gone.

In high-alert mode, Adam pushed us all back down the road toward home. Nothing more tried to kill us before we made it into the kitchen.

I made a beeline for Adam's office. Emerging a few minutes later, wearing my clothes and in human form, I found Aiden waiting for me at the table. Like mine, his hair was still wet.

"Adam went upstairs," Aiden said. "I think he's going to change and come back down. I told him that I needed to talk."

"Are you okay?" I asked.

He laughed, sounding tired. "I am never okay, Mercy. But some days I am more okay than others. This is one of the 'other' days. Wulfe did something to me. Look."

He held up his hand and nothing happened. I wasn't sure what I was supposed to be looking at.

"Since Underhill made me, Mercy, I have never not been able to call up fire." He wiggled his empty fingers and put them back down on the table. In a small voice he said, "I'm not even sure how I feel about that. I can't protect myself. But at the same time, it might be good to be just . . . ordinary."

"Don't get used to it," I warned him. "If Wulfe did something permanent, I'm pretty sure he would have bragged about it."

"Is that what you wanted to talk about, Aiden?" asked Adam, entering the kitchen still buttoning his shirt. His skin was flushed from the change and he was barefoot.

Jeez, he was sexy.

Aiden shook his head. "I know what killed Mercy's friends," he said. "And it is bad."

73

Adam pulled up a chair opposite Aiden, all business. "What can you tell us?"

"Did you see her wounds?" Aiden asked Adam. "Before Wulfe threw her in the river."

Adam started to shake his head—then stopped. "I thought it was a trick of light. But it looked like there was steam rising from the bite on her neck."

Aiden shook his head. "Not steam. Smoke.

"When I lived with my friends in Underhill"—before they all died, he meant—"there were places we knew not to go. Sometimes it was because one of us saw something—or one of us died. But mostly Tilly would warn us about them. This was before we knew what she was—though we sometimes wondered where she learned all the things she knew. One of the places Tilly warned us about was a cave where a beast lived. If it bit you, it could take your body over. Eventually it would tire of playing with you— and it would kill you. But when it bit you, the smoke that was its magic would fill you up and leak from your wounds. And once you were dead, it could take on your shape and go after your friends." He shivered a little more, as if he couldn't get warm. "She liked to tell those kinds of stories when we were huddled in the dark, already afraid. She called this creature the smoke beast." He bit off the word, shook his head, and looked a little ill.

I recognized that look. When he'd escaped Underhill into the ungentle hands of the fae, they'd gifted him with a translation spell. Even the most finely crafted translation spells, I'd been told, are traumatic. They ruffle through memory and thought for the meaning of the word that needs translation. And the one they'd imposed upon Aiden had been of the quick-and-dirty variety.

"That's not quite the right word," he said. "Maybe 'smoke

demon' is a better translation." His mouth tightened again. "Though not a demon as you understand it. Evidently there is not an adequate word for it in English. I don't know if it was one of a kind or if there are more of its kind loose in the world. I haven't heard anyone saying anything about it." He shook his head. "Anyway—supposedly it can become anyone or any living thing."

"The fae can do that," observed Adam.

Aiden nodded. "Yes. Which makes it interesting that its ability to shapeshift was one of the things Tilly warned us about. Maybe it wasn't fae—but she didn't say that. But the main thing she warned us about was that if he bites you, he takes over your body. I have the distinct impression, though I don't remember why, if it takes you over, your death is inevitable."

Something had bitten Dennis, I thought. *And he had killed Anna and then himself.* I remembered the tight feeling in my head, just before I'd gotten my jaws around that rabbit.

I have a limited and unpredictable resistance to magic. Maybe this was one of those kinds of magic that didn't affect me. I felt a chill of retroactive relief at not being some sort of mind slave to the jackrabbit smoke beast who had bitten me.

"What does it want?" I asked.

Aiden shook his head. "That's all I know about it. Other than that it was dangerous enough that Tilly warned me to stay away. I'll ask Tilly what she knows—but you might also ask Lugh's son if he knows anything. It was imprisoned in a territory of Underhill that his family controlled."

"Did she release it on purpose?" I asked.

Aiden shrugged. "I don't know." He looked at me. "It isn't out of the question."

4

"FIVE IN THE MORNING IS A CRUMMY TIME FOR AN all-hands meeting," said Honey briskly as she came in the door.

"Mercy wanted it to be at three in the morning," said Aiden. "But Adam told her that he needed everyone functional."

He was curled up on one of the living room couches and wrapped in a blanket. He didn't normally feel the cold, but whatever Wulfe had done to him was still lingering.

I was pretty sure I was right that if Wulfe had done something permanent, he would have bragged about it. I didn't think Wulfe had enough power to undo something Underhill had created— but I was less sure of that today than I would have been before last night.

The wolves had given the blanket curious looks, but no one had asked Aiden about it. At his words, though, the stragglers who were lingering in the living room, mostly hovering over too-hot-to-drink coffee they'd gotten from the pot in the kitchen, directed appalled gazes at me.

I hadn't been serious about three a.m. But at two in the morning, Adam had been on the phone, on the Internet, or pacing for hours and hadn't seemed likely to sleep anytime soon. Aiden, who had been seriously spooked by the creature he thought might be wandering around our home—and by having his magic quenched so thoroughly—had kept me company as I made cookies and watched Adam pace until I declared "enough" and went to bed myself.

With the wee-hour light peeking into the windows, the pack accused me of torturing them with their sleep-deprived eyes, if not words. I shrugged. They didn't need to know how wound up Adam had been about the intrusion of another pack into our territory. And his stress was not lessened by the trouble that he had characterized as a lack of control over the wolf (but his wolf seemed to think was something different). Adam would show them what he wanted them to see, what they needed to see: their Alpha strong and resolute.

So instead of explaining, I told them, "Adam said that it wasn't anything that couldn't wait for the morning. It had to be *early* morning so that we could get the whole pack here. You can blame Auriele, who has to be at the high school by seven at the latest. Adam is upstairs if you want to head to the meeting room. He'll start as soon as everyone gets here."

"Do you know what this is about?" asked Ben. He took a sip of his coffee and then exploded into expletives that had a couple of the wolves taking out their phones to look up a few of the words he used. He was British, our Ben, and had the foulest mouth I'd ever heard. One didn't, I was pretty sure, have a lot to do with the other, but both of them occasionally required translations.

"We are holding a meeting," I pointed out to him when he'd calmed down enough to listen, "so we don't have to repeat the same stuff over and over as new people come in."

Sherwood Post opened the door on the end of my sentence with a steaming Starbucks venti cup in one hand.

"Starbucks is open?" asked Luke. "I could have gotten Starbucks?"

"Hey," I said. "Don't diss my coffee."

"How's Pirate?" asked Honey.

Pirate was the one-eyed kitten that Sherwood had rescued. There had been a point at which we had all been certain the kitten wouldn't make it. But as of last week, he'd been freed from the vet's tender care.

Sherwood nodded at Honey, which meant that Pirate was fine. Then he looked at me and asked, "What's up?"

"A meeting," I told him. "So I don't have to repeat myself over and over."

Ben snorted a laugh.

Sherwood looked like a lumberjack in his red flannel shirt and khaki pants. He wore the peg leg today, so he was probably headed to work after this. The foot prosthetic was more expensive and he didn't like to risk it. He'd just gotten a new prosthetic that looked like a modern artist decided to blend the idea of a foot with a spring. It was more useful and stronger than either of the other two, but he wasn't comfortable in it yet, so he only wore it at home or at the gym.

No, he hadn't told me all of that. He still didn't talk much—but the whole damn pack gossiped about him like a bunch of fond mamas. His facility with magic—when his wolf took over—had resulted in a betting pool about the real identity of our amnesiac pack mate. I had instituted a one-dollar limit per bet, winners split the pot. It currently stood at $187.29.

There was, I had learned from the entries, an entire folklore about old wolves and their deeds that I had been unaware of. Being a history major, I was more than a little grumpy that no one had told *me* all those stories—but I was learning. I kept the betting book, and before I would write down the name, I made the wolf doing the betting tell me about their candidate for the position. Maybe sometime I'd record all the stories I learned. I couldn't publish them since a lot of them demonstrated just how dangerous werewolves were—and we were currently trying to soft-pedal that for the humans we lived among so they didn't decide that the only good werewolf was a dead werewolf. But still . . . someone should write them down.

The choices for Sherwood's real identity weren't limited to *werewolf* legends, though. Five people had put their money on Robin Hood.

If they had been older wolves, I would have been excited, but four of them were from the current generation and the other was, I think, joking. Still, Sherwood Post to Sherwood Forest made a certain amount of symbolic sense. And everyone knew that Robin Hood had lived in Sherwood Forest. So had Little John and Alan-a-Dale, Friar Tuck, and Will Scarlet. Little John had gotten two dollars. Alan-a-Dale and Will Scarlet one dollar each. No one had put money on Friar Tuck—our Sherwood just didn't look like the friar type.

As Kelly had pointed out when he handed me his dollar for Robin Hood, Bran seldom did things without reason. When I told him the story I'd had from both Sherwood and Bran, that he'd picked the name because Bran had had a book by Sherwood Anderson and the treatise on manners by Emily Post on his desk, Kelly had snorted.

"Please," he said. "Everyone knows that Bran keeps his books in his bookshelves and not on his desk unless he is actively reading. We had that from several different sources. Also, no one has ever seen Bran read Sherwood Anderson, before or since that day."

I blinked at him. Apparently there had been a lot more serious investigation into Sherwood than I'd been aware of.

Misreading my expression, Kelly backtracked a little. "Elliot knows a couple of wolves from the Marrok's pack. Luke knows a few more."

"Might be right," I said. "I don't remember."

Most of what I remembered about Bran's study had to do with keeping my eyes down and pretending I was sorry (or mystified, if the evidence against me wasn't strong) for whatever it was Bran was mad at me about. I hadn't been paying attention to whether he had books on his desk.

Before I took his dollar, though, I told Kelly, "You should know that historians are not sure that Robin Hood was a real person. Or if he was, if he was as significant a figure as the stories about him make it appear."

Kelly shoved the dollar into my hand and pointed to where three other names were behind "Robin Hood" on my notebook page. "And maybe he was a werewolf," he said.

When someone asked Sherwood directly about the Robin Hood identity, he hunted me down and asked to see the betting book. Sherwood put a dollar down on Robin Hood himself—and another dollar on William Shakespeare.

"I can shoot arrows," he'd said. "But I'd rather have been a poet."

I still wasn't sure how to take that. Sherwood certainly had given no sign of wanting to be good with words. On the other hand, poets don't need to use a lot of words to get their point across, even if Shakespeare had.

This morning, our mysterious Sherwood gave me a nod. "Upstairs?"

"Yes," I said.

He nodded again, this time at all the wolves gathered in the living room, raised his cup to me, and then headed up. After milling around a little more than they had been, the rest of the wolves in the living room followed him. Still wrapped in a blanket, Aiden tagged along behind. Adam had asked him to attend the meeting, too.

Darryl and Auriele came in a few minutes later.

Auriele brushed past me and up the stairs. She pretended not to notice me, and I was pretty sure it wasn't embarrassment or regret or anything like that driving her. She was still mad at me.

Darryl gave me an apologetic shrug—because he knew she was still mad at me, too—and followed her up.

Warren was the last one to arrive.

"Everyone else is here," I told him. "But you have fifteen minutes before the meeting starts." Something struck me suddenly. "You know? This is the most punctual group of any I've ever seen."

"Adam," Warren said, taking off his hat and tapping it against his thigh, "appreciates promptness. He explained that by holding meetings every four hours until the whole pack managed not to be late. It took two days and nearly resulted in Paul's death when he was late for the next-to-last meeting."

Paul had died by other means. We both sucked in a breath before I said, "I could see that. Punctuality was never really his thing. It is yours. Usually you aren't the last to arrive."

Warren was wearing jeans and boots, as he had since I met him. But his jeans now fit with an edge that said designer, and his shirt was a polo that clung to the muscles of his shoulders. His clothes had been getting an upgrade lately. In well-fitted, flattering-colored clothing, Warren looked pretty good except for the drawn face and circles under his eyes that were due to more than a single early-morning meeting.

"I would have been here sooner, except the case I've been working has me pinched for time," he explained. "It's a rough one."

"A case for Kyle?" I asked.

"Yeah," he answered, and there was a little smile on his tired face as he started for the meeting room. "For Kyle."

Kyle was his boyfriend, though that didn't quite encompass what they were to each other. They hadn't taken the final step—the human final step—of getting married. But Adam had told me that they were mates. I couldn't read the pack bonds that well, but I trusted that Adam could.

Kyle was very human and a divorce lawyer—and was more than likely responsible for Warren's wardrobe's improvement. Warren worked for him as a licensed investigator who doubled as protection and intimidation where needed.

I've always heard it said that it wasn't wise for people who were involved romantically to work together, especially when one of them worked for the other. But it seemed to be a good thing between Warren and Kyle.

I didn't ask Warren what Kyle had him doing—Kyle didn't believe in gossiping about clients. If there was something they needed from the pack, I'd hear about it. If not, it might show up in the nightly news.

Warren paused on his way up the stairs and gave me a long look. Then he walked back over, wrapped his arms around me, and kissed the top of my head. He was tall, made of whipcord and rawhide, my foster father would have said. He smelled like himself and a little like a new cologne or bodywash. I sank into the uncomplicated embrace; I hadn't realized how much I needed a hug.

"Heard about Auriele," Warren told me when I finally stepped away. "That woman is going to get herself killed trying to protect Christy from things she don't need protecting from."

"Truthfully," I told him, "I'm more worried about Wulfe."

I told him about my new stalker in as few words as I could manage. Warren knew Wulfe, so that cut down on unneeded explanations.

"A hobby, eh?" he said, the words casual enough, but there was a harsh edge to his voice.

"That's what he said," I agreed.

"That kind of hobby could get a vampire taken out of this world—you say he was immune to Aiden's fire?"

"Yes," I said. "And he was able to stop Aiden from being able to use his magic. And he can come into our house. When Ogden brought him here the night of the zombies—I don't know that he was invited in, Warren. I think he just came."

Warren's mouth tightened, but what he said was, "Well, don't that beat all. Guess you should have a conversation about him with Stefan."

"That's the plan," I agreed. "I have a call in to him, but I expect that he won't call now until tonight. We should go up so Adam can start the meeting."

The door to the meeting room was shut, and Jesse, waiting just outside her bedroom door, flagged us down before we could go in.

"What's the meeting about?" she asked.

"Jesse doesn't know?" Warren asked.

"Jesse was a smart person," I told him. "She came in and went to bed last night so she didn't hear about how we found a nasty creature that might be some sort of boogeyman for the fae and another nasty creature who has decided to take up stalking me for a hobby. If she'd gotten up earlier this morning, I would have told her all about it then. But now we have to go have a meeting."

Jesse raised her eyebrow in interest.

"Don't worry, though," I said, even though I'd made the whole situation sound funny so she *wouldn't* be worried. "The stalker saved me from the evil nasty."

"That's just wrong," Jesse said with a grin.

"I know, right?" I shook my head. "But that's not why the whole pack got called in. Or that's not the only reason why. There's a strange group of wolves nosing into our territory."

Warren stiffened. "Invaders?"

I shrugged. "Looks like. Adam's been on the phone to various old friends all night putting together a possible list of suspects. He plans on introducing our guests to all of us digitally before we meet them."

"Aiden went into the meeting," Jesse said carefully.

As a rule, pack meetings were for pack members only. Aiden was there so he could inform the pack about our escapee from Underhill.

"Since the pack is the reason you had to shuffle your life around," I told her, "I'd guess that you have a place in our meetings. Come on in if you want to—it will save me having to tell you everything again, anyway."

"Awesome," she said.

Warren looked at Jesse and gave a solemn shake of his head. "I thought you had more sense. I, for one, have always been grateful for the meetings I have not attended. But if'n you want to come in with us, I guess I'm a big enough shield that none of the others will try to drive you out."

"Except Dad," she said in a small voice.

I narrowed my eyes at the door. "He's abject in misery and wallowing in guilt after falling into Christy's"—I glanced at Christy's daughter and exchanged "trap" for—"situation. He won't object."

She looked down at herself. "I'm in pajamas."

"Go change," I said. "We'll wait." I glanced at my watch. "You have three minutes."

She jumped into her room and shut the door.

"Why?" Warren asked me.

"She deserves to be involved," I said. "She's making life-defining decisions because of the pack. Likely all three of our current crises will affect her one way or the other."

"And because it will drive Auriele to distraction," said Jesse, emerging from her room now clad in jeans and a shirt sporting a cat with an innocent look and a tail emerging from its mouth with the words *Got Mouse?* underneath. "Mercy is sneaky that way. Maybe I am, too." She twirled. "Do I look ready for the vengeance games?"

I decided that the mouse T-shirt was calculated. Though we weren't going to play cat-and-mouse games with anyone. I was not unaware that Auriele was going to squirm at the sight of Jesse, but that wasn't the reason I'd included her.

I couldn't stand to see her isolated. Not this morning, anyway.

Warren looked at me.

"I don't know what you're talking about," I said, and opened the door with fifteen seconds to spare.

And if I found Auriele's face before I stepped aside so Jesse could enter? Maybe making Auriele squirm a little didn't bother me at all.

From the front of the room, Adam looked up from his notes. He saw Jesse—and smiled at her. His smile widened when he saw me. Like Warren, he looked worn-out. I was pretty sure that he hadn't gotten any sleep at all last night.

"By my count, that's all of us," I told him.

"George isn't here," said Elliot, one of the more dominant wolves in the room. He was a big man, massive if not as tall as Warren. Like several of the other wolves, he worked for Adam's security company. Ex-military, I knew, but I didn't think his military service had been in the last hundred years.

Elliot had bet one dollar on Sherwood being Rasputin, the mad monk of Russia. Which was ridiculous because there were photos of Rasputin and he didn't look anything like Sherwood. Which I had told him at the time.

Elliot had grinned at me. "It's the eyes," he'd said. "You can tell by the eyes."

Which meant that he was, like several of the others, putting out bets to tease Sherwood. Sherwood, when he'd seen it, had grunted, then said something in Russian. I'm not sure what it had meant, but it had sounded exasperated.

Unlike others, I didn't put any stock in Sherwood's prowess in Russian being a clue to who he had been. Adam spoke Russian, and he'd been born in Alabama. Bran, as far as I could tell, spoke every language on the planet—if sometimes in archaic versions. Living centuries gave a wolf plenty of time to become fluent in any language they wanted to make the effort to learn.

New languages would be especially easy for Sherwood to acquire. He wouldn't need a large vocabulary because he didn't talk a lot.

"George couldn't get off work," Adam told the room. George was a police officer with the Pasco PD—it got him out of a lot of meetings. "He'll be here tonight and I'll update him."

Warren glanced at a couple of wolves and they got up, freeing the seats next to Aiden—who rolled his eyes at us.

"I don't need a protection detail," said Aiden, pulling his blanket closer around himself. "I don't think there's anyone here who wants to kill me." He didn't speak particularly loudly, but everyone in the room heard him just fine.

Jesse rolled her eyes back at him. She was better at it. "Just me," she said in syrupy tones. She continued with sisterly affection as she sat down, "Stupidhead—we *have* to sit next to you. How else am I going to pass notes back and forth? And why are you wrapped in a blanket?"

"Shh," said Aiden. "I'll tell you later."

Adam had leaned back against the table, legs crossed at the ankles and arms folded. "Anytime you are ready," he said with faux patience.

"Sure, Dad," Jesse told him, as Warren and I took our seats and the rest of the pack quieted down. "Go right ahead."

He grinned at her cheeky response, showing a dimple. Properly, I suppose, he should have enforced discipline. But our pack was very stable at the moment, forced there by the gigantic task of keeping the peace in our territory.

Since I'd made us responsible for the safety of the citizens of the Tri-Cities area, and the fae had taken it a step further and signed a treaty that established the Tri-Cities as a neutral place, we'd been kept hopping, what with minor actors coming in to test our mettle and major offenses like the latest one with the zombies. We were too busy to stoop to squabbles—as a result, our pack was a tightly knit bunch.

I glanced at Auriele and amended my thought. As long as Christy quit sticking her fingers into our business, we were a tightly knit bunch. Today there was a thread of tension in the room that hadn't been there a few weeks ago—or that I hadn't noticed a few weeks ago.

Adam took a breath and looked around the room. "I didn't ask you all here on a whim," he said. "Yesterday brought us some problems."

He explained yesterday in a concise and cogent manner—beginning with Underhill's addition to the landscaping of the backyard, through Anna's and Dennis's deaths, and ending with the final act of the jackrabbit hunt that left us with the realization that we had an unknown but magically capable foe, probably an escapee from Underhill.

I noted that he left out my vampire stalker. I wasn't sure why. I hoped that he wasn't trying to spare me any attacks by Auriele, who had become very quick to point her finger at me since Christy had resunk her claws into the pack. I didn't need him to protect me from Auriele; she didn't worry me. Made me sad, yes; worried, no.

Of course, he'd left out the werewolves, too, so maybe he was just working his way down the list of our new and newly active opponents, one at a time.

"Aiden has some insight as to what we might be facing," Adam said. "Since our adversary and the door to Underhill appeared on the same evening, we are making a guarded assumption that one has to do with the other. Aiden?"

Aiden stood up and gave the same précis he'd given Adam and me last night.

Darryl stood up when Aiden finished. Adam nodded.

"What makes you certain that Mercy's jackrabbit and your . . . smoke demon are the same creature?" Darryl asked. "I'm not doubting you. Just asking for clarification."

"Her wound smoked," Aiden said. "I don't know of any other creature that leaves smoking wounds with only a bite. Not in Underhill, at least."

Darryl sat down and Honey stood up.

"Are you certain it is something that escaped from Underhill?" Honey asked. "There are a lot of magically gifted others who are not werewolf, vampire, or fae. Could one of them have been attracted by all of the notice being paid to us? Maybe its appearance at the same time as the new door is just a coincidence."

Downstairs, the doorbell rang.

Jesse said, "Since I'm only here for curiosity's sake, I'll go get it."

"Wait." Adam held up a hand.

I gave voice to his thought. "It's five thirty in the morning and someone is ringing the doorbell?"

"Warren," Adam said. "Would you go down with Mercy and see who it is?"

By traditional accounting, Warren was third in the pack, after Adam and Darryl. As Adam's mate, I shared his rank—because women didn't get their own rank—traditionally speaking, anyway.

Our pack had started to . . . broaden our reality a bit. Pack members could still easily rattle off the ranking of wolves according to tradition—but they treated Honey as if she were ranked in the pack just below Warren, instead of the bottom-of-the-pack ranking where an unmated female would normally be accounted.

Honey blamed me for this—and she might have been right. Sometimes she chafed at it, but more and more she owned that rank. Auriele, as Darryl's wife, outranked everyone except for Adam, me, and Darryl in that order. But the pack had started treating her as if she were right behind Honey. And it felt like a promotion—even though technically she had dropped in rank.

Adam told me that he was just holding his breath and hoping that it continued. Werewolves are volatile creatures. It is hard for the human to hold the wolf in check—and when it didn't work . . . Well, there was only one thing to be done with an out-of-control werewolf. And now that the wolves were outed to the human world, there were no second chances.

Anything that could be done to strengthen the ties that bound the pack together also helped everyone manage better. Adam maintained that by actually paying attention to the real order of dominance, our pack members were better adjusted and not nearly so likely to go off on another member of the pack because their wolf was confused about who was actually dominant.

To that end we all pretended that we didn't see what was really going on, and only occasionally did it pop up in conversations. We weren't ignoring it—but we were pretending that nothing had changed.

The Marrok's son Charles, who treated his own wolf spirit as if it were another sentient being who shared his skin, once told me that wolves were straightforward creatures on the whole, and that most of the mess that was werewolf culture had been brought about by the human halves of the werewolves. I was beginning to see what he meant.

We also pretended—Adam, Darryl, Warren, and I—that Warren was not more dominant than Darryl. Warren was gay—and a lot of our werewolves had grown up in eras in which that was something not tolerated. The survival rate for gay or lesbian werewolves was far lower than for straight werewolves—which wasn't anything to brag about, either. Warren was the only gay werewolf I knew. The bigoted members of our pack had been bludgeoned (literally and figuratively) into first tolerating Warren and then appreciating him. But none of us was sure if that would hold should Warren become Adam's second—who would be counted upon to lead the pack should something happen to Adam.

All of that meant that Adam had just picked out the most dangerous werewolf in the pack besides himself to escort me downstairs. Maybe it was only because Warren had been sitting next to me, but I doubted it.

The doorbell rang again as Warren held the door for me and followed me down, as if I outranked him.

I STOPPED IN THE BEDROOM TO GRAB MY CARRY GUN and tucked it, loaded and ready to go, in the back of my jeans. Warren didn't say anything about it, just patted his lower back—he was carrying, too.

As we got to the bottom step, doors slammed and a car took off.

"Honda V6," I told Warren.

J-series, if it mattered. But that didn't tell him any more than it told me. There were a lot of Hondas with a V6 J-series, and there were different versions of the J-series. Hondas weren't my manufacturer, so I couldn't tell one version from another without having two different versions in front of me.

"Probably not a rental car," said Warren.

Okay, so it told us something. Rental cars tended to be the stripped-down versions and the V6 was mostly an upgrade.

We were both speaking very quietly as we closed in on the door. Warren kept his eyes on the windows where people could look in. It was darker in the house than it was outside now, so it would be hard for someone to see us, but not impossible.

"Adam needs to get opaque curtains and use them," said Warren.

"Then we can't see out," I told him, not paying as much attention to what I said as to the front door.

"I know he has cameras," Warren answered. "He doesn't need windows."

He bent down and cautiously looked through the peephole and shook his head.

"Maybe it's a Girl Scout," I told him. "They're short."

"There, you've done it," said Warren, reaching for the door. "Now I want a Thin Mint and it's the wrong time of the year."

He opened the door quickly, stepping away and to the side, but there was no attack. Instead, there was a body on the porch. It took me an instant that felt heart-stoppingly long to realize the body was breathing.

Warren leaned his head down, took a good scent, and then leaped across the porch and started running down the road as fast as he could—which was impressively fast, even in human form.

I was pretty sure that we were too late for catching the people who'd driven off, unless they had parked and come back to see what we did—which was possible. I checked out the man on our porch. I smelled unfamiliar werewolves, but I didn't smell any blood. He appeared undamaged except for the part about him being unconscious.

Good. Because I liked him.

"Mary Jo," I called out. "You want to come down. It's Renny."

The gift our werewolf invaders had left for us was Deputy Alexander Renton of the Franklin County Sheriff's Office. He was in uniform, so presumably they'd abducted him while he was on patrol.

Wolves in human form boiled down the stairs and out to the porch. Darryl and Auriele did the same sniff-and-go that Warren had done. Mary Jo dropped to her knees beside him.

"Damn it, Renny," she muttered to the unconscious man as she peeled back his eyelids to check his eyes. "I told you it wasn't a good idea for us to start dating again."

She checked his pulse, then looked up at Adam. "I think he's fine. His heart rate is normal, his color's good. They hit him with a tranq of some sort, I think. His department is going to be in the middle of a mad hunt for him. We should call them." That last was a request for permission.

"Do it," said Adam. Narrow-eyed, he looked out at our surroundings—pausing at a small boat on the far side of the river, maybe a quarter of a mile away. "That boat has binoculars pointed at us," he said in a conversational tone.

Virtually as one, the pack glanced at him to see where he was looking, then followed his gaze out to the river. They were intent enough that the pack magic rose among us and we, the pack, understood that there was no chance of getting to the boat before they fled, because Adam knew that. We also rejected using the handguns that some of us were carrying because it was too far for a clean shot, and besides, we weren't sure Adam wanted them dead.

The boat's engine got louder as the boat swung around and took its passengers upriver and out of our sight. The pack hunting magic subsided.

"We could intercept," suggested Ben, who did some boating with friends from work. "That small engine is good for being quiet, but pushing even that little boat upriver will be slow going."

Adam shook his head. "I don't want them yet," he said.

"I take it," said Honey, brushing her honey-colored hair out of her eyes, "that the wolves who did this were another of the interesting discoveries you made last night?"

"Because by Saint Peter's peter," said Ben, "an arse-licking boogeyman wasn't enough. We needed a bishop-beating bunch of mangy invading werewolves, too."

Luke laughed and in a fake British accent said, "Fecking right, Ben, my lad. But it would be take a real gobshite to try to invade us right this moment."

"Agreed," said Honey, while I was still trying to figure out what a gobshite was. "They should wait a few more months until attrition has winnowed our numbers down sufficiently."

A silence followed her words, broken only by Mary Jo's quiet voice as she talked to the sheriff's department.

It was true. Since we weren't connected with the rest of the packs (for various political and doubtless correct reasons) in the Americas, when our wolves left, there were no replacements. We'd lost eight wolves since we'd broken with the Marrok. One of us had died, and the other seven had moved for the usual reasons—better jobs, family necessity, and the war-ready tension our pack had to operate under right now. Adam could have made them stay, but he refused to do that. Our pack, which used to have between thirty and forty people in it, was down to twenty-six.

Our wolves had given up on the chase and were jogging back to the house.

"They want to talk to you," said Mary Jo, handing her phone over to Adam. "I'll take him inside."

"Put him in the spare bedroom," I told her as Adam explained that he understood that the sheriff's office was not happy with one of their people being taken. "The sheets on the bed are clean."

She picked him up in a fireman's carry. He was quite a bit taller and more massive than she was, so it looked a little odd.

"I'll get the doors," volunteered Ben.

It took Adam about ten minutes to negotiate a path forward with Renny's sheriff that didn't involve the sheriff's department taking the town apart to look for the perpetrators. The chill effect of Honey's words kept the rest of the pack quiet. Adam and I had talked about our declining numbers, but apparently it was a new thought for most of the pack. Or maybe hearing it said out loud made it harder to ignore.

Auriele, Darryl, and Warren were jogging up to the porch by the time Adam disconnected.

"Let's go back upstairs," Adam said. "I have some information for you about the wolves who dropped Deputy Renton on our porch."

ONCE EVERYONE WAS SEATED AGAIN—INCLUDING Mary Jo and Ben, who'd returned from settling Renny, who appeared to be sleeping comfortably—Adam ran down the details of the wolf kill the night before.

"I identified two of the werewolves from last night, and I made some calls," Adam said. "I have a pretty good idea who the leader of this pack is."

He let that sink in a moment, then continued, "And we can put some other names in the probable category. I don't think it's a big group; more than likely there are only six of them. Warren, could you get the lights?"

Warren reached over his shoulder and flipped the light switch. Adam pulled down the shades and turned on the projector.

A somewhat grainy photograph of the top quarter of a man appeared on the screen. He had a narrow, aquiline face, a long nose, and big dark eyes.

"Harolford," said Elliot as soon the photo came up. He didn't sound happy. The big man growled. "Bastard. Nasty opponent in a one-on-one fight—wiped the floor with me." Elliot looked at Adam. "That was before I came here—and I'm a better fighter now. But I don't have any appetite to go at it again with him. He's a good strategist—thinks a few steps ahead. I don't like him. At all. But he isn't stupid."

Adam looked around the room. "I haven't met him," Adam said. "Does anyone else know anything about him?"

"Maybe," said Auriele. "I don't know him, but if that is Sven Harolford—"

"It is," said Adam.

"Then I've had two women—werewolves both—who told me never to be alone with him," she said. Then she smiled, a dark and hungry smile. "Which makes me want very much to do exactly that."

There was a short silence.

"Don't remember him," said Sherwood. "But my wolf is pretty unhappy about him. I'd be okay with killing him."

When no one else said anything, Adam pulled up another face. No one knew that one.

"He has been going by the name Lincoln Stuart, though he is old and that is not his original name."

"Was he the guy who was second to . . ." Mary Jo snapped her fingers impatiently. "A pack in Nebraska, but I can't think of the Alpha's name."

"I know who you mean," Adam said. "And no, you're thinking about Lincoln Thorson. He's still second in the Lincoln, Nebraska, pack—which is why everyone remembers him. This isn't that Lincoln."

He brought up another photo; this one was the kind of photo taken on vacations. An Asian man and woman were standing in front of what I was pretty sure was the Grand Canyon. The shot looked as though it had been taken thirty years ago. The man was smiling at the woman, who was pointing up at him with both of her index fingers in a "look what I caught" pose that was completed by her over-the-moon smile.

"Chen Li Qiang." Carlos was not a big man, nor did he look like the badass he was. He worked for Adam, and his specialty, I knew, was de-escalating FUBAR situations. "Damn it, Adam," Carlos said with feeling. "Damn it. Li Qiang, he's a friend. I served with him in Korea."

"His name is Chinese," said Darryl. "And he looks Chinese."

"He is," said Carlos. "But he's lived in the States since he came over to work on the railroad and ran into a werewolf. He worked as a translator for the USMC because his Korean is almost as good as his Cantonese and Mandarin." Carlos rubbed his hands together and shook his head. "That girl in the photo was his wife. She died about five years ago—I went to the funeral."

"I remember," said Adam.

"I haven't seen him since," Carlos admitted. "I heard he didn't adjust to his wife's death well and he left his pack."

Honey knew the next one, a soft-faced man with gray eyes and medium-brown hair.

"That's Kent Schwabe," she said, sorrow in her voice. "He was a good man, Adam. Ended up in a bad pack, though—I think in Florida. Charles killed that Alpha back in the 1960s, and the whole pack was dismantled. We were casual acquaintances, though, so I don't know what happened to Kent after that."

"He moved to Texas," Adam told her. "He ended up in Galveston."

"That's Gartman's pack," said Warren, sitting up a little straighter.

It hadn't been a question, but Adam nodded. "That's right."

Warren growled. "Some damn fool should take that Alpha right out of existence. World would be a better place."

Adam tipped his head toward Warren. "Oh?"

"I expect you've heard people say he keeps the peace. That his wolves don't cause no trouble and they never say a bad word about him," said Warren. "I know, because I talked to Bran about that one a few times. Bran is watching him, but he can't do anything until he gets a complaint or something happens."

Adam said, carefully, "I understand that he's a hard man."

"Hell," Warren said. "I don't mind a hard man."

"I've heard that," said Ben, his British accent carrying through the room.

Warren gave him a roguish look—he and Ben were friends.

"Kyle aside," Warren said—and there were a few soft laughs from the pack. "Gartman's not hard, Adam, he's polecat mean. Some of his pack stay with him because they like that—he allows them to be mean, too. Most of them are too afraid to squeak."

"Good to know," Adam said. "I hadn't heard anything bad about him—until last night." He changed the photo again.

This time it was a thin-faced woman in profile. No one knew her.

"This is Nonnie Palsic. She's old. My informant—"

Charles, I thought, though officially Charles shouldn't be giving us information since we weren't affiliated with the Marrok. I'm sure the Marrok told Charles that, too, knowing exactly how well his son would follow that directive.

"—tells me that she's around four hundred years old. She's mated to this man."

He changed the screen to show an ordinary-looking guy with a baseball in one hand and a bat over his shoulder.

Adam looked over the room, and when no one spoke up, he announced, "This is James Palsic. He is older than his mate, possibly a lot older than his mate. I met James about twenty years ago—so did any of you who were in my pack when we were in Los Alamos. He was an engineer on assignment. Worked at the National Lab down there for two months before he went back to Washington, D.C."

When no one said anything, Adam smiled. "I have noticed that people don't tend to remember him. I've been told that it's not magic. Not sure I believe it. It is true that he is very low-key. He was one of the wolves I scented last night. Li Qiang was the other."

"I didn't know that you knew Li Qiang," said Carlos.

"I've never met him," Adam told him. "But I picked you up at the airport when you came back from the funeral."

Carlos flushed and looked away.

"Hey," said Adam. When Carlos looked at him, Adam told him, "Not anyone's business."

The words and the tone had a bite to them, were a reproof. But

Carlos relaxed, gave a nod, and settled back in his seat. "All right," he said.

"About six months ago," Adam continued, "there was a distur-bance in Gartman's pack. By the time Bran found out about it, it was over. Gartman had executed four wolves, and Harolford and a few of the remaining rebels were on the run. No sign of them since then, though Bran and Gartman have both been looking."

"Those six you just showed us," said Warren.

"Yes," Adam agreed.

"I've also heard of Gartman," said Darryl, his voice so deep that if Gartman had been in the room, he'd better have hoped he could run faster than our second. "Harolford and the others, they are in trouble and they have to find somewhere out of Gartman's reach. Our pack, not affiliated with the Marrok, might look like a good place to make a stand—if they can take us."

"They hunted on our territory until you noticed," Honey said. "To see how alert we are."

"No telling how long they've been in the Tri-Cities," Elliot said.

I cleared my throat. "The goblins keep a pretty thorough watch. Unless they have someone with Adam's skills, if they had been here long, we'd have known about it."

We paid the goblins to keep watch for us—as did the vam-pires. There just weren't enough werewolves to cover the whole of the Tri-Cities and the surrounding areas. I didn't have any idea how many goblins there were. But if a supernaturally gifted being stepped foot on our territory, mostly we knew about it within a few hours.

"Maybe they paid off the goblins," said Auriele.

I was about to disagree when Adam said, "Or maybe they are owed a favor—the goblins wouldn't betray us for money. But all of the fae have to abide by the bargains they make. These wolves have done a couple of things that make me think they've been watching us awhile—or that maybe they have a way to get information on us that doesn't involve them being here."

"Renny?" asked Mary Jo.

Adam nodded. "That's one. How would they know about Renny without being here?"

Jesse stood up.

Adam nodded at her.

"Facebook," she said. "Mary Jo posted a photo of their last date together." She sat down triumphantly.

Mary Jo slumped lower in her seat, but she nodded when she did.

"Facebook," said Adam, sounding blindsided.

Darryl stood up. "It would be a good idea for the pack members who are out to avoid having a social media presence."

"Make it so," Adam said as Darryl sat down. "Too many people know who you are—and that makes your friends and families targets."

"To those who want to take the pack from us," said Darryl heavily, his dark eyes flecked with gold.

Adam smiled—and for the first time in weeks it was a happy smile. Though nothing could erase the exhaustion on his face, that expression lit his face and sweetened the beautiful features.

"Yes," he agreed.

5

"IS THERE A REASON WE'RE HAPPY ABOUT THIS, BOSS?" asked Warren warily.

I happened to be watching Sherwood and saw him grin in sudden comprehension. He knew what Adam was doing.

Adam nodded in answer to Warren's question. "I think so. I'm going to conscript them, if I can. We need more bodies. They need a place to be safe. It might take some negotiation."

Auriele looked at Adam, and there was just a hint of a sneer on her mouth when she said, "Try to take them before they take the pack from you?"

Beside her, Darryl stiffened.

The smile melted from Adam's face and his eyes grew cold. "Make no mistake, Auriele. They cannot take this pack from me." He stared at her a moment, until she dropped her eyes. It was not voluntary, that averting of Auriele's eyes. I could see it in the stiffness of her shoulders.

"What the hell, 'Riele?" said Darryl in a voice that I don't think he intended to carry.

She shot him a venomous look.

"Auriele," said Adam in a soft, dangerous voice. "Do you want to challenge me for the pack?"

She shot to her feet. "Darryl—"

"Darryl is welcome to make his own decisions," Adam told her, without looking at Darryl, who was shaking his head vehemently.

"No," said Darryl. "Absolutely not." Obviously he didn't want Adam—or maybe Auriele, who was also not looking at her mate—to be under any misapprehension of his intentions.

"Auriele," said Adam. "Go to my office and wait for me there."

I was pretty unhappy with Auriele at that point. But that didn't stop the hackles rising on the back of my neck at his tone of voice. Auriele was a strong member of the pack, and I didn't like her being talked to like she was a misbehaving twelve-year-old. It brought up shadows in my memory of just such pronouncements from the Marrok.

But I was not a werewolf, and not caught up in the need for pack and order that the werewolves were. I knew that the argument she wanted was something that Adam could not tolerate here with the whole pack in attendance. If he didn't stop her right now, she might force him to do something that he didn't want to do.

The wolves were all of them dangerous—to other members of the pack, to the community, and to themselves. A wolf without boundaries killed people that their human halves would not want killed. Auriele knew how far she could push the rules of the pack—and she was pushing beyond them. That wasn't safe for her or the people around her.

Still, it struck me that Auriele and Adam were both acting a little out of character. I looked around the room and felt the tension in the air—but there had been something hovering in the meeting room since I'd first come in—before the Renny incident even. And I wondered, if Adam was locking down the bond between the two of us because he didn't want to damage/pollute/scare me (or whatever excuse he was using), what had been happening with the pack bonds? He couldn't shut those down—so what was he doing? And how was it affecting the pack?

Auriele hesitated for a heartbeat, then wrapped herself in righteous fury that I was not wholly unsympathetic with given Adam's tone of voice, before she headed out the door. I wondered how much of her over-the-top behavior had been pushed on her by the pack bonds she shared with Adam. I'd had a few members of the pack make me act stupidly before. They had been doing it on purpose—but I knew that it could happen. For that matter, I wondered if Adam's patronizing tone came from the same source that had made him act weird yesterday.

Adam watched her leave, then looked at Darryl.

"I would like to bring you into that conversation, too," he told Darryl.

"My mate is passionate in defense of those she loves," Darryl growled defensively.

Yes, but she wasn't stupid, I thought, sitting back. Yesterday and today she had been acting entirely out of character. Something else besides Christy was going on. Something maybe like Adam's struggles and the pack bonds.

"Her loyalty is one of her best qualities," Adam told Darryl sincerely—though he was quite aware that the rest of the pack were listening. "And so is her intelligence. So when I'm done here, we are going to sit down with her and figure out what is interfering with her usual good sense. It isn't that she suddenly decided she needs to take over the pack. If Auriele wanted this pack, I'd figure that out a few months after I'd agreed to take a twenty-year sabbatical in the Yucatán Peninsula and left y'all in her tender and competent care."

The stress level in the room resolved into a wry wave of amused agreement. Darryl . . . Darryl kept a game face on. I couldn't tell if he knew what was bothering Auriele or not. Adam, I thought, would know about what the pack bonds could do better than I did. He'd do his best to keep the pack safe and stable. But for how long?

Adam swept his gaze over the room again. And I saw how tired he looked, saw the weight on his shoulders—and I was the only one in the room who knew that there was a reason that had nothing to do with no sleep, Auriele's dramatic moment, mind-bending escapees from Underhill, or invading werewolves. That meant that I was going to have to be the one who helped him out.

"So," said Adam. "We have an invasion commencing and something of mostly unknown capabilities out creating havoc. Be careful out there. Watch your backs. Tell your families what's going on and tell them to keep an eye out. Don't hesitate to contact me if you think something is wrong. If you want to bring your families here to stay until matters clear up—we can do that. That they hit Mary Jo's boyfriend—"

"Of two weeks," said Mary Jo.

"Of two weeks," agreed Adam, "implies that they are watching us. They have spent some time studying how we function."

"What do you plan to do?" asked Elliot.

Adam smiled. "At its heart, taking over a pack is simple: kill the Alpha in a challenge. I plan on not dying. Go home." He waved his hand.

There was a rumble of laughter as the mass exodus took place. Darryl wasn't laughing. He stayed in his chair and stretched out his legs, his arms folded across his chest.

Adam caught my eye and nodded for me to stay where I was. Warren gathered Jesse and Aiden and exited with the rest. When everyone was gone, I shut the door.

Darryl glanced around to make sure the door was closed, then looked at Adam. "I don't know what it is, either. She's been upset—you know, the kind of upset that when I ask about it I get the 'nothing is wrong' answer." He grimaced at Adam. "Which is highly irritating when she *knows* that I can tell she's lying, but telling her that—something she already knows—will only give her an excuse to blow up at me. And she is looking for excuses to blow up."

At least, I thought, Adam isn't giving *me* that "nothing is wrong" answer anymore. I wasn't entirely sure that it was an improvement. If he'd been lying to me, I could be mad at him. That might feel better than this lump in my throat.

"Let's go see what we can do for her," Adam said.

"Why am I here?" I asked him. "You don't need me for this. She doesn't even like me."

"Sure she does," said Darryl unexpectedly. "Why do you think she's so mad at you about Christy?"

"That makes sense how?" I asked, flummoxed.

"As much sense as lying to your mate who is a werewolf," Darryl answered. "She is smart, passionate, and loyal. In situations that draw on all three of those, logic flies out the window."

"Agreed," I said. "But that doesn't tell me why you need me to come."

"I don't know about him," Darryl said. "But I'm hoping she'll be so focused on you that she'll forget to be mad at me. I want to be able to sleep tonight without having to keep one eye open."

"Thanks," I said dryly. "Happy to help."

ADAM'S OFFICE WAS NOT LARGE ENOUGH FOR FOUR people to fit comfortably. That was even more evident when three of them were dominant werewolves.

Adam sat in the chair behind his desk. Auriele occupied the other chair, a leather and maple work of art that Christy had given Adam for their anniversary one year. That left Darryl holding up a wall and me sitting on Adam's desk.

Auriele was sitting as though she were modeling for a portrait, she was that still. She held her body like a dancer just before the music starts, back upright and body tense. Her legs were tucked back, ready to push her to her feet at any time.

She had barely acknowledged any of us.

Adam pursed his lips. "So how do you think Harolford— always assuming he is the one in charge—will work his attack? Slow and steady? Or blitzkrieg with all barrels firing?"

Auriele finally looked up. "Are you asking me?" Her tone was incredulous.

Adam looked at Darryl, who was keeping his face neutral, and then me before looking at Auriele. *His* face was slightly amused. "Yes."

She glared at him. He raised an eyebrow.

"I thought we were going to talk about my behavior," she said, her voice a growl.

Adam tilted his head. "Why? *You* know what you did today was stupid. *We* know that there is something behind it that's a lot more traumatic than my ex-wife's disappointment about Jesse's choice of schools. I'm not going to ask you about it. Just inform you that"—his voice dropped low and softened dangerously as his eyes turned yellow—"you need to stop letting it affect you to the point where you are useless to the pack."

She met his eyes for a long moment before water gathered on her lower lids. I twisted around and opened a drawer in Adam's desk to grab a tissue. When I turned around, Darryl was kneeling beside her, one of his big arms wrapped around her. To accommodate his hold, she had slid to the very edge of the chair.

I handed her the tissue. She grabbed it and wiped her eyes.

"Damn it," she muttered. "I'm sorry, Mercy. I should have talked to you before I acted. I know that Christy isn't logical about you."

I made a humming noise. "It's probably the blue hair dye that I may or may not have put in the shampoo container she left in my shower," I told her. "I wouldn't like me, either, if I were her."

Her lips turned up and she gave a half laugh. "Yes, Mercy. I'm sure that the blue dye is the real reason that Christy doesn't like you."

She looked at Adam. "I'm sorry. I had some family news a few days ago." She drew in a breath, and when she spoke again, she was talking to Darryl. "My youngest sister is pregnant with twins."

The silence that followed was full of sharp edges.

Auriele and Darryl had no children. Male werewolves could

father children—but female werewolves could not carry them. The moon's call ensured that all werewolves had to change. The change from human to wolf is violent, too violent for a fetus to survive the first trimester.

Auriele's youngest sister was not a werewolf.

"Surrogate," said Darryl, his voice decisive.

"Who would be a surrogate for a werewolf?" Auriele shot back. The speed of her response told me that this was an old argument.

"Someone who wanted to become a werewolf anyway," answered Adam. "Let me speak to Bran."

They both blinked at Adam as if it had not occurred to them.

"I don't know that there is such a woman," he continued. "And even if we can locate one, it might be hard to find a reproductive specialist willing to work with our situation."

"And if you find someone like that," said Auriele, "there will be a long line of werewolves who want children. And our pack is not affiliated with the Marrok anymore."

Adam shrugged. "You have time. As long as you don't force me to kill you or Darryl in the meantime."

"So don't start that fight, *mi vida*," said Darryl.

She laughed, though it sounded shaky. "I'll keep that in mind." She rubbed her hands together, rolling the damp tissue into a ball. She leaned a little harder into Darryl and said. "Blitzkrieg. There is no other way for them to succeed. This is our territory and we have resources here. They need to make you look weak, make the pack feel unprotected. So they have to hit us hard and heavy. Mary Jo's beau won't be the only family member hit."

"He wasn't hurt," I said.

"First salvo," said Darryl. "They are telling our pack, 'Look at us, we can take yours and return him unharmed because we are just that powerful.'"

"I agree," said Adam. "None of our vulnerable is safe."

"Should we call them into the pack house?" I asked.

Auriele shook her head. "No. Not yet. We have to trust our people. Adam's been instilling fighting skills in all of us, willing or not, way before Darryl or I joined the pack. We can protect our own. If someone needs support, then they can call for help."

"How about assigning some of the single wolves to help keep watch over the families?" I suggested.

"I'll get that done," said Darryl.

"Okay," said Adam, checking his watch. "If you leave now, Auriele won't be late for work."

They left and shut the door behind them. I turned around on the desk until I was facing Adam. I took a moment and just looked at him, seeing the stress of whatever was bothering him, the cost of the sleepless nights, and the toll that came with being the Alpha of the pack. I'd been toying with an idea that might help him, and looking at his careworn face gave me the hit of courage I needed.

I slid off the desk on Adam's side and grabbed his hand. He grabbed my hand in return—just a little tighter than he normally would have. I leaned back and hauled him out of his chair—he didn't resist, so I didn't have to pull too hard.

"Come on," I said grimly.

"Come where?" he asked.

"I have something you need to see." I kept his hand in mine as I went back upstairs, ignoring the sounds of lingering pack members from the kitchen and living room.

"What is it?" Adam asked me.

I shook my head. "Wait."

I took him into our bedroom and closed the door, letting go of his hand as I did so. I leaned an ear against the door.

"What are you doing?" he asked. He moved farther into the room, rubbing his neck tiredly.

"Making sure that there isn't anyone to overhear," I whispered.

He gave me a frown. "There isn't anyone upstairs, Mercy. You and I can both tell that. What is this all about?"

I turned back to him. "For what I'm going to reveal to you," I said seriously, "I want to be absolutely sure that we are alone."

He hadn't had a good night's sleep in weeks. He'd been stressed and exhausted before all hell had broken loose yesterday. Something needed to give before the invading werewolf pack was the least of our worries.

I pulled down the roller shades over the windows, explaining, "I don't want my stalker to see or hear anything, either."

"It's daytime," he said.

"I don't trust daytime to stop Wulfe," I said, half-seriously. "And I don't want him to see this."

He made a growling noise. "Mercy—"

I pulled my shirt over my head and dropped it on the floor. Unhooking my bra, I shrugged it off, too.

Adam went silent.

"I told you I had something to show you," I murmured in what I hoped was a sexy purr.

I was not sexually brave—had not been even before my assault a while back. Without Adam, it was not unimaginable that I would never have opened up enough after that to even take a lover, let alone a mate. But resisting Adam was never in my cards—this morning, I hoped he felt the same way.

He didn't say anything, nor could I read the expression on his face. Maybe he was suppressing what he felt—or maybe with the shades drawn to darken the room and his head bent to put his eyes even deeper into the shadows, I just couldn't see him well enough to interpret his expression.

My heart was in my mouth and I was too . . . "frightened" was not quite the right word, but it was fear that kept my breathing shallow. Fear of rejection. Fear that whatever had him all but strangling our mating bond would stop him from taking up my invitation—and what that would mean about our relationship going forward from this moment. So maybe "frightened" was exactly the right word.

Without a reaction from him, I had two choices.

First, I could grab my clothes and tell him I had to go to work—and it wouldn't be a lie even though I had texted Tad during the meeting that I would not be in today until after lunch (along with a warning to watch his back because there were some interesting things happening).

My business didn't need me to go into work this morning, but I would need a place to lick my wounds and the garage would do. If I lost my nerve here, I had a place to run.

My second choice was to keep braving on—and trust Adam not to leave me hanging out on a limb.

My fingers numb with terror, I unzipped my jeans. I didn't say anything, because I was afraid that my voice would tell him that it wasn't desire I was feeling—though while hauling him up the stairs my skin had been hot with anticipation.

I was risking my marriage.

Men couldn't fake desire the way a woman could. Not that I

could, and certainly no woman with a werewolf for a lover could fake it for long. But a man's desire was obvious and unmistakable.

There were a dozen reasons floating around in my head, in my heart, for why Adam might not be interested. There were werewolves invading our territory. There was whatever had him putting up barriers between us. There was the fact that he hadn't had a full night's sleep in however long. It was daytime and he should be getting ready for work.

And if he rejected me—however gently he did it—I would never find the courage to open up like this to him again.

There were tears gathering in my eyes at the thought of losing us, losing what we were. But I felt that it would say something equally bad about our relationship if I didn't take this risk. So I tipped my head down and blinked hard as I slid my jeans and—the hell with it—switched my grip so my panties slid off my hips at the same time.

I couldn't look at him as the cloth puddled on the carpet. I could barely breathe. I knew it was a balmy sixty-eight degrees in the room, but I felt like I was in an ice cave. Naked, I stepped away from my clothes and then stopped, forcing my hands to remain at my sides and not move to protect my bareness from his sight.

Adam had seen me naked before—but I don't think I'd ever felt more vulnerable. Because this wasn't about being naked in flesh—it was about risking myself to help him. Help us.

Possible disastrous story lines ran in my head as I stood there. I imagined him expressing his sadness that I had put him on the spot. I heard him tell me that this wasn't the time for such a thing—that he'd made it clear that sex was off the table until he'd figured out whatever knotty problem his head was all tangled up in. Rapidly I conjured up failure, and imagining that was nearly as traumatic as the real thing might be.

I was seriously considering throwing up, when warm hands closed over my shoulders and Adam's face pressed against my neck.

"Fucking hell," Adam said about the same time I realized that my neck was damp with his tears. "I don't deserve you, my love. I don't deserve this, Mercy—but by God I will take it. I love you, too."

And on his last word, our bond blazed open between us, but, in this moment, it conveyed only emotions, not thoughts. I didn't know if opening the bond was intentional on his part, or if it was a product of his control slipping. Carried by that tie, the deluge of his emotions crashed through me, a complex mix of incredu-lousness (I had, by golly, surprised the heck out of him), exhaus-tion, and love before it was all consumed in a blaze of desire.

Sheer relief let my own tears, now quite out-of-date, fall down my face. Oh thank God, it had worked. There would be a tomor-row for us. I hadn't screwed everything up even more than it al-ready had been.

"Why are you cryin', darlin'?" he asked me in a murmur—then stiffened a little, as if remembering the place he'd brought us to over the past few weeks.

"Fear," I answered him honestly. "If you hadn't touched me when you did, I was making a beeline to the bathroom so I could throw up."

He laughed, as I meant him to. I didn't ask why he'd been crying. Maybe he would think I hadn't noticed. Maybe *he* hadn't noticed. But today was to give him a safe space to be, work off some stress, then rest. He wasn't in a place, I didn't think, where honesty about what he was feeling outside this moment was going to do any of those things for him.

His strong hands were so very warm on my chilled skin. His arms, restrictively tight around my ribs, nonetheless let me breathe. I took a moment to take in his scent. The force of relief rushing through me temporarily short-circuited the arousal I would normally have felt naked and in my husband's arms.

That was okay, though, because the touch of Adam's fingers that ran with hot, slow possession from my shoulders, down my back, and around my butt would have been enough to spark passion from an icicle. His hard body, both familiar and more necessary for the time we had not touched, softened my stress-tensioned muscles.

"Shhh," he whispered in my ear. "We're good. We're good."

That hand on my butt lifted me, and I wrapped my legs around his waist as he took us toward the bed—before diverting to a side table, where he set me down.

With the thin light streaming through the edges of the blinds, Adam slid to his knees without ever losing contact with my body and loved me with his mouth and hands until I forgot my grand scheme to get Adam to loosen up and give him some peace, no matter how temporary. I forgot everything except his touch. Adam was usually a generous lover, and today was no exception.

I lost track of time a bit, drowning in the heat he brought with him. The next thing I knew he was pushing inside me, the zipper of his jeans rough on my skin. He was hot and hard and *mine*.

I bit him on the neck, and he laughed, a husky, aroused sound that I hadn't heard from him in far too long.

"You make this fun," he said in a rough voice that contrasted with the smooth movement of his hips.

"Back atcha," I managed, tight and full and wishing I could stay in this space for the rest of my life.

He moved again and I quit talking—but then so did he.

If his first acquiescence to my seduction was driven, as I thought it might have been, by his understanding of how hard it was for me to strip for him when I wasn't sure how it would be received, there was no question of his need. When we both came, I was surprised in retrospect that the side table—sturdy as it was—had survived its encounter with us.

Adam picked me up again and took me to our bed. He looked at me sprawled languorously where he had put me and began stripping off his own clothes. Where I had jerked mine off in nervous rawness, he pulled his off slowly as his eyes—and other parts of his body—told me that he liked me naked on the bed. That was only fair because watching Adam remove his clothes was a treat I would never tire of.

He didn't put any striptease in it, just a slow, predatory intent that made my heart, my eyes, and the rest of my insides pretty happy about it.

Werewolves, all of them, are hard-muscled because the wolf is a restless creature. Adam, though, considered staying in shape a thing of paramount importance—part of the need to protect those around him that made him an Alpha. His body was a weapon, like his guns, his knives, and his swords—and it would not fail him.

As a purely unintentional side effect, watching him pull off his shirt was very much like watching someone pull a sheet off a great work of art. Muscles bunched and slid as he dropped the shirt and took off his jeans and underwear.

"Mmm," I said.

He smiled—and the tiredness around his eyes melted away. "Mmm back," he said, putting a knee on the bed.

And after a while, with me lying on him like a sweaty limp noodle, he fell asleep. I lay very still to let him rest—and soon fell asleep, too.

Something was moving me around, sliding me across the sheets—but I was tired and buried my face in a pillow with an indignant and not-awake grunt. Warm hands on my rump hesitated. A big warm body—naked male body—pressed into my back.

"No?" he said.

I wiggled my hips in invitation, still mostly asleep.

His head moved next to mine. His mouth tickled my ear as he said, "Nudge." And it wasn't a question because he picked up my hips and slid inside.

I laughed, not because I was amused at anything—or at least not just because he amused me. I laughed because he made me happy. He gripped my hips and I joined the dance.

I WOKE UP SORE, RESTED, AND FRANTIC BECAUSE ONE of the blinds was up and I could tell that it was well past noon. There was a note on the pillow next to me. Written on it in thick black Sharpie and pretty decent calligraphy was:

AND SO IS THE FATE OF ALL THOSE WHO AWAKEN THE NUDGE.

On the other side of the paper, in regular pen and Adam's angular all-cap printing, was:

THANK YOU, SLEEPING BEAUTY. HEADING TO THE OFFICE. WAS AFRAID IF I WOKE YOU UP I WOULD NEVER GET OUT OF THE ROOM.

The effect of this morning's exercise, a few hours of needed rest, and the note was that I smiled all the way through my shower. The hot water eased the edge of soreness nicely, and by the time I got out I was ready to go to work.

It had been a lovely cease-fire, but I knew that the morning had not solved anything except, maybe, given Adam some happiness and rest in the middle of an unknown battlefield. I would know when Adam had worked out whatever was bothering him because he would tell me—and he would open up our mating bond, which was once again shut as tightly as a drum.

I dressed and pulled out the phone to text Tad that I was on my way—and found I'd missed a phone call from Stefan last night. He hadn't left me a message. There was also a text from Jesse: **Out with friends—took Aiden with. My friends think he is cute—if they only knew :P Back for dinner. Dad was cheerful when he came down! Go you!**

I felt my cheeks heat up. But I knew that seducing Adam in the middle of the day was not going to be a secret.

I texted Tad and started out—pausing at the spare bedroom where Renny had been installed. But the room was empty and the bed was made. I texted Mary Jo to see if everything was okay, though I expected that it was. Had there been more trouble, or had Renny not recovered as well as expected, I wouldn't have been allowed to sleep in this late.

Mary Jo texted back: **Renny's fine. Headache. Sorry to have missed his own kidnapping. He doesn't remember anything at all. Poor Renny.**

There was no one home downstairs, either.

I found a note from Lucia on the table:

Took Joel out to check on the progress Adam's contractor is making on our house.

Their house had been trashed when Joel had been cursed with the volcano spirit that kept him in dog form a large percentage of the time. It had taken him and Lucia a while to decide what to do about it.

Once the insurance policy kicked in, they finally hired Adam's go-to contractor to fix their house. Until Joel had better control of his fiery half, they would have to stay with us at pack central because Aiden was able to stop it when Joel's spirit decided to lose its cool. But they had options. They could rent the house out, sell it and buy another later, or just keep maintaining it empty and let it wait for Joel to recover.

Medea yowled at me and stropped my leg, broadcasting the information that no one had fed her. Cats lie, and I was pretty sure she was lying. But feeding her made me happy and made her happy.

Tad called as I was putting away her kibble.

"Nice to hear that you got some" was the first thing that he said.

I disconnected. My cheeks might be bright red, but I had a grin on my face. I had indeed. But that didn't mean that I'd accept teasing without fighting back.

He called again and the first thing he said was "Jesse said her dad looked like the cat who ate the canary." A pause.

I decided he was waiting for me to hang up again, so I didn't.

"If you ask me if I'm a canary, you'd better sleep with your lights on," I warned him.

He laughed. "Okay. So if you are coming to the shop anyway— the parts we've been waiting on are in, but they dropped them off at another garage over in Pasco by mistake. They can redeliver but it will take them two days. The other shop offered to drop them by tonight when they close down."

"No worries," I said. "I'll pick them up." I wrote down the address of the other shop. It would take me out of the way, but someone had to pick them up. And I was pretty hungry; I could stop at a fast-food place on the trip. "Do you want me to bring some food?"

"Mercy, it's three in the afternoon," he responded with stentorian disapproval.

I had been trying not to pay attention to the time.

"Okay," I said. I would not apologize for being late, I thought, all but squirming in fresh embarrassment. *I own the shop. If I don't come in, no one will fire me.* Which was sometimes hard to remember, since I'd worked for Zee for years before I bought the garage from him—and both he and Tad (more rarely) gave me orders instead of the other way around.

I locked the house and headed out to my car.

"Sorry," I said despite myself.

Tad laughed. "Dad dropped by with an early lunch and stayed. If you get the parts here by four, we should be able to knock out those two cars that are waiting for them and we'll be all caught up until the next disaster strikes."

"Super," I said. I paused by the door of my car and turned in a slow circle, inhaling slowly to give myself time to process the scents around me. No strange wolves. No jackrabbits. The scent of Wulfe lingered a bit, but it was an old scent. It was coming from the hood of my car. He'd spent some time sitting on it last night.

I was pretty sure that he wouldn't have done anything to it.

"Mercy?"

"Sorry, got distracted."

"Are you all right?" he asked. "I got your warning—thank you, by the way, for being vague. I always appreciate vague warnings." More seriously he said, "Jesse also said that something went down last night, but I'd have to ask you about it because she wasn't sure what was top secret hush-hush and what wasn't."

"You talked to Jesse a lot today," I said, suddenly struck.

"She stopped by with some friends—including that poor girl who can't do anything but look at me, blush, and giggle. Unless Jesse just wanted to pass on her version of vague warnings, I don't actually know why they stopped. I am very much afraid it was so the silly girl could giggle at me."

He sounded exasperated. Yes, I thought, Jesse's friend's crush was doomed.

"I'll fill you in when I get to the garage," I said.

He growled at me.

"I have to go," I told him. "The most advanced technology my car has is a tape deck and it doesn't work. So I can't talk and drive."

"Mercy," said Tad. "I have been really patient."

I took another deep breath—still no strange werewolves, no jackrabbits, no fresh vampire scent. Yes, it was still daytime. Yes, vampires do not go out in the daytime. But as I'd told Adam, I wouldn't trust the light of day to stop Wulfe. The wind was breezy—if there had been something around, I'd have smelled it.

I popped open the car door and stuck my head in. No scents that shouldn't be there.

So I told Tad, succinctly, about the werewolves and the possible escapee from Underhill. I left out Wulfe because it was as embarrassing as it was terrifying—and because I couldn't see how it would impact Tad's or Zee's safety.

"Underhill put a gate to the Fair Lands in your backyard?" said Tad, sounding nonplussed. Behind him, I heard Zee say something in German about Underhill. I didn't catch it all but it didn't sound complimentary.

"Has to stay for a year and a day," I told them—because Zee could hear what I was saying. His ears were nearly as good as mine, maybe better. "I don't know how she managed it—or why she agreed to take it down at all."

"Aiden *is* a member of your household," said Tad.

"Yes?" I inquired. Aiden would never have allowed a door to Underhill so close to him if he could have prevented it. I believed that the same way I believed the sun would rise in the sky tomorrow.

"Oh, I don't think he did anything on purpose," Tad said. "She just used him to gain permission somehow. A polite 'I wish I could see you more often' might have done it. I'm a little surprised it didn't happen sooner—but Aiden survived her reign for a long time. It probably took her a while to elicit exactly the right response."

I thought about Aiden's guilt. No doubt Tad was right.

"Well," I said, "we knew he was dangerous when we invited him to stay."

Zee said something. I could hear it quite clearly, but it was in German and I wasn't up to translating anything that complex.

"Dad says he doesn't remember a creature that fits your description or that was called a smoke demon or smoke beast—

other than a Japanese spirit. And he can't see what a Japanese demon—as in a being from a different plane of existence, not a Christian demon . . ." He paused and asked, *"Sag mal Dad, hatte die alte katholische Kirche eigentlich Recht mit dem, was sie über Dämonen sagte?"*

"*Ja,*" answered Zee. "*Mehr oder weniger. Aber nicht auf die Weise, wie sie glaubten.*"

"Huh," said Tad. "That's interesting."

"Did he just confirm the existence of demons as espoused by the medieval Catholic church?" I asked.

They had it right, Zee had said. *More or less. But not in the way they believed.*

Those demons weren't only the property of the medieval church—there were churches now that believed in them. Demon stories had appeared in the Bible and various apocrypha, too. But it had been the medieval church that had built castes and characters based upon the biblical references, cataloging and defining demons. And using the existence of demons to cement the church's power.

I'd run into a demon once, but it hadn't . . . I didn't think it had been one of those.

"That's off topic," Tad said before I could ask for clarification. "Dad doesn't know of anything that quite fits your jackrabbit. But it could be something that lived only in Underhill—and he didn't go there much."

A spate of German interrupted him.

"Though he says it could be that you just don't know enough about it yet. Or it could be that he's forgotten and it will take a while for him to remember. He'll also ask around. If it is something that was imprisoned in Underhill—and it would be useful to know for certain—maybe Uncle Mike or some of the other fae will remember."

"It would be useful," I said. Thanking Zee was safe enough, I was sure, but it worried him that I might forget and thank some other fae. So I tried not to do it.

There was a hesitation and then Tad said, "Did Jesse talk to you about Gabriel's note?"

"No. Did she talk to you?" I asked.

"She let me read it." He swallowed. "Look, I think it helped Jesse, but now I'm worried about Gabriel."

"When did he leave the letter?" I asked.

"He didn't date it," he told me. "But some of the things he said made it clear that he put it there the day he moved all of his stuff out."

"He has a new girlfriend," I told him. "As of two weeks *after* he left that letter." Close to that by my reckoning.

Tad swore softly. "Bastard didn't waste any time mending his heart." I guess he wasn't worried about Gabriel anymore.

"Heartbreak can be like that, boy," said Zee heavily. "Healthy pain invites healing. Gabriel is a good boy; he'll be a good man. Not all relationships that end are failures."

Then his voice became brisk as if he'd embarrassed himself by being too sentimental. "Mercy, you will have to hurry to get the parts here in time for us to fix those cars. Otherwise they will have to wait until morning."

"I have to hang up before I can get going," I told them both. "Talk to you soon."

I disconnected, got in my car, and drove.

6

THE SHOP WHERE THE PARTS HAD BEEN DROPPED off was in east Pasco, a couple of miles from Uncle Mike's Tavern, where the fae tended to congregate. It hadn't been a bad drive from the shop or my house when the Cable Bridge had been up and running. But a troll, with the help of one of the Gray Lords of the fae, had destroyed it.

Construction had begun just a few days ago on a new bridge— by popular demand, a copy of the old bridge, which had been something of a landmark. It would be a year or more before it was functional, though, and in the meantime the shortest way to Pasco was over the Blue Bridge.

For everyone.

Before the Cable Bridge had been destroyed, I'd avoided the Blue Bridge as much as possible because of the heavy traffic. Now it was miserable, but my options were that or driving all the way through Kennewick and crossing the river on the interstate bridge and driving all the way back through Pasco.

I took the Blue Bridge and crossed it, with all the rest of the traffic, at a walking pace. Not too bad, considering.

Once I turned off onto Lewis Street, the main east-west artery in this part of Pasco, traffic returned to normal speeds. I wondered, briefly, if I should stop in and see if Uncle Mike would talk to me about our jackrabbit. We still weren't sure it was the creature that Aiden thought it might be—we weren't even sure that it was an escapee from Underhill. We were just operating on best guesses.

I decided half a block before the turn that would take me to Uncle Mike's not to go. If that old fae knew something, he was more likely to talk to Zee than he was to me. So I stayed on Lewis and headed toward Oregon Avenue, where a host of industrial businesses were located: heavy farm and construction machinery sales and services, metalworks, industrial fasteners, agricultural irrigation—and the auto shop where the people had dropped off our parts.

A block or so before Oregon Avenue, a collection of train tracks crossed Lewis—and all other east-west traffic in Pasco. The trains were active here and stopped traffic on a regular basis.

Lewis Street was the major thoroughfare on the east side of Pasco because of the short tunnel that dropped under the railroad tracks to allow the free flow of traffic from the city to Oregon Avenue.

The tunnel itself, built around World War II, was . . . odd. Lewis Street narrowed from four lanes to two lanes and dropped below ground level before burrowing under the tracks with pedestrian walkways on either side. That narrowing was the root cause of the accidents that happened around the tunnel.

The pedestrian walkways in the tunnel were creepy. They were unlit, and the decorative concrete barricades with pillars that kept the walkways safe from traffic also kept them safe from light. Even on the brightest summer day, those walkways were an invitation to trouble.

The weirdest thing about the tunnel was the way it was just plopped into the middle of the intersection with South Tacoma Street. On the south side of the old intersection, South Tacoma took an awkward ninety-degree turn to parallel the tunnel traffic and rejoin Lewis, where it broadened to four lanes again.

On the north side, South Tacoma dead-ended at the tunnel—which wasn't too surprising. However, the dead end was announced by shabby but movable wooden barricades flanked by orange cones—after *seventy* years of not being a through street. It was as though they put in the tunnel and then forgot about finishing the project so that it looked like it belonged there—forgot about it for decades.

Like everyone else still traveling down Lewis, I had planned on taking the tunnel to Oregon Avenue, but it was blocked off with police cars and yellow tape—and what looked like a semi that had tried to jump into the tunnel rather than take that ninety-degree turn onto Tacoma. I wasn't sure a semi could have taken that ninety-degree turn.

I slowed, with the rest of the traffic, with the intention of taking another, much longer route—and I would have except that my Jetta had no air conditioning. Nights might be starting to cool off, but it was ninety-seven degrees Fahrenheit this afternoon so

I had the windows down. And through those open windows I scented the magic I'd first found on Dennis Cather.

I pulled out of the line of traffic and looked for a parking spot. This part of Pasco was on the edge of the only-Spanish-spoken-here business district where bakeries, restaurants, and clothing shops sporting quinceañera and First Communion dresses in the windows all prospered. I parallel parked in a tight space in front of a Mexican bakery, which was emitting delicious smells that almost drowned out the scent I'd caught nearer the tunnel.

I still didn't have the locks working properly on my Jetta, but it looked disreputable enough that I didn't think anyone would bother breaking into it. Towing it as an eyesore was a possibility, but not breaking into it.

I hurried over to the mess at the tunnel and wondered how I was going to talk my way into the area—and saw a familiar face. It must be a pretty bad accident if George was here, because traffic wasn't his usual job. And if he had been working at five in the morning . . .

A wave of magic washed over me and the bite mark the jack-rabbit had left on my neck burned uncomfortably. I clamped a hand to my neck and quit trying to work out George's schedule because there were more important things to worry about.

I waited, but I didn't feel any homicidal or suicidal urges and my breathing was unhindered. But my head felt pressurized, there was a faint ringing in my ears—and the scent of the magic was powerful.

Deciding that scaring myself was unproductive, I dropped my hand off my neck (because that wasn't making it hurt any less) and started for the tunnel bridge again. I gave a sharp whistle before I got close enough for the officer directing traffic to send me on my way. George looked up and I met his gaze. He said something to the uniformed officer he was standing next to and jogged over.

"It's okay," he told the traffic officer, with a hand on his shoulder. "She's with me."

The officer took a second look at my face and his eyes widened. Being the wife of the Alpha of the Columbia Basin Pack made me something of a celebrity.

"Of course," he said. Then he turned his attention back to his job.

"Did anyone catch you up on the meeting this morning?" I asked him as we walked past the police line.

"Werewolves and a demonic jackrabbit," he said. "And you banged happy back into our Alpha—for which not only the pack but everyone who works for him is very grateful. That last I have from both Carlos and Elliot."

I rolled my eyes and ignored my blush. I was getting better at that—better at ignoring the blush. "Well, the scent of that jackrabbit's magic is all over this place."

"Yeah, color me not surprised," George said, "because what we have here is an abnormal incident. I just got through texting Adam some photos."

"Lots of police," I commented, looking around.

"Yep, people are safe to speed anywhere in Pasco at the moment," George said. "I'm off duty—and I'm not the only off-duty cop here, either. When the sheriff's department and the fire department hear about this, we'll be drowning in them, too."

The burning sensation in my neck was growing.

"Hey, George," I said casually.

"Yes?"

"If I suddenly quit breathing or"—heaven help me—"start to act really weird, throw me in the river, would you?"

"Sure thing," he said without hesitation. "I heard you got bitten."

"Yes," I said. "But I am working under the assumption that this magic is one of those that have bounced up against my coyote weirdness and failed. But still, if I try to hurt someone who doesn't obviously deserve it—"

"The river," George finished for me. "I've got it."

"Okay."

We rounded the trailer portion, which looked pretty normal, and I got my first good look at the tractor, which had climbed up the decoratively functional concrete barrier. It hung, tilted awkwardly, the front four feet of the rig over the open roadway below. But the tractor wasn't in any danger of falling—the bottom half of the big rig had literally melted into the concrete barrier.

I touched the top part of the tire, which was level with my chin and somehow still holding air. I ran my fingers down the rubber and paused over the transition between rubber and concrete.

"Huh," I said.

"'Huh' is right," agreed George. "The accident probably happened because the guy driving the rig is high as a kite. He claims he hit the barrier to avoid killing a bunch of kids. Says his girlfriend grabbed the wheel and aimed at the kids. After the truck wrecked, she said, 'Good luck with your beloved truck.' Expletives deleted. Then she took off."

"Witnesses?" I asked.

"Yes. We've got two ladies who were heading into the bakery to order a wedding cake who saw the whole thing. Truck looked like it was going to go down the tunnel—suddenly swerved to the right—and there was a group of maybe six kids walking across the street. Ladies thought for sure that truck was going to hit them, when it jerked suddenly and impacted the barricade where so many other vehicles have met their doom. They did not see the girlfriend."

"So do we believe the girlfriend exists?" I asked.

"And did she have a bite mark?" He paused dramatically. "Yes, yes, she did. Our driver, who did not know his own girl-friend's name on account of him picking her up at a gas station in Finley, said she had a—and I quote—'weird-ass mark on her arm, man—like she'd been bitten by a vampire'—unquote."

It fit. Everything except the way the truck had melded with the barricade, anyway. It didn't seem like the mind-control stuff went together with changing the bottom of a semi tractor into concrete. But my nose didn't lie—the smoke beast had been here.

"Is the driver still here?" I asked.

"Nope, they took him in for questioning."

I'd been casually looking around. Funny how easy it was to tell the cops, in uniform and out, from everyone else—and there were a few onlookers now. It was a subtle thing—an in-crowd, out-crowd. Pasco wasn't that big—all of the police officers knew each other and their body language gave it away.

My eyes caught on one of the onlookers. A dark-complexioned girl wearing shorts and a pink tank top—and her expression was wrong. She was looking at the wrecked vehicle and she didn't look amazed or worried or excited like everyone else. She looked smug.

"George," I asked, not taking my eyes off the girl. "Do you have a description for the missing girlfriend?"

She looked up at me at just that moment. There were probably a dozen yards and twenty people between us—and she looked at me as if she had known exactly where I was standing.

She smiled at me and the bite on my neck flared in a bone-shivering spike of pain that made me stagger before it died completely, like something had short-circuited. As it did, her face twisted with pain—and then malevolent anger.

"That's her," said George, coming to alert as he saw who I was looking at. "Hispanic female, pink top."

He didn't speak loudly, but I think, from her change of expression, she heard him, so her hearing was at least as good as ours. As we started toward her, she looked around at all the police surrounding her. Briefly she looked frustrated—and then she looked at us again. Her shoulders relaxed and she smiled—right before she ran.

George bolted after her—and I bolted after him.

"George," I called out, because—wouldn't you know it—George was one of the very few werewolves who were faster than I was. "Let her go—if she bites you, you belong to her! Then you die! George, wait!"

I couldn't tell if he was paying attention or not. The call of a hunt is pretty strong, and I wasn't Adam.

The woman fled down a side street that was edged with automotive boneyards, warehouses, and empty lots. She reeked of that distinctive magic and she was moving as fast as a werewolf. I was pretty sure we'd found our jackrabbit. George was hot on her heels, gaining a few inches with every stride.

I was twenty or thirty feet behind them and losing ground rapidly. Neither of them seemed to be having trouble with the rough and uneven sidewalk, but it tripped me up once and I almost tumbled head over heels. I kept my feet but it slowed me down.

The woman dropped out of sight down a narrow dirt track

between a pair of industrial-looking buildings that wore an air of abandonment. When George disappeared around the corner, too, I found an extra burst of speed from somewhere.

At the same time, I ripped at the closed bond between Adam and me. It gave in to my frantic attempt, but I'd done something to our bond . . . it felt wounded somehow, bleeding. But I would worry about that later. I needed to keep George safe.

I turned the corner and saw George closing in on the woman quickly—I was pretty sure she had deliberately slowed her pace. There was a woman curled up against the building in a fetal position, her face pressed against the wall as if she were trying to hide. But she wasn't moving and my instincts told me she wasn't a threat, so I ran past her.

"George, stop!" The command rang with the power of an Alpha werewolf because I had stolen it from Adam.

George stopped in his tracks, and so did the woman—who was the smoke beast. They had run past the building and stood in what might have been, in better days, a small parking lot. I stopped, too.

"Get back here," I told George. In my back pocket, my cell phone started to ring. Probably Adam wondering why I'd torn at our bond. But I was busy. I told George again, "If it bites you, it will steal your will. Aiden says that once it takes you over, it will kill you." Or he would die. Aiden hadn't been clear on that point, so I wasn't, either.

When it hadn't been able to steal my will, it had tried to kill me, though, so I thought what I'd said was a good bet. The running water had severed the connection between it and the bite—but I thought of the smoke I had swallowed. Maybe there had been enough left in me for it to try again today. It hadn't worked.

George kept his eyes on the woman, but he obeyed me—backing up rapidly until we stood shoulder to shoulder.

"George," I said. "There's someone on the ground against the wall of the building behind us, to my left."

He glanced over my shoulder and growled, "Missed that." He strode behind me—paying me the compliment of trusting me to guard us from the creature.

The woman stayed where she was, frowning at me.

"Who are you?" she asked. She spoke as if English was difficult for her, and not as if she spoke Spanish. Her accent was nothing I'd heard before. If her word choice was odd, it didn't take away from the edge of rage in her voice. "My power is big. Why are you not mine?"

"I don't know," I told her. "What do you want?"

She narrowed her eyes at me. "If the stupid man had not stopped us. There would be many dead and I would have more power. More enough to take you."

"You get power from the people you kill?" I asked.

"Stupid you," she sneered. "Death is powerful magic. My puppets kill and give me magic to be this."

George approached me and stood just to my right. "Dead body," he told me—and he sounded a little freaked out. It took a lot to freak out a police officer who was also a werewolf. "Her dead body."

"Dead that one," the woman said, running her hands down her body in a way that was a little obscene without being sexy at all. "I own this now. In this shape I kill you and the magic is wasted. Cannot eat death in my own body, only through puppets. Rules. Stupid rules."

She was giving us a lot of information, I thought—but it was almost as if she weren't talking to George and me. As if she were clarifying her thoughts.

This creature had lived in Underhill for who knew how long—

and Underhill was a place where magic was plentiful. Maybe the rules were different here than in Underhill—and this creature was working them out aloud. It sounded like she had trouble powering her own magic and she was killing people to make up for it.

She made up her mind about something—I saw it in her eyes before she spoke. "Dead and you are not a problem, little dog. Regret because much power to eat from you. But prefer dead now to power later."

And she charged us.

I skidded back, drawing my Sig as George engaged her. He hadn't had to warn me off—we both knew who was the better fighter in this kind of scenario. I had the gun out and pointed, but the fight was moving too fast for a safe shot.

George wasn't just better than me, he was one of our best fighters in unarmed human combat. He'd had experience, Adam had told me, before Adam took over his pack, and Adam had pushed him to sharpen those skills.

The beast seemed to be having a little trouble fighting in the form of the woman. I could tell that she was used to being heavier by the way she tried to use her weight. She was also used to fighting with teeth and claws instead of leverage and blunt force. Even so, the fight looked pretty even to me.

"Don't let her bite you," I reminded George, though he already knew that. That I repeated it again was more because I was horrified at the idea of something being able to take over your mind.

I wasn't even certain that it was useful advice, because I wasn't sure that it was only a bite he had to worry about. She'd turned a semi into concrete. I didn't understand the rules of her magic and that scared me. Without knowing what she could do, I couldn't keep anyone safe.

Her weight might not be what she was used to, but she was strong. And as she and George fought, she was getting better at using what she had. She twisted and George—who looked like he should be able to crumple her up and put her in a trash can—flew through the air.

I shot her three times before George hit the side of the building. My Sig held a ten-round magazine and I didn't quit shooting until it was empty. I wasn't standing more than fifteen feet away—every shot was on target.

She stopped dead in her tracks when the first shot hit her in the middle of her forehead. The second and third shots went into her cheekbone, just below the eye. The first three shots had jerked her torso a little toward me, angling her body so that I had a three-quarter frontal view.

I put the next three in her chest where a human's heart would be. Because I didn't know what she really was, the next three took the other side of her chest. I put the final round in her right eye.

I kept the empty gun in my hand because it could make a pretty good weapon. I set my feet into horse stance—a good balanced position. George had bounced back to his feet and taken two running steps to stand just in front of me, so he'd be the first to engage her again.

She . . . she just stood there—swaying a little. There were dark holes where the bullets had gone in. But there was no blood, nor even the scent of blood, only the acrid scent of gunpowder and the smell I'd come to associate with this creature.

Behind us, pounding footsteps announced that the police officers gathered at the semi accident had heard the shots and were coming. The creature heard them, too, tipped her head, smiled at me—and dissolved into smoke that quickly dissipated, taking with it the scent of magic. A soft metallic sound accompanied ten bullets hitting the hard-packed gravel.

"Fuck," said a woman's voice behind me.

I turned to see a police officer in uniform, her gun out and aimed at the place the woman had been. The next officer, who hadn't seen the beast dissolve, had his gun pointed at me.

"Drop your weapon," he said.

George flung his hands up into the air and growled. "Green-horn." He sucked in a breath, trying to get a handle on his wolf, as the little space between buildings filled up with Pasco PD. His eyes flashed bright yellow, a sign that the wolf was still ready for a fight, when he said, "We're all good guys here. Stand down, Patton."

I set my gun on the ground anyway, not wanting to get shot by an overzealous or scared officer. It wasn't like it was going to be much of a defense against a creature that I could shoot ten times with a .40-caliber weapon and not do much more than surprise it.

"What was that thing?" asked the police officer who'd been first on scene.

"We don't know," growled George. "But that's what turned the semi to cement."

"Concrete," said one of the police officers in a small voice. "Cement is what you mix with water to get concrete."

George ignored him, instead stalking over to the body still curled up against the old building just beneath a wannabe gang tag. He knelt without touching.

"She's about sixteen," he told . . . me, I thought. "Her scent is all over that tractor. Freaking driver is forty if he's a day."

"Forty-two," said someone. "We can get him for statutory."

I left my empty gun on the ground and walked over to the

body. I couldn't smell anything out of the ordinary. I dropped to one knee beside George and said, "I have to touch her to be sure."

"Do it," he said.

I put a finger on her neck—and realized that she was wearing the same clothing the creature . . . beast had been. Before I could process it, the smell of magic flooded over me. It was as if, I thought, sitting all the way on the ground, the magic had been entirely encased in the body until I touched it and released it.

"That sucks," said a voice just behind me.

I turned my head and started, bumping into George pretty hard. As he put a hand out to steady himself, he turned to look where I was looking, his body tight and ready to move.

The beast had seemed old, even in the shape of a young woman. This girl looking over my shoulder at the body, at her body, was very young. It was the same face and body the beast had worn—but whatever animated this one, it was not our monster.

She met my eyes, her arms wrapped around her rib cage.

"Damn," she said. "Guess Mama was right. She told me that someday I'd regret jumping in a car with any stranger willing to pick me up." Her voice was similar to the smoke beast's, but her English was unaccented and the rhythm of her words was smoother.

She might not have ID on her, I thought reluctantly. She might have information we needed. I decided to risk strengthening her, though condemning anyone to haunt this sad little space didn't seem kind. Maybe she could make it to the cheerful bakery down the street.

"What's your name?" I asked.

"Liv—like that actress, the one on the white horse in the movie with the monsters," she said. "Liv Mendoza."

"Can you tell me what happened?" I asked.

The ghost shivered. "I was out behind the gas station—" She gave me a guilty look. "Never mind what I was doing. Not your business. Anyway this rabbit just came out and bit me—right here." She stretched out her arm—and two crusted wounds appeared. "And then something sat in my head and ran the show. It just took over." A tear appeared and she wiped it off with the back of her wrist. "I couldn't even make a phone call. And when it was done with me, it discarded my body like a, like a snake sheds its skin." She looked away from me. "I wish," she said, "I had died on a beach somewhere. Or in one of those meadows you see in movies, the ones with flowers. I like flowers."

"Who are you talking to, Mercy?" asked George.

I held up a hand—but she was gone, leaving me with most of the Pasco PD staring at me. Hopefully she was gone for good.

I shrugged, sighed, and told them, "I see dead people."

MY PHONE RANG AS I WAS CRAWLING BACK OVER THE Blue Bridge toward the garage with the parts in the trunk of my car. I took a chance and glanced at the screen. It was Adam. It took me another five or six minutes to get across the bridge and on a street where I could pull over to call him back. I had six missed phone calls from Adam.

"Hey," I said.

"I have a headache," Adam said without preamble. "What happened?"

I did, too, now that the adrenaline from the confrontation with the smoke beast was starting to die down. I prodded our bond. The weird bleeding sensation was gone, though the bond was definitely the cause of my headache. My fooling around with it made me wince.

"Quit that," Adam said. "Tell me what happened."

So I did.

I HAD TO REPEAT THE WHOLE STORY TO TAD AND ZEE when I got to the shop, parts in hand. I restarted the story from my first sighting of Anna's ghost up through today's confrontation, adding in the pieces that I'd left off or glossed over when I'd talked to them earlier.

"Is it a skinwalker?" asked Tad when I was done.

Zee just grunted and continued to loosen bolts with his ratchet, which had chattered at us most of the time I'd been talking. Tad had stopped working about halfway through the story, but Zee, although his expression had been getting grimmer and grimmer, had continued to work.

My phone chimed with a text—and with the way things were, I couldn't ignore it.

"I don't think so," I said, getting out my phone. "There are vampires in Underhill, but I don't know that I'd believe in skinwalkers there." I'd never run into one of those, and I didn't care to do so, either.

The text was from Aiden, sent to both Adam and me.

Tilly confirms smoke beast. Says no other escapees. She is sad she cannot help hunt him. Knows from me that you are good at killing monsters. Wishes you good luck. This is my fault, I am VERY sorry.

I read Aiden's text to them out loud—everything except for the last sentence, which was nonsense.

140

"No," said Zee. "It is not a skinwalker. Skinwalkers are native to this land. This is something from the Old Country."

"You know what it is?" I asked.

"*Nein*," he said. "A creature who transforms one thing into another. Who can infest someone with magic that appears as smoke. Using that magic, it turns its victims into puppets to kill for it, in order to gain power from those deaths. And then can mimic the forms of those it has used as puppets." He frowned. "Magic has rules, Mercy. Especially for the fae. Transformation magic—that is rare and belongs to only a few types of fae—but, with the exception of several of the Gray Lords, generally those are not powerful creatures."

I thought about what it had done and not done. "It didn't turn George or me into concrete," I told him. "Though maybe it can only do that with nonliving things?"

"Generally living or nonliving doesn't matter to that kind of magic," Zee said. "But that it didn't transform you suggests that it had used up all of its magic."

"Okay," I said.

"So," he agreed. "But this other magic that it has—this is oddly complicated for fae magic."

He shook his head. "Bite and infest a living being with magic that manifests as smoke that allows it to take over the body. Then it has to use that body to kill in order to gain enough power to assume the shape of the person it has killed."

"It sounds so weird when you put it like that," Tad said.

Zee nodded. "More like something you'd find on a cursed artifact. A series of steps followed by results that allow you to take the next steps. I know of a few of the fae who have magic that is like this—it allows weaker fae to work complex magic. But their magic uses none of these steps."

He shook his head again. "I will go tonight and speak with Uncle Mike." He gave me a speculative look. "You might contact Beauclaire. He will talk to you before he does me."

Aiden had suggested that, too—I raised my hands. "I am not in the personal communication circle for Lugh's son. The Gray Lords are, one and all, above my pay grade."

Zee eyed me suspiciously for a moment before shrugging. "All right, *Liebchen*. Perhaps Uncle Mike can talk to Beauclaire."

My phone chimed again, this time from Darryl—also addressed to Adam and me.

Ogden called. Worried that there is something amiss at his house. Auriele and I are joining him and the three of us will go back to his house. Will update you as necessary.

Adam responded almost immediately.

Do you need help?

To which Darryl said: **No. Might be an attempt to move resources. Auriele has sent out a general warning to pack.**

Adam responded: **Okay. Keep me updated.**

Watching my face, Tad asked, "What's up?"

"Auriele was right," I said. "The invading wolves have begun their game."

Tad grabbed my phone and read the texts. "Who is Ogden?"

"One of our wolves," I said. "He is quiet. Keeps to himself and doesn't cause trouble. He's a contracts lawyer."

Ogden was one of the less dominant wolves. He showed up for the moon hunts and enough of the pack breakfasts that Darryl or Warren didn't appear at his door and haul him over. I had maybe spoken four words to him since I'd joined the pack. But he was well-liked and respected by the pack mates who knew him.

"Do you need an escort home?" asked Zee.

I thought about it. "Maybe a good idea—but let's get those two cars done first. That way I might have enough money to pay you for today."

"I am not worried," said Zee serenely. "People always pay me one way or the other."

He was joking—a little. But not really.

ADAM STOPPED BY TO ESCORT ME HOME JUST AS WE were finishing the last of the cars for the day.

We all looked at him when he walked into the office, but it was Tad who asked, "Did you hear from Darryl? Is everyone okay?"

Adam snorted. "What do you do here all day besides gossip?" He grinned at Tad. "They're fine. No bodies on either side."

He seemed in a better mood than I'd seen him in for a long time. I thought of why that might be—and managed, finally, not to blush.

"So what happened?" I asked.

"Darryl and Auriele found two of Harolford's pack hiding in Ogden's backyard, both in wolf form. There was a fight, but it was brief because the others had obviously been told not to engage. We aren't sure if they ran because they didn't expect to face Darryl and Auriele, too, or if they had never intended to do anything more than scare Ogden."

Adam grinned suddenly. "Ogden called me to tell me the whole story and he could not have sounded more exhilarated if they had killed all six of the invading army. To celebrate their victory, the three of them are on their way to our house with pizza." He glanced at Tad and Zee. "There will be enough to feed you, if you'd like to join us."

"No," said Tad. "I've been enlisted to take Jesse and her friends to the roller-skating arena. I can't figure out if she asked me to go because she knows you won't let her go without a bodyguard until the strange-wolf thing clears up. Or if she's trying to play matchmaker with the girl who keeps trying to talk to me but can't make herself say a word. Or trying to prove to that girl that I'm the last person in the world she should have a crush on." He gave Adam a droll look. "I have decided to be amused by the whole thing."

ADAM FOLLOWED MY BATTERED BUT RECOVERING Jetta in his new SUV. The old SUV had been hit by a semi driven by vampires—this one looked black and shiny, just like the old one except that it was newer. He had resisted my attempt to get him to buy something more daring—like dark gray.

I had the thought that this journey homeward was symbolic of our lives right now. He in his fortress of solitude, me in my battered vehicle that was doing pretty good just getting down the road. Together, but apart. Adam protecting me as best he could from any outside force that might try to hurt me, but not letting me in.

DARRYL, AURIELE, AND OGDEN STORMED INTO THE house bearing pizza and the remnants of battle. Mostly, by that point, those remnants were dirt and torn clothing that was stained with the blood of wounds that had already closed—and the battle-born adrenaline high of a successful fight. They brought a wave of laughter and chatter as they revisited moments from the fight, their beasts in their eyes.

"I called," announced Ogden to the whole household. "I drove to my house on the way home from work and there was something not right." He gave Adam a shy look. "Minding what you said, sir, I did not stop. I drove to the Uptown Mall and called Darryl."

"And we," purred Auriele, as happy as I had seen her in months, "found a couple of strays in Ogden's backyard. Wolf form—so we don't know which ones. Sent them home with their tails between their legs."

There was another incident that night. Four wolves tried to blindside Warren as he drove to his house. Kyle came out with a loaded rifle and shot one in the hip. The rest retreated.

"I expect," said Warren on the phone, "that Kyle and I will get another letter from the HOA. We've been looking at moving somewhere with fewer neighbors, but Kyle doesn't want to leave Dick and Jane behind."

Dick and Jane were two life-sized naked statues in Kyle's foyer. They'd been in the house when Kyle bought it. He took great joy in finding outrageous outfits to dress them in. Last time I'd seen them, Jane was wearing a grass skirt and nothing else, and Dick was sporting a squirrel puppet on his manly bits.

"Statues can be moved," I commented.

Adam was the one on the phone, but we were all listening in.

"Kyle's stubborn," Warren said. "And when Mr. Francis, our old contentious neighbor, died, it deflated the HOA's sails. They are a little afraid of Kyle because he's a lawyer."

"And because they've met Kyle," said Ogden; the aftereffects of successfully defending his home had left him chattier than usual. It was said in a low tone, though, so I don't think Warren was supposed to hear it—but he did.

"And because they've met Kyle," Warren agreed cheerfully. "I don't know whether they are more afraid of his shark reputation in his chosen field or that if they push him he'll find some horrible thing to do—like fly a giant penis kite over the house—that is not against the HOA agreement."

"Could you tell which four wolves?" I asked.

"The two Palsics were in human form," said Warren. "The other two were wolves and I don't know which ones. Kyle shot the bigger of the two. He'll recover—it wasn't silver ammunition— but it will take him a while. That rifle isn't as big as Mercy's .444 Marlin but it was a .30-06 and that has a lot of stopping power. They had to carry him off."

"Were you injured?" asked Adam.

"No, boss," said Warren. "Kyle kept the big bad wolves from hurting me. Even though I told him to stay inside and call you."

"Four to one," said Kyle clearly. "They didn't have a chance." He lied, but he didn't intend anyone to believe it. "But how many times am I going to get an opportunity to shoot someone without consequences?"

Warren made a noise. I couldn't tell if it was a growl or a purr. "Got to go, boss. Gotta talk sense into someone."

I TRIED TO CALL STEFAN TWICE THAT NIGHT. THE SECOND time I left a message on his phone. He didn't return my call.

7

I GOT HOME LATE FROM WORK ON SATURDAY. LUCIA had saved me dinner, which I ate by myself. That's not to say that I was alone.

We were keeping an extra werewolf at the pack home because of the various threats—though since the night Kyle had shot one of the wolves, we had seen neither hide nor hair of the outsiders be they werewolves, smoke beasts, or vampires. Tonight our extra werewolf was Ben. He sat at the kitchen table opposite me while I ate and told me an incident in the ongoing efforts of the subversive IT personnel (which included computer programmers, system operators, and database administrators) to play mind games with the unfortunate corporate minions who were supposed to be in charge.

In this episode they'd (I was pretty sure that the unnamed perpetrator of most of these was Ben himself) adjusted the e-mail of one of the most disliked executives so that every e-mail he sent out also sent a copy to his wife and his boss. These e-mails included X-rated love letters between the executive and one of the HR people. Ben assured me—with example encounters as proof—that it couldn't happen to a nicer pair of people. Since this had just happened today, the final outcome was yet to be determined.

He made me laugh, which was the point, I think, before he left me to go do some work he'd brought with him.

Jesse had some friends over and, after Ben left, they twice made forays into the kitchen for sustenance. They made popcorn and had to come back for it. On both incursions, Jesse's friend Izzy kept giving me oddly apologetic looks. But I was too distracted by my own growing misery to worry about what Izzy had to apologize for.

Despite my initial victory, Adam had resumed his efforts to stay out until after I had to go to bed. He'd slept in the guest room the last few nights so as not to wake me up. My misery was complicated by my absolute conviction that if Adam didn't want to make an effort, it didn't matter what I did. A relationship was a two-way street. I would fight—but he had to fight, too.

Jesse's friends went to their various homes. Jesse went to bed. And after a half an hour of internal debate, I gave up on Adam and followed her example.

I don't know what made me glance out the window as I was getting ready to go to bed.

Wulfe was stretched out on the roof of my parts car. He'd placed small LED lanterns on the four corners of his chosen stage—all had been set to the night-vision-saving red light. The Rabbit was a small car, so Wulfe's legs and bare feet dropped down the windshield.

And there went any chance that I was going to sleep anytime soon.

I was pretty sure he was naked, but it was hard to tell because the naughty bits were covered by a large piece of white cardboard. There was a picture drawn on the cardboard—a crudely drawn red flower with two leaves at the bottom of a long stem that looked remarkably like the pieces of anatomy that the cardboard was covering. Wulfe had died when he was still a teenager. His pale hair framed a face that would never grow old but also would never fulfill the promise of his not-quite-mature features. He looked younger than Jesse.

I wasn't sure of the effect that he'd intended his theatrical staging to have on me—but I was pretty sure he hadn't intended to make me sad.

The vampire saw me looking at him and blew me a kiss just as someone knocked on my door.

"A minute," I said, grabbing my robe and wrapping myself in it.

It was Ben.

"Mercy," he said. "Is there any legitimate reason for Wulfe to be running around outside? I'm catching his scent all over." Apparently, he hadn't seen Wulfe's passion play on my Rabbit.

It was a sign of how much Wulfe bothered him that he didn't use any swear words at all.

"He's stalking me," I told him. I'd forgotten that Wulfe hadn't been one of the threats Adam had presented to the pack.

Ben's eyebrows shot to his hairline. "Excuse the fuck out of me? Could you repeat that?"

And he was back to normal.

"He told us that he is stalking me," I said again, though I knew Ben had heard me perfectly well the first time.

"Okay," he said, then added a few sentences creatively spiced with expletives that boiled down to, "That would have been a good thing to let your security know in advance, don't you think?"

He was right, and I had thought about it. "Adam didn't tell the pack," I told him. "So I didn't know if he wanted it to be kept secret or not, and he hasn't been around to ask."

Ben tightened his lips and I decided without proof that he was upset with Adam, too. I knew that the pack was watching the two of us with concern. But Adam wasn't the issue right now.

"Wulfe hasn't made any aggressive moves so far," I told Ben—reminding myself at the same time. "In fact, he's the one who dumped me in the river to break the smoke demon . . . smoke beast's hold on me, which saved my life." The last thing I wanted was Ben going out and picking a fight with Wulfe. Werewolves were tough, no doubt, but Ben was not in Wulfe's weight class. So I said, lamely, "Maybe he doesn't intend any harm."

"*Saint Elmo's hairy ass* he doesn't intend any harm," Ben exploded. "If Wulfe is following you around, it's not to sell you magazine subscriptions. Fucking hell, Mercy."

I shrugged, though I agreed wholeheartedly with his assessment. It just wasn't useful to run around shrieking in fear. "So far, Ben, all that he's done is save my life."

Ben opened his mouth, then frowned at the window. "Where's that light coming from?" he muttered, and not to me. He pushed his way into the bedroom and stalked up to the window. He stared out for a few seconds and then pulled down the blinds. He gave me an unreadable look and pulled the blinds down on the other windows, too.

He walked back to me and, in a very gentle voice, swore for a solid thirty seconds without repeating himself once.

When he wound down, he said, "Mercy, he can walk right into this house because some damn fool brought him in when we thought he was dying."

"I think he might have been able to come in anyway," I said. "Even if a vampire is unconscious, you have to invite them into your home or they can't come. Ogden says he did not invite him in, not that he remembers, anyway."

Ben said, "I don't know that I'm comfortable with you sleeping up here alone. Where is Adam?"

"Darned if I know," I told him. There must have been something in my voice because his face softened.

"What is up with him?" Ben asked. "He has been a right bastard these past few weeks."

There was a sudden wary look in his eye at the tail end of his sentence—as if he had been thinking awhile about how to bring it up. But he hadn't really expected to bring it up just now.

"I know as much as he does," I told Ben firmly. The pack didn't need to know that neither of us really understood what was going on. "I'm not going to discuss it with anyone else."

"Private," he said, with a nod. There was relief in his posture. It was enough for him that he believed that I knew what was wrong. "I get that. Do you want me to go drive the vampire off?"

There was not a sparrow's chance in hell that Ben's going out to drive Wulfe away would end up with Wulfe leaving. But I could find a galaxy's worth of scenarios where that ended in disaster.

"No," I said. "I think he's just playing right now. Testing us, maybe. I don't want to do anything that makes him think that we are taking him seriously." And that gave me an idea.

I pulled a blanket out of the hall closet—one of those fuzzy ones sold at Costco. This one was wine red, suitable for a vampire. I'd never had it on my bed. I think the last one to use it had been Christy, so it wouldn't smell like me or Adam. Vampires have keen senses and I wanted to be very careful about the message I was sending with this blanket.

"Here," I said, shoving it at Ben. "Take this out to Wulfe. Tell him I . . . no. Tell him *we* don't want him to get cold."

Ben took the blanket, but as I spoke, he'd frozen in place. He frowned at me a moment, then shook his head and finally grinned. "He doesn't know who he is messing with."

That Ben thought I was a match for Wulfe was nice—but it might be dangerous for him to continue to hold that misapprehension.

"He scares the socks off me," I told Ben seriously. "He should scare the socks off you, too. Don't underestimate him. Don't let him lure you into thinking he is harmless. Or that Adam or I or even the Mistress of the vampire seethe can keep him from doing anything he decides to do. Take him the blanket, and get back into the house. If we keep him amused, then he won't have to kill anyone out of sheer boredom."

His face grew sober. "I get that," he said. "I'll be back in a moment."

He left and I waited for him to return. I wanted to watch out the window, but I was afraid that if I gave him an audience, Wulfe might do something horrible. I'd seen him do horrible things before.

Instead I went down to the kitchen and pulled out a bowl. I needed to get to sleep, but I wasn't going to manage that for a while. I mixed up chocolate chip cookies. Just a double batch.

I heard the murmur of Lucia's voice in the suite she shared with Joel. There was no answering voice—Joel had not managed to shift to human for the past few days.

Aiden's fire had rekindled itself, but it wasn't up to normal levels yet and he hadn't been able to quiet the volcano spirit enough to allow Joel to emerge. That was a little disheartening because we'd been hoping that Joel had been gaining more control. Apparently, Aiden had been getting better at shutting Joel's fire down instead. At least Joel had been able to stay in his presa Canario form so we didn't have to worry about him burning down the house inadvertently.

The sounds of me making food in the kitchen lured Medea out of whatever dark corner she'd been sleeping in. She hovered around my ankles because she knew that hopping on the counters was forbidden. I gave her a small dab of dough before I mixed in the chocolate chips and walnuts. She purred as she ate, and the sound soothed me. Cats are good company when you are sad or worried.

Walnuts were a matter of contention in the pack, but I liked them and I was making these for me. I needed chocolate because Adam wasn't here. And because it was taking a very long time for Ben to walk out and hand over a blanket.

Adam's SUV purred into our driveway about the same time that the back door opened and Ben walked in sans blanket.

"What took so long?" I asked, trying not to listen to Adam's door shut. Now that Adam was actually here, I was nervous. What if he was unhappy when he saw me? I didn't want the sight of me to make Adam unhappy.

"I will trade information for cookie dough," Ben bargained— so it wasn't anything bad that had kept him.

I got a clean spoon from the silverware drawer, dipped it into the dough, then held it out toward him. When he reached to take it, his long sleeve slipped down to reveal two small red marks on his wrist. And from those two marks, faint wisps of smoke emerged. Aiden had identified our foe from the smoke that had, apparently, emerged from my wounds after the rabbit had bitten me. At the time, I'd been too busy trying not to die to pay attention to much of anything else.

I now understood what Aiden had been talking about. My heart stopped. Ben had been bitten by the smoke beast.

I pretended not to see the marks, hoping that my sudden terror went unnoticed, blended as it was with the adrenaline already racing in my veins after the sight of a naked Wulfe on the roof of my old Rabbit.

I didn't know enough to save Ben. Not nearly enough. I knew the smoke beast took over its victims' bodies and piloted them. I knew that it used those victims to kill others to gain power—and that it then killed its puppet and could shape itself into a copy of that person. I had no idea what it wanted or why. I had no idea how to save someone bitten by the beast—and if I couldn't figure it out, Ben was lost. And I didn't know that I could bear a world without our foul-mouthed wolf.

First problems first, I decided. First problem was to survive the next few minutes. Ben was a werewolf. That meant he was stronger than I was—and he outweighed me. Unlike George, Ben was significantly slower than I was. Maybe I could get him to chase me into the river.

I heard Adam's footsteps on the porch, but Ben, licking the spoon clean, seemed oblivious. I gave a hard, panicked tug on my mating bond and the sound of Adam's approach stopped. I had to hope that he had understood that there was something wrong.

"Want some with chocolate chips?" I asked.

He handed the spoon back to me. I dumped in a bag of chips and stirred with my bigger spoon before dipping his teaspoon in the mix—ignoring sanitary issues in favor of keeping him distracted.

Adam hadn't just come in through the door, so I had a reasonable hope that I'd warned him enough. But what would allow him to connect my warning to Ben?

Ben closed his eyes, absorbing the buttery-sweetness-and-bitter-chocolate combination. Was there a difference in his expression? Or was it just that I knew that someone else might be home inside Ben's head that made me think so?

Could I be mistaken? Was this Ben?

"So what's the information you owe me?" I asked when his eyes opened again.

He took a step closer to me and I had to fight my instincts that would have sent me scuttling to the far side of the kitchen.

"What do you want to know?" he asked, his voice flirty. The British accent was the same, but the rhythm of speech was wrong. And there were no swear words for me to edit out.

"Was Wulfe actually naked?" I asked.

"Wolves are usually naked," he said as if he were joking.

"For sure," I agreed easily.

Upstairs a soft *shsh*ing of a window sliding up. I knew it was Jesse's window, but if someone wasn't familiar with the sounds of the house, maybe it would just blend into the various creaks and groans that were the normal sounds of any house. I didn't know if Ben would know what that sound meant. I didn't know how much of Ben's memories the beast who had bitten him would have.

Jesse's window was accessible from the porch roof—which was a security concern, but it was also an escape path if something bad was happening in the house. Adam had decided that risk and benefit balanced out. I listened, but no further noise emerged from upstairs. Either Adam had managed not to wake Jesse up, or she had realized that there was something going on.

Ben held out the spoon to me again. I scooped up more dough and held it out. But this time he grabbed my wrist.

"I have a secret," he said.

He wasn't hurting me. I let my wrist lie limp in his grip.

"What's that?" I asked.

"I let you see the marks," he told me. "I even made sure to mark this body when I was wearing the rabbit so that you would know what you were looking at."

"Why did you do that?" I asked.

Was there a squeak on the stairs? I took a deep breath and smelled the smoke beast's magic. It filled my lungs and I couldn't smell anything else over it.

"I wanted to see what you would do," he said. "Why can't I take you? I can kill you—I almost did the other night. But I am supposed to be able to take any but the most powerful of the lords of the fae. You are not fae at all. What are you?"

"Chaos," I told him.

His eyebrows furrowed and his eyes narrowed with the beginnings of anger. He would have said something more. But quick footsteps came up from the basement and Aiden bounded into the kitchen.

The beast's magic surged. Visions of that semi tractor melded with the concrete of the Pasco tunnel's safety rail danced in my head. I didn't know that he could do that to a living being—life affects magic. We might be just carbon compounds, but there was something about the state of living that was magical.

But if the beast was amassing magic at the sight of Aiden, I wasn't willing to wait to see what it could do. While he was distracted by Aiden, I twisted my wrist, grabbed his wrist with mine, and swiveled my hips to pull him off balance. At the same time, I kicked his knee as hard as I could. He grunted as his knee popped audibly and he released me involuntarily, and I let go and jumped back.

There were a number of counters to that move—Ben knew them, but the creature controlling his body made no effort to use any defense. My attack had been quick and instinctive, and it had taken the beast by surprise. Impossible to say how much of Ben's knowledge the beast had access to. Earlier he hadn't known the difference between Wulfe and a wolf, but with the evidence I had I couldn't assume that he couldn't fight as well as Ben.

I also didn't know if he would feel pain occupying Ben's body, but it didn't matter much at that moment. The damage to Ben's knee was a physical thing that slowed his body down.

I grabbed for a weapon and came up with my marble rolling pin, but by the time I turned to face Ben again, Adam was there. I hadn't heard him. I missed the first move, just heard the noise as Ben's shoulder broke from a joint lock. As Ben fell, pushed by Adam's hold, Adam brought his knee over and landed on the small of Ben's back. I heard those bones crack, too.

"It won't hold him long," said Adam, but I was already running. I jumped over them both and ran down the stairs to the cage that would be our safe room once construction wrapped it in more civilized trappings. But the cage itself was finished and the silver cuffs and chains were hanging from a hook on a post just outside it.

I dropped the rolling pin—cracking it on the exposed concrete floor. I would feel bad about that later, because it had belonged to my mother's mother. But at the moment, I was too busy grabbing the cuffs and chains. Beast or not, the creature was wearing Ben's body and these bindings would hold a werewolf.

I ran back up the stairs to find the tableau unchanged. Ben writhed and jerked under Adam, seemingly unbothered by the pain of the broken bones—though his lower extremities were unmoving. Adam kept him down. About ten feet from them, fitful fire wreathing his hands, Aiden watched them with wary eyes.

I bound Ben's legs together, then closed one of the cuffs on the wrist connected to his broken shoulder. Adam took over from there. Without consideration of the pain of Ben's broken bones, he pulled Ben's arms behind his back and cuffed his wrists tightly together. Then Adam connected the leg manacles until Ben was effectively hog-tied with steel and silver, his skin blackening where the metal touched him.

As soon as he was held immobile, Ben's body went limp.

"God, oh God," he whispered. "Don't let me go. He's still in my head. He wants her dead. She scares him and he wants me to kill her. No more fucking around asking questions, just kill her. Find out why later."

Ben took a deep shuddering breath. "Don't let me go."

"Okay," Adam said.

"Don't let Mercy anywhere near me," he said. "Oh God. He's in my head and I can't. I can't . . . I can't." He went limp again.

"Is he breathing?" I asked, panicked. "This is my fault, Adam. I sent him out there."

"He's breathing," Adam said. "Pulse is strong. Takes more than a few broken bones and an uncanny thing's possession to kill a werewolf." He looked at me. "He was on guard duty—in harm's way. That was his job tonight."

I wrapped my arms around myself. "I sent him out to talk to Wulfe," I told Adam. "I forgot about the smoke beast."

"It didn't forget about us," said Adam.

RUNNING WATER DIDN'T HELP BEN.

Warren and Kyle showed up about ten minutes before Darryl because they'd been working at Kyle's office. Ben's bones had mended themselves by that time and he was half sitting, half lying on the fainting couch in the living room. Adam had put him there after deciding he didn't want to try to get him down the stairs and into the cage by himself for fear of having to hurt Ben further. Werewolves healed fast, but even Adam, drawing on the power of the pack, would have had a hard time healing the kind of damage Ben had suffered in the half hour or so that had elapsed.

I couldn't smell the beast's magic anymore, but I didn't make the mistake of thinking it was gone. Ben's periodic bouts of madness would have disabused me of that if I'd trusted my nose too much. I already knew that sometimes I couldn't detect this magic.

"Well," Warren told Ben, in a squeaky voice that was an obvious attempt to imitate someone, "here's another nice mess you've gotten *you* into."

"I suppose by that I'm to assume I'm Laurel?" asked Ben, trying to sound like himself, but his voice was tight and there was a rough growl on the edges.

"You aren't Hardy," said Adam.

I hadn't made the connection. Laurel and Hardy were well before my time, before Ben's time, too, as he was actually about my age. Adam, on the other hand, had a whole four decades more of cultural references than I did. It had never mattered to me before this moment.

I was discouraged to discover that I could be terrified for Ben—and still worried about the distance between Adam and me.

Warren glanced at me and then at Adam—so apparently I didn't hide what I was feeling well enough.

Adam said, "We are just waiting on Darryl."

Warren shook his head. "He's not that heavy. You and I can carry him down to the river."

"It's not the carrying me that's the problem," said Ben, his voice shaky. "Anytime anyone comes within spitting distance I turn into that girl from *The Exorcist*."

"Your head doesn't spin around," I said, trying not to sound as scared as I was.

"Don't give it any helpful fucking ideas," Ben scolded me.

He'd bounced around between calling the creature who controlled him by the masculine pronoun and by "it." I was withholding judgment.

Darryl arrived eventually. "Sorry. Flat tire."

"No worries," said Ben. "Just sitting here possessed by an evil fae."

The minute they touched him, Ben started to struggle. Undeterred, the three werewolves dragged Ben kicking and screaming out to the river.

I followed them, feeling sick. Kyle walked next to me, his hand on my shoulder. I almost didn't flinch when another hand landed on my other shoulder and Wulfe, wrapped toga-style in the fuzzy red blanket, took up the space on my right.

"Nasty business," said Wulfe conversationally.

"Yes," I agreed. There was no way to signal to Kyle to back away—and I knew him well enough to know that he wouldn't, even if I could ask him. I would just have to keep Wulfe's attention on me and off the vulnerable human on my other side. Kyle, helpfully, kept silent.

Warren caught sight of Wulfe and got Ben's bound feet in his stomach for his troubles. He was forced to pay attention to what he was doing.

"Interesting to see if the river works," Wulfe continued.

"You don't think it will?" I asked.

He pursed his lips, looking, in his toga, like an escapee from a frat party gone wrong. I knew he was older than Stefan, who had been made a vampire early in the Renaissance era, but he would never grow up to look like an adult. His feet were bare, but the rocks and tackweed didn't seem to bother him.

"Should work," he said, at last. "I don't know why it would work for you but not for your little red riding wolf." Ben's wolf was red. I didn't like that Wulfe knew that.

Wulfe tilted his head to watch the struggling wolves just ahead of us.

"But I have an odd feeling that it won't," he said in casual tones. "Shame. It was nice of him to bring me a blanket, don't you think? Though that might have been your idea—I forget what he said."

His hand tightened on my neck. When had he moved his hand to my neck?

I must have made some sound because Adam glanced over at me and asked if I needed help with a single look. I shook my head briefly. He needed to pay attention to Ben. I didn't know if Ben could spread his contagion with a bite, but I'd feel better if no one had to worry about it.

Besides, I was fairly certain that Wulfe wasn't ready to quit playing at whatever game he'd decided upon yet, so I should be safe enough. I wished Stefan would call me back. It wasn't like him to not return my calls.

"I'm not supposed to be here, you know," said Wulfe.

"Oh?" I asked.

"Marsilia has called all the vampires to the seethe because . . . oh. That's why."

I tried to make his words make sense, then realized he'd been talking to himself for the last bit. "That's why what?"

"That's why I don't think running water will help your wolf. It didn't help Stefan."

I stopped. "Stefan?"

"We tried to dump him in the river," Wulfe said obligingly. "But all that accomplished was getting a whole bunch of us wet. Good thing we don't need to breathe or several members of the seethe would have drowned. He took one out anyway. But I didn't like her, so I'm not sorry."

I thought of all those phone calls I'd made.

I struggled to imagine Stefan caught up by the smoke beast and failed. Stefan was . . . reserved, controlled. I had a sudden memory of him in a rage, his face contorted. But even then Stefan had never moved even when the demon killed a hotel maid in front of him, and used demonic powers to inspire visceral bloodlust in my friend. There was no dignity in Ben's desperate struggles—I didn't *want* to imagine Stefan in the same condition.

"What else have you tried?" I asked, starting toward the river again. There was nothing I could do for Stefan right this moment.

Wulfe shrugged. "The usual. After the river, salt, silver, torture, fire. Nothing seems to work."

"Do you know how to kill it? Or if killing it will save Ben and Stefan?" I asked, fighting not to visualize someone torturing Stefan. Wulfe was old—Middle Ages old. And he was a sorcerer, a witch, and a vampire. He should know something about this beast.

"I meant to ask you what you knew about it," he responded, as if we were walking to tea instead of watching Adam, Warren, and Darryl struggle to hold on to the bound form of Ben long enough to get to the water's edge.

I told him everything I knew. It didn't take long.

"Smoke beast," said Wulfe as Ben arced out over the water and entered with a splash. "Never heard of it. Smoking bites don't ring any bells, either—and I know a lot about things that bite." He snapped his teeth together.

Kyle let me go and I broke free of Wulfe so I could get a better look at Adam, Warren, and Darryl trying to drag Ben out of the water. He seemed to be trying to slip out of their fingers, and werewolves don't float—they sink. Too much muscle, not enough fat. Or maybe it was something about the way their magic worked.

All four of them were wet by the time they dragged Ben back to shore. He choked up water in great heaving coughs that strained his bound limbs. The river had almost succeeded in drowning him.

When Adam reached for the cuffs, Ben shook his head. "No!" And after he spoke that single word, he coughed up another burst of river, only to collapse in a limp heap.

"He's in me," he said. Then tears leaked out as if he'd absorbed some of the river into his eyes as well as his lungs. "He's still here. Don't let me free."

"Shh," said Adam. He looked at me.

"Did you hear Wulfe?" I asked.

He nodded, then kissed the top of Ben's head—avoiding the snap of Ben's teeth without apparent effort. "We have a problem. Let's get him back to the cage where I can at least get him out of the cuffs. I'll call Marsilia and check on Stefan."

That would work better, I acknowledged silently. She liked Adam and she really didn't like me. Especially she wouldn't like me asking about Stefan. She tended to view him as her property—and viewed me as the reason he'd broken free of the seethe. He was the only vampire in the Tri-Cities who did not belong to her. We could work together when we had to, but there was no reason to push it now.

And all of that gave me something to think about other than our poor Ben and Stefan caught up in the same hell. And I had nothing I could do to help.

"Where did the scary vampire go?" asked Kyle in a low voice.

"Wherever scary vampires go," answered Warren. His voice acquired a hard edge. "Don't worry. He'll be back."

WE SETTLED BEN IN THE CAGE WITH A MATTRESS ON the floor and the chains and cuffs off.

Releasing him from the cuffs had almost resulted in disaster.

If Kyle hadn't been carrying a stun gun and been unafraid to use it, Ben would have broken free.

Adam called Marsilia and she confirmed what Wulfe had told us. The beast had indeed gotten Stefan, though when asked, she said the bite marks on his shoulder were more akin to a big snake—a very big snake—than to a rabbit. She sent photos. Two red marks, the size of a dime, marred the white flesh of his left shoulder. According to the measuring tape, the marks were four and three quarters of an inch apart.

"That's the size of a horse's mouth," Warren said. "More or less."

"Does he know what bit him?" Adam asked.

"He has not been able to share coherent information with us," said Marsilia. "We can keep him . . . indefinitely, I suppose. But I would not keep anyone I cared about in this state for long."

"No," agreed Adam, watching Ben, who stared back at him with eyes that were not Ben's. "But we are working on it."

"Except for Wulfe—with whom it is not practical—I have brought all of my people and their flocks to our seethe and locked us in," Marsilia said. "I understand that you think that you need to do something about this, but I advise you to do the same. Think about what the news organizations will do when one of your wolves is bitten and goes on a killing spree."

"Is that what Stefan did?" I asked. Then I had a panicked thought: "What about his people?"

Vampire hearing was good, too. She said, "All of his sheep are safe."

I did not add "those who survived," but I wanted to. Marsilia had killed some of Stefan's people (he had never, in my hearing, referred to them as sheep or his flock) in order to perpetrate some desperate scheme or other. He had never forgiven her.

She blamed me. Not for her having to kill his people, but for his lack of forgiveness. It didn't make sense, but emotions don't have to make sense.

"How did you discover what had happened?" Adam asked.

"Wulfe brought him in," she said. "It was not pretty—and there was no doubt that something or someone else was controlling him. He did not try to blend in. At all."

"Thank you for the information," Adam said. "If we find out anything useful, I'll make sure you get word."

"I would appreciate that," Marsilia told him.

Warren and Kyle left to go home and sleep. Darryl settled in as our guard, since Ben had been retired from the field. Adam and Darryl were still discussing how to patrol safely when I went up to bed. I was pretty sure that Adam wouldn't come up to bed until I was safely asleep, so I left them talking and went upstairs.

I paused in front of Jesse's door, then gave in to my need to see someone safe tonight and cracked the door. She was curled up on the bed with a stuffed elephant that I knew Gabriel had gotten her. I shut the door again and left her to her dreams.

I was just pulling the bedding up to my chin when my phone rang. Caller ID said the number was unavailable. I hesitated—but it was the wrong time of night for a robocall.

"Mercedes," said Beauclaire, son of Lugh and Gray Lord of the fae. "Uncle Mike asked me to call you tonight. A few days ago, he informed me that Underhill created a door to her realm in your backyard and in the process, she released a predator, one that Aiden told you was called the smoke beast."

"Yes," I told him.

"I know of that one," Beauclaire told me, and I felt a shiver of relief.

Beauclaire knew things about the creature who held Ben and Stefan. He would know what to do about it so we could save Ben, and save Stefan.

"You know that Marsilia has locked down her seethe because Stefan was taken."

"Yes," I said.

"Did you hear about the accident on Highway 240? The terrible tragic accident where a tanker sideswiped two other cars? All three drivers and their passengers died. Eight people in all."

That accident had happened the same night that Kyle had shot one of the werewolves. It had made the front page and relegated Kyle and Warren's encounter to the Public Records section of the newspaper.

"Yes," I said, sick to my stomach because Marsilia was fond of using car wrecks or house fires to account for "problem bodies" that needed to be explained. She had told me that Stefan's people were safe, but she had not answered my first question about a killing spree—and I hadn't noticed until just now.

"A few hours ago, one of the fae, not a Gray Lord, but one who had power and skill, walked into Uncle Mike's with a sword and used it and her magic to kill as many as she could. Fourteen fae died and also three humans and two goblins. Uncle Mike was on other business so he was not present. Had Larry the goblin king and the snow elf not been there, more people would have died."

There was no such thing, as far as I knew, as a snow elf. It was just what our resident frost giant liked to be called. I thought about how powerful a fae had to be if it took both the goblin king and a frost giant to subdue.

"Some of those who died were very old and very powerful

beings," Beauclaire told me. "Uncle Mike says that your previous encounters with the smoke beast seemed to indicate that it was having difficulty acquiring power. I thought you should be warned that, as of tonight, that is no longer the case."

"I see," I said. I no longer was hopeful that Beauclaire was going to provide me with an easy way to save my friends.

"Because of tonight's incident—and because of the problems the vampires have experienced—I have called all the fae in the area back to the reservation, including Siebold Adelbertsmiter and his son." There was a bite to Zee's full name. Zee had killed Beauclaire's father a zillion years ago—but the fae have long memories.

"Is there anything that you can tell me that would help us defeat it?" I asked.

"Yes." A pause, as if Beauclaire was being careful with his words. More careful than usual. "I cannot tell you who he is."

And that was important or it wouldn't have been the first thing he said in answer to my question.

"Cannot," I said. "As opposed to will not. Like a geas?"

"To you, perhaps that is the best way to explain it. It is a quirk of his nature. I can tell you a few, very few things about him."

"*Please*," I said, tightening my grip on the phone.

"In addition to 'smoke beast,' some call him 'smoke weaver' or 'smoke dragon,' all three referring to his nature—none of them are his name or bear any resemblance to his name."

"Because you cannot speak his name," I said, to tell him that I caught the import of what he was telling me.

"That is so," he said. "Long ago he was captured by Underhill, a result of a bargain he made with her. He needed to bargain, as a part of the nature of the creature he was. A human woman gained the upper hand that somehow triggered the terms of his bargain with Underhill. Underhill swallowed him and we . . . I had thought him safely caught up in her nets for all these years."

"Needed," I said. "As in no longer needs."

He didn't answer me right away. "Any answer I make to you may be misleading," he said.

"We think Underhill let him out on purpose," I told him.

"Do you?" he asked, but more as if he found the idea interesting. "To what purpose, I wonder? And why at the door in your backyard instead of in one of those in the reservation where his prey would be so much more interesting, where he could cause so much more death?"

"And become so much more powerful?" I half asked, half stated. Then I had a worrying realization. "As he did tonight at Uncle Mike's?"

"I am speculating now," Beauclaire said in apology—or as close to an apology as a Gray Lord was comfortable giving. It was a matter of tone rather than words. "I do not know why Underhill does what she does. But it is interesting that the first thing that happened when she put a door in your yard was that the smoke beast escaped."

"Do you know what he wants? What his goal is?" I asked. "He seems to be sticking around here."

"I don't know what he wants," said Beauclaire, and again there was an apology in his tone. "I myself never met him personally. But he can take any of the fae—"

"He said he couldn't," I interrupted him. "To me. He's taken one of our wolves. He said he could take all but the most powerful of the fae lords."

"Interesting," said Beauclaire. "But we cannot risk it. The one he took tonight was powerful. Our gates are closed indefinitely."

"How do I save them?" I asked. "My friends who he has taken?"

"I don't know," he said. And he was fae, so it had to be true. "But I will ask if any do. Should I gain that knowledge, I will see that you are told."

"How many can he take and hold at a time?" I asked.

"I don't know that, either. Likely that depends upon the power he amasses."

In other words, more people now than he could have controlled before tonight.

"How do I kill him?" I asked.

"I don't know that, either," he answered. "No one has managed to do so yet. I do know that he can only be harmed in his own form, whatever shape he wears, not in the bodies of those he takes. That his own form shifts to smoke as he wills, so he cannot be easily imprisoned. Underhill managed—you might speak to her." He paused. "There is a story about him. And it has to do with bargains." He stopped again. "My incomplete knowledge of the smoke weaver—and creatures of his ilk—makes me leery of telling you more than this—"

His voice changed, deepened, and developed an odd resonance. It sounded more feminine—and that voice was familiar. "The key to his undoing is in his basic nature. Do not pay attention to smoke and appearances."

"Baba Yaga?" I asked.

Beauclaire sighed. "She will have her games," he said. "But her advice is good."

He disconnected. I set my phone on the bedside table—and then realized that Adam was standing in the doorway. I didn't know how long he'd been there. There was something . . . alien in his eyes that reminded me of the night we'd had the fight over Jesse's school.

"How much of that did you hear?" I asked cautiously.

"I came up when the phone rang," he said. "I wonder why Beauclaire called you instead of me." There was an edge of anger in his voice. Probably, I decided, that was because Ben was locked up in a cage, possessed by an escapee from Underhill, and we couldn't do anything about it.

"I don't know," I said. And that was true. He could have called Adam. I wondered if Beauclaire's calling me instead was a message, too. The fae could be very subtle creatures.

Adam's jaw tightened at my reply, but he didn't say anything. He just shut the door and went back downstairs. I waited for him for a while, but it was nearing one in the morning and I was going to have to get up early to post a *Closed until Further Notice* sign on my business and call everyone who had an appointment at the shop.

Without Tad or Zee, the shop made me a target. Not just for invading werewolves or escaped prisoners of Underhill, but also any crackpot, supernatural or not, who wanted to launch an attack on our pack. Most people, even most preternatural people, thought I was a mundane human. That I could turn into a coyote was pretty cool—but it didn't make me a superhero.

I set my alarm, pulled the covers over my head, and closed my eyes, but I didn't really go to sleep until I felt the mattress sink under Adam's weight. For whatever reason, he hadn't gone to the spare room to sleep tonight, and I was grateful.

I WOKE UP FACEDOWN ON MY PILLOW WITH THE URgent feeling that I was under threat. I could feel eyes on me, feel the hunt engaged with me as its target. I lay very still and breathed shallowly through my mouth.

Was it Wulfe? I couldn't smell anyone but Adam and me in the room.

Adam moved on the bed and the feeling gradually faded. Probably it was the leftover of a very bad dream. I rolled until I could touch Adam—and my fingers slid through his fur. I was pretty sure that he'd been in his human form when he'd come to bed, but I'd been mostly asleep so I could have been wrong.

I buried my face in the fur at his neck, and the scent and feel of him brushed away the last of that paranoid feeling that had awoken me. I was very tired, so it didn't take long to start drifting back to sleep.

"Good night," I murmured.

Sleep, the wolf told me through our bond, *the threat is over for tonight.*

8

ADAM WAS GONE WHEN MY ALARM WOKE ME UP. Downstairs, Darryl had been replaced by George, who was taking his coffee down to keep watch over Ben.

"How is he?" I asked.

"Not good," said George, pausing halfway to the basement. "He's himself this morning, but he says that thing still has a hold on him." He hesitated. "He doesn't want you down there. He says that thing in his head wants to kill you in the worst way."

I didn't know what to say to that. The urge to go down and watch over him was a pain in my heart. He was my friend and in trouble that he'd gotten into following my wishes. But if the thing was leaving him alone, more or less, as long as I was out of reach, I wasn't going to make matters worse for him. The image of him crying on the bank of the river last night was a strong one.

I didn't have any comment on Ben's situation that I wished to share out loud. So I said, "Beauclaire called me last night." I needed a sounding board, but Adam had obviously not wanted to talk to me about the call; who better to talk to than George, who solved crimes for a living.

"So I heard," George said. "Adam talked to Darryl, Darryl told me." He frowned at me, then said, "Darryl said Beauclaire didn't have much to say." He glanced downstairs and then started walking toward Adam's office. "But both Adam and Darryl indicated that all important conversations should happen in the upstairs bedrooms with the doors shut or in Adam's office."

So Ben wouldn't overhear us.

George took the fancy chair; I closed the office door and took my usual seat on Adam's desk.

"Did Adam and Darryl have their conversation in here or out there?" I asked.

"In here," George said, his eyes shrewd.

I felt sick. Beauclaire had been subtle, but Adam understood subtle better than I did. Reading between the lines was admittedly dangerous with the fae. But Beauclaire did not want to keep his people locked up in the reservation. Without Underhill being a safe refuge for the fae—which she decidedly was not—the reservation was a limited-time solution. If all the fae remained trapped inside those walls, they would start feeding upon each other—in both a figurative and literal sense. Beauclaire had already proven that his primary goal was the survival of his people, and his people were all of the fae.

Beauclaire had been subtle, for sure. But he'd given me a lot of information. That Adam hadn't seen it scared me.

"Beauclaire thinks that there is a reason Underhill let the smoke beast escape in our yard instead of the reservation, where it could have had access to fae who could kill hundreds if not thousands of people in very short order." And that last was why Beauclaire had pulled all of his people to safety. It was also why Marsilia had sealed her people in, too.

"So she didn't want to create chaos or kill lots of fae," said George.

"Right," I agreed. "When Aiden discovered the door, Underhill told him, 'I need a door to Mercy's backyard. I miss you. The fae aren't playing nice.'" I frowned, trying to remember exactly what Aiden had told me. There had been something about not wanting to owe the fae anything.

But George said, "She meant those statements to be put together." He'd seen what I had. "That she wanted a door to your backyard so she could see Aiden—because she didn't trust the fae with him, or they were using his visits as bargaining chips or some such thing."

I nodded. "But why would she need to let him go in my backyard? She likes Adam better than me. She could have said Adam's backyard. And Aiden lives here—so she could have said your backyard."

"The smoke beast bit you," George said. "And it couldn't control you."

"Okay," I said. "I think that is significant. And later she told Aiden something about me being good at killing monsters." I grabbed a small spiral notebook out of Adam's top drawer, ruthlessly ripped out all the pages with writing on them, and shoved them back in the drawer. Then I wrote:

Underhill released smoke beast here because of me. Smoke beast's bite doesn't let him control me.

"It still almost killed you," he reminded me.

"Why didn't it just turn me into concrete like it did that semi?"

I asked him. "Or, for that matter, why didn't it just turn you and me both into concrete?"

"Because we're living?" George postulated.

I shook my head. "Zee says that for fae magic—transformation is transformation."

"Power," suggested George—that was what Zee had concluded as well. "She said that she killed things for power. And she hadn't been able to kill those kids crossing the road. Maybe she used all her power transforming the semi—and that's why the whole semi wasn't concrete when we got there. I've been wondering why, when she was mad at the driver, she only transformed part of the semi. What if she was trying to transform the whole thing, driver and all, but didn't have the juice to do it? She took Dennis—and Dennis killed Anna, but didn't kill anyone else. You didn't kill anyone or die yourself. She took this poor hitchhiker and still didn't manage to kill anyone—that we know of. That's a lot of power outlay."

"That sounds right," I said, writing:

Did not have enough power to transform George and me and only ½ semi.

"So if we can keep the people the beast takes from killing anyone, we can keep it powered down," George said. "We have Ben contained."

He sounded so hopeful.

"Did Adam tell Darryl, and Darryl tell you, that one of the fae was bitten, went into Uncle Mike's, and killed a whole bunch of people—fae and human and goblin? That Larry and the frost giant stopped it?"

George frowned. "No," he said. "Just that the fae, like the vampires, are holed up until the smoke beast is dealt with. By us."

"Do you remember the big car wreck that pushed Kyle's discharging of a firearm to protect Warren off the front page?" I asked.

George looked sick. "Stefan," he said.

I nodded. "That's what Beauclaire indicated. I think that the smoke beast has plenty of power right now."

"What else did Beauclaire tell you?" George asked.

"He said that they called it the smoke dragon and smoke weaver—that both of those terms spoke to its nature—that it had a name, but Beauclaire could not speak it. Nor could any fae. And that that was because of the rules under which the smoke weaver operated."

George started to say something, but I held up a hand. "Sorry, there is something Zee told me. He said . . . he said that what the smoke beast—" I hesitated because Beauclaire had told me what they called the creature for a reason. "What the smoke *weaver* is doing with the whole body snatching and killing to power up is more like the way an artifact would have been made. He said that the transformations like what the weaver did with the semi are a power that belong to a group of lesser fae."

"Huh," said George. "That would explain the power problem it has. I have never noticed that the fae have trouble powering their own magic. Maybe it has an artifact it's using? All you have to do is figure out what it is and take it away."

That sounded like an interesting plan. I wished I had the book Ariana, a powerful fae I knew, had written about her people. It had a whole section on artifacts—but I didn't remember any of them operating quite like that. If Zee had known of one (or built one), he would have told me. The book was gone, but I would call Ariana and see if she knew of something like this. Last I had heard from her, she was somewhere in Africa with her mate, Samuel, and communication was tricky.

George had moved on. "Are we sure this is fae? You said her magic—its magic—didn't smell fae."

I shrugged. "I haven't run into it before. There are a lot of fae; maybe this one is like the platypus—or the goblins, for that matter. It doesn't quite fit in."

"What else did Beauclaire say?" asked George, half closing his eyes, which was what he did when he was thinking hard.

"That we're unlikely to be able to kill it"—and Beauclaire hadn't mentioned an artifact—"and that trick it has of transforming itself to smoke makes it hard to capture. He then said that Underhill had imprisoned it because of a bargain it made. And that there is a story about that bargain I should find. Then Baba Yaga shut him up and told me that the key to the smoke weaver's undoing is to be found in his basic nature." Huh. "*His* basic nature," I said again.

"So we have a start," said George. "That's more than we knew when Ben got bitten. I have a few contacts that might know something about artifacts. Even if they're locked up in Fairyland, cell phones still work. I'll do some sleuthing."

"I'd appreciate that." I hopped off the desk and opened the door.

"I need to go put some signs up at my garage," I told George. "I'm trusting you to keep Ben from killing anyone—or himself—while I'm gone."

"He doesn't seem suicidal," George said. "He ate a hearty breakfast—muffin with bacon, eggs, and cheese—all off a paper plate without even so much as a fork or spoon. He's not exactly cheery—but Ben isn't usually a cheery sort of guy."

Hmm. Ben was usually pretty cheery around me. Foul-mouthed

and sarcastic, maybe, but cheerful enough. For sure he hadn't started out that way. Maybe he was grumpier around other people—or they avoided him so much that they didn't know he'd changed.

"So you played cook this morning?" I asked. George didn't strike me as the homemaker type. Toast and eggs maybe, but not a better-than version of a fast-food staple.

"Adam cooked it up for all of us." George frowned at me. "He was cooking when I got here at five—and Darryl said you didn't get to sleep until the wee hours. *You* look like you could use another eight hours to sleep. You both need to get more rest or you aren't going to be any good for anything."

"News at eleven," I said dryly, and he grinned.

"Telling you things you already know is the job of all of your friends," he said, and headed down to the basement.

When had George become my friend?

I had a smile on my face when I opened the fridge, but it dropped away when I saw the deconstructed breakfast sandwich on the large plate with assembly instructions written out in Adam's handwriting.

The sandwich was for me. And another time I would have taken it as a thoughtful love-note kind of thing. But we weren't in that place right now, so that limited the reasons for this gesture. Apologies or guilt—which were both kind of the same thing.

I thought, just then, of waking up in the middle of the night knowing there was a predator watching me with hostile eyes. Of reaching out and finding Adam in wolf form.

I don't trust myself, he'd said. *I've been a werewolf for longer than you've been alive and it's been decades since I've had trouble with it. But now I wake up and I'm in my wolf's shape—without remembering how I got there.*

Could that hostile presence have been Adam?

Shaken, I microwaved the things that needed to be microwaved and toasted the English muffin. Adam had said he didn't know what had caused his problem controlling his shapeshifting—but his wolf had blamed the witches.

Adam was smart, but beyond that he was perceptive. He didn't usually have blinders on when he was looking at people, even if he was looking into a mirror.

I bit into the sandwich.

He was, in fact, overly harsh when looking into a mirror. He still thought he was a monster. I swallowed and considered that. Could it be that the witches had done something to him and he thought it was his own inner demons breaking free? That the wolf was right and Adam was wrong?

And what the freak could I do about that? Find another witch? I thought of Elizaveta, who had been our pack's witch for decades before Adam had had to kill her. I didn't know that there was a witch I would trust Adam to. Maybe I should talk to Bran? That was an idea with some merit.

I finished the sandwich and punished myself with a glass of orange juice for health. Followed that up by punishing myself with a cup of coffee to stay awake for the day. Coffee I found nearly as vile as orange juice, but hopefully both of them would do their jobs.

I was dumping the last half of my coffee in the sink when the front door opened and my nose told me that Auriele had walked in.

"We are both being chastised," she told me as she walked into the kitchen. "I am to accompany you on whatever you are doing today."

Her tone was neutral, as was her body language. I had no idea what she was feeling about doing guard duty for me. Maybe it was time to put the cards on the table.

I dusted my hands off and gave her a somber look. "I like you. I think that you are too easily led by your need to protect Christy, who needs protecting about as much as a . . . a jaguar needs protecting." I didn't call Christy either a shark or viper—go me!

Auriele gave me a look that told me that she'd heard "viper" instead of the sexier "jaguar" just fine.

"I like you," she told me without sounding like she was going to choke on it. "You are a Goody Two-shoes sometimes, but you'd fall on a grenade for Adam or Jesse or a member of the pack. You fell on a grenade for Christy, even. But you would also fall on a grenade for a total stranger—and that makes you a liability to the pack."

I thought about what she said.

"That's fair," I told her. "But I don't open other people's mail."

"That's fair, too," she said. "Where are we going and when? Adam said he thought you'd be moving by eight."

It was seven and if she'd been five minutes later I'd have been gone. Normally I'd have been headed to church (although not at seven a.m.), but the garage was more urgent today.

I grabbed my purse and said, "The garage. The fae have recalled everyone into the reservation. Without Zee and Tad there, under the circumstances, working in the garage by myself is a liability to the pack." I deliberately chose her words.

She nodded approvingly. "Good decision." Implying that most of my decisions were not.

But I was a grown-up and didn't bring up her decision to open Jesse's mail again.

———

I USED THE SHOP COMPUTER AND PRINTED OUT SIGNS after Auriele observed that my handwritten signs looked like something her students would do if they were trying to flunk her class. I am not a computer whiz and wasn't sure the ones I'd put together were any better than the handwritten ones, but I put them up anyway while Auriele played on her phone. And I hid the signs I'd previously scrawled with a marker for everyday use: *Lunch break, back in five* and *Unexpected drama, will return eventually.* On that sign I had initially spelled "eventually" with one "l." In my defense I'd been in a panic when I'd written it. Tad later corrected it for me using a different color marker than I'd used. It probably said something about me that it didn't bother me to display it for my clients, but I didn't want Auriele to see it.

I called and canceled the appointments for that week that I could, and streamlined the rest. I'd come in on Monday and fix a few desperately needed vehicles. I sent some of my clients with newer cars to the dealership—and a few who couldn't afford the dealership to another garage. Fifty-fifty chance that those clients would stay with that garage afterward, because he was good and nearly as inexpensive as I was.

"I thought you were closing the garage until further notice," Auriele said as I locked up.

"That's right."

"But you are still coming back Monday," she said.

"There are some cars I can't trust to anyone else," I said. "And a few customers who need special handling. I'll get one of the wolves to come in with me. People need their cars to work."

We got back in my Jetta.

"We could have taken my car," she said, not for the first time.

"I don't want to get oil stains on any car that Darryl half owns," I told her seriously. "He might have a heart attack and we can't afford to lose any more wolves until Adam succeeds in bringing the invaders into our fold."

She laughed. "Ah. So it is not the gas mileage, or the need to be in the driver's seat." Which were the answers that I'd given her the first two times she'd complained about the Jetta. "It is out of a deep and abiding concern for my husband's health."

"Absolutely," I said. "I like Darryl."

"We aren't going back?" she asked as I turned the wrong way to head home.

"Nope," I said. "It's been a rough few days. I'm going for doughnuts. Spudnuts." Spudnuts were called spudnuts because the dough was made from potato flour. Ben loved spudnuts.

"Okay," she said. "I could do a doughnut."

Spudnuts was in the Uptown in Richland—a fair commute from my garage in east Kennewick, but it was totally worth the trip. Except when it was closed—which apparently it was.

"Well, that's sad," I said. Why did I not know it was closed on Sundays? I was sure I'd come here on Sunday once or twice.

"Safeway has good doughnuts," Auriele offered soberly.

I sighed. Grocery store doughnuts and spudnuts shouldn't be mentioned in the same breath. With the garage closed for the foreseeable future, it looked like I was going to have some extra time on my hands. Maybe I should try making doughnuts. My homemade bread was good. I already knew how to make fry bread—and there wasn't a whole lot of—

My brain lit up with information.

I didn't know if the other wolves saw their connections to the pack the way I did. To me, it was like a web of Christmas garland, sparkly and metallic with unexpected lights here and there, the mating bond between Adam and me a thick, glowing rope. That one changed every time I observed. Today it was a sullen red with orange light moving within, almost like a lava lamp. The orange light, I was sure, was information the bond wanted me to have but Adam was keeping from me. Under normal circumstances that bond informed me of things like Adam's mood, where he was, what music he was listening to, or what he was thinking about.

The pack bonds, on the other hand, very seldom told me much. Mostly I could tell when someone died. I knew that Adam got a lot more information than that. But the only time the pack bonds really gave me much was when we were on a hunt. Then it was overwhelming, as if the whole pack was one beast.

I would have thought I'd freak out when I was consumed by the pack bonds—but it was the best feeling in the world. There was no sadness, no worry, nothing except for a wild joy that seared my nerve endings. No hesitation, no questioning, just knowing that the pack is one.

Granted, if the bonds had done that all the time, turning us into a hive mind like the Borg from *Star Trek*, I'd be moving to Istanbul or Outer Mongolia or some other faraway place to get away. But once or twice a month in a planned and organized hunt? That was pretty cool.

Today was different.

I froze where I was, standing in the parking lot with my hand on the top of the open door of my disreputable Jetta, my head and fingertips buzzing with the urgency of the call. The power of it made the air I breathed feel electric. And as on the nights of the hunt, I knew things I had no business knowing. I knew that Kelly was down and scared and—

"Makaya," said Auriele, putting her butt in the passenger seat of the Jetta.

I'd gotten that, too. Makaya was Kelly's six-year-old daughter— and she was in trouble. We were less than two miles from Kelly's house. I was peeling rubber before Auriele slammed her door shut.

On the whole, '80s Jettas looked like pedestrian cars, something built along the lines of the Chevette or Echo. Useful, but unpretty and unremarkable. My Jetta, midway through restorations, was remarkable for all the wrong reasons. But unlike my beloved Vanagon, which was lucky to attain highway speed, the Jetta was built to move, not only quick but also maneuverable.

I was doing sixty when I took the corner from Jadwin onto Kelly's street, and the wheels stayed on the ground when I did it. Ahead, right by Kelly's house, I could see a large man with a small child in his hands—he was holding her above his head. Just beyond them was a large construction dumpster.

"She's alive," said Auriele, her voice raspy with wolf. "She's moving her legs."

"If I hit him with the car," I asked her, "can you make the grab from the hood of the car to protect her?"

I braked pretty hard as I spoke, slowing the car until we were going about twenty-five miles an hour. Much faster and Auriele wouldn't have a chance. Much slower and I risked not doing enough damage to the werewolf to get him to drop Makaya. This was an old car, well-designed, but what I was planning was going to hurt me, too, because it didn't have airbags. That thought was a rueful one, and didn't change my plans. Makaya was a child. And also a smart aleck. And I adored her.

Auriele didn't bother to answer me. She just broke out the side window with one definite hit of her elbow and climbed out over the shattered glass. The Jetta's windows rolled up and down manually—she'd still have been lowering the glass ten seconds after we passed Kelly's house if she'd tried it that way.

Being a werewolf gave her the strength to break the window efficiently and crawl outside without risk of falling on the ground. But it was her own natural grace that let her stand on the hood of the Jetta while I drove over a pothole-pocked road, aiming my two-thousand-pound weapon at the bad guy holding the little girl.

He dropped Makaya, holding her by one leg. Apparently his intent was to scare her family, because his focus was toward Kelly's house. I couldn't see Kelly or his mate, Hannah, but I couldn't imagine that they weren't out there, just hidden from my sight by their picket fence and the neighbor's hedge.

I started to slow. I didn't want to risk hitting Makaya with the car. We were barely half a block away—I was going to have to abort.

And then he swung her up over his head again, dancing around in a circle. He didn't even look at us—though he had to have heard the engine. He was having too much fun.

On the hood of my car, Auriele remained crouched, knees slightly bent. There wasn't another wolf in the pack that I would even have thought of asking to try this in human form. I wasn't asking Auriele just to survive the accident. I was asking her to keep six-year-old Makaya safe. But I'd seen her fight a volcano god; I was reasonably certain that if anyone outside a movie could do this, it would be Auriele.

Even so, I wouldn't have tried it—except that even when I'd

turned the corner and he'd been six blocks away, I could read madness in the enemy wolf's body language. I'd grown up in the Marrok's pack, where every year, people who had been newly Changed failed to control their wolf. Some of them went completely mad. I'd probably seen a dozen of them, but one would have been enough. They were scary enough to imprint on my brain the first time.

If I'd had any doubt, the expression on the face of the man holding Makaya would have cleared it right up. Whether Lincoln Stuart—I recognized him from Adam's photo presentation—lived or died today, he was never going to have a human heart again.

I could see Hannah and Kelly now. Hannah, a scarlet streak across one shoulder, was frozen just inside the gate. Kelly was on the grass, elbow crawling toward her.

And then the time for observation was over.

Auriele launched herself, stretching out in the instant before the Jetta hit the werewolf. He was tall, so the bumper caught him just below the knee, obliterating the bone. The sound was loud, but dull as if I'd hit something soft. The velocity folded him sideways over the hood as the car crushed him into the dumpster.

The seat belt holding me in my seat gave up the ghost—I'd been worried about that; it was on my list to fix. Even so, the car crumpled, as it had been designed to do, absorbing a good bit of the power of the collision. The seat belt held on long enough that I didn't go through the windshield.

The impact rang my bell pretty good—and maybe broke my nose on the steering wheel. There was enough blood for that, and my nose hurt sufficiently. Dazed, I backed the car up until it died—about six feet from the dumpster, which had not moved with the impact. I popped the door open and struggled out amid dripping glass. I had to spin around awkwardly once to get rid of the remains of the seat belt.

The car was more damaged than I'd expected—maybe the speedometer had needed some work. I stared at the car for a moment and decided the speedometer was a moot point. I was going to be looking for another car, again.

About that time, I realized I could hear a lot of noise—and that there were a lot more important things going on than the wreck of my car.

I pulled out my gun and stepped around the car to point it at Lincoln, who was howling and snarling and trying to pull the remains of his left leg out of my radiator, where it was caught. That both of his legs were hideously broken did not apparently register because in among the other sounds he was making were threats. They seemed pretty undirected at the moment, but I believed him.

I'd seen this kind of behavior before. Pain meant nothing to someone who was lost in his wolf. But then his shirt slid back—and I saw a wound on the top of his shoulder.

My breathing was labored—because I had to breathe through my mouth because of my nose. I was starting to think, as the shock of the collision (I could hardly term it an accident) receded a bit, that I had broken a rib or two as well. Woozy as I was, I couldn't afford to take my eyes off Lincoln. The shirt slid a little more and I saw a second scab on his skin where another tooth had penetrated. They weren't small holes—like the rabbit bite that Ben and I had gotten. These were bigger—more like the photos that Marsilia had sent of Stefan's wounds. As much as I wanted to go rip the shirt off to be sure, I didn't dare go any nearer to him. He might be bitten, but he was also a werewolf.

"Makaya?" I called. "Auriele?"

"Safe," said Auriele, sounding remarkably composed.

The sounds had died down to just children crying—near and far—and Lincoln's frenzy.

"Injuries?" I asked.

"Makaya looks like she has a broken wrist and maybe an ankle," Auriele said. "Hannah has a bad cut on her shoulder that will need stitches. A lot of stitches. Kelly—"

"Will survive," he growled. "Changing now."

"Any bites?" I asked. "This wolf has been bitten like Ben."

Auriele said something pungent. After a moment, relief in her voice, she said, "Not Makaya. Not Hannah. Kelly?"

"No," said Kelly. "He hit me with a baseball bat. Then he hit me with my tool chest."

"And the sledgehammer," said Hannah, sounding broken.

"And the sledgehammer. But no bites. Will survive," said Kelly again. "No bites, Mercy."

I was pretty sure the last word he said was my name, but Kelly's voice had dropped and lost clarity because he was changing.

Shifting to wolf and food should fix most of it over the next couple of days—as long as nothing was misaligned. I had to trust Auriele to make sure Kelly would be okay, too. My job was to figure out what to do with this wolf.

I had my gun and my cutlass, which was still in its case in the car, but I couldn't just kill him, not here in the open with door cameras and cell phone cameras (I could see some curtains moving at Kelly's neighbor's house). He hadn't killed anyone here for anyone to see. Broken by the impact with my car, he appeared not to be an immediate threat. He was, especially with those bite marks, but the human authorities wouldn't know that if I killed him. And if I waited until he was up on his feet—he might manage to kill me.

"What about the other kids?" Auriele asked—not me, obviously.

"Safe," said Hannah. "Sean and Patrick are at a friend's house. I locked the baby in our bedroom; she's not happy, but she's safe." Sean and Patrick were their two boys, ages twelve and ten. The baby was three—so not really a baby anymore.

A truck drove up. I didn't look up from Lincoln, but I heard it just fine. A late-model Ford diesel, I thought from the sounds of it. It didn't belong to any of the pack—I knew the sounds of the pack's vehicles.

The truck stopped across the street and a pair of doors opened. I heard three people get out of the truck and stop on the other side of the road. Three people who were werewolves, and not our werewolves. I wasn't smelling them—my nose was definitely broken—but I could hear the werewolf in the way they moved. I knew they were our invaders because of the truck.

"People are watching," I told them. "Think about what you do next." Then in a softer voice I asked, "Auriele?"

"They don't look like they're coming for a fight," she told me, quietly. "That could change." The enemy werewolves would be able to hear us, but not the humans in their houses.

I needed to move, to get my back to Auriele and my front toward the new threat. The problem was I was still dizzy, my eyes were having trouble focusing, and I wasn't sure how far I needed to keep away from the downed wolf-mad Lincoln. I had to be close enough to shoot him if he started to regain mobility.

The new werewolves stayed where they were.

"Kids okay?" called a man's voice.

"The one he manhandled has broken bones," I said. "She is six."

"Seven," said Makaya, her voice wobbly. "I am seven."

"I told you," the stranger said. "I told you that he wasn't right. But you thought you knew better."

"Lincoln said he was fine. He had eighty years of controlling his beast," said a woman.

I frowned. I'd heard that voice before. But I didn't know Nonnie Palsic, the only woman in the group of invading werewolves, according to the data Adam had compiled. Maybe I'd only heard her voice, on the phone or something.

I wished my nose were working. My memory for scent was much better than my memory for voices.

"We were supposed to go out and create a little havoc today," said the man—I think he was speaking to me. "The houses with kids were *supposed* to be strictly out-of-bounds."

I chanced a quick look at the new werewolves.

The man was hard to focus on—as if I were a human looking at a werewolf pulling on the pack bonds to hide themself in the guise of a big dog. I didn't have time to do more than glance at him, but it didn't take a genius to know this was James Palsic. Standing just behind him was Nonnie Palsic. Her hair was dark brown, though in the photo Adam had shown the pack it had been lighter. Her face was thinner, but unmistakable. The third person was also a woman, both short and slight, who was faintly familiar.

I turned my focus back to Lincoln as he finally managed to rip his leg free of the ruined front of my car. He hadn't shown any sign of noticing me at all, up to this point. But, still without looking at me, he rolled sideways with speed, slashing at my knee with a knife I hadn't noticed him having.

Having two good legs, I managed to get out of his way, but

that put me in the middle of the street. And closer to the Palsics and the oddly familiar woman.

James Palsic said, "Would you mind if I took care of him?"

I couldn't tell if he was asking me.

"Put him in the back of the truck," the woman with the familiar voice ordered. "We'll figure out what to do with him when we get back."

"Go ahead," I said.

I put the gun up in the air so I wasn't aiming at anyone and backed up a dozen feet down the middle of the road, so it didn't put me any closer to the enemy. Auriele, who had given Makaya to her mother, put herself in front of the little family. I wondered if I should tell them what was wrong with Lincoln.

Palsic stalked past me and said something in a Romance language that wasn't Spanish or Italian—Portuguese maybe, or Romanian. It sounded sorrowful and resolute. He avoided Lincoln's attack, and the maneuver put him at the damaged werewolf's back. With a quick and easy movement he picked up the struggling werewolf.

"Don't let him bite you," I told him—and he raised an eyebrow at me.

"Don't intend to," he said.

"Kill him," said Nonnie.

"There are about six cell phones pointed at us through windows," James told her. He didn't seem to be having trouble keeping Lincoln's mouth away from him.

"I *said* we will decide what to do when we get back." There was ice in the other woman's voice—and for some reason that made everything click.

I had met her before, in the Marrok's office. I'd been cleaning it after Bran had been the victim of a glitter bomb. For some reason he'd blamed me—even though I'd only been responsible for the first three or four of the things. Someone who was not me had been gutsy enough to break into Bran's office and suspend the glitter bomb over his desk. Bran was not interested in my defense—though he must have known I wasn't lying—so I got to clean the room. It did not take much glitter to make a real mess.

Bran must have forgotten about it—or else he'd assumed that it would only take a half hour or so to clean up. He clearly hadn't expected to find me there, two hours later, when he came in with a tiny blond woman with a sweet face. But he'd introduced us and explained about the glitter bomb to her—which, as I recall, she'd had very little reaction to. He'd sent me off so they could conduct their business.

He'd summoned me back a few hours later. His room was absolutely sparkle-less, which was more than could be said about me. He had apologized—told me the real culprit had confessed (without telling me who it was) and cleaned the room. Then he told me that if I ever saw Fiona again, to steer clear of her.

It had made an impression—because he'd never warned me about another werewolf like that. Because she was so small—smaller than I had been at fourteen or fifteen. And because her eyes had been a cold, clear green—not the green of hazel eyes. But like someone with light blue eyes had put in green-tinted contacts. I'd never seen anyone with eyes that color.

I later learned that she was one of a group of wolves that Bran used to keep the werewolves in order. Charles was only the most obvious and feared one. But Charles had limits—he knew right from wrong. This woman did exactly what she was told, and enjoyed assassin work the most.

"Fiona," I said, and she turned to focus on me. From this distance I couldn't see her eye color beyond that they were light. Her hair was dark, not blond, but her body language was the same.

"Mercy Hauptman," she said, without smiling. "Bran's little coyote pet."

"How unexpected," I said—though clearly she was not surprised to find *me* here. "Are you still . . ." I couldn't think of how to phrase it.

"Running errands," she said.

"Still running errands for Bran?" I asked, using her phrase.

She shook her head. "No, actually. I found my mate and changed my ways."

"Not Lincoln Stuart," I said, more to let her know that she wasn't the only one who knew their enemies than because I thought there was a chance that it was Lincoln. She'd have been a lot more concerned about Lincoln than she was if he had been her mate. "And the Palsics are mated to each other."

James, still standing beside my car with the struggling Lincoln in his arms, met my eyes.

"Adam remembered you," I told him. Let them think we'd had eyes on them, too, instead of good intel from Charles.

Fiona gave me a sharp smile. "Sven Harolford is my mate, Mercedes Thompson . . . Hauptman. We are here to take over your pack. We will allow Hauptman to take three wolves with him— and you. You should be grateful."

I smiled back at her, centering my weight over my feet. I was in no shape to fight, between broken nose and sore ribs, but I wasn't going to let her see that.

"Shivering in my boots, here," I told her. Fiona was probably a game changer. We had a lot of wolves in our pack who had killed people. But we didn't have any killers—wolves who enjoyed murder. I didn't want Fiona in our pack. "You won't take my advice, but you should move on. If you need a refuge from Gartman and his pack, Bran will help you."

"No," said Fiona, a faint bitterness in her voice. "He won't. James? What are you waiting around for? Get Lincoln in the truck." She turned around and stalked back to the truck herself.

James nodded to me as he passed by with Lincoln. I stared at him, trying to fix his features in my head. I knew what he looked like from Adam's picture. But I couldn't get a lock on his face.

James tossed the other wolf ungently into the back of the truck. Onlookers who did not have supernatural hearing wouldn't have heard the pop as he broke Lincoln's neck in the middle of that toss.

"*Idiot*," snapped Fiona. "Who do you think gives the orders around here?"

He stared at the truck bed for a long moment, tension in his body. Then he turned back to *me*.

"I told them," he said in a soft voice. "No children. And Fiona and Sven sent him here anyway." He looked at Fiona. "He did not find this place on his own. He's been so wild that he could barely put his own clothes on." He met my gaze.

I felt a spark. There was a little pop in my head, like when my ears depressurized. A zing of magic darted down my spine—and I could see his face at last.

Fiona said, "We thought he was stable. Today he was better."

And she'd sent a wolf here to cause havoc. To Kelly's house where there were children.

I looked back at James. "Green Beetle," I said to him. "Nicely restored. You needed a new generator."

He'd come into the shop a couple of weeks ago—and I hadn't even noticed he was a werewolf. Hadn't remembered his features or recognized him when Adam had shown his face to the pack. More worrisome, Zee had been working with me that day—and he hadn't noticed that James was a werewolf, either. Adam's information was wrong. James Palsic's ability to go unnoticed was definitely magic. I was pretty sure it wouldn't work on me anymore.

He smiled at me, a genuine, open smile. Which felt a little odd coming from an enemy werewolf who had just killed one of his compatriots.

"That's right," he said. "Nice shop you have there."

"I've closed it temporarily," I told them. "Because you folks are not the monsters we are worried about just now."

"Having trouble with the fae?" asked Fiona. "You should let us handle them."

I smiled at her and debated telling her that the smoke beast had already taken one victim from her people. "Not all the fae— they have locked themselves in the reservation because this one, *this one* they are afraid of."

"Sirens are getting closer," Nonnie said. "If you really don't want to meet the human authorities until later, Fi, we should get going right now."

They listened to her and got in the truck without another word. They drove off just as flashing lights rounded the corner I'd taken at sixty. The police cruiser took it considerably slower than I had. The truck passed them, took a right turn, and disappeared from view.

And I wondered why Fiona had asked me about the fae. There

were vampires here—and other things that defied classification. Had she known about the bite?

THEY SET MY NOSE AT THE HOSPITAL. AS SOON AS the medical professionals left me to my own devices, I decamped and went looking for Makaya. I found Auriele and Kelly waiting in one of the other emergency bays and wandered in.

"Nice shirt," said Auriele.

Mine had made me look like an extra from a horror movie because broken noses bleed. So I'd been issued a hospital top. The hospital issue was a pale beige color that made my Native-toned skin look greenish. Solemnly I turned around so she could get a good look at the open back.

"I don't think I'll be setting any fashion trends soon," I told her. "Makaya in X-ray?"

"Yes," Auriele nodded. "Hannah went with her. She'll let them stitch her up in another room as soon as Makaya is taken care of. Makaya is pretty traumatized and wanted her mother."

"How bad is Hannah's cut?" I asked.

"Long," she said. "But not deep. It will need stitches at the top, but the bottom is okay. He cut her with that knife he pulled on you."

I knelt to talk to Kelly. "How are you doing?"

His muzzle wrinkled up and he let out a low, angry growl.

"He walked in here on his own," Auriele said. "But it wasn't easy for him. I checked him over pretty thoroughly. I don't think any of his bones were misaligned."

She meant none of them would have to be rebroken.

Kelly was still growling.

"I know," I said. "Me, too. Those people are not becoming members of *our* pack. But you have to stop growling now, before you scare someone."

"They don't intend to join us, remember," said Auriele dryly. "They will let Adam take three of his people and you. Who *are* you going to pick?" She knew Adam and me well enough to know that wandering off and leaving the pack to someone else was not going to happen.

I snorted with more dismissal than I actually felt. "They have no chance now. If they wanted to take the pack from us, they shouldn't have gone for Kelly's home. No one will follow a wolf who allows children to be attacked."

I stood up abruptly. "Adam is here." I didn't smell him. My bond was currently telling me nothing. But I heard his voice. At least my ears were working.

I stepped out of the alcove and looked around, finding him talking to a nurse. I'd called him as soon as the truck carrying Fiona and the Palsics had left and told him what had happened.

Adam had been about an hour's drive away, out in the Hanford Area, nearly six hundred square miles of government access-restricted land surrounding the numerous nuclear reactors and reprocessing facilities being slowly deactivated and cleaned up. He'd known Kelly was hurt—had tried calling him. Then he'd called Darryl and Warren. Apparently, no one except Auriele and me had been alerted by the pack bonds—we had been the closest to the trouble. I was, once I'd had a chance to think about it, a little uncomfortable with what that said about the pack bonds—implying an intelligence at work that did not belong to anyone in the pack.

Darryl and Warren had arrived at Kelly's not long after I got off the phone with Adam. They bundled up the other three kids—Sean and Patrick having been recalled—and took them to our house, where they should be safe. Safer, anyway.

Adam had said he would meet us at the hospital—and here he was, as promised.

I gave a soft whistle, and Adam looked up. He said something more to the nurse and then strode over.

He stopped in front of me and took my head in his hands. He looked gutted. Whatever weirdness was going on—it could not be what was between us. Because that face said that he cared what happened to me. He was being a stubborn bastard, trying to keep his troubles to himself. Maybe I'd wait until the rest of this—the stray wolves and the smoke weaver—were dealt with. But I wasn't going to let him continue carrying whatever was bothering him alone.

"No worries," I told the stubborn bastard. "I broke my nose on the steering wheel. Probably I'll have two black eyes to go with it. But the good news is that my ribs aren't broken or cracked, just bruised."

"I'll spend the next week telling the press I didn't hit you," he said, but he looked like he could breathe again.

"Good for you," I said encouragingly.

He smiled wryly and kissed my forehead. "Do you think that your next car could have airbags?"

Retrofitting airbags was a fool's game—and dangerous. It was a matter of pride for me as a mechanic that I drove an old car.

"I just need to quit hitting people with my cars and we'll be good," I told him.

"If only," he murmured, "you don't run into any more who

need to be hit." Proving he knew me. "I suppose I should be grateful that you aren't under arrest."

"Might have been," I told him. "Except that Kelly's neighbor came running out of his house. He'd caught most everything on his cell phone. Just wait until you see the part with Auriele making the grab for Makaya as I rammed Lincoln with the Jetta. It looks like a scene from Cirque du Soleil. The police decided I was justified and warned me not to do it again. I pointed out that I couldn't do it again because the car is totaled—and was, at that moment, getting towed to my garage, where I can mine it for parts."

Adam smiled, but his eyes were worried.

9

BECAUSE MAKAYA WAS IN THE CAR WITH US ON THE
way home, and I didn't want to scare her, I didn't talk to Adam
about Fiona or how Lincoln had been bitten. He knew what I
knew, because I'd talked to him about it on the phone when I'd
called him from Kelly's house. There were still some important
implications that we should discuss—but it would have to wait
until we got home.

So for the ride home, I stayed quiet, nursing my broken nose,
as Auriele organized a pack bunk-up on her phone. Bunk-up was
one step shy of "everyone to the Batcave"—our house being the
Batcave. Bunk-up meant that the wolves stayed in groups of two
to four and avoided going anywhere alone.

I wasn't sure how a bunk-up was going to keep anyone safe
from the smoke weaver—though it probably would be effective
against Fiona's band, at least in the short run. But I didn't say
anything. What else could we do?

We could pull the human families of the pack into our home; we'd done that when the witches had become a problem. But we had too many werewolves to take them all into our home for long—and if we did, there was no way to lock the doors to keep them in and the smoke weaver out. Packed in like that for more than a few hours, we'd start having fights. Our wolves needed freedom to move. We literally could not do what the fae and the vampires had done to protect themselves. We also could not do it figuratively. We were the protectors of the Tri-Cities. It was our job to face the scary bad things—if we retreated, we left the field to the villains.

We arrived home and the mass chaos of too many people in too small a space was whipped into shape by the combined efforts of Auriele, Hannah, and Jesse. I tried to get Adam's attention a couple of times—but he kept retreating with different people to confer in his office, where Ben couldn't hear them. But also where there wasn't enough room for me, not even on his desk.

"You look like you hurt," Adam told me. "I know you have some things we need to discuss. I'll come up as soon as I can. Take a bag of frozen peas and lie down. I'll find you as soon as I have the security schedules lined out."

We had ice packs, but I liked frozen peas better. They were gentler on swollen tissue. Frozen peas on my poor nose was a good idea, and finding a quiet place sounded amazing. I grabbed a bag from the freezer and went to our bedroom and shut the door.

Our bedroom was more or less soundproofed—not like Adam's office, where the soundproofing was a serious thing. If the bedroom door was shut and the house was quiet, the werewolves could hear noise from the bedroom but probably not actual conversation. With the mass chaos in the house, being overheard was not a consideration.

I pulled out my phone and dialed a number by memory.

"Mercy."

Just hearing the Marrok's voice took a chunk of stress out of my day. Not that he couldn't return the stress and add stomach-acid-producing interest, but just now he was the person I needed to talk to the most.

"We are in trouble," I told him. Then considered who I was talking to and said, "Not anything we can't handle."

"I feel as though you should amend that," Bran said. "Other-wise you wouldn't have called me."

I thought of the vampires and the fae locking themselves away. And Ben down in the basement pretending there was nothing wrong.

Before anyone could stop them, Kelly's kids had boiled down to the basement, where the electronic toys waited. And they had found Ben in the cage. Ben had dutifully admired Makaya's bright pink casts, adorned with hot-glued glitter and plastic gemstones thanks to Jesse. And he'd begged us all with his eyes to get the kids upstairs before he lost it again.

We hadn't quite made it, but Jesse told Makaya that Ben was playing.

Makaya had put her head down on Darryl's shoulder (for all that he was scary as anything, kids loved Darryl) and said sadly, "Maybe I would have laughed like he wanted but that man scared me today. I don't want to be scared again for a while."

Yes, so maybe we were having trouble handling it.

"Okay. Let's say that I have some concerns," I hedged. "I think you might help with a couple of them."

"You have some wolves invading your territory," he said.

That photo montage and information organization had been

mostly Charles. I would have known that even if I hadn't heard Adam talking to him. Charles handed out information that was useful, organized, and succinct. But if Charles knew about our invaders, so would Bran.

Bran was more Socratic when delivering aid. "Adam," he might have said, "where do you think you should go looking for information? If I were you I might look at . . . Texas."

Which was why Adam had gone to Charles for help and not Bran. Well, that and Bran had formally washed his hands of our pack as a necessary step in the experiment of a werewolf pack being the neutral party while the humans and the fae worked out how they were going to live in the same world together. Our pack had to be independent so that if matters didn't go well, we wouldn't drag every werewolf in North and South America into a war with the fae or the humans—or both.

I had gone to Bran because I wasn't looking for loads of information—I needed advice. Advice was Bran's best thing.

"One of the invading wolves is Fiona," I told him. I wasn't actually sure of her last name, but I didn't need it.

Bran inhaled, then said, "She's dead."

"Nope," I said. "I just saw her tiny as life about three . . . no, five hours ago. Time flies when you are in the emergency room." And I shouldn't have said that last.

"Are you all right?" he demanded.

"Yes."

"Mercy."

"*Jeez,*" I complained, feeling about four. "I broke my nose running my car into a possessed wolf who was hurting one of the pack's children. Because I broke my nose, she only has a broken wrist and ankle, and the wolf is dead. I'm *all right* with the results of today."

"Semantics," he growled.

"Truth," I told him. "What can you tell me about Fiona?"

"Stay away from her," he said.

I hoped he could hear my eyes rolling. "That's what you told me when I was fourteen. I was hoping for something more useful now that I'm an adult and she's trying to take over my pack."

"Don't roll your eyes at me," he snapped. "And you were fifteen."

I looked at the phone. "You remember how old I was?" I asked incredulously.

"It was the day Charles glitter-bombed my office," Bran said darkly. "Of course I remember."

"Charles?" There was no way. "Charles glitter-bombed your office." Cold, scary, efficient, deadly—those were words that suited Charles. That the term "glitter bomb" and Charles's name were in the same sentence was dumbfounding except maybe in something like "Charles discovered the glitter-bomber's secret identity and hanged her by her toenails to teach the other people who stole her idea never to do that ever again."

"Why did he glitter-bomb your office?" I asked.

"It was something I said," Bran told me. "And not your business. What do you know about Fiona?"

"You told me to stay away from her," I said, "which left me insatiably curious."

"Of course it did," Bran returned dryly. "I don't know what I was thinking."

"Like a carrot in front of a horse," I agreed. "But no one knew very much. She was your assassin that you sent out to do work that Charles wouldn't do."

"Yes," agreed Bran.

"That she is as deadly as Charles."

"Differently deadly," he said. "Charles or Adam could take her in a fight. But she won't engage them unless she has to. She will use people . . . Charles told me that there were six wolves invading your territory. Since he didn't mention Fiona—and he would have—are there any others you know of?"

"No. The only ones I have personally seen are James and Nonnie Palsic," I told him. "Oh. And Lincoln Stuart, but he doesn't count because he is dead."

"He is the one you killed?"

"He's the one I hit with my car. I would have shot him, but there were too many onlookers. James Palsic killed him." I could see that I had the choice of telling Bran what happened today one sentence at a time, or I could tell him the whole story. Actually, I was probably better off throwing everything into the mix in order to save time.

"I think," I told him, "that I really need to start with the jackrabbit."

"If that is what you think," he said. "Then by all means, start with the jackrabbit."

He was utterly silent while I was talking—so I really didn't know how he persuaded me to tell him about Wulfe when I hadn't intended to. Or Adam's growing problem with whatever it was that was making him shift without meaning to and that was causing him to close down our mating bond. Or that was what Adam had *implied* as the reason for closing down our mating bond—

sometimes just talking about something out loud pointed out information I'd missed.

I did manage to keep to myself that cold feeling I'd awoken to last night, when only Adam and I had been in the room. I know what it feels like to be the subject of a hunt. To be prey. It could have been my imagination, despite the I'm-sorry breakfast sandwich.

When I finally finished up with Ben scaring Makaya in the basement, I was a little hoarse. I waited for Bran's response. It took long enough that I checked my phone to make sure we were still connected. I'd feel pretty stupid if I'd spent the last hour talking to myself.

"Bran?" I asked. "Are you still there?"

"Tell Adam to kill Fiona, whenever and wherever he gets a chance," he answered briskly. "She is selling her services to the highest bidder. She doesn't share her money with a team, so the others are probably useful tools. She does not make a good ally for anyone or anything she is not terrified of. If she has made, as you are concerned about, an alliance with the smoke weaver—proceed with caution."

"You said that she was supposed to be dead," I said as I wondered who Fiona was working for—and didn't like the obvious answer much. There were other people who wanted us dead besides the witches. She had been sincere when she told me that Adam and I could take three of our people and leave—so maybe she was here to create a base for herself, a pack independent from the Marrok and too important to his schemes for him to destroy.

"I was assured of her demise five or six years ago," he agreed. He could remember that I had *not* glitter-bombed his office when I was fifteen, but he didn't remember how long ago Fiona had died?

"Did you have her killed?" I asked, remembering the bitterness in Fiona's voice.

"I would have," he told me. "But no. She was working for a witch and the deal went bad."

"Deals with witches frequently go bad," I muttered.

"Exactly so," he said gently. "You should tell Adam that the Palsics and Chen Li Qiang I would prefer saved if possible. Kent? Other than which pack he is affiliated or not affiliated with, I haven't heard anything about Kent since the sixties, which I find concerning. Either he is hiding from me, or he has settled down into a boring life with a small blip when he joined the rebels in Galveston."

"We don't work for you anymore," I said dryly. "You can't just dictate to us."

"Why am I helping you, then?" he asked equally dryly.

He had a point. And we'd try to do what he asked as far as the Palsics and Chen were concerned. I'd seen Carlos's face when he talked about Chen. And I'd found myself liking James Palsic. I didn't know about Nonnie—she hadn't done or said anything remarkable, but it might be nice to have another woman in the pack. But I'd had to give Bran a hard time about his assumption that we'd obey his orders, if only for form's sake.

"Okay," I conceded. "I will inform Adam that you *suggest* that we should kill Fiona—and her mate?"

"Mate?" Bran asked.

"Harolford," I told him.

"I'd forgotten about Harolford," he said. "But by all means kill Harolford, too. Just remember that Fiona is the more dangerous of the two."

"Okay," I agreed. "We'll do our best to absorb the Palsics and Chen into the pack and make up our own minds about Kent."

"Good girl," he said, and I could hear the squeak of his chair and knew he was leaning back in it. That was how you always knew he was happy with you.

And if I was pleased about making him happy, I was sure as shooting not going to let him know that.

"So have I solved one of your problems?" he asked.

"Nope," I told him promptly. "But you've told me how you see it—and you have more information than we do. And I know that you are rooting for this experiment—our pack, the fae, and the vampires working together for the good of all—to work, so you are on our side in this. Which means we will take your advice seriously. And *that*, oh Marrok, makes it easier for us to solve our own problem."

"Good," he said, sounding pleased again. Making me think for myself, was he? As long as I thought what he wanted me to think, he liked it when I thought for myself.

"Now, about your problem with Wulfe." His voice grew darker and arctic.

Just from that tone, I realized that someone had told Bran that Wulfe had been the reason that Bonarata, the king of the vampires (or at least the de facto ruler of the vampires), had captured me and taken me to Europe. Bonarata had asked Wulfe who the most dangerous person in the Tri-Cities was. Wulfe, who has an abysmal sense of humor as well as an almost fae-like ability to lie with the truth, told Bonarata that it was me. I am still not quite sure of the logic that Wulfe used.

"I think you can leave Wulfe to Adam and me," I said hastily.

"He's just playing, I think. He saved my life. I don't mean that he's one of the good guys, but . . ." I drew in a breath and centered myself.

I didn't want Bran to come destroy Wulfe, because it would be wrong. He had done nothing, up to this point, that deserved aiming Bran at him. Besides, I tried really hard not to aim Bran at anyone. I had a policy of not using nuclear devices to take out pesky flies because that tended to yield mixed results. I tamped down the small voice that wondered if even Bran could take on Wulfe. I needed Bran to be immortal and unstoppable.

Right this moment, I had to convince Bran not to kill Wulfe.

"I hurt him—badly, I think," I told Bran. "He was trying to help us for whatever twisted reason guides him—maybe because Marsilia asked him, maybe because he was bored. But he was trying to help us and got caught in the backlash of me trying to lay the spirits of zombies to rest. It broke something inside him."

Bran muttered something that might have been, "I can break something inside him, too."

"Bonarata broke him for real a long time ago," I told Bran. "Wulfe is a wizard and a vampire and a witch." That last might be a secret. I certainly hadn't known it before the Night of the Zombies, as Ben liked to call it. But I needed Bran to understand about Wulfe so he didn't just have him eliminated the way he'd just assigned us to eliminate Fiona. "He has spilled blood for Bonarata and for Marsilia for centuries. Tortured and killed for centuries."

Into my dramatic pause, Bran said, with palpable irony, "Yes, Mercy, I know."

"And his witchcraft is white."

This time the pause was his.

"Exactly," I said. "He is a lost soul wandering in the darkness..."

"Drivel," said Bran, who had written that particular line for a rather beautiful song I'd heard him sing once. I think the song was a few centuries old—but he had written it.

"Mawkish sentimentality doesn't make it untrue," I told him. And that was a Bran quote as well. One he used both ways—true or untrue—depending upon the circumstances.

"He is dangerous," I told Bran, "and unpredictable and all of that. But maybe he can be turned into an ally. Adam has made Marsilia an ally."

"Adam thought Elizaveta was his ally."

"So did Elizaveta," I returned. "But that is beside the point."

He took a long breath, and I pictured him holding the bridge of his nose. The breath had that sort of sound to it.

"I will leave him to you and Adam, then," he said finally. "For now."

"Thank you," I said, and he growled at me.

"A third problem," said Bran. "The creature who escaped Underhill. What you know about him, even with Beauclaire's additions, is not enough for me to figure out who he is. It may be that I do not know him, or that I only know him through attributes that you haven't run into."

"Okay," I said. I had really, really hoped that Bran could help us with this one. "He has Ben and Stefan," I reminded Bran.

"I know," he said gently. "And I would not like to lose either of them. To that end, I have some conjectures that may be useful."

"Okay," I said hopefully.

"First—that Beauclaire could not give you the creature's name. The fae place great store by names. There are a number of fae who protect their names by not allowing others to speak them."

"Okay, so the name could be important, once we figure out who this creature is. But we are unlikely to find him just by looking for someone hiding his name—because they all do that."

"Exactly." He sounded pleased again.

I wasn't a child anymore. I shouldn't be happy that he thought I was a good pupil for his Socratic method of teaching.

"I think you should focus on the bargaining part of what Beauclaire told you," he told me. And now I could hear in his voice that he thought I'd missed something obvious.

"But they all *bargain*, too," I said. And maybe I was a little sharp.

"Indeed," he said. And the patience in his voice made me want to dye all of his underwear purple, though that hadn't worked out so well the first time I'd tried it.

But I was a grown-up now, so I set aside petty vengeance and thought about what Beauclaire had said about the bargain.

"But not all of the fae had a bargain with Underhill," I said finally.

My reward for seeing what Bran had seen was him saying, "And someone I know has a door to Underhill in her backyard, and one whom Underhill treasures to knock upon it and ask her to come out."

I thought about Tilly and sighed. "You don't happen to have any hints for dealing with a bloodthirsty immortal being with the attention span of a ten-year-old, do you?"

"Feed her sweets," he said promptly. "Or call Ariana and ask her. But I think something sweet, especially if you bake it yourself, might be a way to coax out whatever information she might have." He paused and then said, "And treat her like a co-conspirator, not a naughty child who has loosed doom upon the world. She may not be able to tell you much, but she may be useful to you all the same. Something within the boundaries of the bargain she has with him."

"Okay," I said. "Thank you.

"And Adam?" I asked him hesitantly. All I had told him about Adam was that Adam had shut down our bond after we'd killed all the witches.

"Blow up the bond," Bran said. "See what happens."

And he hung up.

I stared at my phone. I called him back, but he didn't pick up. I guess he thought that I needed to figure it out. Did he mean that I should try to destroy the bond between Adam and me? How in the world would I do something like that? I didn't *want* to do that.

I tried to call him back again. Maybe if I explained that it wasn't just Adam changing to the wolf involuntarily? It was . . . what? What did I know? That Adam thought I'd be harmed if the bond between us was open?

What did Adam think it would do to me? Did he think I would get caught up in his madness—assuming he thought that he was becoming a monster? *"Argh,"* I said in frustration, and hit the red button on the screen.

Bran had obviously decided not to take any more calls from me tonight.

Someone knocked on the door.

"Who is it?" I grumped, trying to figure out what I could text to Bran so that he'd call me back.

"Me," said Adam, opening the door. "Who were you on the phone with?"

"Bran," I told him. "You and I need to talk."

His eyes were so unhappy.

But his face was locked in his I-deal-with-messes expression, so I figured he didn't know that I could see through it. It was easier to read him with our bond up and functioning—but I'd known him for a long time before we'd been mated, and I'd paid attention.

"I agree," he said after a moment's consideration. "But not here."

"Not here," I agreed. Too many sharp ears—and at least one of them had been co-opted by the enemy. But it wasn't just that. With this many of the pack in the house, we wouldn't have much time before someone needed Adam's attention—as had been amply demonstrated when I'd been trying to talk to him earlier.

"Your house?" he asked, tipping his head toward my empty manufactured house.

I started to say yes, then hesitated. "I don't want to run into Anna again," I told him. "How about the garage? I can check the phone while we're there."

I had forwarded that phone to mine, but no one had called for the garage since this morning. That might mean that no one needed their car repaired. It might also mean that I'd flubbed it.

"Okay," he said, holding the bedroom door wider and stepping back in invitation. "I'll drive. Your cars are under the weather."

"Ha-ha," I grumbled, walking past him. "Poor Jetta."

I was going to have to find time to work on the Vanagon, I thought, resigned. I hated to drive it until I got all the air bubbles out. The air bubbles wouldn't actually hurt anything. All they would do was make the gauges tell me the van was overheating when it wasn't. The big problem with that was that if the engine really did overheat, I'd ignore it because I'd think it was just air bubbles. That would ruin the engine.

"I will buy you a new Jetta," Adam said, stepping into my path so I stopped.

He reached up and caressed my cheeks on either side of my broken nose. His touch was gentle enough that it didn't make my nose hurt worse than it already did.

"I'm onto your devious plot," I said, rising up on my toes to kiss his cheek. I did not wince when the move caused my ribs to remind me that they'd been injured, too. I didn't want to devolve into a "Mercy is hurt" conversation again.

"No *new* Jettas," I said, putting the emphasis on the word he'd tried to skate by me as I started for the stairs. "Even though they have airbags. I will be laughed at by all VW mechanics everywhere if I get caught driving a new car. I just have to find another old car. Those old VWs are engineered to fold around you so even without an airbag they do okay in accidents."

I caught myself before confessing that I'd probably have been all right, or at least my nose would have been okay, if the seat belt hadn't given way. Because that would feed his argument and not mine.

I thought about where I could start looking for another car as I started walking. It had taken me a while to find the Jetta. I'd call all the scrapyards here, in Yakima, and in Spokane, let them know I was looking for a car that was reasonably restorable. Maybe I'd have to give in and pay a little more—it was hard to find them cheap. At least those old Jettas and Rabbits weren't doing what the Vanagons had done—Vanagons were more expensive to buy used than they'd sold fresh off the assembly line. My Syncro was worth a *lot* more now than it had been new.

"Maybe another Rabbit," I mused. "My old Rabbit lasted me more than a decade. The Jetta didn't even make it a year."

"No more Rabbits," said Adam. "At least not this week. I think we've had quite enough rabbits for one week."

He trailed me down the stairs. Or maybe he was herding me down the stairs. I was starting to get an odd vibe from him.

I snuck a peek over my shoulder at him. Caught off guard, his eyes were still as unhappy as they had been when I opened the bedroom door.

"What?" Adam asked me.

But before I had to answer, Warren approached to ask him about the schedule for guard duty—and if we were still running with that plan after everyone had been told to bunk up.

IT TOOK US ABOUT A HALF HOUR BEFORE WE ACTU- ally got going. We didn't talk in the SUV on the way to my office. I wasn't sure why not.

I mean, of course I knew why *I* didn't say anything. I was still mulling over what Bran had said, trying to organize it so it made sense. Sorting through the things Bran had actually said—and the things I'd extrapolated from those. The first being important, the second being a little more suspect.

But I didn't know why *Adam* didn't say anything. Maybe he'd forgotten what he wanted to talk to me about in the avalanche of questions he'd dealt with on our way out the door.

When I looked at him, his eyes were opaque in the shadows. For a moment, though, I was caught by the way the dashboard illuminated the planes and curves of his face. He had the kind of beauty that would make maidens in old tales throw themselves off cliffs in order to attract his attention. Mesmerizing.

He didn't notice me watching him, though—too focused on whatever had been keeping him quiet the rest of the drive. Whatever it was, it wasn't a good thought, judging by the tension in his shoulders.

I put my hand on his thigh. I wasn't sure he noticed. That was really not like him at all. By the time we made it to the garage, I was starting to worry about him—or about what he had to say. Maybe he knew something more than I did about our current circumstances, but it didn't feel quite like that.

The parking lot was lit up a lot better than it had been before we'd rebuilt the garage. I could have sat on the front step and read a book. The light made it easier for Adam's security cameras to get clear pictures.

I stopped on the way to the office and stared at one of the cameras. Not that I could see it—it was really small. But I knew where it was.

"Adam," I said thoughtfully. "How often do you purge the surveillance video from here?"

"I don't," he said.

That distracted me. "Really? Never? Doesn't that take up a lot of data storage?"

"Data storage is cheap at twice the price," he said. "You have been attacked here by werewolves, vampires, volcano gods, and—" He stopped and grimaced.

"A Tim," I told him stoutly. "Though he came out the worst in that encounter."

He gave me a short nod. "I don't erase anything."

"Okay," I said, getting my brain off Tim and onto more current matters. "If you don't erase it, do you have some nifty way of sorting through it?"

"What do you need?" he asked.

"James Palsic brought a car in for me to repair a couple of weeks ago. I didn't notice him then, because I am pretty sure that remember-me-not thing he has going is a variation of pack magic that he's learned to twist to his own use. Zee was here that day—and he didn't even notice James was a werewolf."

"If you didn't recognize him then, how did you figure out he came in?" he asked. "Did he tell you?"

I shook my head. "Something clicked while we were exchanging words at Kelly's house and that magic quit working on me. Apparently, it quit retroactively, too. Because as soon as it quit working, I remembered him.

"If you can find him on the feed, maybe he left some clue about where they are staying," I said.

We had the plates to the Ford truck, but they were registered to a fictional address, according to George. They did tell us that the wolves had been here for long enough to acquire Washington plates. I didn't expect the plates on his VW bug to be any more use. Especially because I was pretty sure those plates had been from out of state. But he had given us a phone number that might be of use.

Adam nodded and sounded more like himself when he said briskly, "Sounds like a good idea."

I keyed in the sequence that would unlock the door—for a garage that specializes in inexpensive repairs to cars that tend to be older than I am, my shop's security is pretty high-end.

"I know it's a long shot," I told him. "But I hate waiting for the bad guys to make a move. We could head to your office after we get done here."

"I don't like defensive wars, either," Adam agreed. "I can access the video files from here."

I let us in but didn't turn the lights on in the office. There were windows all the way around, which was awesome for working there. But just now, lighting up the office would make us a perfect target for someone sitting outside with a gun.

It was true that the immediate threats I knew about were unlikely to be sitting outside with a gun. Though werewolves (and I supposed Wulfe, too) could use guns just fine, shooting us in an attempt to take over the pack would make them look weak. A bullet wouldn't be enough fun for Wulfe to try.

But there were a lot of people who were unhappy about the changes taking place in the world, and everyone knew that the Columbia Basin Pack's Alpha was mated to Mercy, who owned that garage in east Kennewick.

There were shades on the windows for just that reason, but they were a pain in the butt. They were supposed to be electronic, but that had lasted exactly a week. We were in discussions with the manufacturer that felt like they might take a long time.

"Can you see well enough to get into the video system?" I asked Adam. "I could just pull the shades and turn on the lights if that's useful."

"I can see fine." He walked toward the door to the bays instead of to the corner of the office where a monitor that scrolled through the cameras sat on an expensive-looking pile of electronics.

"Adam?" I asked. "Where are you going?"

"The controls in the office are dummy controls," he told me. "The real controls are in the garage proper."

"Huh," I said.

"We give the bad guys something to 'shut down' and they quit looking," he explained. Which was why he made the big money in security.

"Okay," I said. "While you do that, I'll search the receipts. We require a phone number and an address. The address may be bogus—but we called him to get his car." I was pretty sure he hadn't given the name James Palsic. That was an odd enough last name, I'd have remembered it. And a pseudonym might be a clue, too.

"So he'll be on the cameras twice," Adam said.

"Yep. He came in about four p.m., maybe as early as three thirty, but no earlier than that. Not last week but sometime in the previous two weeks," I told him.

"Okay."

He waited in the open doorway while I settled myself on a box behind the counter and pulled the office keyboard and monitor down where I could use them. Tucked behind the counter, they were low enough that no one would see the light from the monitor from the outside.

"Why did we put all the windows in here, again?" Adam asked as I sat down. I think he was trying for a teasing tone, but his eyes were focused on my face. On my nose. The tape strapped across the bridge of my nose was going to be my friend for a week or so; I'd get rid of it about the same time my black eyes would turn yellow. At least they hadn't had to pack it.

"Because windows are more friendly than walls," I told him, touching my nose a little self-consciously. "And mostly we are in the bays anyway." Having our bond shut down was making me ridiculous. Adam loved me, broken nose and all. I reassured myself of that with the memory of his face when he'd first seen me in the hospital. Even so, I couldn't help but say, in a voice that was a little wobbly, "They said it would heal without a bump."

"You get hurt a lot," he said softly.

I couldn't read his body language or his tone, which was unusual. But where he was standing was oddly shadowed, the strong light from the window obscuring the lower half of his face.

"This was *my* choice," I told him. "Me or Makaya. My nose or her life—it wasn't even a difficult decision."

Adam grunted and disappeared into the bays, where he'd hidden the real controls to the surveillance system. Good to know that if I wanted to shut the system down, I'd have to go looking for the secondary controls . . .

I wanted to say something more to him. Something that would feel better than that last exchange did. Still, Adam was pretty good at communication—better than I was. Maybe I just needed to give him some space. Resolutely I turned my attention to the files.

We fixed maybe fifteen cars on a good day with all three of us working. That didn't count the parts we sold, but it wasn't an insurmountable number. It took me about ten minutes to find the right bill, but only because we hadn't put the year and model of the car in the computer.

But the notes jibed with what I remembered.

Generator not charging, does not respond to polarizing. Recommend new generator. Customer agrees.

The bill was complete with address and phone number. He'd paid with a credit card in the name of John Leeman, his address was out in north Richland near the Uptown Mall, an area with a lot of apartments, and looked suspiciously like the false address that had been used to register the plates on the truck. But the phone number could be useful.

"Got it," I said, and told Adam the date of the bill. "Time stamp on the charge is eleven twenty-eight."

Adam grunted.

He sounded odd.

"Adam?"

"What did you want to talk to me about, Mercy? That we couldn't talk about at home?" He was speaking so softly I could barely make out his words—and my hearing was coyote-good.

"I have a few insights I wanted to share about the werewolves we are facing," I told him cautiously.

There was a long pause. I didn't want to conduct a serious discussion with him in there and me out in the office. I set the keyboard on top of the counter and bent to heft the monitor.

"I thought you might want to discuss last night."

The monitor skidded on the counter as I set it back where it belonged, so I thought I might have misheard him. "Last night?"

Locking up Ben? But he made it sound as if something had happened that needed discussion. Something personal. Oh.

"Are you talking about the reason you made me an apology breakfast sandwich? Thank you, by the way." I had everything put away in the office. I could have headed into the bays to talk to him, but I hesitated, my instincts keeping me right where I was.

"I put you in danger," he said.

I loved Adam and trusted him in a way I'd never trusted anyone. I had never been afraid of him. Not really. Okay. He was a werewolf—but this was different. It was the way his voice was traveling out of the darkness. My heartbeat picked up.

"I put myself in danger," I told him. "You certainly had nothing to do with my broken nose today."

He didn't answer. Aching cold shivered through me like a blade drawn through my chest—and it wasn't an emotion, it was my mating bond, our mating bond. I reached out for it in that place where I could see the ties that bound me.

I understood that no one else in the pack had a place like that they could go. I supposed my place, my otherness, had something to do with the fact that the first time I beheld the pack bonds was when a fairy queen locked me into my own head while she held me imprisoned. The Marrok, possibly with the help of a rogue fae walking stick, used the bonds to locate me. In the process, he pulled me someplace where he could show me the spiritual and magical ties I bore. Over time, I had learned how to get there on my own. Mostly this otherness had a dreamlike quality in that it was changeable and responsive to my subconscious. But in some ways, it was more real than any other place I had ever been.

The pack bonds were still there. This time there were no lights, but they were still bright-colored and festive Christmas garlands strung in all directions as if they were part of a giant spider's web. Sometimes I perceived the wolves in the pack as rocks or bricks. Once, they were flowers, and I never did figure out why. But this time the bonds just stretched out into the darkness. If I'd needed to know which was which, I could have grabbed one and yanked on it, but for now, none of those were the bond I was looking for.

The bond I usually tried not to pay too much attention to was there as well. Visually that one changed a lot more than the other bonds. Even so, another time it would worry me that the tie that existed between me and Stefan was a gossamer black weaving that looked as though a good wind would blow it away. Not that I enjoyed being bound to a vampire, even Stefan—but that frailty didn't say good things about my friend and his battle with the smoke weaver.

Sometimes the most important thing I looked for, here in the otherness, was the last thing I found. The bond between Adam and me was wrapped securely around my waist—where it burned me with its cold. The cord itself had changed from the thick red cord I'd last seen to something like a flexible cable made of ice.

I blinked that image away and stood once more in my garage office, feeling neither enlightened nor reassured. Having our bond turn to ice, even if only in the imagery of my other place, could not possibly be a good thing.

"Adam?" I said cautiously, not moving from where I stood behind the counter. "What are you doing to our bond? I don't like it."

"You need to get out of here."

That wasn't Adam. That was the wolf speaking from Adam's throat. I heard a ripping noise.

"Adam, are you okay?" I asked, ignoring the wolf's advice.

The silence was so deep that I started when Adam spoke, his voice gravelly as it sometimes got when he was changing into his wolf form. I could usually smell the magic gathering when one of the wolves was changing form—but my nose was broken. For all that Adam maintained that I wasn't really smelling magic, that I was just interpreting it as a scent, I couldn't tell if he was really changing or not without my nose working.

"When you spoke to Bran, did you talk to him about me, Mercy mine?"

That didn't sound like any tone I'd ever heard from Adam. It didn't sound like Adam or the wolf.

I remembered the way Ben had sounded. Had the smoke weaver bitten *Adam*?

The creature hadn't been able to fool me for more than a few minutes when he'd been using Ben. And my instincts, which had never steered me wrong so far, told me that this had nothing to do with the smoke weaver. Stefan's bond in my otherness, I now remembered, though I hadn't noticed at the time, had an odd odor—just like the jackrabbit. It had smelled like the smoke weaver. Apparently even with a broken nose I could smell when I was in that other place.

The bond between Adam and me had still smelled . . . tasted like us. This, whatever this was, was about whatever had been troubling Adam long before the smoke weaver had escaped.

"I asked you a question," he growled from the depths of the big space beyond the office door. "Did you go to Bran with the trouble you are having? With *me*?" The last was a roar that sounded more wolf than human and hurt my ears with the sudden volume.

I didn't answer, didn't know how to answer.

"Mercy?" The soft question came out singsong, emerging from the echoing bays, sounding more menacing than the blast of sound that had preceded it.

I didn't think that telling him yes would be smart right then. But I wouldn't lie to him. And I didn't think this was a conversation we should be having while I cowered behind a counter that would be no barrier against a werewolf.

This is Adam, I reminded myself. Whatever his troubles, whatever was happening to him, he would not hurt me if he could help it. He was in trouble and I had to help him.

I walked to the door to the bays. Inky darkness stretched out endlessly in front of me. I can see in the dark pretty well, but my eyes were adjusted to the relative light of the office, and the bays were as dark as a cave. I reached for the lights.

Adam said, "Don't."

"What's going on?" I asked. I couldn't use my nose, and the sound effects of the empty bays kept me from pinpointing where Adam was.

"You should leave," he said, his voice gritted, almost vicious. "God damn it, Mercy." Desperate. "Obey me for once in your life and get the fuck out of here."

I heard him open the under-the-counter gun safe that held a loaded gun. However cautious I was around agitated werewolves, I was absolutely certain that Adam wasn't about to shoot *me*.

I hit the light.

10

I EXPECTED TO SEE ADAM, GUN IN HAND.

I did not expect him to be eight or nine feet tall, looking like something horrible had happened to his change from human to wolf. I'd seen him in an in-between stage before, a blend between wolf and human that was oddly graceful, no matter how frightening. This wasn't that.

This was a monster.

His skin was red and mottled with oversized veins standing out like tree roots on the forest floor. The only hair or fur on his body was a strip that started at the back of his neck and ended at the top of his hips. Even his pinned, oversized ears and his tail were bare.

His hulking shoulders bulged unnaturally and supported disproportionately long arms ending in clawed hands so massive that they made the big Ruger Redhawk look like a child's toy from a bygone era. I had no idea how he'd managed to open the gun safe with those hands.

His torso gave a nod to a humanoid shape in that it was upright, but it was too long and bent too much, as if weighed down by those shoulders. His hips and legs were shaped more like a wolf's and ended in paws that were two or three times the size of his own wolf's.

The claws on his toes scored the concrete floor. By those marks, I could track him backward to the pile of clothes, which looked as though something had exploded in them. They weren't ripped—they were confettied—including the heavy leather combat-type boots.

He had, I noted, taken a direct path straight to the gun safe.

His face was a nightmare version of a werewolf's face, like something dreamed up by a comic book illustrator who was more worried about making something look scary than how viable what he drew was.

Adam's massive lower jaw was undershot and more like a bull-dog's than a wolf's, but it was wider than the upper jaw, too. The whole muzzle was too long for the width of his face.

Werewolves have lots and lots of big sharp teeth—but Adam's teeth now would have done credit to a T. rex. They were black and looked as though you could drop a piece of paper on one and end up with two pieces. I could see most of his teeth because his lips were pulled back in a snarl.

But the most disturbing thing was his eyes. They were entirely human, entirely Adam's eyes, trapped within the monster. And that was just wrong, because when a werewolf takes his wolf form, the first thing to change is his eyes.

Ugly. He was ugly.

I stood frozen, my hand on the light switch.

He ducked and twisted his head impossibly and let out a sound that was part scream and part wail, impossibly high-pitched with a bass rumble that followed behind and sent my hindbrain into fits. He took an aggressive step toward me and then two slow steps backward.

"After," he said—and his voice was oddly clear, emerging from that mouth. Werewolves couldn't talk in their wolf form. Like the eyes, his ability to speak just made this form more wrong. "Go to Bran. Follow his advice."

And my stunned brain remembered why I'd been so worried about Adam having a gun.

I had a bare moment to figure out what to do. He was a soldier. That gun was going to go off and he would be dead. No hesitation, no fumble.

Worse than useless to wish that I'd been clearer when I told Bran that Adam and I were having troubles. Hard to get good advice from him when he didn't have all the information.

Blow up the mating bond, Bran had said. Without those words, and if I hadn't just inspected our bond, maybe I'd have tried something different. Maybe if there had been time to actually think about what to do, I'd have formed a clever plan. But all I had were my instincts. I needed time.

I stepped back into the otherness, where such a thing might be possible. Ever since this place had proven to be useful when I was lost in Europe, I'd been practicing. It was sort of like lucid dreaming, in that I could influence, both on purpose and by accident, what I found there—though that was not to say that I was in control. In this instance, needing time, I imagined a pocket of existence where time moved while no time passed in the real world.

As soon as I entered, I knew that I'd only been partially successful. This gift of time was not infinite. Adam's gun was still moving and I had only bought myself a little grace to do some-thing about it.

I could see our bond, still frozen, though this time I could see that there were deep fractures in the structure, awaiting just one hard hit to shatter into nothingness. It made me reluctant to move for fear I would shatter it. Bran had not said "shatter" or "cut," either, for that matter. He had told me to blow it up.

I just needed a bomb.

I'd been reading a lot of fairy tales since I'd put the pack in the place of peacekeeper of the Tri-Cities. Fairy tales weren't factual, for the most part. But there was a surprising amount of informa-tion to be gleaned from them.

Since our Underhill escapee had started killing people, I'd read and reread a few more. The last fairy tale I'd read was the Perrault story "Diamonds and Toads," where a girl is kind to an old woman at a well, and as a consequence, beautiful and valuable items spilled from her mouth every time she talked.

In the otherness, as in dreams, what I perceived was influ-enced with apparent randomness by the things that I'd been doing or thinking about.

Blow up the bond.

I opened my mouth and took out the golf-ball-sized pearl that emerged. It wasn't exactly a bomb, for all that it was round. How was I going to blow up our bond with it? The pearl was luminous, the color a reminder that white was not colorlessness—in being white, the pearl reflected all colors. It struck me as something hope-ful, that pearl.

Words are powerful things.

I don't know where that thought came from. Maybe something I'd read, or something someone had told me. Maybe it was just a universal truth that came to me in that moment.

I brought the pearl up to my mouth and spoke to it. Then I took it and smashed it against the icy bond that stretched from my waist into the dark mist surrounding the little clearing I stood in. When the pearl hit, the bond cracked around it like the safety glass on my Jetta. I shoved the pearl inside and folded the cracked sheet of glass back around the hole. I wrapped my hands over where I'd damaged the bond, and it re-formed beneath my skin, becoming first smooth and then so cold I had to jerk my hands away.

What did you say?

I looked over and saw that a wolf whose gray coat, lighter on his back and darker on his face and feet, shimmered in the odd sourceless light of the otherness. He was curled up in the hollow of a tree growing on the edge of the mist. His tail wrapped around his body and draped over the top of his nose.

He was too small, too thin, and I'd never seen him hide from anything—but I knew him for Adam's wolf.

"What are you doing here?" I asked him. This was my otherness and I had not summoned him—or Adam—here.

I've been driven out by the monster, he said, closing his eyes and starting to fade from my sight.

"Wolf!" I said, desperate to keep him with me. I was deathly afraid that when he disappeared, I would never see him again.

Do you have a question for me? he asked.

I opened my mouth to ask him something, anything to keep him here with me. And the words that came out of my mouth were: "What did the witch do?"

Ah, he said, lifting up his head. *That is a good question.*

Between us, separating us, a stage the size of a Manhattan apartment kitchen table rose until it was waist high. Mist from the edges of the clearing drifted to the top of the table and solidified until the witch Elizaveta and Adam stood facing each other upon the stage, both naked.

From this perspective I was struck by how perfect they both were. Her body was tall and strong with beautiful pale skin that looked very like the pearl I'd held in my hands. Her hair was long and dark. She looked like some artist's rendition of an idealized female. And Adam . . . was Adam.

I'd seen this scene before but not from this observation point. Standing with the mists playing about their feet, they looked like something out of a Russian fairy tale—as if they belonged together.

Do not, warned the wolf harshly. *Such thoughts have power here. We cannot afford to feed her magic with your foolish insecurities.*

Right. I cleared my mind and tried to pay attention without judgment. There was something here that I needed to know.

The first time I'd seen this, I'd been in a position to watch Adam's face. This time I could see Elizaveta's as she stepped into his space, leaning her tall, naked body against his. She tilted her head and bent forward to kiss him.

Her lips touched his—and even though I knew what had happened and why, fierce possessiveness swept through me.

He was *mine.* She had no right to touch him.

Yes, said the wolf. *We were yours.*

Are mine, I thought fiercely. *Are.*

I didn't say the words aloud, and I couldn't tell if he'd heard me.

One of Adam's arms wrapped around her waist, holding her to him, his hand flat against the small of her back.

He liked to hold me like that, protective and possessive.

His other hand cupped her face, then threaded through her long silky hair on its fatal journey to the back of her head.

As his fingers tightened, her eyes, which had been closed to savor his kiss, flashed open and comprehension slid across her face. In that second, when she knew she was going to die, magic slid from her mouth and into his.

Her magic carried her voice, *her* words, into him. *You are the monster you think yourself to be.*

He broke her neck, stepping away from her, allowing her body to fall away. But he put distance between them too late. Her death-gift sank into him, disappearing beneath his skin as he looked up and fell into parade rest.

Waiting, I remembered, for *my* judgment. I reached out for him and the scene faded away. My fingers brushed the stage and it altered under my touch, becoming the stump of a tree that some giant saw had cut more or less flat. The wood bit my finger and a drop of blood welled and landed on the stump.

This was my otherness, formed of things I knew. My stomach tight, I looked at the wolf and asked, "Was that something I saw, but didn't—" That night had been one horror after another, I'd been so tired by that point. "—didn't pay attention to?"

It is what was, the wolf said, seeming a little less substantial than he had before.

He said, *He was lost in that moment, for he believed the truth of her words before she gave them to him.* His voice faded, growing softer. *Twice born those words, his and then hers. So they took hold in his belief and made it true.*

I walked around the tree stump and knelt beside him. He was smaller now, the size of a German shepherd maybe.

"What's happening to you?" I asked.

He is becoming, answered the wolf tiredly. *I am unmaking.*

I pulled another gemstone out of my mouth. This one was an amethyst about the size of a marble, uncut and rough-sided. I took it and spoke to it, too. When I was finished, I held it out to the wolf, who eyed it.

What do you have for me? he asked.

"It won't work if I tell you," I said, following my instincts. "Eat it."

He opened his mouth and consumed the purple stone. I waited, but there seemed to be no effect for good or ill. Maybe it would take time—real time, not otherness time.

He was no bigger. He didn't move his body, had not moved anything but his head the whole time we'd been here.

But his voice was steady when he asked, *What did you do to the bond?*

I looked at the bond then. The tie that bound me to Adam was now the same color and texture as the scabby red skin that covered Adam's monstrous form. I touched it and the skin-like surface was rough under my fingertips. My wounded finger left a thin trail of blood behind that melted into the bond, which did not change again. Blood is one of those things, like words, that have unexpected power. The bond was ugly, but it did not look fragile.

"Well," I told him, "I didn't blow it up." I'd intended the pearl to blow it up until that last second before it touched the bond. I didn't want to lose Adam, and I wasn't willing to risk breaking our bond—and the pearl had looked so hopeful.

"But maybe," I said, "I instilled a little common sense and logic into the situation."

What words did the pearl hold? he asked.

I took a breath and the otherworld faded to nothing. I was back in the auto bay with Adam and a gun that was moving quickly toward his head.

"You are mine," I told him, using the same words I'd given the pearl. "I can't stop you from using that gun. But you know what?"

I was so *angry* at him. As if the whole time I'd been in that otherness, anger had been filling the real me from the bottom of my feet to the top of my head and it was spilling out my mouth—as that pearl had done.

"It doesn't *matter* if you live or die—you are still *mine*," I bit out. "Alpha werewolf, nightmare creature—I don't care. But don't you forget who *I* am. You gave yourself to me, and now you *can't* get away." I took a step closer to him and jutted out my chin. "You die, and I will drag your butt back from the afterlife kicking and screaming. But let me tell you, mister. If you are dead, you'll just have to watch us get hurt—without being able to do a damn thing about it. Because you will be dead and helpless and I won't let you go. And. Every." I pointed my finger at him, stabbing him with it figuratively the way I was tempted to do it literally. "Single. Day. I will say, 'I *told* you that you would regret pulling that trigger, you bastard. I *told* you so.'"

I was shaking with rage when I finished saying the words I had sent inside our bond with the pearl. How dare he? How dare he try to kill himself?

He'd lowered the gun at some point during my speech. There was an odd expression on his face.

"Bastard," I said again, though I had intended to stop after I told him the words I'd sealed into that pearl.

But the single word didn't provide any relief for what I felt. I stomped my foot like a two-year-old. My eyes burned and tears formed . . . tears of something huge, bigger than grief, bigger than rage, and they burned down my face.

"Go talk to Bran, you said." I was enraged at the thought. He'd given me words like a pat on the head—something to make him feel as though he weren't leaving me alone. "Fuck that. You just try to leave me, you bastard, see how far that gets you—" I might have devolved into incoherence after that.

Adam put the gun slowly down on the counter. He tried to uncock it, but his oversized hands equipped with oversized claws apparently weren't up to that, so he pointed the muzzle away from us both. I realized (and this didn't lessen my anger one iota) that if I'd listened to him and replaced the gun in the safe with a 1911 instead of the Redhawk, he wouldn't have been able to even try to kill himself with it because it would have been too small.

The gun safely dealt with (as safely as a loaded and cocked gun could be dealt with, anyway), Adam started walking toward me. He did it slowly, cautiously, as if he were afraid of me.

Or more probably, under the circumstances, because he was worried that his unusual form might scare me—or revolt me as it evidently did him.

Slowly he wrapped those too-long arms around me and hauled me to him, lifting me so my face could press against his neck. I was still yelling at him.

"Shhhh," he said. "Sorry. You're right. Of course you're right."

"I'll *monster* you," I growled.

"Of course you will," he soothed. But there was something in his voice.

I was so mad I wouldn't have been surprised if I gave him steam burns. "Are you laughing at me?"

"Maybe—" he began, and then choked. His arms jerked convulsively.

He set me down on my own feet abruptly. Took a step back and then dropped to the concrete on his hands and knees. He didn't make any noise as he transformed from monster to human, but it was so fast it must have hurt. Under other circumstances, the popping and crunching sounds of bones doing something that bones aren't really designed to do might have made me feel sorry for him. Made me worry for him. But I was still too . . . too *something*.

He wasn't dying—anything else he did was his own problem.

I stalked to the gun, uncocked it, and put it back in the safe. I closed the safe door and stalked back past him and into the bathroom. I shut the door behind me and grabbed a washcloth to wipe my eyes and stopped when I saw myself in the mirror.

Holy cow.

My usually brown skin was blanched until it looked green. The two black eyes that had been oncoming after the accident were definitely bruised, and my nose was swollen with a trickle of blood dried on my upper lip. There was another bruise along the cheek next to the white scar that usually looked sort of like war paint. But now that I looked like an extra from *The Walking Dead*, it just completed the effect.

"I see your monster," I muttered, turning on the water. "And raise you another one." I leaned closer to the mirror. "Brainssss."

As I held the washcloth under the flow, I tipped my chin to see if I looked better from another angle. Huh. There was a bruise and a friction burn on my neck where the seat belt caught me before it let me go too soon. I pulled back my shirt and . . . wowza.

I'd been in worse wrecks—and I'd been hurt worse in them.

But I didn't remember *looking* worse after a collision. No wonder Adam had been on edge. Well, that and apparently Elizaveta had gotten him with a curse as she died.

I didn't know what to do about that curse. I'd bought us some more time, I thought. Bran might have an idea or two . . . but I was a little leery of contacting him after Adam's over-the-top reaction. And Bran was weird about witchcraft. Maybe I'd call Charles; Charles had his own sort of magic.

I put the washcloth against my eyelids—very careful of my nose—and waited for a while. When I pulled the washcloth away, my eyes were still red like I'd been wearing bad contacts for a week, but they felt better. I wiped the blood off my lip.

I was tired of all the emotion. I didn't want to open the door. I wanted to magically wake up tomorrow with the relationship between Adam and me reset to a normal place. My heart hurt.

I tried to think of a logical path to get home and in bed. First step: get in the car. But Adam, assuming he was changing back to his human form, which was what it had looked like, would be naked.

Tad had clothes here that might fit Adam, but werewolves could be funny about wearing someone else's clothing—especially if that someone wasn't pack. On a good day, maybe it would have worked. This day had been a whole bad year all by itself.

Adam's SUV would have a change of clothes. Probably not footwear, but he had made his own bed and he could lie in it.

Second step: drive home and . . .

I had to put the washcloth on my eyes again. My hands were still shaking. If he had pulled that trigger . . . I could have been alone again.

Maybe ten minutes later, Adam knocked on the door. "Mercy? Are you planning on taking up residence in there?"

"Might as well," I bit out. "My mate is an idiot."

After I said it, I knew that those two things didn't go together, except that I really had needed to say that last.

"Yes," he agreed. "So why don't we go home and you can punish me by telling everyone there how you feel."

I froze. "We can't do that," I told him. "We have an invasion and a killer bunny. They need you invulnerable."

"God," he said with feeling, "are they going to be disappointed if that's what they need."

Then he laughed, and it sounded a little like I felt—shaky and damaged. Yes, tonight had altered the game board a little, but no one had won, yet. There was a soft thump as his forehead (I was pretty sure) hit the door.

"Elizaveta cursed you," I told him.

"I know," he admitted.

"How long have you known?" I asked gently. He and I both knew exactly how much anger was behind my tone. I had, after all, learned that from him.

"That is a complicated question."

Holding a conversation through a closed door was stupid. I wasn't afraid of him—and if I didn't open the door, I would never be able to go home and pull the blankets over my head. I unlocked the door and opened it.

He was his usual gorgeous self, no monster to be seen. He was also naked as a jaybird. His unclothed and glorious body might have distracted me had he not looked at my face and winced.

I would have liked to think that he'd flinched from my wrath. But I was pretty sure it was the damage to my face. Just as well I'd been able to hide most of the bruising on the rest of me with the shirt.

"How complicated?" I asked.

"The wolf knew," he said. "But I didn't know until he told you."

Just after my neighbors had died.

"And you kept it to yourself afterward because why?" I asked—more sharply than I meant to. But we had people who could help with witch curses, Bran and Zee—we even had Wulfe. The one thing that I knew about witch curses was that ignoring them—as tonight had made obvious—didn't make them get better.

He looked away from me.

I was going to tell him exactly how smart I thought that keeping this to himself had been. I opened my mouth, and hesitated. Hadn't he . . . hadn't we been through enough today? He was going to have to put on his clothes and go back to the pack house and pretend that everything was okay. That he was fit and ready to face off with . . . heaven help us, Fiona. And the killer bunny. And Wulfe and whatever else decided to rain down on our heads because the universe was just generous like that.

He couldn't afford to let anyone but me see the mess he was in. Because our pack was short of people to do the job we had to do. They were bearing up wonderfully for the most part—but the pressure wasn't going to let up anytime soon.

"So," I said, to change the subject. "Why did you want to get me alone to talk to me?"

"Because I thought you'd called Bran for advice, and he'd told you to get away from me."

I blinked at him, utterly flummoxed. "What?"

He spoke more slowly. "Because I thought you'd called Bran for advice, and he'd told you to get away from me."

"Funny guy," I said. "I heard you the first time. I just never thought that you would utter such absolute . . . drivel."

"It seemed logical at the time," he said.

"Huh," I growled at him. "What in the world makes you think that even if Bran told me to leave you, that that would be something I would ever do?"

And that started the waterworks again. I hated to cry—in this case it felt manipulative, as if I were punishing him somehow—when that was the furthest thing from my mind at the moment. I wiped my eyes with the bottom of my shirt—and caught my nose.

"Damn it," I growled, batting away his hands.

"I'm cursed," he said mildly. "It interferes with my thinking. Stop that. You're hurting yourself."

Both were true. I stopped trying to wipe my eyes with my shirt and used my hands instead.

I wasn't going to cut him any slack on his muddled thinking, curse or no curse. He thought I was going to tell him I was leaving him. And then I put it together with his actions tonight.

"So your thinking was that I was going to tell you I was leaving you—so you were going to kill yourself and save me the trouble?"

His face went still. Then he said, "It sounds so stupid when you say it that way."

"Good," I snapped. I started to pinch my nose—Bran style—and Adam caught my hand.

He kissed my knuckles (which was pretty brave when he knew how much I wanted to hurt him) and folded my hand in his. "Don't do that," he said. "You'll hurt yourself again." He sighed. "I think I've done enough of that today."

It echoed my earlier thought about him, that he'd been through enough today. I took a deep breath.

"This is maybe not the best time to hash this out," I said.

"Agreed," he said, his voice heartfelt. "What did you want to talk to me about? Or is that another minefield?"

It took me a moment to remember.

I held up a finger. "Bran thinks that we, that you, need to kill Fiona at first opportunity."

"Fiona?" he said blankly, as if he'd forgotten who she was.

"Fiona," I said. "Apparently she went rogue a while ago. Started selling her skills to whoever paid her. Bran thought that she died in a deal gone bad while she was working with some witches. You should maybe call Bran and talk to him about her." He wasn't taking my calls. "Bran has decided what we need to do with our invading wolves. Harolford is on the kill list, but less urgently so. Kent Schwabe is a question mark, but he'd like us to save Chen and the Palsics."

"I'll talk to him," he told me.

He was still naked. It was distracting me—though I didn't think he knew that yet.

I held up a second finger. "He told me that we should talk to Underhill about the smoke weaver."

Adam's eyebrow raised. "And that is a revelation how?"

"He told me to ask her about the bargain Underhill has with him or that she had with him. He told me to bribe her with something sweet that I've cooked myself. And he told me to approach her like we have a common problem and not like she released someone who killed innocents and now holds two people I care about in his thrall."

"Okay," he said. "That's useful."

I held up a third finger. "And he told me that if you kept shutting me out, I should blow up our mating bond."

"Excuse me?"

"He hung up and won't answer my calls," I said. "I have no idea what he meant. Just what he said."

"You did something to our bond, though," he said slowly, and I felt a faint pull on the bond, a softening that, after a moment, stiffened back to where it had been.

"I didn't blow it up," I told him.

I decided not to tell him exactly what I had done.

I'd been influenced by the pack bonds and hadn't enjoyed the experience. Let him think that it was just me yelling at him that had made him put down the gun.

He didn't need to know that I'd sent those words through our mating bond in a pearl before I'd given them out loud. Maybe yelling alone would have worked. It would have if he'd been in a normal headspace—but if he'd been in a normal headspace, he wouldn't have been trying to kill himself. I was hoping that the words I'd given him would linger. That they would keep him from doing anything rash until we had a chance to talk to someone.

He'd been under the influence of Elizaveta's spell. I was pretty sure that it had been my pearl that let me break through the effect of her curse—my hopeful pearl against her words.

"Why couldn't you have told me this at home?" he asked. "Our bedroom is private enough."

I gave him a wry smile. "Because I thought you were looking really tired and our house was full of people. I also wanted to see if I could get you to tell me what was wrong."

He grinned at me abruptly and said, "Well, you got that part done in true Mercy fashion."

"Anything worth doing is worth overdoing," I intoned solemnly. I took in a deep breath and sighed loudly. "I suppose that I should quit enjoying the view and go get you some clothes from the SUV."

I rose up on my toes and kissed him. "Don't you give up on us, my love."

"Okay," he said. He kissed me back. "Nudge?"

Yes. Oh yes. There was so much emotion that my insides felt scoured with the tides. Sex . . . making love wouldn't fix any of it. Wouldn't break what Elizaveta had done to my husband. Wouldn't change the reality that Adam hated himself so much that he thought he deserved to die. I did not lie to myself. I had spoken to his wolf. Elizaveta's words would not have taken fruit if Adam hadn't had the garden plowed and fertilized for it.

Sex wouldn't fix that. But . . . sharing is a very powerful thing. And making love with Adam was generous and warm—powerful magic of its own kind. And ten minutes of not thinking sounded like heaven just now and I was pretty sure Adam felt the same way. It was not passion he was seeking with his "nudge"—it was surcease.

But . . . no way in hell was I going to let him see me naked while Elizaveta's magic was still working on him. I knew my mate. Guilt—the failure of living up to his own expectations—was driving that curse. Adam had an overabundant sense of responsibility. My poor face had been the tipping point today, I was pretty sure. I wasn't going to let him see that my entire right side was black where it hadn't been scraped raw.

"Not tonight," I told him. "We have wolves to kill and Underhill to talk to. Busy, busy." And after misquoting *The Princess Bride*, I admitted the truth—a little of the truth. "As much as I'd like some nudging of my own, I think I need to give my body a break for a day or so." I paused, and since it was true and I deserved a chance to whine a little, I said, "And my nose is *throbbing*."

He hugged me gently and I didn't so much as stiffen at the pain in my ribs—which I hadn't actually noticed until I saw them in the mirror. I'd been too focused on a lot of things more painful than bruised ribs. Once all the drama had subsided, my body was more sore than it had felt before the whole Adam's-got-a-gun scene had played out.

EVERYONE WAS TUCKED INTO BED BY THE TIME WE got home. Jesse called a good night to us as we passed her room, so they hadn't been in bed for long.

I found the pajamas that I wore when I was sick—Adam wouldn't think it strange for me to grab them when I had a broken nose. They were a gift from my mom—nothing I would ever have bought myself. It was ridiculous how much I loved them.

They were mint green and covered with pink ponies with improbable purple manes and tails. My mom had a thing for horses. But the important thing about them tonight was that they covered me from neck to feet.

I showered and dressed and by the time I was through I hurt so badly I wasn't sure I could sleep. Every muscle in my body was stiff and sore. I crawled into bed and finally just lay facedown with a pillow under my chest and my face turned aside so that my nose didn't hit the mattress. Nothing else was comfortable, either.

Adam showered and I must have dozed despite the discomfort because the next thing I knew the bed was moving under his weight.

"Mercy," he told me. "Take off your shirt."

I lay very still. Maybe he would think I was asleep.

"Your shirt rode up while you were poking your finger at me," he said. "Threatening me with the dire consequences of dying around a ticked-off daughter of Coyote who can call the dead. You don't have to hide your injuries from me—that's our deal, remember?"

"You knew?" I asked.

"I just wanted to see how far you would take it. Strip off your shirt, tough girl, and I'll see what I can do about making you feel better."

He didn't know I'd been hiding my bruises so that he didn't have one more thing to feel responsible for. One more thing for Elizaveta's curse to dig into him with. He wasn't wearing a monster, so apparently I hadn't needed to try to hide anything from him.

"I can't move," I whined, now that I didn't have to pretend. "It hurts."

He helped me roll over and gave me a bag of frozen peas, which he must have brought upstairs while I was dozing, for my nose.

"No, don't press it," he said. "Just let it rest there."

And my nose settled down while he lit a vanilla candle I couldn't smell and turned out the lights.

"I'm not being romantic," he advised me. "The lights are going to hurt your eyes. The candle is warming the oil I'm going to use to help your poor abused muscles relax."

I thought that sounded like a pretty romantic thing to do. Romantic didn't always have to do with sex.

He unbuttoned the shirt of my pajamas and managed to get it off me without hurting me more. I had a bag of peas over my eyes so I couldn't see what he looked like after getting a fully detailed report on my body.

What he said, after a moment, was "Okay, pants off, too."

And he lifted and moved my limp body around. At one point he stopped and said, "These are your favorite pajamas."

"Yes," I said.

He grunted. "Easier if I could rip them off, but I'll manage." And so he did.

Then he rubbed warmed oil all over my sore muscles. Not a

massage, just gentle repetitive motions that took the edge off. I fell asleep with his strong hands rubbing my shoulders. I still hurt, but I didn't care as much as I had.

I DON'T KNOW WHAT TIME IT WAS THAT I WOKE UP TO the hairs on the back of my neck crawling.

"Adam?"

A low growl from the far side of the room answered me. It wasn't Adam's usual growl, but it was him. I thought about the ugly, ugly monster.

"For Pete's sake," I complained after a moment of thought. "Get back to bed. I'm cold."

Something very, very heavy got into bed beside me. I was worried the bed was going to break. A very big, hot body curled around me and rough skin touched my own. Adam rested his very large chin on the top of my head.

"Better," I grumped, snuggling into his warmth. "Go to sleep."

HE WAS GONE WHEN I WOKE UP IN THE MORNING—AND I woke up early because moving hurt. It didn't hurt as much as it might have if Adam hadn't given me a hot oil treatment. Today was Monday, and though I was shutting down the garage until further notice, on Monday I had promised to fix the cars that absolutely only I could do. If I was going to have to go to work this morning, it was probably a good thing that I'd gotten up early.

Hannah was in the kitchen when I finally came down, feeling like I was a hundred and ten years old. She took one look at me and winced.

"Adam said you'd be in rough shape this morning," she said. Then she walked over and kissed me on the cheek. "I'd hug you if it wouldn't hurt both of us. Thank you for saving my little girl."

"You've got me mixed up," I told her. "Auriele saved Makaya. I just hit the bastard with my car."

"Yes, well, thanks for that, too," she said. "I hurt too much to sleep in, so I thought I'd come down and make my granny's secret recipe for all that ails you."

She brewed it all up in a double boiler, then poured it into two cups, took out a flask that had *Granny's Secret Ingredient* engraved on the side, and added generously to the result.

She sniffed one of the cups, then added a teaspoon of honey. She sniffed it again.

"That's smells right," she said. Then she added another teaspoon of honey to both cups and shoved one in front of me. "Drink that."

I looked at her. I knew what had gone into that pot. Moreover, I had a fair suspicion that there was something potent in Granny's flask of alcoholic splendor.

"Just plug your nose," she advised.

"Ha-ha," I told her. "Funny."

She drank it down. All of it in one gulp. When she was done, her eyes watered and she couldn't talk—but she pointed her finger at the cup in front of me.

It was a gift, I knew. A thank-you that she'd gotten up ungodly early to prepare and feed to me.

It was the kind of gift that was unrefusable.

I followed her lead and drank the whole thing before I could think too much about what I'd seen her put in the brew.

When I was in college, after my first and only drunken bout,

I realized that I knew too many people's secrets to be drinking. After that, I'd made a habit of avoiding alcohol of any kind—so I didn't know if my reaction to Hannah's gift would have been the same if I'd gulped a glass of any old alcohol.

My skin warmed, my ears tingled, and so did the backs of my knees. My broken nose buzzed with a feeling that I was worried was going to wake up nerve endings that didn't need to be roused. Instead, it settled into a pleasant sort of hum that drove the soreness away.

I couldn't breathe or see for as much as a full minute, and my taste buds would have run away from my mouth in full revolt if they could have. But that was a fair price to pay for the lack of pain.

When I could focus properly again, Hannah said, "Warren's going with you to the garage today. He'll be here pretty soon. I would let him drive. But by the time you get to the garage, you should be okay for handling tools again."

I moved my right shoulder, working it around in a circle. "I just might live," I told her.

11

A LITTLE BUZZED AND A LOT LESS SORE, I LEFT HAN-
nah making breakfast waffles in the kitchen and went down to
the basement.

A red wolf paced restlessly back and forth in the cage. He
didn't seem to take any note of me, even when I stopped in to say,
"Hello, Ben."

Luke, on watch duty, looked up from the video game he was
playing to say, "He shifted to wolf about two in the morning. I
don't know why or if it was his decision. And so I told Adam
about two hours ago."

It was six in the morning. That made yet another night of very
little sleep for Adam. It was obvious from Luke's tone of voice that
he was worried, too. The last thing we needed in the middle of
multiple crises was Adam impaired by lack of sleep.

I couldn't do anything about Adam just then, but I did have
one avenue of progress on other matters. If Adam had been home,

I'd have taken him because he was better at negotiations than I was—as long as he didn't lose his temper. And he'd have been better at this negotiation because Underhill, like most females, had a soft spot for Adam.

I knocked on Aiden's door. "Up and at 'em. Hannah's making waffles."

"I'll dress and be out," he said, sounding alert. To survive terrible conditions, you learn to be alert.

I put my hand on his door.

"Waffles?" said Luke hopefully, and I let my hand fall as I turned to face him.

"I think you are on the top of the list," I told him.

He smiled and went back to his game.

BY THE TIME AIDEN MADE IT UPSTAIRS, I'D CARRIED Luke's waffles down to him along with a cup of fresh-made coffee, and was arranging a second plate. Aiden had dressed in a sweater and jeans, even though the day outside looked to be warming up nicely. His fire had mostly returned, he'd told me, but there were lingering effects from what Wulfe had done to him.

The waffles I'd taken from Hannah's second batch were an even golden brown. I'd poured a thin layer of homemade (by Christy) raspberry syrup and topped that with fresh whipped cream. I'd already dribbled some blueberries around and was slicing strawberries, which were the final touch on my gift for Underhill.

Aiden looked at the plate, raised his eyebrows, and said, "For me?"

"We'll take it outside," I told him, and comprehension lit his face.

He opened his mouth, glanced down the stairs, and simply nodded. "Sounds good."

I started to pick up the plate and remembered another thing from my recent study of fairy tales. I got a small glass from the cupboards and said, "Hey, Hannah? Can I borrow your flask?"

I CARRIED A GLASS THREE FINGERS FULL OF KENTUCKY bourbon, made twenty years ago by Hannah's grandmother in a batch she'd intended for family use only, out to the door in the wall in our backyard. Aiden brought the plate of waffles.

"I don't know if she'll come if you knock," he told me.

"She's a guest in our backyard. She'll come," I said with more confidence than I felt. I rapped the rough wood with my knuckles as if I meant business. Three times, because three is important in fairy tales.

Nothing happened.

Multiples of three are important, too, I told myself.

I knocked three more times. Waited. Knocked three more times. If this didn't work, I'd take the plate and Aiden would knock. But my instincts told me that since I was asking her for information, I needed to be the one requesting her presence.

The door popped open and a cranky-looking Tilly stuck her head out. Her hair was dripping wet and had something that looked like seaweed in it. Even with my nose out of action, I caught a whiff of brine. Through the partially open door I heard surf and wind.

"What is it?" she snapped. "I'm drowning things and you're inter—" She looked at my face and brightened. "Is there a fight?" Then her smile deepened. "Are you *wounded*?"

"She mostly killed a werewolf with her car," Aiden said. "All he needed was the coup de grâce." He paused and then in a mournful voice he said, "The car was sacrificed for the good of all."

Tilly's smile disappeared. "Alas," she said. Tilly liked cars. She couldn't get far enough from one of her doors to ride in one—and then there was all the cold iron. But she liked them anyway.

Aiden nodded his head in acknowledgment, then said, in a more hearty tone, "She managed the blow without harming the child the werewolf held over his head. She used one of her own werewolves—tossed her wolf onto the front of the car to catch the child. Mercy is a little hurt—but her enemy is dead."

"You told that backward," I said. And skipped most of the parts that would have made that story make sense.

"Important parts first," said Tilly thoughtfully. "That's how to tell a story. Skip the boring parts. End with the results, though. Good job, Fire. That was a good story—I especially liked the part where the car died. I do so love tragedy."

She stepped through the door and closed it behind her, running a dirty finger around the latch. The magic she used sent a zing up my spine. Her white shift was drenched with water until she looked at it. Under her gaze, the cloth dried in a few seconds but looked stiff and crusted with salt. There were smears of green here and there. Something I was pretty sure was blood had soaked the bottom of her hem, which was about knee height.

"I need to ask you a few things," I told her. "I brought you a gift as an exchange."

Aiden held the plate out to her. She gave me a considering look before turning her attention to the food. She stuck a finger in the cream and licked it off. She ate a slice of strawberry. Waited. Then ate one of the blueberries as if it might be poisonous.

"Did you make this?" she asked.

And I wished I'd taken the time to make brownies or cookies or something, because the way she asked it, I knew it was important.

"I assembled it," I told her. "My friend made the waffles fresh this morning and my stepdaughter's mother made the syrup from the first fruits of summer. I whipped the cream"—thus ensuring that anyone in the house who was trying to sleep was awakened—"sliced the strawberries, and put it all together for you."

"Friends and enemies," she said. I couldn't tell if it was a good thing or a bad thing. "Bitter and sweet. And the fruits of the earth. I accept."

And she ate with the manners and speed of a starving stray dog as Aiden held the plate for her. She took it from him and licked it clean before handing it back. Her face was covered with whipped cream and syrup, and she wiped her hands on her white shift, leaving streaks of pink behind.

"Interesting," she said. "I liked it." She looked pointedly at the glass in my hand.

Aiden shook his head at me, so I didn't say anything. Finally, she sighed, rolled her eyes, and said, "What do you have in your glass?"

"My friend's grandmother's bourbon," I told her.

She had been reaching for the glass, but she hesitated. "I do not know bourbon."

"Whiskey," said Aiden. "Local variety."

She reached for it again and I gave it to her. She said, suspiciously, "This has some magic within."

"Huh," I said. "It *was* more than just alcohol. I had some this morning and it took the ache out of my muscles. The woman who crafted it gave it to her granddaughter. She made it specifically for her family."

Tilly sniffed it warily, then tipped the glass so she could touch her tongue to it. She smacked her lips together a couple of times. "Good," she said. "Very good." Then she drank the whole of it in one swallow.

She handed the glass back to me and said, "That is brewed with fae magic. Your friend's grandmother has fae blood. It is an old magic she used, for healing and health."

She dusted her hands and gave me a look out from under her hair. "Before you get all romantic about it, that spell was developed *specifically*"—she added weight to the word I'd used—"to keep human slaves working at full strength for as long as possible."

I shrugged. "That was not the *intent* of this particular magic when it was mixed in with the drink."

"No," agreed Tilly. "But I thought it was interesting in the present company."

"I am only half-human," I told her. It was not something I said a lot, but it was important that she did not view me with the contempt she felt for humans—and fae, for that matter. Adam really would have been better for this. "My father is Coyote."

She frowned at me. "I know that. It's why I find you interesting."

"I find you interesting, too," I told her truthfully—and I meant it to be exactly as complimentary as she had.

She bounced up and down for a minute, then gave me a sly look. "Aren't you going to ask me your questions?"

"Yes," I said. "But first I wanted to tell you that it's too bad the smoke weaver ran away. It seems to me that when someone loses a bargain, they should abide by the terms of that bargain and not scamper at the first opportunity."

I was doing a little bit of guessing.

She scuffed her foot in the dirt. "Right? He cheated." She sighed. "Okay, he didn't cheat. I could do things to him if he had cheated. Our bargain was that I got to take him; I didn't specify that he couldn't leave."

"Things" was not a nice word in that context.

"Is your bargain with him still in effect?" I asked.

She blinked at me, then tilted her head in thought. At last, she said, "There wasn't a final term to it. And the whole thing was nonspecific. 'Lose our bargain,' I said to him—I think we were drinking mead—'lose our bargain and I get to bring you here.' He said, 'What do I get in return?'"

She looked at Aiden fondly. "I thought about giving him Fire, because that's my favorite, but I'm glad I gave it to you instead. You are a lot better friend than he was."

"So what did you give him?" I asked.

"Body snatching," she said with relish. "One of my favorite residents—because he was a hunter and brought me back such interesting beings to keep prisoner. He even had me help design his cells . . ." She got a faraway look in her eye. "He had a body snatcher. *Those* cells I never did open when I let loose the rest of the prisoners and slaves. Some of his prey might not play nicely with others."

Aiden exchanged a look with me.

"That sounds like a smart thing," I told her, and then kept going because I had the feeling that the world didn't want her to keep thinking about those cells and whatever they held. "So you gave the smoke weaver the ability to take over bodies?"

She nodded. "He was primarily a transmogrifier—a shape changer." She looked at me. "Better than you. He could change himself and others. The body snatching just made changing to new shapes easier." Virtuously she said, "It wasn't much of an alteration—and I gave it limits. He had to bite his prey, pilot them for a while to prime them for his use. When they were dead, their essence—their shape—was his to use until he wore them out. He wasn't powerful enough for the magic, though." She pouted. "He said it was a bad gift. I fixed it so that if he made his puppets kill some people, he could use that for power."

She looked at Aiden. "If he'd known about Fire, he'd have bargained for that." She paused. "I wouldn't have given it to him. He didn't need that much power. I just gave him a useful twist on his own."

She had wanted to let him shapeshift more easily. To accomplish that she devised a method that involved taking over someone's mind. Killing them—but not before they killed as many people as they could in order to power the magic—because the complex ability she gave the smoke weaver required more magic than he had. I thought of Ben and Stefan, Anna and Dennis, and even the poor hitchhiker who I had met only after she'd died, and I kept my mouth shut. No words that would come out of my mouth at that moment would be helpful.

"Very clever," said Aiden, coming to my rescue.

Tilly beamed and curtsied. "I am clever," she agreed.

"If the bargain is still in effect," Aiden said after I remained silent, "does that mean you could recapture him?"

"Yes," she said. "Oh, that would be lovely. I miss him." She gave Aiden a scowl. "All of my friends leave me."

He wisely ignored that.

"How can we help you invoke the bargain?" he asked. "What are the terms?"

"We were drinking very good mead," she told him apologetically. "So it isn't very complicated. He has a secret—and you have to tell him what that secret is."

"I will do my best to see that your friend is returned," I told her.

She looked at me, then sighed. "Your best. And you raised my hopes, too. That was silly of me. Okay, go on. Do your best." She looked at Aiden. "The food and drink were very good. When she is dead"—she pointed her finger at me—"I hope you remember who your friends are. I shall be very lonely without you *or* the smoke weaver to talk to."

She looked at me. "I'm sorry," she told me. "I forgot who I was dealing with. I hope you die soon. Then, at least, I'll get Aiden back."

"No," Aiden said. "I will always be your friend, Tilly. But I am not living in Underhill ever again."

"Not ever," she said, "means never. But never is a long time. I do not think it will be never."

He bowed to her but didn't say anything.

She pouted. "You aren't being nice. I think I will go kill some things."

She left, closing the door behind her with a thud.

"That could have been more useful," Aiden told me. "I'm sorry."

I shook my head. "It was useful, I think."

I WAS GLAD TO BE WORKING ALONE AT THE SHOP; IT gave me plenty of time to think. I thought about Adam, mostly.

But also I picked apart everything that Tilly had said, everything Beauclaire had said, and everything I had ever read about bargains. I was looking for a path through that did not involve me getting into a bargain in which I gave away my firstborn child.

Warren stayed in the office reading. He was a voracious reader—he'd told me once that he'd learned to love books when he'd been out for months on cattle drives. Warren had been a cowboy in the nineteenth century and it had become as much a part of him as the wolf was.

He'd brought three books with him and I was pretty sure there were a couple in the truck in case he wanted something different to read. He usually had six or eight books midread at any given time.

He was on his third year of working his way through *War and Peace*. He'd told me privately once, in a bout of frustration, "I think you have to be Russian in order to read this book. Especially if you are going to try to remember who is who."

To combat his frustration with Tolstoy, he'd brought his old copy of *The Princess and the Goblin*. It had been read to tatters, and sometimes he'd quote from it. "Seeing is not believing—it is only seeing." Or "That is the way fear serves us: it always sides with the thing we are afraid of."

The third book he'd brought, the one he was really reading today, was Stephen Ambrose's *Band of Brothers*. It struck me that this book was something very interesting for a werewolf to be reading. What was a pack, really, but a military unit that sought to keep its members alive and make the world a better, safer place?

He'd offered to help—and he wasn't a bad mechanic—but I needed to be alone in the bays so I could fix things and ponder.

We ate lunch at the soup-and-sandwich shop not too far from the garage. He read *War and Peace* (because he welcomed interruptions while he was reading it), and I did Internet searches on my phone to find more fairy bargain stories. "The Pied Piper" was promising in that all of the children and the piper disappeared at the end. But it didn't fit anything else.

I was pretty sure that I knew which story our smoke weaver had come from—and that story told me his secret. Beauclaire had given me most of it. But I was also pretty sure that defeating the smoke weaver could not be as simple as shouting his secret to him—especially if I wanted to also save Stefan and Ben.

When we got back, I sat down at the office computer. I had been calling Ariana off and on since our first encounter with the smoke weaver. Now I composed an e-mail with everything I knew about the creature, and all the conclusions I'd come to. And I asked her about fae bargains—not the bargains made by Gray Lords or the most powerful of the fae, but the bargains the lesser fae made. And I sent that e-mail to Ariana and to her mate, Samuel, who was Bran's firstborn son, and hoped that somewhere in Africa or wherever they were they could get e-mail.

As I was getting up to go back to work, I noticed a piece of paper on the floor in front of the printer. I picked it up and found myself looking at the bill for a generator.

I hesitated, then called the phone number Mr. John Leeman had left for us.

"Hello?" said a cautious voice—one I recognized.

"James Palsic," I said. "This is Mercy Hauptman. Is Fiona there?"

"No," he said. "What do you want, Ms. Hauptman?"

"I have information you should know—" And I told him what

Bran had told me. Told him what he'd said about Chen, the Palsics, Schwabe, and Harolford. And I told him what Bran had said about Fiona.

"She's not rogue for hire," he said with conviction. "She's killed a lot of people—in Bran's service, I might add. But she is not for sale to the highest bidder."

"Bran doesn't lie," I told him. "And his truths are generally not the kind of shaded truths the fae use, either. Look. You are going to do what you are going to do. I understand that. But I think that you should call Bran"—I gave him Bran's number, and I heard the sound of a pen moving across paper as he wrote it down—"and you should talk to him. Ask him your questions and why Fiona told you that you could not go to Bran for help."

"Is that all?" he asked.

"Yes," I told him, and I hit the button on my phone that disconnected us.

Warren was watching me. "That might be putting the fox in the henhouse."

"If he calls Bran," I said. "If not—jeez. I should have called him on the shop phone because I just gave him my cell number to trace. I probably should have discussed that with Adam first."

"Your cell number is on your card." Warren tapped his finger on the counter just in front of the card holder with my business cards. "But if you had Palsic's number, why didn't you do that sooner?"

"I got distracted and didn't think about it," I told him—and I kept right on talking, hoping he wouldn't ask me what had distracted me. I was not telling anyone in the pack about Adam's monster until I was sure that was the right thing to do.

"I found the bill last night in hopes that it might have information we could use, but Adam and I got to *talking*—"

That wasn't a lie, and if Warren drew the wrong inference—and he had, judging by his grin—it wasn't my fault. It also wasn't my fault that the whole pack seemed to be way too interested in Adam's and my sex life. I didn't feel guilty about using it against Warren.

"But when I picked that bill up just now, I thought, Palsic was horrified that Lincoln had been sent to attack Kelly's house, where there were children. Bran seems to think Palsic is one of the good guys—why not give him the information he needs to save himself?"

Warren nodded. "Sounds like good thinking to me."

"Nothing might come of it," I told him as I texted Adam what I'd just done.

"I don't see how it could hurt us," Warren said.

Adam asked me to text him the number, so I did.

I will try to put a trace on it so we can follow his movements, Adam texted. **It will take time. I think what you did might bear more fruit.**

BY SIX I'D FINISHED EVERYTHING I'D PROMISED AND the last car went home with its owner—who had grumped at me over the bill to the point that I was casting worried glances at Warren, who was supposedly reading his book. He finally paid his bill so I would give him the keys to his car and stormed out, vowing never to come back. He always did that. That was why he was one of my special customers whose car I had to fix instead of sending him elsewhere. Someone else might overreact or hurt his feelings—or overcharge him.

"Someone once told him that if he made a big fuss, people would give him discounts," I told Warren. "And then it worked.

So now he does this every time." I watched him drive sedately off. "I think this might be his only social outlet. I'm not as fun as Tad. Tad can keep him going for twenty minutes some days."

"If he had come an inch closer to you, he would not ever bother you again," Warren said, closing his book with a snap.

Yep. I had been right to be worried.

"The day I need protection from Pat Henderson is the day you decide that pink is a real color."

He grunted. "I've worn pink."

"Because you love Kyle," I said. I looked at him more closely. "You look better."

He grunted. "We had a case turn bad. Leaves a sour taste in your mouth when you know something is going to happen and you can't do anything about it."

I watched him, watched his eyes brighten to gold.

"Oh?" I asked softly.

"Happens I did something about it," he said. "Kyle will start speaking to me again in a few days. I didn't do anything he wouldn't have done if he could have—and I reckon that makes him madder."

"Good guys must win?" I asked.

"And bad guys must lose," he agreed, and we fist-bumped.

ADAM CAME IN LATE, BUT I WAS WAITING UP FOR HIM.

"Bed," I said sternly.

His eyebrows rose and I could all but hear the occupants of the house prick their ears—even the ones in human form.

"Oh?" he said slowly. Trying to decide if he should take offense at my tone.

"Oh," I said. "Yes. You. Me. *Bed*. Now." I could raise my eyebrows, too. "Is that simple enough? Or do you need poetry? I might be able to do a haiku if you'd like."

"I vote for a limerick," called George from the basement. "There was a young lady named Mercy . . ."

"You don't get a vote," I called back.

There was a general round of friendly and interested laughter from various places in the house.

"It seems I am summoned," said Adam, giving in—as I had hoped—to the pressure of the house's expectations.

He had a smile on his face, but his eyes were worried.

"You bet, buster," I told him, and I led him up to the room where I already had the oil warming. Because every good deed deserves reciprocity.

THAT NIGHT I DREAMED OF STEFAN, DREAMS THAT had me sitting up in a cold sweat. Adam was asleep so deeply that I didn't wake him. By my count he'd been averaging two or three hours a night for weeks; it was hardly surprising that he was out.

Still . . .

I touched his well-oiled shoulder and he grumbled, wiggling down until his face was tucked against my hip, his hand gripping my knee briefly. Apparently reassured, he went limp again.

Leaving my hand on his shoulder, I slipped back into my otherness so I could look at the bonds that tied me to my people. This time, somewhat to my surprise, I took both the bedroom *and* Adam with me. Adam . . . was lit up with tiny strings of light that crossed and crisscrossed his skin before they went off in all directions. Our mating bond was thicker than it had been but was still the same monster-skin texture and color. It felt . . . sated. Which was, I hoped, a good thing.

But that wasn't what I was looking for tonight. I found the bond I shared with Stefan. This time it was a strand of lace the color of coffee grounds. It was so brittle that when I touched it, a small piece broke off.

I opened my mouth and pulled out a dandelion in full flower, fuzzily golden and cheerful. I stared at it a moment, because I had thought I was reaching for a gemstone—though in the Perrault story, the virtuous daughter also had flowers fall from her mouth.

Had I considered it beforehand, I would have envisioned roses or orchids, but maybe Stefan needed something less hothouse and more tenacious. That sounded right—because I needed him to be tenacious.

I put it to my lips and said, "Here is a bit of hope for you. Stay strong, my friend." I would have said more, but that felt like all the words the little flower could carry.

I held the flower over the lacy ribbon and hesitated. There was no way to open this bond, which was already so fragile that it crumbled at my touch.

After a moment's thought, I crushed the flower between my fingers and let the small bits of gold and green fall on the lace. When all of the flower was scattered in small bits, they melted into the bond—and a small spark popped and skittered from where the flower bits had been toward Stefan. Who now lay supine on the floor, though Adam and I had been alone in my otherness just a moment ago.

I slid out of the bed, knowing with certainty that Adam would not awaken here. I was still naked, but my bathrobe was awaiting me on the foot of the bed. I put it on and tied it securely before going to Stefan.

It took a lot more steps than it should have to cover the distance to him. And each step was weighty, as if I were traveling much more than the ten or twelve feet that lay between Stefan and my bed. Like dreams, the otherspace was sometimes richly symbolic and sometimes just weird. The trick was in figuring out which kind of weirdness I was dealing with.

As I neared Stefan, the carpet vanished between one step and the next, becoming the polished concrete of my garage auto bays, complete with the scratches from Adam's monster's claws. My bathrobe altered to jeans and a red T-shirt that said *Scooby Snacks Forever* in black letters across my chest. Little black bats began at the final "r" in "Forever" and concentrated over my left shoulder so that the shoulder of the shirt and left sleeve were black.

I didn't own a T-shirt like that. Why my subconscious thought I should be wearing something so Stefan-like, I didn't know.

Stefan himself was wearing all black, like a stagehand in a play. His eyes were closed and his face was tilted toward where the bay doors would have been if they had made an appearance here, but instead it was only inky blackness—like when I met Adam's monster. There was a distant rumble of sound, and I forced myself to quit thinking about the monster.

Instead, I knelt beside Stefan and put my hand on his shoulder. The result was explosive.

He went from still to full speed in the blink of an eye, rolling away from me and up and onto his feet in what was obviously some sort of martial and practiced maneuver. But once on his feet he stood swaying, his hands to his face, covering his eyes.

"Stefan?" I asked tentatively. Because I suddenly had the worrying thought that it might not be Stefan. The smoke weaver could take his shape.

But as soon as the worry found me, I knew that whatever shape he wore in the real world, here in my otherness, he would still be the smoke weaver. And unless I summoned him, the smoke weaver could not visit me here.

Stefan let his hands fall to his sides and gave me a wild look. "Go," he said. "You shouldn't be here."

"No," I told him patiently without rising to my feet. "It's okay. This is my space. You can come here because you are invited." I indicated the coffee-colored lace bond that was tied around my right ankle and stretched to his left ankle.

He dropped to the ground as if his knees just quit working. If he'd been human, in the real world, and had fallen like that onto my concrete floor, he'd have been in agony. But it hadn't seemed to have hurt Stefan—maybe because I hadn't wanted Stefan hurt.

We sat there for a moment, about four feet apart.

Finally, he said, in a voice filled with wonder, "It's so quiet here."

"Yes," I agreed.

His fingers played with a small place on the floor where Adam's claws had left a stuttering arc. "Sorry," he said, seeming to gather himself together, a mask suitable for social interaction forming on his face. "It's been a long time since it was quiet in my head."

"I need you to listen to me," I told him.

He looked up—and there was such . . . despair in his eyes. "I killed people, Mercy," he told me. "Innocents in the wrong place at the wrong time. I've done it before." He opened his arms to

267

remind me of what he was. "But I swore that I would never do so again. And until *this*, I kept my vow."

I crawled over to him and put my hand on his jaw. "Hang on, Stefan. I promise you that there is help coming if you can just hang on."

He said, sadly, "I am not a hero to be holding on for one minute longer."

I recognized the reference, though I couldn't remember the author—someone German, I thought.

"I disagree," I told him. "Just hold on, Stefan. Help is coming."

He shook his head. "Marsilia won't let me die by his hand," he told me. "But he will not let me feed. I weaken moment by moment until soon, there will be no more of me."

I thought about that one. Then, wordlessly, I held out my arm to him.

Stefan bit my wrist—and I let him, just as I had let him before. The feeding wasn't real except as dreams were real, or powerful except as dreams were powerful. He didn't drink blood from my veins—he drank strength, conviction, and hope.

When he had finished, he kissed my wrist, then rubbed it with his thumbs until the small wounds disappeared. He looked up. "I don't know whether to thank you or to curse you."

"I don't care," I said. "As long as you hang on."

Much as an actor in an artsy one-act play might have done, he lay down on the ground and faded into the darkness that now surrounded me.

I ran my finger over the same mark on the floor that Stefan had touched, feeling the roughness against my skin. I looked around and like the spotlight that lit where I sat, the bed was illuminated. I could see my mate lying asleep, his face turned away from me. Faintly, I could see the hulking monster curled around him like a lover.

I got up and walked through the darkness to the bed. When I finally reached it, I climbed in and wrapped my body around Adam as if I could protect him from himself.

"Hope," I said out loud, because I didn't have another pearl for him. "Hope, my love." And then I closed my eyes and slept.

ADAM WAS STILL ASLEEP BESIDE ME WHEN I WOKE UP the next morning. He didn't stir when I got up and hastily pulled on clothes as quietly as I could—I didn't see my bathrobe anywhere.

I had made it all the way to the door when Adam said, with lazy satisfaction, "You should shower, Mercy. You smell like sex."

"I was trying to let you sleep," I told him, coming back to the bed.

He smiled without opening his eyes. "Go shower. I'll sleep until you get out." And as I walked to the bathroom he said, "Thank you."

"No, sir," I said. "Thank *you*."

I TOOK BREAKFAST—EGGS AND BACON AND FRENCH toast—down to Ben, who was still in wolf form.

Luke, back on guard duty, shook his head as I walked by him. "He hasn't eaten anything since yesterday morning."

I frowned and approached the cage. I started to tell Ben that he needed to keep up his strength—and remembered Stefan, and what he'd said. I remembered how the last time I'd come down here, Ben had ignored me. But the time before that—when I knew it had been our Ben speaking—that time he hadn't wanted me anywhere near him.

Ben would be telling me to leave.

Instead of addressing Ben, I said, conversationally, "It takes a long time to starve a werewolf to death. As they grow more desperate for food, their wolf takes over from the man. I wonder if you can hold the wild beast you will be letting loose." I slid the plate through the long, narrow opening designed for that purpose and left Ben's breakfast in front of him. "If you can, it will take a lot of magic. You couldn't even hold me."

Ben's wolf gave me a baleful glare—but he got up and ate the food. He ate the second plate I brought down, too. And then he curled up with his back to the room and I couldn't help but remember how Adam's wolf had taken the same position when I fed him the amethyst. I hadn't seen the wolf since.

"Hope," I told Ben. I said it to myself, too.

I did some laundry—the sheets and bedding had gotten oil-stained. I didn't flinch at the knowing looks that were sent my way by everyone from Kelly to Medea. The cat might have been my imagination, but she purred from her perch on top of the warm, clean bedding. She didn't stop even when I lifted her off so I could fold them.

Adam worked from his office most of the morning, but he came up to the laundry room as I folded the last of the sheets.

"Have you been getting the looks, too?" I complained.

He laughed and took the folded sheets from me. "If you hadn't issued your invitation so that the whole household overheard, you might have avoided some of this."

I was pretty sure if I hadn't issued the invitation in front of the whole house, he wouldn't have taken me up on it. I grabbed the comforter, rolled it together until it made a manageable bundle, and said, "Sure I would have."

He laughed again and followed me as I took the comforter back to our bedroom. "How about I take you away from all of this for an hour or so. Want to go out to lunch?"

Get out of the house filled with werewolves with sharp ears and noses—and one werewolf trapped in a cage. I liked the hustle and bustle and organized chaos. But getting away from the pleased and knowing looks?

"That would be amazing," I told him.

12

THE FOOD AT THE RESTAURANT WE'D DECIDED UPON was good, but it was the river view that brought people here. We took an outside table on the deck, which hung out over the water, and we weren't the only ones who chose to brave possible bugs for the sunshine and river-freshened air.

The temperature had subsided as it sometimes did late in the summer. A few days ago, it had been in the triple digits, but this afternoon it was in the mideighties with a light breeze off the water. I saw a couple of people in light jackets and sweaters—ridiculous on the face of it. But the sudden drop in temperatures affected some people more than others.

Neither Adam nor I were wearing sweaters—I was a little chilled, but werewolves don't feel the cold as much. I'd seen them run around naked in the middle of a Montana winter without so much as a shiver. Hot weather bothered them, but not cold.

Out in the late-summer sun, wearing a button-up shirt I'd bought him, Adam looked more relaxed than I'd seen him in a while. He also looked gaunt. He'd lost maybe ten or fifteen pounds over the last week. Werewolves need fuel for shapeshifting. I suspected that the monster needed even more fuel. Adam was eating, but he was burning it all.

"Hey, Mercy," said someone I didn't know as they passed by our table on the way out. "I read about your car accident. I'm so sorry—I've broken my nose a couple of times. It really sucks."

One of the problems with being a local celebrity was that the newspaper and TV stations tended to cover any excitement. It provided an opportunity to frighten the daylights out of people, but also to do some PR. From the sounds of it, my Jetta's fate had been used for the latter.

"I liked that car," I told him with a friendly smile. "*I'll* be fine, but we're having a private funeral for the car on Wednesday."

I'd said that last to be funny. We'd had a funeral for my old Rabbit, but the Jetta would actually just end up in my parts car graveyard without ceremony—though I might say a few words over her.

"Good to hear," he said, and then his partner pushed him on with a nod to us and a "Let them eat, dear" to him.

When they left, I said, "I didn't know the local news caught my high jinks with the car."

Adam grunted. "Someone interviewed the police officers and got an official version. They called us, and my office sent a press release to all the news organizations. All of which downplayed the injuries so that your car's death was the biggest news. Kept it off the front page of the newspaper and in the last five minutes of on-air news."

"Huh," I said.

"Do you want me to keep you up on when you make the news?" he asked. "One of my guys in the office tracks it for me—all the reporters have his name and contact information."

"Like a movie star's promotional manager," I said, fluttering my eyelashes at him. "Assistant to Mr. Hauptman."

He laughed. "I'll tell him you said so. His main job is being big and scary to reassure clients we can protect them. He seems to be enjoying schmoozing the press—it's a different look for him. He tells me that he's just waiting until one of them actually sees him."

"Butch?" I asked incredulously. "Butch is your PR guy?"

Butch was six-eight and over three hundred pounds of ex–football player and Marine. Aided by some facial scarring, he could compete with Darryl for scary.

"Yes."

"You need to get him on the air," I said. "No one will pay attention to a few werewolves if they can follow Butch around."

"Do you want me to tell him to keep you updated?"

"Yeah," I said. "I know I should track that on my own, but . . ." I shrugged. "If I can get a heads-up, I won't react to people like a goldfish." I opened my eyes wide and made bubble-blowing motions with my mouth to illustrate my point. "It isn't a good look for me."

"I have to agree," he told me with an appreciative grin. "Especially with the tape on your nose."

I had forgotten all about the tape somehow between the mirror in my bathroom and the front door of the restaurant. Now I remembered. And the way the bruising on my left eye was darker and bigger than the one on my right. It gave me a lopsided appearance.

Self-consciously, I glanced around at the tables where people were studiously *not* looking at us: the very handsome—if too thin—man and the lopsided woman, who had just been making goldfish faces. Maybe, if they didn't know Adam, they would just think that slender was his normal build.

"I think you are beautiful no matter how much tape is on your nose," he said consolingly.

He wasn't lying. There was a reason why—even though he had shut down our bond; now turned into a terrifying monster instead of a beautiful, terrifying werewolf; and could be completely unreasonable at times—I loved him to bits.

"I know a good optometrist who can help you with that," I told him, and he smiled at me.

"So everyone knows about the car wreck," I said, because I couldn't say, *Let me take you to Bran and have him fix you.* I wasn't sure Bran could fix him—and I knew that he wouldn't go as long as the smoke weaver and Fiona's wolves were still running around.

"Better that than everyone wondering if I beat you up," he replied.

"Hah," I agreed.

The waitress came and took our orders. She didn't even widen her eyes at the size of Adam's—we'd eaten here before.

After she left, I said, "I don't know why it's so different eating here than it is eating on the river shore by our house."

"We could clear the river area and put up picnic tables down on the shore," Adam said. "But I like it better the way it is."

"With weeds and rocks and mud for all the river wildlife to use," I agreed.

"And," said Adam, raising his water glass to me, "*here* we have a chance to eat an intimate meal without the pack interrupting four times an hour."

"With the added benefit that neither of us has to cook," I said lightly. How could it be an intimate lunch when Adam still had our mating bond locked down tighter than a miser's penny jar?

I knew about the monster he'd been hiding, and he still wouldn't let me in.

Conscious that we were under surveillance by the curious, we avoided talking about the smoke weaver, the intruding were-wolves, or Wulfe. Instead we discussed Jesse's plans for school and whether she should get an apartment near the campus in Richland, which would give her some independence and a lot less daily travel time.

"Larry's people," said Adam, meaning the goblins, "would probably keep a close watch on her and alert us if there are any problems—as long as we pay them."

"We have a number of werewolves who live in Richland near the school," I said. "That way if there was trouble, someone could get to her over there pretty darn quickly. The question is, would Jesse want to do that?"

"Let's see," said Adam, and he texted her, his mouth quirked up, knowing that whatever her decision on the matter, Jesse would be excited to consider it.

He liked making Jesse happy. I wanted him to be happy, too.

"Have you thought about talking to Bran or Charles about what Elizaveta did?" I asked very quietly so no one else would hear.

This was neither the time nor place for that question, but I was so worried about him. He stopped texting and the small smile left his face. He didn't look at me. "I called Charles yesterday. I was going to tell you about it last night, but . . ."

He smiled ruefully, his eyes carefully on a cormorant on the river. If he'd had good news, he'd have been looking at me.

"Charles," Adam continued, "told me that witchcrafted spells usually dissipate when the witch dies, which we all know already.

Death curses are a lot more difficult to deal with. He'll look into it and get back to me."

"Okay," I said. I'd been hopeful that Charles would know what to do. Tonight I'd call Bran—assuming he was taking my calls again—lay everything on the table, and see what he said. Maybe he'd have more useful advice than "blow up the bond" if he knew what was really going on.

I wasn't sure I'd tell Adam before I called Bran. Better, maybe, in this case, to ask forgiveness than permission. I was already feeling guilty in advance because of Adam's weird reaction to the last call I'd made to Bran—and wasn't that interesting.

Adam had gone back to his texting, so he didn't see my assessing gaze. Maybe I was only feeling like this was a private, hush-hush matter because Adam was treating it that way. As if getting wham-mied by a scary and powerful witch was something to be ashamed of. He knew better than that. It must be something the curse was doing to him.

An e-mail came through on my phone. I checked it—it was from Ariana. Short and sweet, it read:

I agree with your conclusions. Bargaining is a thing of rules, espe-cially for the lesser fae, with balance being the most important part. Bargains, properly made, are complicated things. Above all else, a proper bargain is balanced. Each party gets something they want that is of equal value. I save your life—you give me your firstborn child. That is a balance. You give me your bubble gum, I give you my balloon. That is also balanced. Unbalanced bargains have no power—and you need a bargain with power. Good luck, my friend.

Adam finished his text to Jesse, glanced casually around, then said, "Let's save other important things for the car. We are getting a lot of surreptitious attention."

"Sounds like a smart thing to do," I said agreeably, and watched his shoulders ease down.

Don't worry, my love, I won't peel open your pain until after I talk to Bran about how to do it most efficiently, I thought. But better to do that than to find out that Adam had given in to despair sometime when I wasn't around to stop him.

Elizaveta had broken open something inside him, and I wasn't sure that just getting rid of the spell was going to fix him.

"You are healing remarkably quickly from the car wreck," he said. Apparently picking at *my* wounds was a good subject change.

Fair enough, mine weren't as deep, and they were getting better.

"Right?" I said. "I'm still achy here and there—and my nose still hurts. But I'm a lot better than I expected to be at this point. I'm pretty sure it's Hannah's fault."

I told him about Hannah's granny's bourbon and what Underhill had said about it. I'd told him the gist of the conversation with Underhill yesterday, but I'd forgotten about Hannah's bourbon.

"It's not going to bring anyone back from death's door," I told him judiciously. "But it beats any over-the-counter painkiller all to heck."

"I wonder if Hannah's granny's fae blood is the reason that Kelly and Hannah have so many kids," Adam mused. "Though it seems like the fae blood should work against them, because the fae have more trouble reproducing than werewolves do."

"Maybe it's Hannah's granny's secret ingredient," I told him. "Take one sip before bedtime as needed for conception."

He rewarded me with a laugh.

My cell phone rang. I dug it out of my purse and looked at the caller ID. Palsic. I turned it toward Adam so he could see.

His smile fled, and he nodded.

I answered it warily. "This is Mercy."

"This is Nonnie Palsic." She sounded rattled down to her bones. "Could you help us? I don't know . . . I don't know what to do. He's . . . like the trolls in *The Hobbit*."

I had to think a moment—and then realized what she was saying. "You mean when they turned to stone?"

Adam had already taken out his wallet and was counting out bills on the table, paying for the food that hadn't come yet. There were protein bars in the SUV. I would feed him on the way.

"Sort of," she said. "But like that. Yes. Can you help?"

"We're coming," I told her. "Who did the smoke weaver get?"

"Smoke weaver?" she said.

"Fae," I told her. "He bites people and makes them kill. And he can change one thing into another—like the old alchemists tried to change lead into gold. That kind of thing."

"God help us," she said, and then she took a shaky breath. When she spoke again, her voice was steadier. "Your smoke weaver has changed my mate into stone."

"Where are you?" I asked her as we hurried through the restaurant toward the parking lot. Adam paused briefly to talk to our waitress and then caught up as Nonnie rattled off an address.

Adam took out his phone and keyed in the location. As soon as we were outside, we both broke into a jog. I wasn't sure there was a reason to hurry, though. James Palsic had been turned to stone. Even Tolkien's trolls hadn't come back from that.

———————

"IS FIONA THERE WITH YOU?" I ASKED, BELTING IN.

"No, I—wait." She took another deep breath. And again, it seemed to help. When she started talking, she was calmer. "Things you need to know. Fiona and Sven are on their way to kill Warren Smith's boyfriend, the one who shot Sven."

I glanced at Adam.

"Kyle's at work," he said. "Both Warren and Zack are on guard duty at his work, too."

"Fiona likes to shoot people," Nonnie told us in a weary voice. "She hits what she aims at." Almost to herself she muttered, "I told James that she was bad news—but, as he pointed out, we didn't have a lot of options at the time."

"Who is with you?" I asked, as Adam pulled out his phone and called Warren.

"Li Qiang and Kent," she said. "James said you told him to call Bran yesterday." She hesitated, then said, "We've been trying to fly under Bran's radar. Fiona said that our defection from the Galveston pack would be a capital offense—that he'd send Charles out to hunt us. He would kill us all. Fiona said that once Harolford was Alpha here, we'd be safe from retaliation because your pack isn't one of the Marrok's."

"We exist independently because Bran allows it," I said dryly. "Bran hasn't given our pack carte blanche, and he wouldn't have overlooked Harolford taking over. Did James call Bran yesterday?"

"Yes," she said. "And talked to him for a while, apparently. But he didn't say anything until Fiona and Sven left to go after their target—we were supposed to go after ours then. That doesn't matter. We didn't. Once the four of us were alone, James explained to us that Fiona had been lying to us all along: we could have gone to Bran for help—but Fiona is under a death sentence. *She* needed *us*."

"Bran would have killed her, even if she and Harolford had succeeded here," I told her.

"So James said," she agreed.

"So how did James get turned to stone?" I asked.

"Bran invited us to Montana. As soon as Fiona and Sven left, we started packing," she said. "James finished first so he went to get the car. He never came back. We were looking for him—and Li said . . . Li said, 'Hey, Nonnie, do you remember a rock being there?' And it was James."

There was horror in her voice. I didn't want to push her over the edge until she'd given us all of the information that we needed, so I didn't ask her any more about James. I'd see him soon enough.

"When are you expecting Fiona back?" I asked. "We will help if we can, but I need to know what my people will be walking into."

"Sven and Fiona are supposed to be back here by five," she said. "But Fiona likes to savor her kills—and if you manage to keep her from her target . . . she doesn't give up."

I looked at Adam, who had just set his phone down. I hadn't tried to follow his conversation.

"The three of them will stay indoors and away from windows until we give them an all-clear. Warren and Zack are armed. Kyle is sending everyone in his office home. We can hunt Fiona and Harolford down at our leisure."

"Did you hear that?" I asked.

"No," she said. "Sorry. I wasn't paying attention."

"Kyle Brooks is safe and likely to stay that way. We have time. I am going to hang up now and confer with Adam. Expect us about a half hour from now."

"Okay," she said mournfully. "We'll wait."

I hung up.

"We can't help Ben," Adam said. "And no one turned him to stone."

"I've been working on how to deal with the weaver," I told him. I grabbed the backpack we kept on the floor of the back seat and came up with the protein bars. "I'd like to have had more time to make sure I'm right. But I know who our villain is—and I think I know what we need to do."

"Tell me," Adam said.

"I can't tell you his name—I think that might attract his attention in the wrong way."

"But you've worked it out?" he asked.

I nodded. "Maybe. Probably. He's not powerful as the fae go."

Adam gave me a look.

"Really. Outside of the power that Underhill gave him, he is one of the lesser fae."

"How do you know that?" he asked.

"The fae are creatures whose lives are bound by rules. That they cannot lie being the core rule all of them must follow." I handed him a protein bar. "Here, eat this."

"I never thought of them that way," Adam said, taking the bar and starting in on it. I immediately felt a little calmer.

"That's because you usually deal with the powerful fae," I told him. "The Gray Lords, Zee, Baba Yaga, and the like. The powerful fae have a lot fewer rules and they are bendy."

"Okay," he said. "Yes, I've noticed that."

"The other important thing to remember about the rules is that they constrain all the fae. But only the fae." I frowned. "Dang it. I think that the rule about lying has to be an exception, because we know that the fae actually can lie—they just suffer a horrible fate if they do."

"Maybe that is the rule," Adam suggested. "If a fae lies, they will suffer a horrible fate."

"Okay," I said, feeling better. "That fits. And the fae can't lie without suffering a horrible fate. But we could lie to a fae."

"Only if we have a death wish," said Adam. "But I know what you mean. I could tell Zee that you love orange juice. Which he knows isn't true. But I could say the words and not suffer a horrible fate."

"Right," I told him.

"The weaker the fae, the more rules they have?" Adam asked, pulling the conversation back to the point.

"Yes." I looked up and realized he was taking the most direct route to the address we'd been given. "Could we make a stop at home before we go see what the smoke weaver has done to James Palsic?"

His eyebrows went up, but he made a minor course correction that would take us home first. I unwrapped another protein bar and handed it to him. His lip quirked up, but he took the bar.

I watched him eat and thought about how I wanted to frame the information I'd put together. I needed him to believe me so that he would agree to the plan I'd devoted a lot of time to yesterday while I had been fixing cars. Because that plan required a certain amount of risk on my part—which was something that was hard for Adam. But I was the only person who could do it.

"Take brownies," I said. "The lowest caste of brownies have very specific rules. They must find good people. Once they do, they clean their homes or do work for them—and this makes the brownies happy. But they can do these things only so long as the people they are working for never see them and never say anything about them. They must be given milk and bread—but cannot be thanked aloud. If they are seen, thanked, or not fed, the brownies have to move on and find someone else to serve. They have no choice about any of it."

"What rules does the smoke weaver have?" Adam asked.

"He has to make bargains," I told him. "If one is offered to him properly, he has to accept. That's how Underhill caught him in the first place. And there's a rule about his name, too. People who know it can't tell anyone what it is. Before Underhill got ahold of him, he had only one power, to transform one thing into another. It is an impressive power—but it is also very limited."

"Tell that to James Palsic," said Adam.

"Yes, well." I waved that away. It shouldn't matter to my plan. I hoped. "Tilly told me that the intent of her upgrade was that he would have an easier time making himself look like a specific person. It made me think that was a problem for him before she changed him. Like maybe he couldn't make himself look very much like a person at all."

Sorting through the implications of Tilly's story had taken me most of yesterday.

"The way to defeat him is to use the rules that he has to follow," I said. Baba Yaga had told me something of the sort.

"I can already tell," Adam said, "that I'm not going to like this."

"Here," I said. "Eat another protein bar."

I DROVE JESSE'S CAR TO THE ADDRESS THAT NONNIE Palsic had given me. Adam would collect what I needed from home and then follow me out; hopefully it wouldn't take too long.

It wasn't that far from our house—maybe ten minutes in a
direction I seldom took, one of those out-of-the-way places that
didn't lie on a direct route between our house and anywhere I was
likely to need to go. It was out in the hill country between the
Tri-Cities and Oregon where there was no water available for irrigation and not enough houses that the city would pipe water
out. This late in the summer the hills were a pale dirt brown
dusted with sparse remains of grass.

I turned up a well-tended gravel road and followed it for a
quarter of a mile that twisted around with the lay of the land, no
houses in sight. It took a final turn, climbed a steep grade, and
popped out on the top of a hill, where it ended in an asphalt circular driveway laid out before a huge house. The house had been
carefully placed to hide itself from the highway below without
impacting the panoramic views. A narrow ring of bright green
grass circled the house, and there were a few raised flower beds
that were unplanted.

I parked the car near the front door, as far as I could get it
from the three people on the other edge of the driveway. It left me
with about twenty yards to walk—it was a big circular drive. But
I didn't want Jesse's car to suffer the same fate my last two cars
had, so I wanted it well out of the action. I couldn't do anything
until Adam got here anyway.

I didn't say anything as I approached the three werewolves because I was too busy looking at the tall, pillar-like rock they were
huddled around. I had expected a detailed sculpture in stone—
maybe because of Nonnie's comparison to *The Hobbit*, or maybe
because of how detailed the concrete version of the semi tractor's
tire at the Lewis Street tunnel had been. But this looked sort of like
a basalt columnar joint—the kind houses like this used as land-

scaping focal points—except that it lacked the sharp-edged hexagonal structure.

I walked around to the side that the others were standing in front of, and I realized that the image I should have been imagining was more like Han Solo's encasement than Peter Jackson's stone trolls. This side of the rock had eyes and an opening through which I could hear the faint slide of air.

Nonnie looked at me with a tear-stained face and said, "He's having trouble breathing now."

It did sound shallow and irregular.

"Adam's bringing what I need," I told her.

"What kind of a place *is* this?" asked Kent, sounding traumatized.

"The kind of place where fairy tales live," said Chen Li Qiang in a dreamy voice, "and monsters dwell."

I gave him a concerned look, but he just hugged himself.

"We are the monsters," he told me seriously. "And we are damned."

I frowned at him and asked the others, "Has he been bitten recently? By anything, a rabbit, maybe?"

"No, he just falls into bad poetry when he's sad. It was—" Kent Schwabe stopped as Adam's big black SUV topped the rise and drove directly to where we stood.

Li Qiang watched it for a minute, then said, "Is there something wrong with the suspension? It seems to be bouncing more than nec—"

One of the rear windows exploded outward in a shower of glass.

"Nothing wrong with the SUV," I said, and turned my attention back to James. His eyes, encased in stone, were red and dry.

He couldn't blink because he did not have lids. I wondered if the smoke weaver had done that deliberately, or if it had been a cruel accident. Regardless, they didn't move. I couldn't tell if that was because he couldn't move them—or because he didn't move them.

If it weren't for the shaky breathing, I would never have believed that he was still alive.

"Oh my God," said Jesse beside me.

"What are you doing here?" I said, horrified.

"There wasn't anyone to drive the car," she told me.

"Oh," said Aiden in a small voice. "This. He'll take a day or two to die all the way."

"Not going to happen," I said, with a lot more sangfroid than I actually felt.

I looked around and said, "Li Qiang? I am putting you in charge of making sure that Jesse and Aiden don't get hurt. Jesse"—I tapped her on the shoulder—"is our *human* daughter. This is our son, Aiden." I tapped him. I met Chen Li Qiang's eyes. "I am trusting you because everyone else I trust will have their hands full—and Carlos has vouched for you. I trust Carlos's judgment."

Li Qiang gave me an oddly formal bow that would have been more at home on another continent. "You can help my friend?"

"I hope so," I told him.

"Then I will keep them safe this day as long as I have breath in my body."

I turned to Jesse and Aiden and started to say something, but Aiden beat me to the punch. "Your son."

I raised an eyebrow. "It would be weird the other way around, don't you think?"

His smile was a little tentative and he gave me a nod.

"Okay—you two and Li Qiang, I want you to stand . . ." There was nowhere safe, not until I was further into my gambit.

"Next to each other out of the way," said Jesse.

"I'll help keep them safe," Kent said to me. He had to raise his voice a little to be heard over the sounds coming from the SUV. "If you are what I have heard, you will know I am telling the truth."

He was. But he was also the one that Bran had been unsure of. I hesitated—but Aiden was capable of protecting himself, now that his fire was mostly recovered from what Wulfe had done to it.

"Thank you," I said, nodding toward Li Qiang, so he would know I meant him, too. I liked having the (more or less) innocent bystanders innocently bystanding instead of getting hurt.

I looked at the SUV and said, "Hey, Jesse. You and Aiden are here. And that looks like Luke, Kelly, and your father in the car. Who is minding the fort?"

"Joel is there," she said. "Darryl and Auriele are on their way—about twenty minutes out. Dad was going to leave Kelly behind but"—another of the back windows in the rocking SUV exploded—"they were having more trouble than they expected. It took all three of them to get him into Dad's SUV, and it took all three of them to keep him in. Finally, Dad said that given that Fiona and Harol-somebody were out fruitlessly hunting Kyle, the house should be safe enough for twenty minutes."

Ben would have heard that—which meant the smoke weaver knew it, too. So I should hurry and get started. Once I had begun, hopefully he would be too busy to launch a counterattack.

Aiden touched my arm. "Joel is good protection," he said. "Hard to bite a tibicena." And that was very true. Some of my worry left me. "I thought I might be useful here given my background. But maybe I should have stayed home, too?"

"I don't know," I told him honestly. "Tough call to make. For what it's worth, I'm happy to have you here. If you hear me about to do something stupid, you might warn me."

He nodded. "Don't put me so far away I can't help."

Nonnie touched the rock and then told me, "I will help guard your children. Help Li and Kent. I will keep them safe if it is in my power."

"I will do my best for James," I said, nodding. "I have a couple of guys who need rescuing from the smoke weaver, too. I'm going to try to do it all at once."

She nodded mutely. Frowned and then said, "You aren't the Alpha. You aren't even a werewolf. Fiona says that your only gift is turning into a coyote. Why are you in charge?"

"Because Fiona is wrong about me," I told her.

I didn't say anything more, because I had no idea who else or what else might be listening. And because they were not pack—and they didn't need my secrets.

When Li Qiang led the group the short distance to the lamppost that I had indicated, Nonnie followed. About that time, Adam, Luke, and Kelly managed to get Ben—shackled, chained, and in werewolf form—out of the back of the SUV, which now looked as though I was going to get a second chance to try to talk Adam into something other than black.

"Over here," I said.

And they half carried, half dragged Ben to where I stood. All three of the men were bloody—all four if you included Ben. His rear legs looked like hamburger from the car windows. Ben, on his own, was no match for any of them by themselves, let alone all three. But they didn't want to hurt him—and the smoke weaver had no reason to worry about hurting any of them, including Ben.

"Ben," I said. "Hold on."

"Don't get any closer," growled Adam.

He was right. I didn't heal the way that the werewolves did, and I was not nearly as strong. So I stood back and did not touch him the way I wanted to.

"I see you," I said. "And I have a bargain for you."

Ben quit thrashing.

Adam murmured, "Set him down."

The other two gave him incredulous looks. But he was their Alpha and they were used to doing what he told them to.

"A bargain," I told him, "must have something that I want—and something that you want."

And I realized I had a problem. "I need Ben to be able to talk," I told Adam.

He didn't tell me it was impossible, as he had every reason to do. I thought it might be impossible, too. Poor James's breathing didn't sound like he had time to wait at all. But this wouldn't work if Ben's body couldn't speak.

Usually it doesn't matter much that werewolves cannot speak in their wolf form. They communicate very well using body language, and they can scratch out letters if something is very important. If a matter is truly urgent, then sometimes the pack bonds provide a way to communicate with Adam.

None of that would work for the smoke weaver—what I needed to do required a voice.

Adam sent Jesse to the SUV to grab a ring of keys that was in the glove compartment. She had to rummage a bit but found it. She threw the keys to me before going back to where I'd asked her to wait.

Adam unlocked all of the chains that bound Ben. Undid the silver muzzle and the band around his chest. The only binding he left on was a heavy silver collar and a thick chain attached to it, which Adam kept hold of. Ben's fur was burned where the bindings had wrapped him.

If there were any other way to hold a crazed werewolf, Adam would have done that instead. But the wolf had very few weaknesses, and steel bindings alone were not enough to hold the strongest of them. And, Bran had told me once, never assume that you have one of the werewolves who can be restrained without silver. If you make that mistake, it might be the last time you get a chance to be wrong.

Ben sat still for it all.

Adam glanced my way—and that was when the smoke weaver went for him. I knew it was not Ben. I didn't need to see it in his eyes to know that Ben would never attack Adam.

Adam had the other wolf on the ground so fast I didn't see him move. He put his head next to the great mouth as it snapped and growled.

"*Change,*" said Adam.

I felt the hard tug from the pack bonds as he pulled power from all of us. Kelly staggered and Luke reached out to steady him.

Adam leaned closer and licked Ben's face where blood gathered from a small wound. "*Change.*

"Hold him down," Adam said, his voice strained.

Luke and Kelly piled on. Changing for a werewolf is a horrible, painful, and slow process. The more dominant wolves can change relatively quickly—ten or fifteen minutes, a little faster if they pull hard on pack bonds. Wolves lower in the pecking order, like Ben, took longer—except when their Alpha forced power into the change.

But the painful part was important. I tried really hard not to touch a werewolf who had recently changed to either form for a few minutes because their skin was hypersensitive—and their muscles and bones ached from being reshaped and moved. Ben, changing to human with Adam, Luke, and Kelly on top of him, had to be in agony.

I hoped the smoke weaver would feel some of that, too.

I glanced away from Ben and my eyes fell upon the rock that held—or that *was*—James Palsic, and I found myself wondering why he'd been turned to stone instead of made a puppet.

According to my calculations, the smoke weaver was limited in the number of people he could control, and not being able to take me over at all had made him, according to Ben, obsessed with me. He had taken Ben, who belonged to our pack, and Stefan. How had he known about Stefan? Maybe Stefan had been coming to our house when I didn't answer his call? The hitchhiker didn't count, because she had been earlier. Lincoln could also have been lurking around our house when he'd been bitten, but the weaver had been riding him while still controlling Ben and Stefan—which meant that he should be able to control three people at a time.

It made sense, having taken Lincoln, that the smoke weaver was aware of these wolves and could choose another victim from among them after Lincoln died. But why had he turned James into a rock? Why hadn't he bitten him if he could control one more person?

And I thought of Fiona's reactions to Lincoln. She dealt with witches, why not fae? Assuming that she did not care about Lincoln—which I thought might be a safe assumption to make about her. What if she had bargained with the fae instead of opposing him? They had, after all, a similar goal. The smoke weaver, like Fiona, was driven to attack my pack. I didn't know why.

James was taking Fiona's pack from her, and the weaver had acted against him. That made sense. But again, why turn him to stone when he'd be of more use bitten? His mate would know that he was bitten, I thought. And then I had a terrible thought. What if he had not bitten James—because he had bitten someone else?

Oh. Oh no.

He had bitten someone else. Not Li Qiang, not Kent or Nonnie. I would know if it were one of them; I was pretty confident that I could read the signs. He had bitten either Fiona or her mate. And I was betting on her mate. And that meant—

"He can talk now," said Adam sounding tired.

One enemy at a time, I told myself firmly, squelching panic as far down as I could. This was a chance, possibly my only chance, to send our unwelcome visitor back to Underhill.

Kelly and Luke pulled Ben up to his knees so he was looking at me. Adam kept hold of the chain.

"Mercy," Ben croaked, his eyes terrified. Because he'd known all along what I'd just understood. It hadn't been the smoke weaver kicking the bejeebers out of Adam's SUV. It had been Ben, desperate to convey the information we all equally desperately needed.

"I know," I said. "I just figured it out."

Adam frowned at me and I shook my head. It didn't matter because there was nothing to be done until this was finished.

"We're here now, Ben. Now we have to do it this way or it will be an even bigger disaster."

"Okay," he said. "Hurry."

"Smoke weaver," I said. "I have a bargain."

Bargains, properly made, Ariana's e-mail had read, *are complicated things.*

"Bargains must be made," he said. His voice was Ben's, but it was not Ben.

"If you come here, in your own—"

"Blood and bone," supplied Aiden.

"Blood and bone," I said, trusting him. "You may bite me once to test your power against mine. You in your most powerful form."

I was guessing that this was a factor. What bit Stefan had been much bigger than the rabbit who bit Ben. If the rabbit had been enough, why would the weaver trade up to bite Stefan at nearly the same time and place? Stefan was a very old vampire and a power in his own right among his kind. Ben might be a beloved member of our pack, but his actual age was very close to my own, and he was pretty far down the pack structure in power. Stefan was much tougher prey than Ben.

"If I win?"

"Then I am yours," I told him.

He snorted. "What then the incentive? I could come upon you when you least expect it and have the same result."

Could he? I wondered. Why hadn't he, then? But it is important when dealing with immortal creatures to not allow them to distract you from your goal.

"Ask me what happens should you lose," I told the smoke weaver.

"What happens if I lose?" he asked.

294

"Because I have defeated your magic once before," I said, "it is only fair that I should pay you a penalty for the opportunity to make a bargain where the odds are not in your favor."

Above all else, a proper bargain is balanced. I hoped that I had judged it correctly.

"Yes," he said.

"What would you?" I asked.

"Answer three questions," he said.

I pretended to consider it.

"I will answer one question because you come here where I am," I told him. "I will tell you one true thing because I have already withstood your bite once."

He stared at me. "Why do you bargain?"

"Fair question," Aiden said.

"It is important to know if your bite at fullest power will affect me—or else I will always be worried that you will sneak up behind me in the dark." True—but not the answer to his question.

Flattered, he smiled. It was Ben's face, but it was not Ben's smile. "I come," he said.

And then Ben went limp in Kelly's and Luke's arms, and he began, brokenly, to swear. He looked up at me once, and I shook my head. It would take too long to explain—and at this point there was no good to be had telling the others. The weaver knew that we'd left our vulnerable alone in our home with only one protector—because Ben knew we'd left our vulnerable alone in our home with only one protector. And what Ben knew, the weaver knew, and what the weaver knew—Fiona and her mate knew.

Joel was home. That would have to be enough.

13

I FOUND SPARE CLOTHING, THE METALLIC EMERGENCY blanket, and a real blanket in the back of the SUV. It took me a few minutes because as bad as the outside of the vehicle looked, the inside was worse.

The leather upholstery was slashed, seat stuffing scattered in chunks ranging from baseball size to pea size. One of the inner linings of the doors had been broken into two. The whole of the back two-thirds of the car was liberally sprayed with blood, as were the first two shirts I found.

I took the results of my search to Ben. He was curled up on the ground shivering convulsively. Kelly had wrapped his large body around Ben's to help him keep warm. Luke crouched with his hand on Ben's shoulder, talking to him in a low voice. It didn't matter what the words were, it was the familiar voice that soothed him.

It probably would have looked a little odd to someone who didn't know they were werewolves.

Adam stood a little back from them, holding the chain attached to the collar Ben wore. Adam had to stay far enough back that if the weaver took Ben again, Adam would be able to control the situation. But I could see from the expression on his face that Adam would rather have been in Kelly's or Luke's position.

The lamppost group had ventured nearer. Aidan and Jesse had stopped at the rock that was James Palsic. Jesse stood next to it . . . to him. She glanced up furtively to stare at the eyes that had no recourse but to look back. Aiden touched him, running his hands over the stone gently, as if petting a dog.

I could hear him murmuring, "Remember who you are. Remember." Over and over as if it were a spell, but I couldn't sense any magic.

Li Qiang and Kent were keeping watch over them, but Nonnie approached Adam while Luke and Kelly grabbed the clothes and blankets from me and used them to wrap Ben up.

"He hasn't talked again," Luke said in a low voice. "We think he's in shock."

"No wonder," I said. "My fault. If I'd worked it through better, I could have told you I needed him human. It would have been easier on him if you didn't have to make him change so fast."

"Werewolves are tough," said Luke. "Don't fuss, Mercy."

"So we just wait?" Nonnie said tightly. "How long?"

Adam looked at her thoughtfully. After a moment she started to squirm.

"We wait," he said softly, "for my wife to risk her life for your mate."

He looked over at Ben, who was dressed in sweats that were too big for him on the bottom and just right on the top. Luke wrapped him in the soft blanket first, and then the thin metallic one.

Then he looked at Nonnie, who had lowered her eyes and looked as though she was seriously regretting saying anything. Adam shook his head at himself. I knew that expression.

In a much gentler voice he said, "Mercy is risking her life for Ben and anyone else who might encounter this creature because Mercy is the only one who has the ability to make this bargain."

"Why is that?" Nonnie asked.

Then she held up a hand. "Sorry. Not my business. I'm sorry." She looked at the rock and then back toward Adam. "What I should be saying is thank you. You had no need to come to our aid at all after what we've been doing."

"Desperate people do desperate things" was Adam's reply. "We all understand that."

Kent gave a low warning whistle, then said, "It's getting darker."

He was right. The sun was still high in the intense blue sky, but the area we were standing in was growing shadowed. I inhaled—and bless Hannah's granny's potion—and the magic scent that was unique, as far as I could tell, to the smoke weaver filled the air.

"Ladies and gentlemen, the waiting is over," I said quietly. I kissed Adam, and it was a good kiss even though I had to do it from an awkward angle so that I didn't interfere with his ability to manage Ben.

Then I walked to the middle of the driveway, halfway between Jesse's car and Adam's. Away from all of the people. I was pretty sure that the smoke weaver had to treat with me, and complete our bargain, before he went out biting anyone else. But pretty sure wasn't certain, and I didn't want him closer to anyone else than necessary.

A circle centered, more or less, on my position in the middle of the circular drive, and continued to darken, as if someone were drawing it with shadows.

Kelly and Luke had pulled the blankets off Ben again. And then Adam kissed the top of his head and pinned him to the ground so he could not move. Kelly stood on one side of them, Luke on the other, ready to help in case Ben broke free.

Like a Christmas snow globe, the dome over our head, cutting us off from the rest of the world, was invisible. But I could feel the resulting pressure drop as the circle sealed. Circles like this were something I associated with witchcraft. But this didn't smell like witchcraft—it smelled like the smoke weaver.

The darkened edges of the circle began to fill with smoke, covering the ground in folded layers that grew thicker and rounder until they reminded me of the rolled-up dough for a cinnamon roll before you cut it, or . . . the coils of a snake.

The smoke had left a little area around Adam's group and another around James's rock. I didn't like the look of them separated.

"Kids," I called, "get closer to Adam."

Jesse and Aiden tried, but the smoke between them thickened and grew taller. Just before I lost sight of them in the smoke, I saw Luke make a rolling leap over the top of the coils. Hopefully he made it to Jesse and Aiden. I believed that Kent and Li Qiang had meant it when they told me they would guard my family, but I felt better having one of the pack with them.

I now had a smallish area to stand in, about ten feet around, but clear, more or less to the top of the dome—though even the surface of that dome was darkening. Meanwhile, the layers and layers of coils were becoming more real, and solid. Giant silver scales glinted iridescently in the filtered light that drifted through the smoke.

"Smoke dragon," I said.

Beauclaire had called him that. There was evidently some truth in the appellation, though I thought that "wyvern" or even "serpent" might have been more accurate. The only dragon I had seen had had four legs and wings.

I supposed that there could be more than one kind of dragon, but this creature did not carry the amount of magic that dragons were reputed to have. While I didn't see limbs, there might have been wings in the mists of smoke that filled the space not occupied by the smoke weaver.

The coils stirred, as if the weaver had heard me name him. One of the coils nearby moved and a giant, reptilian head slid over the mounds of his body to look at me through eyes that might have been fist-sized gemstones.

The head was as tall as I was, but still it seemed small for the size of his body. It didn't look exactly like a snake's head, but it resembled that more than a dragon's. The weaver's muzzle was long and almost delicate.

He snorted and a salty, watery gel covered me.

I wiped my face off impatiently. Coyote mates of Alpha werewolves don't care if smoke dragons cover them in snot. We certainly wouldn't squeal.

Instead, I asked him, in what I felt was a reasonably calm tone, "Why the show?"

There is not enough magic in your world to allow me to take my true shape, the smoke weaver said, though he wasn't really talking. There was sound, it was a voice—but it wasn't coming from the serpent's mouth. *I must make a place where I can gather it sufficiently. This takes time.*

"It is an acceptable inconvenience," I told him, not untruthfully. I didn't care about circles—I cared about the time. Joel, I reminded myself, against two werewolves. If Fiona, "equally dangerous" as Charles, weren't one of them, I wouldn't have even worried.

I am here, the smoke weaver told me, *in blood and bone.*

He seemed to be waiting for something, so I said, "Yes, you have thus fulfilled the first part of this bargain."

I don't know why I used forsoothly speech; it just seemed the right thing to do—and when I had no clue, I tended to go with my instincts.

I was still musing about language when he bit me. The strike came without warning. My reactions were fast, but I didn't have time to even flinch. He clamped his teeth over my left shoulder and the upper part of my chest.

I made an involuntary sound, as much of surprise as hurt—and it did hurt. It felt as though someone had stabbed me with something hot. That pain burned, and when he pulled his head back, the breaks in my skin where his teeth had been had trickles of smoke coming from them.

"Mercy," Adam said.

"He surprised me," I said back. "I am fine." But I could have saved my breath.

As if it had been difficult for the smoke weaver to hold on to his enormous shape, the coils dissolved into grayish smoke that covered the globe of the circle so that we could not see out nor anyone outside see in. Then the inner part of the circle cleared until nothing lay between me and the others except for a dozen yards of driveway pavement.

Adam could see for himself that I was fine—so far.

A piece of smoke dropped from over my head, darkening as it fell. It hit the ground in front of me with an audible thump. The smoke drifted away and left a man no more than four feet high. Or someone who looked vaguely like a man, anyway.

He was hairy and very ugly—as if someone had taken a rock and chipped away at it with a crowbar until they made something humanoid, and turned that into a living creature. Then, deciding they hadn't quite managed to make him look human, they covered him with a great beard that fell to the ground. The hair on his head, about the color of cinnamon, was neatly braided and was also floor-length. But there was hair in his ears, and his eyebrows were unusually thick. There was not much room on his face for eyes and nose, and his mouth was lost under a prodigious mustache.

We stared at each other. Smoke still curled out of my burning wounds, but neither the smoke nor the pain or burning sensation increased.

Nothing happened.

I remembered the way the smoke had choked me the first time he had bitten me. That had been a worry. He had already proven he could simply kill me. But the night he'd taken Ben, Ben had told me what the weaver most wanted. Killing me was vital—but it was still secondary to finding out why he could not use Tilly's gift to take me over.

In any case, so far, air continued to flow easily in and out of my lungs.

"You do not look like much," the weaver said finally, his voice gravelly and rough.

"Nor do you," I answered. "Not in this form, anyway. What are you waiting for?"

"For the smoke to do its work," he told me, and I saw that his small beady eyes, mostly hidden under those eyebrows, looked identical to the sky-blue gemstone eyes that he had in his serpentine form.

I glanced down at my wounds and saw that the mists of smoke emerging from the breaks in my skin were thicker, as if I had smoke in my veins instead of blood. There was a viscosity to the smoke that I didn't like. The bite continued to burn painfully.

"What are you waiting for?" asked Adam—asked me, even though he was echoing my words to the smoke weaver. This was where I had planned to call upon the power of the pack.

Cheating is an honored part of any fae bargain—but you can't cheat by breaking your word. *To test your power against mine,* I'd said. I realized that I was hesitating because I was worried about breaking my word.

The pack was a part of my power. I fixed that idea in my head and believed it. It seemed like a very good idea that when dealing with fae bargains, I should be very clear in my own mind why the way I was cheating was not breaking my word.

And it was true that each member of the pack enjoyed the strength of the whole—and I was pack. With that thought in my mind, I called to the ties that bound me to the pack. Some instinct pushed me beyond that, though, and I called upon the mating bond and the bond with Stefan, though I knew that both were compromised. Damaged bonds still belonged to me.

303

Something else stirred, too, but it wasn't unfriendly so I let that be for now. I had other things to worry about.

I did not pull magic, or even power, from my bonds with the pack: I pulled will. We, the Columbia Basin Pack, called no one our master. We lived and died by the will of our Alpha and no other.

As sometimes happened, especially when I had been spending so much time there recently, I found myself standing in the otherness without meaning to. This time, as soon as I stood in that place, the bite from the smoke weaver flared up from slow burn to hot coal and I couldn't help but cry out at the agony of it.

Sweat beaded on my forehead and I had to work to keep my feet, balancing myself by pulling on the garlands I held fisted in my right hand—the pack bonds.

And at that moment, when my balance was fragile and the pain off the scale, I felt another's will press down upon me with suffocating force. Unexpected force.

When I'd brought Stefan here, the weaver had not been able to follow him. One of my contingency plans, should I not be able to resist the weaver's bite using the pack, had been to come here and see if I had other options to fight him with.

The power and unexpectedness of the attack made me stumble sideways and I knew, with absolute conviction, that falling would mean something a great deal worse than a mere scraped knee. In my spiritual place, things like falls could have symbolic consequences that had nothing to do with forces like gravity. Sometimes that was a good thing—but my instincts told me that falling while my body was filling with smoke would be a Very Bad Idea.

Knowing doom was coming and preventing it were two different things.

Fortunately, I was not all alone. Something tightened around my waist and lit my spine with a shiver of strength. I looked down and saw my mate bond. It was still red and rough and closed to me, but it was thicker than it had been when last I saw it. My right ankle had a creamy lace cuff, Stefan's bond, that helped my right foot find balance when my left foot threatened to slip, despite the steadying effect of my tie to Adam.

Once I was solid on my feet, the pressure of that other mind didn't feel so overwhelming. I took a deep breath and realized that the otherness I stood in was different.

Not that my otherness was ever exactly the same place twice, but usually it was based on a forest. Sometimes that forest was pretty weird—like diamond-encrusted trees that wept or grass that was knitting needles.

But this time, I stood in a great cave—a cave that was filling with smoke—and the smoke felt very wrong. It did not belong here—and it was boiling out of the wounds in my chest.

What is this place? asked the smoke, swirling in delight. *I do like this. This has so many possibilities.*

The pressure in my head lightened, the burning of the wounds fading as the smoke poured out of me and into my spiritual home. I had a feeling that wasn't really an improvement, even though the surcease of pain was welcome.

The smoke ran down the glittery garlands of my pack bonds. As it touched them, the bonds sparked with alien magic, revealing the wolves on the other side of those bonds. They stood unmoving, like life-sized glass figures. I was all too aware that those figures were hollow—like blown glass. So fragile.

Long strands of graceful red garland wrapped precisely around Auriele and Darryl, binding them together. That red garland formed a braid as it stretched from them toward me.

Ben stood with his head bowed, leaning forward as if bracing himself against something I couldn't perceive. His glass was not clear, and was instead the bright blue of the weaver's serpent eyes. But his white garland, his pack bond, was solid.

Honey stood strong and resolute. Her right hand was held up and forward, extending the green-and-silver garland toward me. Her left arm was held a little behind her, and that hand held a few strands of tarnished tinsel that drifted limply in the light breeze that filled the cave.

Each and every member of our pack was caught in a single frame of their lives. Some of them, like Mary Jo and George, were in their wolf form. Joel was, surprisingly, his human self, and part of me knew that I'd been worried about him, but I couldn't remember why just then.

All of those strands ended in my mate's right hand. And they reappeared in his left hand, which was extended to me. His head was turned toward me. The half of his body nearest to the pack was his own, strong and true. The half of his body nearest to me was the body of the monster. His head was his own human self—his expression caught midscream. The clear glass that was his shell was spiderwebbed with fractures.

The smoke filled the cave rapidly, first covering the floor and then rising to waist height. It curled around Adam like a cat at the cream.

Ooo, it said. *Pretty. And broken.*

At that moment, I realized that the smoke didn't belong to the weaver. It was familiar, though. Underhill. I had invited Stefan to my otherness, and he had come alone. But when I'd come here, filled with the power of the weaver's bite, power that was a gift from Underhill, the power had come with me, leaving the weaver behind.

As I watched, she started to penetrate the fractures in my mate's altered body.

I needed to stop that—but I was trapped where I was by the bonds that allowed me to keep my feet and resist that smoke. I strained helplessly, but I could not reach Adam.

And that was when that niggling presence I'd felt—that presence that was not pack, not Stefan, but bound to me anyway, by thin spidersilk that smelled of fae magic—that presence whispered in my ear.

Let me Be. *I can help you, if you will only let me* Be.

I chose not to answer it because taking up that new bargain felt dangerous. Instead I addressed the interloper.

"Go home, Tilly. You are not welcome here," I said firmly.

Tilly's voice was much louder than that other, secret whisper. The sound echoed in the hollow cave when she asked, *How can I be unwelcome when you brought me here yourself?*

"Not willingly or knowingly," I said firmly. "Go home."

You can't make me go, she said, and the smoke near Adam became nearly solid and formed Underhill's human avatar. Here, her hair was not dirty and her clothes were not tattered. She turned to Adam's form and bent to the ground, picking up a rock from the cavern floor.

I held out my left hand, which was empty, as if I had known from the beginning that I would need it for something other than holding the ties to my beloveds. And I understood who and what that small secret voice was, and why what I was about to do was dangerous. Maybe I should have thought it over, but Underhill had a rock and my mate was already a little broken.

I said, "*Come.*"

And in my hand a familiar weight settled, so light for the

power it represented in this place where love and hatred meant more than earthly forces like gravity or magic. I pointed Lugh's walking stick toward the smoke assaulting Adam's battered form. Light traced through the runes on the old gray wood and lingered on the silver on the blunt ends of the walking stick.

Find your way home, the walking stick told Underhill as lightning arced into the center of her chest. Its voice was still a whisper, but somehow it rang through the air as definite as and bigger somehow than the lightning that preceded it.

Momentarily, almost as if altered by a stray breeze, Tilly's face softened, then formed a grimace of rage. But as I stepped forward, able at last to move, pointing the walking stick toward her as if I were an extra on a Harry Potter film with an unusually big wand, her body became smoke. Then the smoke retreated, first folding in upon itself and then disappearing altogether.

As the smoke vanished, the glass figures vanished, too. The cave gave way to open air. Between one instant and the next, I stood in the dark heart of a small grove of oak trees. I could feel the ties, but I could not, in this moment, see them. I was alone, except for the walking stick, which was very pleased with itself.

"Mercy." Adam's voice recalled me to the real world.

Breathing heavily, sweat pouring off me, and both hands empty, I looked down to see that the wounds on my shoulder no longer bled. I blinked a couple more times before I could orient myself.

I stood once more on an asphalt driveway. Adam stood between me and the enraged, ugly little man who was screaming in a voice that must have had some magic in it to sound so sharp and wrong.

"I'm here," I said, because Adam's back was to me. Only

afterward did I realize that had probably been the wrong thing to say. To the perception of anyone watching, I had never gone away. "I'm fine. I'm still me."

I flexed my fingers, still feeling the impression of the walking stick in my hand—but there was nothing there.

"Stole it! She stole it!" the weaver screamed.

For a moment I thought that he was talking about the walking stick—then I realized that he meant the power that had followed me to my other place and had not come back to him. I noticed that the smoke was entirely gone from the circle—although the circle, stretching over our heads like a giant snow globe made with darkened glass, was still in place.

Ben, Luke, and Kelly were on their feet. Kelly held the chain to Ben's collar, but they were all staring at the little man and his very noisy rage.

There was no more pillar of rock. Only a cluster of people on their knees beside a very still body. That was something I would have to worry about later.

And the little man raged on.

"*Quiet,*" my mate thundered, the power of an Alpha werewolf in his voice.

And it was evidently as effective on very angry little men as it was on a restless pack of wolves. The weaver stopped his tantrum, though his whole body shook with the effort, his skin, where it showed, several shades redder than his hair.

"I have completed the second part of our bargain," I said into the sudden silence.

"You never said you would *steal* it," the weaver said in despair. "It was mine. Fair and square. I bargained for it. You can't take it."

"Underhill is what she is," I told him. "She isn't a personage, though it pleases her to pretend. Any magic, any power that is hers, remains hers even if she lent it to you. You pushed it all inside me. When all of it was in me, and you held none of it—it became hers once more. It has returned back to where it came from."

Adam, once he had determined that the weaver was no longer a physical threat to me, stepped aside. We faced each other, the weaver and I.

"I have completed the second part of our bargain," I said again. "You came here in your own blood and bone. You bit me and failed, once more, to hold me. Now, as agreed, I will answer one question and then give you one truth. Ask me your question, smoke weaver."

"Why you?" he asked. "Why were you able to resist my power? And you the second person I bit after my escape? How did chance favor me so ill?"

In words it was more than one question—but it felt like they were twined together—something that would balance the truth I would have for him after I answered. For the first time, I really felt the power of a fae bargain. Because certain things became very clear to me that had not been clear until he asked his question. I didn't gain new knowledge, but all the bits and pieces seemed to gather together. I just had not realized, until the weaver's question, how much I actually knew.

"I was supposed to be the first person you bit," I told him.

Underhill had driven me out of my own house, hadn't she? Just after the weaver escaped. She could not break her bargain with the weaver, but she could cheat.

"Your power came from Underhill—was a part of Underhill,"

I told him. "And so it was limited by her limitations. Had you bitten me while I was standing in Underhill's own realm, I might be in your power now. But this is not the heart of Underhill's power." And where I had unwittingly taken her magic was the heart of mine.

"Why you?" repeated the weaver.

"Because I am Coyote's daughter," I told him, though that would mean nothing to him, trapped as he'd been in Underhill. So I explained in a way he could understand. "My father is a primal power and he has jurisdiction over certain spiritual magics. He is an agent of chaos. Underhill's magic, wielded secondhand, could not prevail over that." Not in my otherness.

"I would have killed you if it had not been for the vampire," growled the weaver bitterly. "You are not that powerful."

I nodded. "Yes. Not by myself. But my mate, my pack, and my friends and allies are part of my power. That the vampire saved me was because of my own earlier actions. He was something I had the right to call upon."

"Accepted," said the weaver sadly. "Your answer is full and whole truth. Give me then your truth that I have not asked for, would not ask for."

He knew, I thought.

"There is a more complete answer for your question than what I have given you," I told him. He was right, I didn't owe him more. But I felt that I needed to give it to him to keep the balance of our bargain. It was insight that I wouldn't have had without our bargain, after all. "Underhill released you on purpose—you did not escape against her will. She is girding up for war and so collecting all the bits of herself that she had used to make better playthings."

The fae aren't playing nice, Tilly had told Aiden when she first put the door in our backyard.

The weaver looked up at me.

"She had intended her bargain with you to be small. She told me so. She carefully found something that you wanted—to be able to appear human so you could more easily blend in with humanity."

"To make better bargains," agreed the weaver. "Bargains are more necessary to me than soup or bread. Better that I should starve than to have no one to bargain with."

"She made a mistake. The power she gave you was no small thing." I thought of how I had perceived the smoke in my otherness, how immense and heavy it had felt. It had contained so much of Underhill that she had been able to manifest in the heart of my spirit.

To the weaver I said, "She did not understand how much power she must give up to allow you to overcome another's will, to steal their spirit. And she feels that she needs that power now. She used me to cheat you of your due. But she did it without breaking your bargain. You lost the gift she gave you; she did not take it from you."

That was behind the avarice she felt when she looked at Aiden, as well. If the weaver had consumed a noticeable amount of her magic—how much more of her magic did Aiden hold?

The weaver nodded slowly. "I understand. Now your truth?"

He looked small and powerless—an object of pity.

I turned my head to watch Nonnie Palsic pull James up to a sitting position. Saw him turn his head and heard his voice, soft and rough, say, "Nonnie."

I thought of Anna and Dennis, of Ben who had had all the

trauma he ever needed in his life well before the weaver had bitten him, of Stefan helpless—bound and tortured. Of a young hitch-hiker and Lincoln, a wolf I didn't know but whom James Palsic had mourned.

"Your name," I said, "is Rumpelstiltskin." And then, because it felt like the right thing to do, I said it two more times, pronouncing it carefully each time. "Rumpelstiltskin. Rumpelstiltskin."

In the story, the little man danced about in a rage until the earth opened up beneath his feet and swallowed him, never to be heard from again. Today, the little weaver's rage was spent, but the earth still opened up and swallowed him, shaking under my feet and sending me staggering forward. If Adam's strong hand had not grabbed my wrist, I might have fallen in as well.

That was twice he'd stopped me from falling to my doom. Or at least to my harm. Adam was good at saving people other than himself.

The earth closed again with a final crack, leaving only a thin break in the asphalt of the circular drive where the hole had been.

A voice by my elbow said, "That was fun."

I looked down at Tilly without favor. I swallowed the first three things I wanted to say because none of them would have been smart. Duplicitous, sneaky, and horrible she might be. But she was unimaginably powerful, and old, and we still had to hold to our bargain, another bargain, to make Aiden available to her.

Adam was watching me, letting me take point on this one because I had just demonstrated that I had a little more information than he did.

"I wish you hadn't given him the answer to his question quite as thoroughly as you did," she continued when I didn't say anything. "He's not going to be as fun a playmate as he usually is, at least not for a while. He knows how to hold a grudge."

"How is it that you are able to come here?" I asked, because it was worrisome. There was a limit to the distance she could travel from one of her doorways—or so I had been led to believe. "There is no door to your realm near this place."

"No," she agreed sadly. "But he drew this circle we stand in with power he got from me." She frowned up at me. "I did not intend for you to figure that out."

"I imagine not," I told her.

"Mercedes Thompson Hauptman," she purred with one of her mercurial mood changes. "You are more interesting than I imagined."

And the circle broke. The sun brought light, a breeze blew away the last remnant of smoke—and Tilly disappeared with a crack that sounded like a great rock breaking in half.

Ben said, "Get this freaking collar off me. And get me a phone. We need to check on the house. He was in my head you—you nitwits. And he had Harolford like he had me. Harolford and Fiona *knew* we left the house, left the children, the humans with only Joel to protect them. They *knew*. And I couldn't get you to pay attention, to *listen* to me." As if to make up for the "freaking" and "nitwits," he devolved into a solid stream of swear words.

I lost the gist of what he was saying because I was sprinting for Jesse's car, where I'd left my cell phone.

I had twelve missed calls. I called Lucia on the grounds that she would know what had happened and no one else here would try calling her first. She picked up on the second ring.

"They came," she said, not waiting for me to say anything. "A woman and a man. They shot Joel—he is fine. One thing that tibicena spirit is good for is that it takes more than a bullet to hurt my Joel. Libby grabbed one of the rifles from your gun safe and, from your upstairs window, she shot the man who had the gun. The female carried him back to their car and they left."

I sucked in a deep breath of relief and met Adam's gaze across the twenty yards of driveway—because even as I'd run for my car, Adam had run for the SUV. He, too, had a phone against his ear. I gave him a thumbs-up.

He nodded, then went back to his call.

JAMES WAS GOING TO SURVIVE. ADAM OFFERED THEM all a place in the pack if they wanted it.

James shook his head. "Not that I'm not grateful," he wheezed. "But I had a couple of hours that felt like a year to contemplate what you-all go through living in Crazytown. Bran invited us to Montana. Said we could take some time up there to catch our breath. Maybe find another good pack in a few months."

"Or years," said Nonnie.

James nodded, pointing a finger in her direction.

Kent got to his feet. "Fi and Sven won't be best pleased with us. If we are going to go, I suggest we go now. We're packed. I'll get the car, and Li Qiang and I will get it loaded."

"Careful," said James. "That's what I was doing and then 'poof,' I was a rock."

I called Bran to tell him they were coming, and watched Adam's face out of the corner of my eye. There was a white line on his cheek from the clenching of his teeth.

I hung up. "He says someone will meet you in Spokane to escort you the rest of the way. That way you aren't trying to drive the dirt roads in the mountains of Montana in the middle of the night."

I gave Bran's number to Nonnie—James's phone had not survived its time as part of a rock. And I gave her the number of the pack member they would meet in Spokane.

We saw them off. They drove an Accord with a V6. I don't know what happened to the bug I'd repaired for James.

Once they were gone, we dusted ourselves off and looked at our available rides home.

"My car is fine," Jesse said cheerfully. "Dad, you and Mercy have got to take better care of your stuff. Do you think that money grows on trees?"

JOEL TOOK A FEW HOURS TO DOWNGRADE FROM HIS tibicena form to the presa Canario. But the more-mortal dog showed no signs of having been shot. A few hours later—without help from Aiden—Joel was able to wear his human self for the rest of the night. Despite Adam's belief that Joel's unexpectedly long stint as a human was a result of the time Joel had spent in tibicena form, any number of the pack offered to shoot him again—or get Libby, the sharpshooting heroine of the hour, to do it.

I called Beauclaire and told him most of what happened to Rumpelstiltskin. And warned him that Underhill was amassing power for something.

"Yes," he said, "we have noticed."

I almost said, *Thanks for the warning*, but not thanking the fae is a good general rule for people who want to live a healthy and free life. The same could probably be said for sarcasm.

Instead I said, carefully, "The clues that you gave to me when we talked were instrumental in allowing me to identify Rumpelstiltskin."

"I am happy that I was of service," he said.

"May I ask one question?"

"Of course."

"Why did Rumpelstiltskin's magic not feel like fae magic to me?"

"He is of an older lineage. Most of them were gone when I first came to the earth—and that was a good long time ago. The reason he survives is probably because of the friendship he developed with Underhill."

"Friendship?" I said.

"Not all relationships look alike," he said.

"Indeed," I agreed. "Are we friends?" I probably should have waited until I'd had a good night's sleep before calling him, I thought. That was not a safe question.

He laughed. "Perhaps tentative allies? Definitions are not always useful, are they? Mercedes, thank you for dealing with the smoke weaver. We will open our gates at dawn and allow our people to go about their business."

He had thanked me. I wasn't sure what that meant.

"Good," I said.

I called Marsilia next, but she did not pick up the phone. Five minutes later she called Adam.

He told her basically the same story I'd just conveyed to Beauclaire—edited for the audience.

"Ah, that explains Stefan's sudden improvement," she told him. "We despaired of his survival the past few nights, but he held on."

I remembered how bad he had been when I'd seen him in my otherness. "Can we go see him?"

She heard me. "No. He wouldn't want you to see him this way. I will call you as soon as he is better—or should he worsen again."

And I had to be satisfied with that.

Like Stefan, Ben didn't just step back into who he had been before the weaver had taken him. Being in someone else's power was pretty much a reliving of his worst nightmare. He had four weeks of vacation time built up at work, and he took those and stayed with us.

The goblins found Harolford's body in a shallow grave near the river. Dead from a silver bullet wound, presumably Libby's. I asked, but all of the witnesses were pretty sure that Fiona could not have known who it was that shot him.

The goblins did not bring us the body. They texted photos to Adam's phone. When Adam asked what they'd done with it, Larry the goblin king laughed and said, "Finders keepers," before he disconnected.

Fiona was still a problem.

We stayed on high alert and bunked up for the three days following the banishing of the smoke weaver. But when Charles called with news that Fiona had been sighted in Wichita, Adam told everyone to go back to normal.

"People can only stay alert for so long," he told me. "And she is only one werewolf."

"Charles is only one werewolf," I told him, and he laughed.

Adam was doing . . . "better" was the wrong word. More stable was probably closer to the answer. There had been no further appearances of the monster, and when the moon hunt came, Adam wore his wolf's form just as he usually did.

But I had seen his wolf fading, and I worried. The pack was uneasy, though no violence broke out. Adam still would not open our bond. But he put back on some of the weight he had lost and he did not seem to be getting worse, so I bided my time. I had a date circled on the calendar—and if matters did not change, I was going to have another conversation with Bran.

A month went by. Jesse started school and began looking for an apartment. Aiden started school, too.

We enrolled him in sixth grade, which was a compromise. He would look younger than most of his schoolmates but not so much so as to be an outcast. Tutoring by Jesse and the pack had brought his math skills up to high school level, but his reading skills were below sixth-grade level. The translation spell did not help him read or write in English.

We had none of the paperwork for him, but Adam and I sat down with the school district superintendent and told him the whole story, a heavily edited version of the whole story. We didn't tell him about the fire, just that we'd found Aiden in Underhill, where he'd been trapped for a very long time. We didn't tell him that Aiden could burn the school down if he wanted to. I figured that most kids in sixth grade *could* burn down a school if they wanted to anyway—they would just have to work a little harder at it than Aiden would.

The superintendent agreed that the circumstances were unusual and gave us a paperwork path to follow that would let Aiden start school. We managed to get it done (thanks to Kyle, who knew family law and could make it dance to his tune), and Aiden made it to the first day.

There were a few rough patches the first month of school, but Aiden finally settled in with a group of computer gamers. He still had those moments that reminded me that he was centuries older than he appeared, but mostly he looked happy.

I didn't visit Stefan, but he called me twice and sounded nearly himself the second time. He said that the hope I'd given him was still helping him cope. I didn't know what to say to that.

"I didn't want to lose you," I said, finally.

"Thank you," he'd said. And he'd disconnected shortly thereafter.

The pack killed a pair of ghouls who had tried to settle in near Lourdes Medical Center in Pasco. Apparently hospitals are a favorite hunting ground of ghouls. We helped Marsilia roust a couple of itinerant vampires who tried to set up shop in West Richland. Renny started coming to Sunday breakfasts with Mary Jo and struck up an unlikely friendship with Ben, our candidate for wolf most likely to end up in jail. Anna's ghost waved at me whenever I drove past my old place. I didn't wave back.

Life happened. And we forgot to worry about Fiona.

14

I COULDN'T SLEEP.

A heavy arm wrapped around my shoulders.

"Feeling restless?" The growl in Adam's voice made my toes curl—they knew what that roughness meant and they liked it.

So did I.

"Yes," I answered, my own voice a purr.

"I can help with that," he promised. And boy did he.

His efforts were above and beyond to the point that when his phone rang in the middle of the night, I only woke up long enough to hear a bit of the conversation.

"—false alarm, probably, sir, cameras don't—"

There was no stress in Adam's employee's voice and it didn't sound urgent, so I went back to sleep.

I woke up when Adam patted my butt. I cracked my eye open suspiciously and he laughed.

"Not waking you up for that again—not that it wasn't fun. But we have some equipment problems. The alarms at the garage are going off again, though the cameras aren't showing anything."

The system at my garage had been developing quirks over the last couple of weeks. His IT people couldn't run it down closer than "an intermittent glitch." Adam had finally ordered a whole new system, but it wouldn't be in for a couple of weeks.

"I'm going to check in on that, then drive out to work and give my people a surprise visit." He did those to keep his people on their toes. And to let them know that he wasn't asking them to do anything he wouldn't do—because on his surprise visits, he'd sometimes pick a random pair of guards and do their patrols with them. Sure enough he continued, "I'll be out most of the day. I have a couple of new people to torment."

I grunted at him.

"Why don't you sleep in this morning?" he said.

"How is it that you are this cheerful?" I asked him plaintively. "You didn't get any more sleep than I did."

"I am male," he said, and wiggled his eyebrows like the villain from a B horror movie. "Sex is better than sleep."

"Go away," I moaned, rolling over to bury my face in my pillow.

He laughed and started to do that.

"But kiss me first."

He rolled me back over and did that, too.

When my alarm went off an hour later, I was really tempted to sleep in. Then I remembered that it was Saturday and I would be the only one at work.

Jesse and her friends were going to a concert in Seattle. Adam had fretted about security—so Jesse had called Tad and invited him along as her "muscle." Which was all well and good, but it left me alone to mind the shop. I could have asked Zee to come in, but he had a project of some sort going on and told me not to bother him for a couple of weeks.

My official hours didn't start until noon on Saturday, but I had some cars to finish up and a boatload of paperwork. After a recent IRS audit, I was religious about my paperwork. In the end, I owed them $452.00, which they had graciously rounded down from $452.34. But at one point, before I finally located a box of receipts where I'd used it to balance a transmission, they had claimed I owed them a little over six thousand dollars. Which meant, my accountant (Lucia) pointed out, if I could have found the other missing box, the government would probably have owed me money.

So off to work I needed to go.

I felt better after a shower and some painkiller to ease away the ache of repeated vigorous nighttime activity. I paused as I was brushing my teeth. I never used to have to resort to painkillers. Was I getting old? Or had Adam started to use sex to make up for the fact he was keeping our bond closed down?

Hmm.

When I got to the garage, it was still early enough that the lights in the parking lot were on. I waved to the camera and imagined Carlos or Butch—or Adam—waving back. The office, when I let myself in, smelled overwhelmingly of gasoline.

I grimaced. Fuel odors were par for the course when running a garage—and at least gasoline was volatile and would clear pretty quickly once I opened the bay doors.

I'd parked a '62 Mercedes convertible in the garage last night for safekeeping, and I assumed that was where the fuel smell was coming from. It belonged to a local car collector, the prize of his collection, and it was in for its annual checkup. It wasn't surprising that it had developed a fuel line problem. Even the best auto engineers in the world didn't factor in better than a half century of use.

It was a little odd that Adam hadn't called me about it when he'd been here earlier to check the security system—but he knew I was planning on coming in early. And he knew that he'd left me short of sleep.

I was smiling as I tucked my purse in the safe and locked it. The safe was on the floor under the counter and my back twinged as I stood up. I stretched, touched my toes, and the ache dissipated. The stiff muscles clinched it, though. I would start with finding the fuel line problem, and that would give me plenty of opportunity to work out any lingering stiffness before I started on paperwork.

I turned on the stereo and found a soft-rock station. I hummed along with "Spirit in the Sky," a song nearly as old as the '62 Mercedes, as I opened the door to the bays.

"Hello, Mercedes Thompson," Fiona said. "We have some business to conduct."

She'd been waiting on the far side of the garage, where she had a clear shot at me. And she was standing in classic shooter position with—if I was not mistaken—Adam's carry gun in her hands.

I took a moment to assess the situation.

A gas can had been overturned near the door, leaving a puddle of gasoline—designed to keep me from scenting an intruder. To keep Adam from realizing that he wasn't alone, too. In the corner where the real brains of the security system lurked, Adam lay unmoving on the ground.

He wasn't dead, I told my panicking soul. I would know if he were dead.

"If you cooperate," she said, "I will not kill either of you today.

"There is a chair," she said. "Go sit down."

A couple of weeks ago I'd pulled one of the sturdy metal chairs from the office into the bays—I couldn't remember offhand just why. She had set it in front of the lift in bay one. And on the ground around it were cuffs and chains that looked very businesslike.

I glanced again at Adam—he was breathing.

"Don't worry, *your* mate is alive. He'll stay that way if you follow my directions." She wasn't lying.

"What did you do to him?" I asked.

"Ketamine and silver," she said. "A little trick I learned along the way."

"Gerry Wallace has a lot to answer for," I said. Gerry had been the first to concoct a tranquilizer that would work on werewolves. But I felt a little better. The tranquilizer could be fatal if the silver concentration was too great. But Adam was an Alpha werewolf. It would take a lot of the tranquilizer to kill him.

"Sit in the chair, Mercy."

If I did that, all of my options were gone.

"The alarm glitches were you," I said, to engage her in conversation.

"There is a reason that 'The Boy Who Cried Wolf' is a classic," she answered. "I have a way with electronics." She nodded toward the corner where Adam and the heart of the surveillance system lay. "The video is currently playing a loop—after it replayed a segment of Adam coming in and leaving from a few days ago. His people won't know that there is anything wrong until they don't see you come in at noon."

"But you needed more than just to game the security system," I said. "This is not only your taking advantage of an opportunity. You had to watch us, track our habits—without anyone in a pack of werewolves noticing." I put a little admiration in my voice.

There is very little that arrogant people like more than an appreciative audience. At the moment, I didn't really care about reasons or methods; I was trying to buy time. I didn't know what I would do with it yet—that depended upon her and whatever opportunities she gave me.

"That was trickier," she acknowledged. "And more boring. Your house is supposed to be the home of a werewolf pack—so why are you teaching some kid to read? If I had to listen to another hour of '*H* is for *horse*,' I'd have to shoot someone. Do you know that you have a baby vampire who likes to watch your house?"

"Yes," I told her.

I'd thought she had watched us, but she'd done one better. She had bugged our house. Those lessons with Aiden took place in the kitchen, the heart of the home. But she hadn't managed to bug all of it, I didn't think. We didn't talk about Wulfe a lot because we didn't want to worry the pack, but he made sure that he didn't go unnoticed. Two days ago, I know that Adam and I had talked about Wulfe in our bedroom. If she had overheard us—or come face-to-face with him—she would never have referred to him as a "baby vampire."

After considering my words carefully, I said, "For the past few months we have had the government trying to bug our house on a regular basis. Adam does a daily sweep for bugs. How did you manage?"

I didn't mention the fact that there were werewolves in and out of the house at all hours. She could not have done it without magic—and I didn't remember her being able to use magic. Bran *would* have mentioned that when I talked to him. And magic . . . magic worried me. I thought about how she had called me by my married name that afternoon at Kelly's house. She had known me by my maiden name. If she and her group of lost wolves were searching for a pack to take over, I was not important except as a weakness to exploit. But, in retrospect, I realized she had looked at me like someone addressing a target.

"Not all listening devices are electronic," she told me. "I know a witch who specializes in surveillance."

Suddenly I was a lot more concerned about why Fiona was still here than I had been a few seconds ago. I reevaluated our interactions with Fiona and her pack, adding in witches, and some patterns started to make sense. A wolf trying to take over a pack would not make an alliance with a fae creature—which was why none of the rest of her wolves had known about the smoke weaver. Witchcraft explained why the goblins hadn't found Fiona or her people. Bran had told me that Fiona was selling her services to the highest bidder—and the witches certainly had reason to want revenge. Or worse. I had a bad feeling about why Adam and I weren't dead.

Fiona smiled at me; her expression would have been friendly if I hadn't been able to see her eyes. "Now that you have finished flattering me, go sit in that chair or I shoot Adam in the head. In that case, I'll have to kill you immediately, too, or risk getting caught by your pack. If you cooperate, I will not kill him. I know you can hear that I'm telling the truth. Now, you have three seconds. One . . ."

I sat in the chair. But not because she had started counting. Adam was coming around—I felt the draw on the pack bonds as he started fighting off the effects of the tranq.

I pulled the chair sideways a little so that it gave me a better view of Adam. Hopefully she'd think that was the only reason I'd done it. But it meant that while she was dealing with me, her back would be mostly toward him. I wanted her attention on me, though I didn't think she'd ignore him entirely. If he moved, she'd react. But there was a good chance that she would trust the drug. That tranq was nasty business—but Adam had encountered it before.

"Funny," she said. "But I don't care which direction you face."

I raised my eyebrows and turned the chair to face Adam directly.

"Put on the ankle chains," she said.

The ankle cuffs were nylon and looked to be standard-issue. With them on, I could use my legs with the same grace as the average mermaid on land. I deliberately fumbled with them to give Adam more time. The power that he was pulling made me dizzy. That draw alone was going to alert the pack that something was wrong. Almost as soon as I thought that, Adam's phone rang. Fiona's time had just been limited; all I had to do was keep her occupied until someone figured out where we were.

"And now the wrist cuffs."

She had used two old-fashioned metal handcuffs, attaching each one to opposite chair legs. The bracing on the chair legs ensured that the cuff wouldn't just slide off if I tipped the chair upside down.

She knew I wasn't a werewolf. Nylon cuffs wouldn't hold a werewolf at all. The metal handcuffs would last longer—and really tick off the werewolf who broke them, because breaking them would hurt. She knew that I could change into a coyote. She had called me "Bran's little coyote pet." But she didn't understand *what* I was, because otherwise she would know that the cuffs, any cuffs designed to hold a human, were worse than useless. Maybe she thought that it would take me a while to change shapes—the way it took a werewolf time.

As soon as I had the handcuffs on, she walked up to me. She bent down to tighten the cuffs on my ankles. Then, smiling, she pulled a collar out and wrapped it around my neck. It fit tightly enough that it was decidedly uncomfortable. I heard chain rattle as she attached that to the back of the chair. Unlike the cuffs, the collar would hold me, coyote or no, so maybe she hadn't underestimated me as much as I thought she had.

"Coyote's daughter, Kent told me," she said. "That explains a lot—like why Bran decided out of the goodness of his heart to let bleeding-heart Bryan adopt you. I wonder what Coyote did for Bran for the Marrok to make a deal like that."

I was pretty sure that it was my mother who had pushed Bran into accepting responsibility for me. But Fiona didn't know my mother, so I could see why she would look for someone else. Bran wasn't known for his soft heart.

"Kent?" I asked.

"He's one of mine," she told me. "Witchbound to my service like Sven was." She gave me a thoughtful look that I'd seen on other people's faces before. So I had my abs tight when she punched me in the stomach.

It hurt anyway. But she was a werewolf; if she had wanted to, she could have killed me with that blow.

"Hardesty family paying you?" I asked when I could breathe. I didn't want it to be them, especially when Fiona seemed interested in keeping me alive. I had close-up knowledge of the kinds of things black witches did with living victims, and I didn't know of any witches blacker than the ones in the Hardesty family.

Fiona smiled. "I understand you had a run-in with them recently. They are *very unhappy* with you. I might have been offered a reward should you die and a bigger reward for a live capture. They don't know what you are, Mercy—I haven't told them yet. But they know that you were the key in the deaths of their people—and they think that you might have been the one responsible for destroying a treasure that had taken them generations to build."

Zombies.

"Charles will hunt you down," I told her, and she flinched. She was afraid of Charles.

She should have been afraid of Adam. He had quit drawing power from the pack.

"The witches pay well enough that I can hide for generations if I need to—and they have promised protection, too." She gave me a sisterly smile. "But you and I know how far to trust the word of a black witch. I have some value for them, too; they like to play with werewolves. Too much to ever put myself in their power."

If she had let them witchbond people to her, she was already in their power. I didn't exactly know what she meant by the term, but I knew witches.

"Kent told you what happened with the smoke weaver?" I asked her. It didn't matter to me, but I needed to keep her attention on me. "Bastard. I trusted him." True enough to keep her from reading a lie. But the bite in my voice was fake—I didn't want her knowing that I was wasting time.

Something rose silently from the place where Adam had been lying. Something too big.

Oh, my love, what did you do?

But I knew. He'd had to pull everything he could to wash the silver and ketamine out of his system. He would not have been able to pull more to increase the speed of his shift usefully. Not to mention that she would have noticed if he had tried to shift to his wolf form—it was not a subtle thing. An unarmed human form against a werewolf with his own gun—the odds were not optimal. He'd have taken them, but he had another option.

I did not think it had taken him ten seconds to change from human to monster.

"Fucking Rumpelstiltskin," Fiona said. "What is the world coming to when you have to make deals with a damned fae and he turns out to be Rumpelstiltskin?"

"Rumpelstiltskin" was the last word Fiona ever said. A giant nightmarish monster landed on her from fifteen feet away and ate her neck in the same motion. The gun went off because she'd had her finger on the trigger. She was dead by then, but the gun had been pointed at me and the bullet hit me in the arm.

The monster that had been Adam dragged Fiona's body back into the corner with all the useless surveillance electronics and settled in to feed. Growling defensively, as if I might try to take his prey away.

I didn't need to see his eyes to know that Adam wasn't home. Adrenaline is the enemy of control for a werewolf, and Adam had had to build up adrenaline to fight the tranquilizer, even with the pack's help. He'd changed without a moment to spare for gathering his thoughts, centering himself. If he had changed to his wolf, I would have been surprised if Adam had managed to hang on to control under the circumstances. But that would have been okay. I was the mate of Adam and his wolf; neither of them would ever hurt me.

I did not think I shared that link with the monster.

I shifted to coyote and lost the wrist and ankle cuffs, but my neck was pretty much the same size in either form. I shifted back and found that the monster was staring at me. The sound of the cuffs hitting the floor must have attracted his attention.

He inhaled, nostrils flaring. I didn't know if he could smell my blood over the scent of gasoline. I met his eyes briefly—silver and bright like the moon—then quickly looked away and down.

He didn't make any sound, but I felt him come over to me. His nose touched the top of my head and trailed to my neck. I raised my chin and tilted my head, giving him free access to the pulse that beat wildly there. I was breathing in shallow, openmouthed pants because I was so scared.

I could smell Adam on him—but I could not smell the wolf. Just a sour musk that smelled like rage and hatred and witchcraft. It had grown stronger since I'd last met it. I had made a mistake in not calling Bran sooner.

Something warm and wet hit the top of my shoulder. Drool.

He bit my neck. If I hadn't been wearing that collar, I'd have been dead. I think there must have been silver in it because he yipped and then roared at me. I kept my eyes closed because I didn't want my last sight to be this creature, born of witchcraft and self-hatred. But he retreated back to his meal.

He was so precise in his movements, the chair hadn't even skidded on the floor. He'd bent the collar and it restricted my breathing now. The arm that had been shot wouldn't obey me. But I raised my free arm and felt around the collar. I found the latch—and the lock.

With two good hands and a lockpick I could have opened that thing up in a few seconds. If wishes were horses . . .

I could feel the stirring in the pack bonds—the rise of alarm. They would come here soon, and they would be able to take this monster down—if they worked together. If they didn't hesitate because it was Adam. But some people would die.

And I would be dead before they got here, because though he was eating again, his face was toward me, his eyes focusing on my exposed abdomen.

Blow up the bond, Bran had told me. And then refused to

explain what he meant. And he'd given me that advice without a full explanation of the extent of the problem.

It wasn't like I had a lot of options.

I closed my eyes again, because I couldn't do this with the monster staring at me. Then I put myself in the place where I could see the bonds.

The pack bonds exploded into sound, as if I'd stepped into a firehouse in the middle of an all-hands three-alarm fire. I told them, "Not now—hush." And the otherness quieted.

I stood ankle-deep in a creek so cold it made my feet ache; the bond I shared with Stefan was still wrapped around one ankle and I felt his attention on me even though it was daylight and he should be dead for the day. I could have called him to me, I thought. Stefan would not hesitate when faced with the monster my mate had become.

"No," I told him. "Not now."

The bond around my waist was grotesque and repulsive, the red skin cracked open in places and oozing green slime.

I opened my mouth and pulled out a diamond the size of a baseball. It had been faceted into a princess cut and was clear and flawless—and cold.

I pressed my lips against it to warm it. And I told it the same thing I had told the wolf when I fed him the amethyst.

"I love you," I said.

This was a place where words were powerful things, and feelings even more so. What I imbued that diamond with was more than the words I spoke—it was the huge ball of emotion that those words invoked in me: all the memories, the laughter, the joy.

When I took my mouth away and looked at the gemstone again, it glowed with every color I could imagine. I cupped it in both of my hands and told it sternly, "I am going to feed you into my mating bond—and you are going to blow it wide open for me."

The pearl had been a soft thing; the diamond was a more suitable weapon. I used the pointed end—which was sharper than any reputable gem cutter would have left—to widen one of the damaged places in the mating bond. When I had a hole big enough, I shoved the gemstone inside. The slick green slime acted as lubricant, making my job easier. When the gemstone was entirely covered, I rubbed the poor bond apologetically as the green slime hardened, sealing the wound.

"Not your fault," I told it. "We'll fix this."

I waited for a long time, watching the bump that was the gemstone slide toward Adam's side of our bond. When it felt like the right time, I said, *"Now."*

And the world went white.

I EXPECTED TO WAKE UP BACK IN THE GARAGE, BUT that's not what happened.

I woke up lying on a stone table in a small . . . What was the proper term for a building that had a floor and ceiling but no walls, just archways that held up the roof? It had the form of a temple—though there was no sense of worship here.

The floor and archways—and the stone table I occupied—were hewn from a tawny sandstone the color of a lion's pelt. The whole building sparkled a little in the afternoon sun.

I sat up. I was wearing something that looked very much like the toga I may or may not have worn to a toga party in my dorm when I was a freshman in college. It was the same color as the sandstone right down to the sparkle.

I found that my hands and arms were bedecked with jewels. And there were gemstones on the sandals I wore, too. I stood up and walked over to the edge of the building, and a beautifully carved waist-high barrier appeared in front of me—as if it had always been there and I just hadn't noticed it.

The air was sweet-smelling and the temperature perfect. In the corner of the room on a small table was food and drink. Music began to play, something catchy from the big band era that Adam was still secretly fond of.

"This is ridiculous, Adam," I said.

Because I was in Adam's otherness—on the far side of our bond. I had no real way to be sure of it—I hadn't thought that anyone else even had this weird place they could go to. But my instincts had never steered me wrong, and in the otherness, instincts were strong enough to feel like a guide through the weirdness. I was in Adam's space and, even here, he was trying to protect me.

Below the hill I was on, I could hear mortar fire. I'd never been on a battlefield—not an official battlefield—but I'd seen the movies. I knew what mortar fire sounded like.

I kicked off the shoes, hitched a hip on the barricade, and landed on the hill beyond. The big band music accompanied me as I walked for about a mile on a path that kept trying to take me back up to the top of the hill.

Finally, I stood still, put my hands on my hips, and said, "Adam, that's enough."

Then I stepped off the path and began wading through the dense foliage. About four paces into the woods, the music quieted and a path formed under my bare feet. This path took me down into a valley filled with dead bodies.

I picked my way through them. Some of them I knew. Paul. Mac.

Peter. Others I'd seen pictures of. People from Adam's military past. People who had worked for him. There was a whole section of people in Vietnam-era US military uniforms; some of them were missing body parts—and some of those had the parts they were missing stacked at their feet. Another section was filled with people I was pretty sure were Vietnamese—though that was not an ethnicity I had much experience with. Some of these were in uniform; some of them were not. Every face was unique. I had absolutely no doubt that every body corresponded to a person that Adam had killed—or he felt responsible for their death in some way. Adam organized his guilt in neat rows.

And then there was the field of children—maybe twenty in all. Some of these had faces, but some were featureless, as if there was a blanket of skin hiding who they were.

"That's because I didn't see all of their faces," Adam told me. "The Vietcong used children—so did the South Vietnamese, for that matter. I don't keep the adults whose faces I never saw—but the children were different." He pointed to one faceless body. "That one was up in a tree, keeping us pinned down for two days. I shot him, but Christiansen was the one who found the body and told me our sniper had been a kid. I never saw his body—but I should have gone to find him myself. I was the one who killed him." He gazed out at the row after row of his dead and said, "I owed it to that boy to look at what I had done, but I chose not to."

I reached out to hold Adam's hand, but he stepped away from me. When I turned to face him, I was back on the top of the hill, in the building without walls, but this time there was no sunlight. A rainstorm thundered all around and I was not alone.

Elizaveta Arkadyevna Vyshnevetskaya stood with one hand on the stone barrier, the other holding an apple from the plate on the little table. She, like me, was wearing a toga, but hers was burgundy. Most of the time that I had known her, she'd been an old woman. Here, as on the day she had died, she was young and beautiful.

"He doesn't keep me in his garden of failures," she told me. "I wonder why that is."

"Because he does not regret your death," I told her, but I knew as soon as I said it that it wasn't quite right.

"No," she said. "Because you absolved him of my death."

"You think I am perfect," said Adam's voice behind me. "Beautiful, even. I need to be perfect for you."

"Or she won't love you," said Elizaveta, and here in the otherness her voice had a power that tried to seep into my bones. "She needs you to be her hero, Adam. As beautiful and perfect as your face. You don't want to hurt her with your darkness, do you, Adam? And you carry so much ugly darkness inside you, don't you?"

"Buddy," I said, turning my back to Elizaveta to face Adam, though leaving her behind me made my skin crawl. "If you think I believe that you are perfect, you've got another think coming."

He stood on the other side of the room, and I noticed that that corner of the building was falling apart. The roof was not even sufficient to keep the rain off him.

Off the monster.

He was bound—as I had been bound—to a metal chair, larger than the one in my garage to accommodate his size. And the bindings weren't handcuffs and nylon leg cuffs; they were vines of thorns that smelled of black magic.

"Don't free me," Adam said urgently. "I will destroy you; I destroy everything I touch." He looked away from me. In a low voice he said, "I didn't want you to see me like this."

Elizaveta walked behind him and bent down to whisper in his

ear. I couldn't hear what she said, but Adam looked at me and spoke. "You are so perfect, so strong, my Mercy. I don't deserve you."

"Perfect?" I asked. I looked down at myself and realized that I was missing a few things.

"Ahem," I said, addressing neither Adam nor Elizaveta, but the otherness that made this confrontation possible. "I survived the wounds that gave me my scars; I would like them back, please."

It felt as though a finger touched my skin with sparkly pain that faded quickly but left the marks of my life behind. When it was finished—and I deliberately chose not to hear the faint laughing cry that might have belonged to a coyote—I peeled off my toga and displayed my imperfect self to Adam.

"I jump into things before I think about how it will affect other people," I told him. "I am prickly and overreact when you try to protect me because I don't want to trust anyone to have my back. I dislike your ex-wife and won't make an effort to get along with her anymore—no matter how much easier that would make everyone's life."

I took a deep breath. "I hurt you because sometimes I need to walk out on my own." I frowned at him. "And I'm not going to change any of it—though it would make your life better."

"And you like to make me mad," Adam said in a whisper. "Even though you know I'm dangerous when I'm mad."

I smiled at him and nodded. "Yes. That's your fault, though. I wouldn't do it if you weren't so sexy when you're mad. And I love the knowledge that no matter how angry you are, you would never hurt me."

Elizaveta bent to whisper in his ear again, but I took the walking stick in my hand. I noticed that it had made itself into a spear, as it sometimes did when I needed a sharp weapon. I thrust it into her, forcing her away from Adam. The spear sank deep, and blood the color of her toga bubbled out of the wound. I shoved her into the balustrade.

"You are dead," I told her. "Go away."

She tried to say something, and a viper fell out from between her lips followed by two asps, and then she faded away. The spear had no trouble killing the snakes. I liked snakes. If these hadn't come from Elizaveta, I'd have let them be. But I didn't want to leave anything of Elizaveta's free to roam about in Adam's otherness.

I turned to Adam again—and the vines and the chair were gone, the smell of black magic replaced by pine with a hint of mint. But Adam still wore the monster's guise, wounds weeping where the thorns of Elizaveta's vines had dug in.

"I am ugly inside," he told me.

"Me, too," I said. "And I'm not as pretty as you are on the outside, either."

"I'm jealous and spiteful," he said. "I don't like it when men call you. When Bran calls you—or Beauclaire."

I nodded. "I'm jealous, too. And I think I outmatch you for spite. I hate that Christy was your wife and is Jesse's mother." I looked around and then grabbed his horrible hand and dragged him to the balustrade, still stained with Elizaveta's blood.

I climbed on top of it, and the blood disappeared before it could touch my dirty bare feet. Balanced on top of the stone, with his big hand making sure I did not fall, I leaned over and kissed him.

"I pick you," I said—and the world dissolved around me.

I SAT IN THE STREAM IN MY OWN OTHERNESS. THE WA-ter was really, really cold.

A big gray wolf, his feet and muzzle much darker than the silvery fur on his back, waded in beside me. He put his muzzle on my shoulder.

I wanted to tell you that I love you, too, he said.

I BLINKED UP AT THE SHOP LIGHT THAT WAS SUDDENLY over my head.

"Your arm is broken," said Adam, his voice ferocious. "I have it wrapped to stop the bleeding, but as soon as Carlos gets here we're taking you to the hospital."

"Fiona was working for the witches," I said. His face filled my world, and I realized he was in his own human skin.

"I know that," he told me. "I heard."

"We need to tell Bran that Kent was witchbound, whatever that means."

"I will," he said. "Shut up now. Save your strength."

"I love you even though you aren't perfect," I said.

He met my eyes. "I know that."

"I'm not perfect, either," I told him.

"I know that, too," he said, his voice growly.

"You need to find some clothes to wear, and I think I'm in shock." And I passed out before he could tell me that he knew that, too.

ABOUT A WEEK LATER I WAS SITTING AT THE KITCHEN table and Adam sat down beside me and kissed my shoulder, the one connected to my unbroken arm.

"Hmm," I said, writing down the parts number from the catalog I was ordering from.

The guy who ran this particular parts yard didn't believe in the Internet, but he had parts that no one else carried. The order was made more difficult because I had to write everything down with my left hand.

But mostly I kept writing because I could feel Adam's amusement traveling through our mating bond. He was about to do something or tell me something that he thought was really funny.

"Okay," I said, looking up.

His face was lit with laughter—and it looked good on him.

"First," he said, "I need to tell you that Izzy's mother is very sorry. She didn't realize that the client she was talking to is the sister of a reporter for a tabloid."

Izzy's mother sold essential oils. I couldn't imagine what she . . .

"Butch apologizes," Adam continued, "because when I told him to watch the newspapers and TV news—he did not consider tabloids until he caught one of our new guards reading one of them."

Adam set a stack of tabloid newspapers on the kitchen table in front of me. There must have been ten or twelve of them. The front page headline of the one on top said: *Human(?) Wife Says Alpha Werewolf Is Sex Fiend, Seeks Help from Friend.*

And that wasn't the worst one.

I laughed until I cried. Then Adam picked me up, careful not to jostle my broken arm, and growled, "Nudge."

"Help," I called as he carried me up the stairs. "My mate is a sex fiend. Help."

There was no help for me.

ADAM GOT CALLED INTO WORK THAT NIGHT, SO I WAS alone when the sounds of a guitar and a violin drifted through my closed window. I got up and shoved the window open—which would have been easier without the stupid broken arm.

Sitting cross-legged on the hood of my old Rabbit parts car, Wulfe played a violin. In front of him, standing on the ground but with one foot on the bumper, Stefan played a guitar. They managed a pretty good version of "The Sound of Silence." Small hesitations here and there made me think they hadn't practiced it.

When they were done, Wulfe slid off the car and took a bow with a flourish worthy of a Shakespearean actor. But it was Stefan's grin, not Wulfe's bow or the performance, that put a smile on my face as I closed the window.

On the top of my chest of drawers, just as though it had always been there, the walking stick lay in its usual place.

ACKNOWLEDGMENTS

Thanks to all of those who have helped make this book better: Collin Briggs, Linda Campbell, Dave and Katharine Carson, Ann Peters, and Kaye Roberson. They read this in rougher forms and sometimes at speed. Thanks also to my long-suffering editor Anne Sowards, copy editor Amy J. Schneider, Michelle Kasper, Alexis Nixon, Jessica Plummer, Miranda Hill, and the team at Penguin Random House, without whose skilled guidance this book would be much the less. Thank you to Susann and Michael Bock, who once again have furnished Zee and Tad with their German. (Zee is particularly happy not to be stuck with mine.) I am grateful for my friend Michael Enzweiler, who draws the wonderful and useful maps for my books. Finally, thank you to the readers who enjoy the journeys of my imaginary friends. As always, any mistakes are mine.

ABOUT THE AUTHOR

Patricia Briggs lived a fairly normal life until she learned to read. After that she spent lazy afternoons flying dragon-back and looking for magic swords when she wasn't horseback riding in the Rocky Mountains. Once she graduated from Montana State University with degrees in history and German, she spent her time substitute teaching and writing. She and her family live in the Pacific Northwest, and you can visit her website at www.patriciabriggs.com.

Find out more about Patricia Briggs and other Orbit authors by registering for the free monthly newsletter at www.orbitbooks.net.